Teka

Homecoming

DEE OSAH

For information contact :
inspire@deeosah.com

Book Cover design by Austin M. Pennington (Redbridge Graphics)
Book Formatting by Derek Murphy @Creativindie
ISBN: 978-1-962485-04-3

First Edition: December 2025

10 9 8 7 6 5 4 3 2

To J&J, you are our greatest reward.

This novel is dedicated to those who come home slowly,
Carrying fractured histories and inherited silences,
Learning that belonging is not always about blood,
But about love that stays.

Thank you for giving our words a place in your world.

1

Bart jolted upright from the unforgiving wooden chair beside the hospital bed. The old man lay still, his chest rising and falling in shallow breaths beneath the thin blanket.

"Mr. Banigo," Bart said, slicing into the silence. The name tasted wrong, distant. The man had days—maybe hours—left to live, but Bart still couldn't say the word.

Dad.

It caught in his throat like broken glass. Peter Banigo wasn't his father. He was the coward who'd vanished before Bart ever took his first breath, leaving him to be raised in another world, by people who hadn't owed him anything.

Bart rubbed his eyes, trying to shake the fog of another sleepless night. The bedridden man was a shell, not the confident businessman Bart had seen in old photos, those sharp eyes now dulled, lost in regret. The ghost of a past Bart had spent his life trying to forget.

Peter stirred with a faint wheeze. "Bartimeus."

Bart leaned forward. In Peter's voice, his name always sounded like it belonged to someone else.

"I'm sorry," Peter croaked. "I was talking about your mother."

For three days, they had pieced together fragments of a girl Peter barely knew. A college fling in Texas. He'd called her "J." After learning she was underage, Peter had fled the country, afraid of deportation, leaving her like luggage he never meant to reclaim.

Now in his late fifties, Peter looked decades older, a life spent running from mistakes. A well-traveled man who had avoided America like a plague, afraid of what he'd left behind.

"I tried to look for her," Peter said, each word seeming to peel another second off his life. "I never meant..." He trailed off, eyes glassy.

"Never meant what?" Bart asked, harder than he intended. "Never meant to disappear without a word? It's been thirty-two years. Do you even know if she's alive?"

The question hung between them like a challenge.

Peter finally shook his head. "I was scared. I didn't know what to do."

Bart laughed under his breath. His gaze dropped to Peter's wrinkled hands, the stubby fingers uncannily familiar. Even their heads were shaped the same. Genes were cruel like that.

Outside the window, Port Harcourt pulsed with life. The city's muffled chaos spilled into the room—voices, horns—drowning the machines humming around Peter's bed, casting him in a ghostly glow, a song of sorrow and death.

"I'm sorry, my son."

Bart snapped to his feet, the chair scraping behind him. "I didn't ask for this," he muttered. He'd never wanted to meet his birth father, let alone watch him die. Yonas and Ester Teka were the only parents he ever needed. They had loved him and his four adopted siblings—Abe, Junior, Darah, and Eli—with a steadiness that never flinched.

"Dad" was a word that belonged to Yonas Teka, not this

stranger.

"I'll be back," Bart said, heading for the door. His head was pounding. He needed to find the pharmacy.

"Wait." Peter's strangled whisper stopped him mid-step. "I don't have much time left." His hand lifted, then dropped on the bed. "Could you ever find it in your heart..."

The words hit like a sucker punch. Bart stood there with his hand on the doorknob. Of course, it had come to this. From the moment they first met here—three days ago—he knew what Peter wanted. Forgiveness. A final mercy before death. A clean slate.

No way. Thirty-two years of absence couldn't be erased with just "sorry." Why should Peter get to go in peace when Bart had spent his whole life trying to stitch together the broken pieces?

"No," Bart whispered. The word burned.

He turned, met Peter's eyes. For a second, guilt scraped at him, but it wasn't his to carry. Not for a man who'd never carried him.

"I don't think I can, Mr. Banigo." He never knew how much he hated the man. Not until now.

Peter's whole face trembled, but he said nothing.

Bart walked out into the hallway, past the nurses and visitors in the packed lobby. The antiseptic haze stung his eyes as he reached the empty stairwell. He leaned against the wall and released a long breath. He'd come to Nigeria for closure, but all he'd found was a broken man who reminded him of his own demons.

Laughter drifted from above. Bart bolted down the stairs, skipping steps like he could outrun the memories, the years spent being shuttled from one home to another, years stitched together with the silence of survival.

Stumbling outside the hospital, the air hit thick and hot, Port

3

Harcourt alive with blaring horns and engine smoke. It twisted the nausea in his gut. He pressed his palms to his face. Peter's plea clung to him like the unbearable heat.

His phone buzzed. Kasey. His ex. Finally calling him back. He'd called yesterday to make sure she was okay after the hurricane. He hadn't talked to her since she'd broken up with him again, right when he'd needed her most. Always leaving. Always when it mattered.

He slipped the phone back into his pocket. He didn't have the headspace to deal with her drama. Not today.

His headache flared. He'd expected meeting his birth father to be tough. But there wasn't a word that could cover the frustration of watching a man he couldn't hate enough to abandon, but couldn't love enough to mourn.

Bart stepped back into the hospital. There was no running. Not from Peter. Not from himself. He needed to finish this chapter, close it for good, so he could go home and finally move on with the life he'd built.

Could you ever forgive me? The words chased him like shadows.

"Screw that," Bart muttered. He wouldn't.

Not now. Not ever.

2

At the pharmacy, the pain medication shelves were cleaned out. Not even Panadol.

Bart stood in line, headache pounding, hoping the frazzled pharmacist had an alternative.

"There's no Panadol at all?" a woman at the counter asked.

Her voice struck him like a jolt. Her back was turned, partly blocked by an elderly man leaning on a cane, his arms full of incontinence pads, frail hands trembling as he tried to balance the stack.

The pharmacist glanced at Bart, who lifted a finger, motioning for a single box. The man disappeared into the back and returned with five boxes.

The old man shifted, almost fumbling the pads. Bart grabbed a basket and held it out to him. The man nodded thanks, looking between the pads and the counter like he was calculating how many he could afford.

"Two boxes," the woman said. Maybe it was her Texas drawl that made her sound familiar.

Bart pulled out his wallet. "I'll pay for him," he said, gesturing to the elderly man. "And for her Panadol, too. Three boxes."

The woman spun around. "No, I can't take your money."

Bart placed the bills on the counter, avoiding her eyes. He didn't need her thinking he was trying to hit on her. "It's fine. I just need to do something good right now. My father's upstairs. He's...dying." The words slipped out, surprising even him.

"So sorry to hear that," the old man muttered.

"You're joking, right?" the woman said.

Bart turned. A sharp breath escaped his lips. He'd stared into those amber eyes before. He'd dreamed of them.

"Bart? Bartimeus Teka? What on earth are you doing here?"

Hearing his name in her voice cracked the well open inside him. She looked different, older, softened with time into this stunning, fragile beauty. And yet it was really her. How could she have changed so much in only four years? As if the memory he'd held on to was merely his imagination. If he'd met her in another part of the world, he might have mistaken her for someone else, but the one thing that hadn't changed about her was those wild curls framing her face. And her smile—that old, defiant smile— she now turned on him.

"Geri," he breathed, like a prayer finally answered.

Before he could stop himself, he pulled her into his arms, like a dream. Only it wasn't. She was no longer the same Geri. She didn't smell like watermelon.

She pulled back, eyes scanning him. "Why are you here?"

Bart laughed, still trying to believe it. She really was different, a quiet guardedness, as if a stranger had taken over the body of the spirited woman he once knew. She looked worn down, her face thinner, and the light in her eyes dimmed. Where was the spicy princess who used to argue with him, who nearly burned down their kitchen?

The day he'd taken her to the hardware store had stayed etched into his mind—her flushed cheeks and reckless laugh. He'd kept the memory like a talisman for four years, a snapshot of Geraldine Pena in her most beautiful moment. But even that didn't compare to her now.

"Did you come here to find me?" she asked.

"Of course not," he said. "I thought you were still in Abuja." He'd spent the last two years trying not to think about her after hearing she was engaged.

"Right. Your dad's dying. Seriously?"

"Long story," he said. She was finally standing in front of him, and yet still felt miles away.

"That's not funny, Bart. I was at the funeral."

He shoved his hands in his pockets, resisting the urge to touch her again. "Remember that last Thanksgiving you spent with us? We talked about our biological fathers." A bitter smile tugged at his mouth. "Well, I met mine. And like some cosmic joke, he's dying."

She stared at him. "Are you okay?"

He wanted to ask her the same. Dark circles under her eyes—like she hadn't slept in days. The panic behind her smile. Why did she need two boxes of painkillers?

Geri flinched, grabbing her phone. "I-I have to go."

"Wait, can we meet up?" His hand shot out. "What's your number?"

"I'll text you," she said, backing away. "Same number?"

"Yeah. Call me."

She was gone before the last word left his mouth.

"She forgot her Panadol," the pharmacist said.

Bart snatched the bag from him and ran after her, calling her name as she disappeared into the stairwell. An elderly woman gingerly made her way down, blocking his path. By the time Bart reached the next floor, the pediatric sign stopped him cold.

Geri had gone in there. Geri was a mother? He hadn't imagined that. But it explained her panic, her exhaustion. Her kid was sick.

A man and a woman entered the pediatric unit. Bart slipped in behind them, smiling at the nurse by the station without being stopped.

Down the hallway, a guard stood outside one of the rooms, a gun visible at his waist. Bart pressed his phone to his ear, pretending to be on a call. As he edged closer, he heard Geri's voice—pleading, arguing with another woman.

The guard looked his way, and Bart walked past as if he was hurrying to one of the rooms down the hall. Once he turned the corner, out of the guard's line of sight, Bart pressed against the wall, straining to catch the words. This wasn't the Geri he knew. She'd never let anyone talk down to her.

Footsteps made him jerk as the guard approached. Bart knocked on a random room door before retreating. He slipped out of the pediatric unit just as his phone vibrated.

It was Tonye. The cousin who'd accidentally lit this fuse three years ago at Abe and Phoebe's wedding. Bart had met Tonye at the candy bar and later found out they were related. This past January, Abe had dropped the bomb: Peter Banigo, Bart's biological father, was alive. Dying. And wanted to meet him.

Just weeks ago, Tonye had orchestrated an intervention where Bart's brothers had demanded that Bart visit Nigeria to see Peter Banigo.

"Where are you?" Bart asked. What were the odds that Peter Banigo and Geraldine Pena were in the same hospital in Tonye's backyard?

"Something urgent came up," Tonye said. "Sorry, I'll be plenty late. You sound like you were running."

"Yeah." Bart exhaled. "I just ran into Geraldine Pena."

Tonye went quiet. Not that he needed to say anything. Tonye was the gift that kept on giving.

"Does your emergency have anything to do with her?" Bart asked.

Tonye sighed. "I'm sorry, Bart."

He gritted his teeth. "Then tell me everything—"

"Bart," a voice shouted.

He turned to see Uncle Paul running toward him, face pale. "Tonye, I'll call you back," Bart said. "Your dad just showed up."

"Bart, come quick," Uncle Paul gasped. "Your father—"

3

Geri didn't have time to process Bart's sudden reappearance. She'd imagined their paths crossing again, but not like this. Not in Port Harcourt, or the bombshell that his birth father was Nigerian—just like her late father.

But today, her thoughts were consumed by Asabe Musa, her mother-in-law, the storm waiting to strike.

After her husband Hakeem's death, Geri had fled Abuja, clinging to the lifeline her friends IB and Tonye had offered. Port Harcourt had become a fragile sanctuary while they worked to secure American passports for her and Joaquin. But fate had conspired with Asabe's endless reach to trap her in Nigeria.

A month ago, Geri had walked into Joaquin's hospital room and found Asabe there, sitting beside her grandson like he belonged to her. It had been nearly two years since Geri last saw

Asabe. The woman hadn't changed. Still cloaked in black, still bitter, blaming Geri for Hakeem's death, and bent on reclaiming what she believed was hers.

Today was no different. The text had come while Geri was at the pharmacy: She's back.

Geri had rushed through the hospital and found Asabe already seated at Joaquin's bedside, towering in her black robes, a suffocating storm cloud of grief and control. Whatever rumors Geri had heard about Asabe's declining health had clearly been exaggerated. Her iron-willed mother-in-law was here for one reason: to take her grandson. The heir to the Musa fortune.

"You remember Fatima?" Asabe said, gesturing to the younger woman beside her.

Fatima had been paraded like a bride-in-waiting at Hakeem's last birthday party, just hours before he threw divorce papers at Geri. Asabe had always wanted Hakeem to marry Fatima, but he'd defied her and married Geri, the outsider, the American.

"She's here to look after Hakeem," Asabe said.

The name was a dagger. Asabe refused to call him Joaquin, as if saying her son's name might validate Geri's presence in the boy's life and unshackle him from his father's legacy.

Fatima stood by the bed, all grace and polished silence. Her fingertips grazed Joaquin's curls.

"No more feeding him this junk," Asabe said, eyes fixed on the empty takeout box on the side table. Her cold gaze slid to Geri. "Is this how you care for a Musa? Like a street orphan?"

Geri's pulse hammered. "He is my son. I'll decide what he eats."

"You'll decide?" Asabe's smile was like a predator. "You can't

11

even decide what to do with your life. When will you stop running, Geraldine?"

Geri dropped her eyes. She knew better than to meet Asabe's gaze head-on. Not here.

"Fatima is a nurse," Asabe continued, voice dripping with fake sweetness. "She'll stay with Hakeem until it's time to bring him home."

"No." She couldn't let Joaquin go back to that viper pit in Abuja that had already cost Hakeem his life. "He already has a nurse," Geri said, her eyes on Fatima's hand. "Don't touch him. You'll wake him."

Fatima glanced at Geri with polite disdain, as if swatting a fly. She spoke to Asabe in Hausa. As much as Geri had tried to learn the language, she could still only understand pieces. But she did catch Joaquin's name.

"Keep my son's name out of your mouth," Geri snapped.

Asabe turned on her. "Did you even understand what she said? You think I expected you to learn our language? When you can't even speak good English. You that couldn't finish school? You were never fit to be a Musa. Always so defiant. Too American."

Geri clenched a fist. One year under this woman's thumb had nearly broken her. She wouldn't let Joaquin be crushed the same way.

Asabe looked down at Joaquin and her face softened. "Last night I prayed for him. That God would spare him." Her eyes lifted back to Geri. "This child means more to me than you'll ever know. He is my blood. My legacy." Her voice broke in a way Geri had never heard. "How could you keep him from me? You didn't even want me to know he existed. While my grandson was suffering in the NICU, I knew nothing. I will never forgive you for that."

For a breath, Geri felt the woman's pain. But just as quickly, the softness vanished.

"As I told you last week, he returns home in two weeks."

"He's not ready to travel," Geri said. "He's safer here."

"Safe? In this place?" Her eyes narrowed. "Do you think you can protect him better than me? You have no idea how dangerous..." She trailed off as if she hadn't meant to stop talking.

Geri bit her tongue. She couldn't tell Asabe what Tonye told her. Hakeem had been murdered. Asabe would never believe it, not from Geri.

"You ran away to put my grandson in this third-rate hospital," Asabe went on. "When we have better ones back home."

Geri's mouth moved before she could think. "Those hospitals couldn't save your son."

Silence. Even Fatima stood wide-eyed.

Asabe rose slowly. Geri braced herself for the slap, but it never came. Asabe stared at Geri, and she might as well have wrapped her thin, wiry fingers around Geri's neck.

"I will bring my grandson home," Asabe said. "With or without you." She swept out, Fatima trailing behind, the guards falling into step.

Joaquin stirred, his soft snores the only sound left. Her son being a deep sleeper was a blessing. Every time Asabe had tried to hold him, he'd cried. Children could sense evil; Geri was sure of it.

She gathered Joaquin into her arms. "Mi querido." Her

precious boy, her reason to keep going. From the day he was born, she'd whispered prayers in two languages, singing lullabies over his tiny form in the NICU. He had survived. He was her miracle, her reward for everything she'd been through.

Her phone buzzed. IB.

Geri's heart sank. It wasn't safe to talk here. Not with Asabe's shadows around every corner.

When Joaquin's doctor entered moments later, he delivered the final blow. "Looks like your time with us is coming to an end," the doctor announced.

Days ago, he'd insisted Joaquin wasn't strong enough for discharge. Now he was changing course. Geri didn't need to ask why. Asabe had gotten to him.

When the doctor left, Geri sat in silence, arms wrapped around her son. Tomorrow, Asabe would come back. Or Fatima, and next time they wouldn't leave quietly.

She had run out of time.

4

The door creaked open and Geri stood. The visitor was IB's assistant—a petite young woman with a kind face and the roundest eyes.

The woman pointed to the walls, then tapped her ear, her message clear. Someone might be listening. She held up her phone and gestured to the door.

Geri glanced once more at Joaquin, still asleep. She would have to trust that no one was coming back tonight. But Asabe's people could be anywhere.

She stepped out of the room. The hallways were quiet now, thinned by the late hour. No sign of Fatima or the guards. No hum of visitors or bustling nurses. Geri kept her head down as she slipped through the pediatric unit and made her way outside.

She found refuge in the empty courtyard, a worn bench beneath a fledgling tree. The stillness hummed with hidden watchers as she made the call.

IB answered, then added Phoebe. Hearing both of their voices instantly steadied her nerves.

"Asabe is using her contacts to get Tonye to back down," IB warned. "We have to get you both on a plane now."

The doctor's earlier reversal echoed like a betrayal. "And what if Joaquin has a seizure again?" Geri asked. "You saw what happened the last time we tried to leave."

"It's gonna be okay," Phoebe said. "Just bring him to Houston. Eli's doctor and the team—"

"No," she refused. "Houston just got hit by a hurricane. It's too risky."

"You don't have a choice," IB said, firm. "This is the window we've been waiting for. And Bart can help. You can go back with him."

Her chest clenched. "I don't want him involved in this." She paused, realizing they both knew he was here. "I can't believe you guys didn't tell me."

"You've had enough on your plate," Phoebe murmured.

Her fingers gripped the phone. "He looked shocked to see me." She'd asked Phoebe to keep her situation from Bart. "And what's this about his birth father being Nigerian?"

"Crazy, right?" IB said. "Small world."

There was movement in the courtyard. A figure stumbled in from the side and slumped onto a bench in the far corner.

Recognition jolted her. "It's Bart," she whispered.

"What?" Phoebe and IB asked in unison.

"He's right here." She squinted to see him better. "And, I think he's crying."

The words felt surreal. Bart, who'd stood like stone at Papa Yonas and Mama Ester's funeral, but now, his shoulders shook, face buried in his hands.

"I have to go," Geri said. Talking about him while he fell apart

16

felt like a betrayal.

"We'll wait for your call," IB replied.

Geri ended the call. She walked slowly across the courtyard until she stood in front of him.

"Bart?"

He looked up, eyes bloodshot. "Geri."

The way he called her name—just Geri, not Geraldine—washed over her like a memory, taking her back to middle school, the coat closet where she had her first kiss, and never could have imagined the heartbreak waiting for her in the future.

"Are you okay?" Geri asked.

He didn't answer, just looked at her like she was the one real thing in his crumbling world. She sat down beside him, knowing she'd have to return soon. He remained quiet for at least a minute. When she shifted, about to stand, his hand brushed hers.

"He, my birth father is in a coma," Bart said, voice hoarse. "He'll probably die soon. He asked me to forgive him... but I couldn't." His tortured eyes met hers. "It's not fair. Am I not allowed to hate him after everything?"

Her heart ached at the despair in his eyes. He wasn't asking for an answer. He was asking for permission. She couldn't bring herself to speak, afraid her own pain might unravel in her voice.

"All I can think about is what Dad would've said," he murmured. "And it pisses me off. I never got to say goodbye to Dad. But now I have to say goodbye to a man who didn't even want me? What a sick joke."

The silence stretched between them. Geri knew she had to say something, but wasn't sure how to answer without making light of his pain.

"Maybe it's not about choosing to hate or forgive right now," she said. "Maybe it's just about being honest. With him. And yourself."

A bitter laugh. "Honest? Like, 'Hi, fake Dad. Thanks for being nothing to me my whole life. And right, I'm supposed to forgive you now because you're dying?"

She turned to face him. "You speak your truth. Even if it's messy. Forgiveness is more about you than the forgiven. It's not about giving them what they want. It's you freeing yourself. You're allowed to feel whatever you're feeling, just don't get stuck in the anger."

Bart let out a deep sigh. "It's not just him. I feel like I cheated Dad. And I can never make it right. I'll never get to tell him how much I love him. How much I miss him."

Tears blurred her own eyes as her memories of his parents rose like ghosts. Their warmth, their words had helped her through the darkest moments of her marriage. She'd even had a dream where Mama Ester had prayed with her, and Papa Yonas had given her one of his big hugs.

"He knew," she whispered. "He knew you loved him."

His head dropped. "I just wish I'd said it more."

"You still can." She nudged the ground with her toe, stirring dry leaves, their edges charred like flame. "I talk to them all the time. Like they're still here."

Bart looked at her. "What do you say?"

Geri scanned the quiet courtyard. What if Joaquin woke up wondering where she was? Or if Fatima came back?

"It's okay if you have to go," he said.

She couldn't leave him. A long time ago, she would have done anything for this moment—Bartimeus Teka needing her. But now, needing him scared her more than anything.

18

"I tell them I miss them," she said. "I tell them about my life. And…it's okay to cry, you know."

He nudged her shoulder. "Who said I was crying?"

"Just saying."

He didn't argue. His shoulders trembled against hers. She blinked back her tears and stayed beside him, letting him grieve the dad who raised him, not the father who abandoned him. Because all dads were fathers. But not all fathers were dads.

For the first time in months, Geri let herself think of her father. She'd come to Nigeria seeking a connection to a man who had always been a shadow in her memories. Instead, she'd met his family and they tried to erase her. Married off to a man who tried to break her.

"Thanks, Geri," Bart said.

His fragile smile pulled her straight back into middle school, when one look from Bart Teka had made her feel like she was flying. Maybe it was the years apart, or everything between. But after all this time, it was still there.

She stood from the bench, and he rose with her. She thought he might reach out, but he didn't.

"Geri, I—"

"I need to go." She turned. He caught her hand.

"I heard everything," he said. "I followed you to give you your meds."

Her stomach twisted at the softness in his voice. He'd heard Asabe. "It's not what you think."

"Let me help."

"You've got enough going on."

"You don't have to do this alone, Geri."

Her anger surged, hot and wild like a flame scorching dry

19

wood. What did he know about her life? About everything she'd lost? This was what she'd become, the kind of woman Bart would pity.

"I can take care of myself," she snapped, pulling her hand free. She walked off before he could say another word and get entangled in her mess. Anyone but him.

She didn't look back, didn't let herself break until she was back in Joaquin's room. He was still asleep, his curls damp against the pillow.

After IB's assistant left, Geri sank into the chair beside the bed. Sleep didn't come. Bart would leave soon. Back to Houston. Back to the life she'd longed for these past four years.

She missed the Tekas. Missed him. But if Asabe had her way, she might never see them again.

A sob clawed to the surface and she pressed a trembling hand over her mouth. Her other hand stroked Joaquin's curls, her anchor in the storm, her heart.

How would she ever escape this nightmare?

5

Bart paced the living room, the truth about Geri's life sinking deeper with every step. After a sleepless night, he'd shown up at IB and Tonye's house around noon.

"I can't believe Abe kept this from me," Bart said. Each revelation had shattered the image he'd built of Geri's life in Nigeria. The woman he remembered—too fierce to tame—had been reduced to someone he barely recognized.

Bart reached into his pocket and found nothing. He'd run out of watermelon gummies several days back.

"How do we get Geri out of here?" Bart asked.

IB leaned on the cushions, one hand on her belly. "Phoebe didn't tell you anything about Geri?"

"No." He had told Phoebe not to. "I looked up her husband. Rich guy from old money. I thought she was happy."

Tonye's voice was low. "Before he died, Hakeem asked me to help her. We think he was poisoned, slowly. Probably by one of his sisters, over the inheritance. He died before Geri could tell him she was pregnant."

"Hakeem was the worst," IB said.

"It wasn't all his fault," Tonye said. "His family treated Geri like a bargaining chip. And after her grandmother passed, she had no one left."

"Hakeem didn't protect her," IB snapped. "From his mother, or his sisters."

Bart sat on the edge of the couch. "Why didn't she just leave? Come home."

"They took her passport," IB replied. "Her marriage was about uniting two families. Geri was the sacrificial lamb."

"Hakeem did love her," Tonye said.

IB scoffed. "He wanted to divorce her because she didn't get pregnant fast enough. And don't forget about the stairs."

"What stairs?"

"She fell," Tonye said.

"She was pushed," IB corrected.

Someone had tried to kill her? "Hakeem pushed her?"

"No," Tonye said. "It could've been anyone. Her dad's people didn't want her to have a child. Neither did Hakeem's half-sisters. Geri's existence threatens both sides. And now Asabe wants Geri's son to inherit the bulk of the Musa fortune."

"This is worse than those dramas Darah watches," Bart muttered, rubbing his face. "We have to get them out. Today. Is the kid okay? What's his name?"

"Joaquin," IB replied.

Bart couldn't help smiling. Joaquin sounded like a name the old Geri would give her son. But wasn't it too close to Hakeem?

"Joaquin has seizures," IB went on. "The doctors haven't figured it out. We were waiting until he was cleared to fly, but now

22

that Asabe's here, it's too risky to wait."

Bart looked between them. "Is there anything we can do?"

"You can," IB said. "Geri needs you."

Bart almost laughed. He'd spent years trying to forget her in the mess of his microwave relationships. "What do you expect me to do?"

"Convince her to leave," Tonye said. "We have a plane ready to fly. Joaquin was cleared for travel this morning, but Geri's scared. The last time they tried, he passed out before they even left the ground."

"But if she doesn't leave now, she might never get another chance," IB warned.

Convince Geri to leave or she might be stuck here? The latter wasn't even an option.

"I'll get her on that plane," Bart said. She'd been cold with him last night, but this was his chance to be there for her in a way he'd never been able to before.

IB kept her eyes on him. She'd always had a way of seeing straight through people, even as a teenager at church. Bart remembered that look—like the one Abe got when he was deciding to trust someone.

"I'll come with you," she said.

"No," Bart refused. Tonye wouldn't want his pregnant wife in any danger. "People know who you are. I'll go alone."

"We have to take a stand," she told Tonye, who had started to object.

Bart stood. Here came the standoff. "IB—"

"I'm going," she said, daring Tonye to challenge her.

Bart watched their familiar rhythm unfold. Every marriage had its battles. Even Abe and sweet Phoebe weren't immune. But seeing IB stand there, fierce and unflinching, reminded Bart of his mother, the quiet woman who never stayed silent in a storm. Tonye had been scandalized once, and IB had left America to stand beside him. They were forged in fire. A love like that was hard to break.

As Bart edged toward the door, IB pulled him back in with a question.

"Why's your cousin so overprotective?"

"Because you're you," Bart replied. "A famous director working on a film about election fraud. And you look like a walking magazine cover. Can you blame a man for wanting to protect the mother of his child?"

IB narrowed her eyes, but the corner of her mouth lifted. Tonye put his arms around her, putting out the fire, for now.

Bart left them hugging. "I'll call after I talk to her," he said, walking out of the house.

He drove straight to the hospital. But he didn't go to Geri. First, he went to Peter's room. Yesterday, Peter had slipped into a coma. The doctors didn't expect him to wake up.

The room was colder now, Peter barely recognizable under the machines crowding his bedside. Bart sat by the bed, trying to trace his own face in this stranger's face who'd given him life and nothing else. Peter looked so small and fragile, yet his existence was a giant shadow over Bart. He'd always told himself he was fine without answers. But now that he had them, they brought no comfort. He could no longer pretend as if he'd never had any parents other than the Tekas.

He stood by the window, staring out at the rain, listening to the soft hiss of oxygen. This wasn't closure. He was too drained, too tired to feel anything.

"I wish I never met you," he said, annoyed that it wasn't even anger anymore. "I might be leaving soon. There's someone who needs me more." The words felt strange but freeing. He watched the slow rise and fall of Peter's chest and again wondered how a man like him could be his father. "I think not seeing you will help me figure things out. Then maybe, I'll be able to—"

He couldn't finish the thought. Forgiveness was too far away. But for a moment, he thought he'd seen Peter twitch his hand.

He waited, heart pounding. But there was nothing. Only the quiet rhythm of Peter's breaths ticking away like the old clock on the wall.

At the door, Bart looked back one last time. "Goodbye, Mr. Banigo."

He walked out, leaving his unwanted past behind. His phone buzzed before he reached the elevator. IB.

"Have you talked to her yet?" she asked, breathless.

"No, I'm just heading there."

"My assistant saw one of Asabe's men talking to Joaquin's doctor. Something's happening."

Bart ran to the pediatric unit. The floor was too quiet, the lobby empty. The electronic doors were open. No nurses were at the station. Down the hallway, a man in black turned the corner toward Geri's room.

On instinct, Bart sprinted after him. He heard the muffled scream as the man shoved a woman into a room—Geri's room. Bart launched himself at the door and was met by a fist to his face. Pain exploded from his nose, but stumbling back he managed to duck the next punch, and drove his boot into the man's knee. A satisfying crack. A scream. The man dropped.

Bart didn't stop. He pinned him, fists flying, blow after blow. "Who sent you?" he shouted.

"Bart!"

Geri's voice broke through his haze. She stood by the

window, Joaquin in her arms. On the floor, another woman lay in blood.

Bart turned back to the unconscious man under him. Not the same guard from yesterday. He threw one last punch at the man and got up.

"We have to go," he said, crossing the room.

"Is Fatima dead?" Geri asked, trembling. "She protected Joaquin."

He knelt, checked the woman's breathing. "She's alive. But we can't stay." He reached for Geri's arm and she pulled back.

"What are you doing?" Geri asked.

"That man was sent by Asabe. You're not safe here."

She clutched Joaquin tighter, shielding his face.

"Please," he said more gently There wasn't time. Thank God he'd arrived when he did. "Just trust me. Let me help you."

Her eyes filled. "Why are you doing this? I haven't seen you in—"

"Three years, eight months," he said. "Would you like the exact number of days? I've counted every one, Geraldine Pena."

Her lips parted, and he seized the moment, taking her hand.

"Please," he said again. "I got you."

This time, she didn't pull away. Together, they ran, down the hall, away from the blood, away from the past, their steps haunted by the threat of another enemy waiting for them.

6

The stale hospital air clung to Geri's skin as she followed Bart out of the pediatric unit, Joaquin heavy in her arms, his face tucked into her chest. Her arms ached, but there was no time to think with a hundred questions attacking her.

"Where are we going?" Geri asked, and Joaquin whimpered. She brushed his curls away from his damp forehead. "We're okay, mi amor," she whispered, her voice trembling despite her effort to sound soothing. She wasn't sure if the words were for him or herself.

"Stay close," Bart said, leading them across the dim lobby.

It wasn't lost on her how much she needed his calm right now. The warmth of his hand when he held hers, his broad back shielding her and Joaquin like a silent promise. When a nurse had tried to stop them from leaving the pediatric unit, Bart had answered without hesitation.

"The boy needs fresh air," he'd said, that smooth voice convincing enough to still any protest, with the kind of smile that could bend the world to his will.

Even Joaquin, wary of strangers, seemed enchanted by this heroic figure who had suddenly dropped into their lives. When they reached the ground floor and Bart paused to make a quick call, Joaquin stretched his arms toward Bart with surprising confidence.

Bart looked at Geri for permission. Not that she had a choice. Joaquin slipped from her arms into Bart's. Her heart warmed at the sight, but she didn't have time to dwell on it. Bart moved faster now with Joaquin in his arms, blending into the streams of people, navigating the halls until they reached a back exit.

"Almost there," he said, grabbing her hand as they pushed through the door.

Outside, an SUV waited with its headlights off in a small lot. Bart helped Geri into the back seat of the car, handed over Joaquin, and climbed in beside her. The vehicle sped away before the door closed.

Geri sank into her seat, trembling as the adrenaline drained from her body. In the front seat, IB's assistant offered a quick smile before launching into a tense discussion with the driver.

Geri looked out the window, watching the city lights blur past in glowing streaks. She turned to ask Bart where they were going, but Joaquin was playing with Bart's fingers.

"He likes you," she said before she could stop herself.

"Smart kid," he replied.

Geri cleared her throat, steeling herself before she got too emotional. She'd trusted before, and look where it had gotten her. But the least she could do was say "Thank you."

The SUV jolted sharply as they turned onto a gravel road.

DEE OSAH

Moments later, an airstrip came into view, a sleek jet gleaming on the small runway. IB and Tonye stood beside it.

Once Geri got out of the car, she ran into IB's arms. The decision to flee had already been made the moment that man stepped into her son's room. There was no going back.

"You're a Godsend," Geri whispered, hugging the woman who had become her lifeline this past year. Without IB and Tonye, she would still be trapped in Abuja, watching her son be used as a bargaining chip in the same deadly game that claimed his father.

IB quickly explained the plan. First, fly to Ghana to throw off any trackers. Then a commercial flight to Amsterdam, and finally Houston. It was complicated, but necessary.

As Geri looked over at Bart saying goodbye to Tonye, she forced back tears. He wasn't part of the plan, but she couldn't imagine doing this without him now.

They boarded the plane together. For a second, Bart's hand rested on the small of her back, a gesture both steadying and unsettling. But there was no space left in her mind to dissect it. The ramp lifted behind them. The doors sealed shut.

Inside, the cabin was softly lit, the seats soft and inviting, a haven of luxury. Geri sat by the window and placed Joaquin in her lap. The last time she'd been on a plane, she was leaving Abuja a month after Hakeem's funeral, her body swollen with grief and pregnancy.

The ground fell away, and the lights of the city that sheltered her disappeared into the darkness. She didn't realize how tightly she was gripping the armrest until Bart's hand covered hers.

Joaquin reached for him again. Bart took his tiny hand, and Joaquin's fingers curled around his like he'd done it a thousand times. His soft gaze stirred gratitude within her, warring with an anger she couldn't shake.

She hated the way she felt. Small, dependent, like a broken bird needing rescue. But when she saw the dried blood still crusted on Bart's nose—a testament to his sacrifice, the fight drained from her. He'd stepped into her nightmare without a thought. That had to mean something.

"Thank you," she whispered again, not knowing what else to say.

"You can thank me when we're back home," Bart said. "I'm here for you."

The words soothed and unsettled her. A balm she hadn't asked for. A burden she wasn't sure how to carry.

The plane leveled off, sky stretching into endless night. Geri let her eyes close. For now, her son was safe in her arms. And for the first time in years, she didn't feel alone.

"We're going home," Bart whispered beside her.

She echoed the word, "Home," her exhaustion pulling her under. A sliver of hope trickled through the chaos. They were finally going home.

7

Home. The word stirred buried images of the life she'd left behind. Four years ago, she'd left America believing in happily-ever-after, swept away by the promise of family. Her grandmother's blessing had brought her Hakeem Musa, a fairytale of a man, all smooth charm and dark skin.

Lust had come first. Then what she thought was love. It hadn't taken much convincing to say yes, deceived by a heart drunk on dreams.

Soon after the glitzy wedding, those dreams curdled. Asabe was the first crack in her fantasy. Her new mother-in-law made it clear that Geri was nothing more than an "exotic" pawn, her value measured in the heir she was expected to bear. When months passed with no pregnancy, civility vanished, and contempt took its place.

Then Geri's grandmother died. Her only protector. The walls

of her gilded cage sealed shut.

Hakeem's passion died a cruel death and was reborn as indifference, hardened into irritation. Her husband—who once couldn't keep his hands off her—refused to share her bed, leaving her to face the cold void of their failing marriage alone.

Her darkest moment came on his birthday. Asabe humiliated her in front of dozens of guests. Hakeem's silence was the final cut.

That night, she'd been ready to leave. A one-way ticket back to America. A quarter-million dollars meant to buy her silence. But Hakeem hadn't let her go.

Two nights later, he had stumbled into her room, drunk and reeking of regret. "I'm sorry, my love," he'd begged. "Why won't you just give me a son? Why do you make me the bad guy? All I ever wanted was to love you, my sweet..."

She must have been insane to give in to him again. But somehow, even after all of it, she'd still wanted to make it work. Still loved him enough to seal her fate. Even now, his voice still echoed, like a shadow haunting her bones.

Geri...

"Geri."

She jolted awake, hands swinging. "No—"

Strong arms caught her before she tumbled from the bed. She clawed at the arm holding her waist, vision blurred with panic.

"Easy, it's me," Bart said, in that steady voice, anchoring her to the present.

He clicked on a bedside lamp and light flooded the room. He stood there, rubbing his arm where she must have dug her nails in. Across the bed, Joaquin slept, unbothered.

"You were having a nightmare," Bart said.

Not a nightmare. A memory. Her lips still tingled with the ghost of that night. Hakeem's kisses, his pleading, she'd never seen him that unhinged before. That was the night Joaquin was conceived.

"Are you okay?" Bart asked. He wore a sleeveless shirt, arms lean, ripped. His face was sharper now, more mature. But the softness in his eyes hadn't changed. No matter how indifferent he'd always tried to act back in the day, he'd always been kind at heart.

Geri nodded, too raw to speak. Bart set a bottle of water on the table beside her. The roar of an airplane overhead drew her gaze to the window.

"What time is it?" She vaguely remembered landing in Accra and checking into a hotel near the airport.

"Almost five," Bart said. "You've been out since we got here."

Her eyes darted to Joaquin. "He didn't wake up?"

"He did. I fed him and got him back to sleep. You were out cold. I didn't want to wake you."

She swallowed. "When?"

"Less than an hour ago."

His voice, edged with quiet pride, made her stomach twist in shame. What kind of mother didn't wake up when her child cried? And Joaquin had let Bart take care of him, trusting a man he barely knew.

"How did you get him to sleep?" she asked, half in wonder.

"I just held him," Bart said, smiling.

She remembered now, what he'd said at the hotel front desk, calling them a family. It was a clever move, but something about the lie felt too real.

"You didn't have to pretend we're a family," Geri said. "We've already inconvenienced you enough—"

"It made things easier. Less questions."

She studied his face, trying to see beneath the façade of his casual response. "Why are you doing all this, Bart? It's not like we were ever really friends, or…" Her words failed her, unsure whether to name the space that had always come between them.

"Or what?" he asked. "You could've ignored me when you saw me that night. You didn't."

It wasn't the same. "Sitting with you doesn't compare to this. You got hurt—because of us."

He leaned back against the wall. "Aren't we friends, Geri?"

Friends. The word didn't fit. Not with the way he'd barely tolerated her back in Houston. But what he'd said at the hospital. Had he really counted the days since she left?

"I'm not sure how to answer that," she whispered.

"All right then." Bart pushed off the wall. "I fed Joaquin some rice and chicken."

"Chicken?" Her eyes snapped back to Joaquin, watching him closely. Joaquin would break out sometimes when he ate meat. The doctors had told her he might be allergic.

She took a deep breath. Hopefully, he would be okay. It wasn't Bart's fault. She should have been awake to tell him.

"There's more food for you," Bart said. "Our flight's tonight, so get some rest after you eat. I'll be on the couch if you need anything."

Geri watched him cross the room, settling on the couch without another word. This wasn't the Bart from years ago, not the smooth guy who always had a comeback with that easy laugh. Now, he seemed like he was holding back, hiding behind a wall that might crack if she dared reach out.

She lay down beside Joaquin. The steady rise and fall of his breath comforted her. But as she stroked his curls, his forehead felt too warm. The instant she pulled back her hand, his body jerked violently. His eyes rolled back. His limbs seized.

"No," she gasped, carrying Joaquin from his bed to the floor. She turned him on his side and held him tight. Sometimes, a simple change in orientation helped fend off the attacks.

Not today. The spasms kept coming.

"Bart, we have to go to the hospital. Now." It was her fault. She'd been too exhausted, too caught in her own mess. Joaquin's body went limp in her arms, knocked the breath from her lungs.

Already by her side, Bart's hand rested on Joaquin's chest. "Thank God. He's still breathing."

A sob broke from her throat. His body wasn't convulsing anymore.

"Just breathe," Bart said, his hand holding hers. "He's going to be okay. God got him."

Hearing those words pierced through the haze. Joaquin had always been in God's hands, long before he'd been hers.

She held Joaquin, whispering prayers, kissing his brow. Her son. Her everything. Why did he have to suffer so much?

"We still have to go to the hospital, right?" Bart asked, his voice shaky.

Geri looked up at him, this man who had become her rock in the middle of her storm, whether she wanted him to be or not. He stretched out his hand to help her stand, and she took it, surrendered to the hope that his presence offered, even as fear clung to her like a shadow in the valley of death.

Within minutes, they were racing down the hotel corridor, Bart leading the way with the same quiet strength that had carried her since the moment God sent him back into her life.

8

"He's stable for now," Bart said, on a three-way call with IB and Phoebe. He stood by the door leading to Joaquin's hospital room. They had missed their flight to Amsterdam the night before. A whole day of tests, no clear answers.

"The doctor's supposed to come back soon with the results," he said.

"We're praying," IB said, and Tonye added, "Hang in there, cuz."

Bart paced the quiet hallway, each step a slow burn. "How's... your uncle?"

The silence stretched just long enough to sting.

"Still unresponsive," Tonye replied. "We moved him to a new facility after recent events."

Back in Port Harcourt, Tonye had mentioned that Asabe might go after Peter Banigo once she realized that Bart and Tonye were part of Geri's disappearance.

"You did the right thing," Tonye said.

Phoebe's voice came next. "We're praying for you, Bart. You're where you need to be."

Bart didn't argue. For the first time in years, he felt exactly that. But Geri needed their prayers more. She had carried this weight alone too long. Joaquin deserved more than a life of hospital ceilings and uncertainty.

Bart looked up as the doctor and a nurse turned the corner and stepped into Joaquin's room. "I have to go."

Inside, the tension hit like a wall. Bart stood near the door, his eyes fixed on the pale child in the bed, the monitor beeping beside him like a timer counting down to heartbreak. They'd tried to get him out, and they'd failed. Was freedom worth this?

"We need more tests," the doctor said. "His fever's high, and the seizure could mean deeper complications. He's stable, but the next twenty-four hours are critical."

Bart tried to keep up, but it all blurred, questions he didn't know how to ask knotting his throat. This wasn't his kid, not his responsibility, so why did it feel like his heart was lying in that hospital bed?

"What can we do to help him?" Bart finally asked. "Tell us what you need."

The doctor looked between him and Geri. "Right now, fluids. Monitoring. Rest. If things worsen, we'll consider transferring him to a larger facility."

Geri looked like she hadn't slept for almost twelve hours the day before. Her eyes burned with defiance, but she simply shook her head.

"Whatever you need, just let me know," Bart said. "Can we move him to one of your best rooms? Since we might be here a while." He looked him in the eye, trying to communicate that money wasn't an issue.

The doctor nodded and scribbled on his pad before walking out with the nurse. The door clicked shut behind them, leaving an oppressive silence that threatened to crack Bart's composure.

Geri was hunched over the bed, Joaquin's tiny arm taped to an IV. The kid looked just like her, only deeper toned.

"He's strong," Bart said. "Just like his mom."

"Please don't try to make this easier," she snipped.

Bart let her anger wash over him. It wasn't about him. She was mad at the sheer unfairness of this situation. Maybe at herself.

"You should go back to the hotel," she said, quieter now.

Bart sat on the couch by the window. "I'll stay until they kick me out. Visiting hours or not"

She didn't respond right away. "They won't kick you out. I told them we're family."

His brows rose. "You mean, like Joaquin's my kid?"

She gave him a look sharp enough to make him grin. "If you want to stay, you can."

He watched her, wondering how much she'd endured to protect her son, the way her fingers threaded through Joaquin's hair again and again. She was holding herself together by habit, not strength.

"You should rest," he said.

Her jaw locked in that stubborn way he remembered. "I'm fine."

"You're not. You look like you haven't slept in months."

"I can't leave him."

Bart stood. "Then don't. Just rest. Let me take care of you both."

She closed her eyes like she was fighting the urge to scream.

Instead, she sat on the chair beside the bed.

"Why are you doing this?" Geri whispered. "Why are you here?"

He knelt beside her. "Because you shouldn't have to do this alone."

She stared at him. "Is that all?"

He paused, a little taken aback. "For now," he wanted to respond, but this wasn't the time.

"It's going to be okay." He gently placed a hand on her shoulder, as if touching a wounded bird. She didn't pull away.

She wasn't the woman he remembered, the hellcat with head-spinning curves and the curious scent of watermelon and old leather. She was something else now. Stronger. Time had stripped her down to her rawest parts, leaving behind the refined beauty of resilience.

He'd seen it before, the marks that loss left on a woman, changing them from the inside out. How Phoebe had crumbled after her first miscarriage, anxiety chipping away at her heart like a chisel carved by a God too complex to understand.

Losing Joaquin would break Geri in a way she might never recover from.

The thought made his hands tremble. All he could do was stay. For Geri. For Joaquin. For whatever came next.

"Your phone's ringing," she said.

His phone had dropped onto the couch. It was Darah calling. She hadn't called him at all since he'd left. He almost picked it up.

"I'll call her back," Bart said.

Geri gave him a look. "Did you talk to Phoebe or IB? I can't find my phone."

"Yeah. Everyone's praying."

Her laugh was hollow. "I don't get it. I mean, I understand

Abe helping—we go way back. But IB, Tonye? Why's everyone sticking out their necks for us?" Her words rang with the quiet disbelief of a woman who'd carried too many burdens alone.

"Because they care," he said. "You're an easy person to love."

Her amber eyes lifted to his, and everything stilled. Then she looked away.

"This past year," she said, the weight of the hard years pooling in her eyes. "I've had to take my faith more seriously. IB and Phoebe have helped me to see God differently. I used to put God and Christians in the same boat. Used to think Christians were all... not like your parents."

She waved the air as if casting out a memory. "Before I came here, I'd been hurt by Christians more than anyone else. My mom gave everything to the church, but they never showed up when it mattered."

"Them probably weren't real Christians." The words slipped before he could season them with the appropriate grace.

"Right? People preaching love but doing the opposite. The ones who're first to lay hands and pray are usually the last to help out. But your parents, they were the real thing."

His last Christmas with his parents, they'd had a silly argument when he refused to go to church with the family, fed up with the hypocrisy and fake church folk.

"Yeah," he said. "They were."

She smiled. "So are Abe and Phoebe. IB and Tonye."

"Yeah, I wanna be like them when I grow up."

Her laughter burst out before she slapped a hand over her mouth. He'd missed that sound.

She glanced at Joaquin and her smile faded. "He's always so tired. Barely eats," she said. "I should've been more careful while I was pregnant."

She sounded like Phoebe, who'd blamed herself for what neither she nor anyone else could control. As though mothers alone bore the weight of life and death.

"I don't know what to do," she whispered.

"Sometimes all we can do is pray."

She pressed a trembling hand to her forehead. "What if God doesn't want to heal him?"

"He will." The words left his mouth with a confidence that surprised him. But somehow, he believed it. "He gave you Joaquin for a reason."

She looked up at him. "But I've prayed so much. What if God's not listening?"

He reached for her hand. "Then we keep asking. Together. Where two or three are gathered..." Her brows rose, but he pressed on. "IB, Tonye, Abe, Phoebe. They're all here because God put them here. Even me. I'm here right now because He wanted me to be."

Her eyes searched his face. "Do you really believe that?"

He thought of Peter, the man he'd left behind to be here. "Yeah, I think I do."

When her hand slipped into his, he squeezed gently. He'd read somewhere that a man couldn't help hurting when he saw the tears of the woman he cared deeply for. But this wasn't just hurt. It was pure devastation ripping up his heart and stitching him back together again with hope.

"What do we do now?" Geri asked.

He looked down at their hands. It had been years since he prayed out loud, but he'd found the best way to express his craziest—most desperate thoughts—was to whisper it into the void, a silence where there was no judgment. Only a peace that never made any sense to him, but somehow had the power to

41

quiet the madness in his own mind.

"How about we start with gratitude?"

She squinted. "Grateful for what?"

For this, he wanted to say. For you. If he'd known what would happen, he never would have let her go.

"You're almost home," he said.

"Closer to Nigeria than Houston," she pointed out.

He'd missed her smart mouth. "But we've started the journey. Let's start there. Close your eyes."

She huffed before doing so. He studied her face, the freckles, the weary yet enduring strength she'd always carried with her. Soft streaks of light seeped through the edges of the curtain, chasing away the shadows in the room.

For the first time in years, Bart found himself praying, not just for Joaquin, but for Geri, and the strength for him to be what they needed.

He spoke the words he'd learned from his dad many years ago.

"Our good Father in heaven..."

9

Darah stretched her legs and got up from the airport bench. The screen listing incoming flights had stopped moving.

"Why's it moving so slow?" Darah groaned. "Their flight already landed ages ago."

"You should've stayed home," Abe said, not bothering to look up.

Darah laughed at the irritation in his voice. "Can you believe that guy didn't even call me back the whole time he was there?"

Abe stood as a new wave of passengers flooded the gates. "He had his hands full."

Darah scanned the crowd, letting her imagination wander, all these people with captivating stories, their luggage trailing behind them like secrets. Somewhere in the rush, Bart and Geri would appear to write another chapter in their story.

"You think they're good now?" Darah asked. "It would've

been awkward spending two weeks together if they're still beefing."

Abe chuckled. "Guess we'll see soon enough."

Darah rolled her eyes. He always left her dangling on the hook, just like a good book. Ever since Phoebe had spilled the tea about Bart and Geri being stuck in Ghana together, Darah had been inspired to write a close proximity slow-burn romance with a plot twist—the hero rescuing the heroine from her villainous mother-in-law. And the baby—a son, no less. It was crazy how no one had told her about Joaquin.

A man in the crowd was pushing a luggage cart with his ball cap pulled low. Beside him, a woman walked quickly, a bundled toddler pressed against her chest.

Abe gave a low whistle and the couple turned. Bart.

"Geri," Darah called. She looked much older than their four years apart. The sparkle in her eyes had dimmed, her rosy cheeks thinned, skin kissed by the African sun.

"Darah?" Geri's voice still had that familiar lilt.

Darah stopped short of hugging Geri with the child sleeping against her chest. "He's so cute," Darah cooed. "I can't believe it's really you."

"It's me," Geri said softly, like she needed convincing.

"Good to have you back," Abe said, clapping Bart on the shoulder. "Well done, bro."

Darah blinked at Bart. "Dude, you look different."

His smile was tilted. "Been gone a month and this is my welcome?"

"I called you," she said.

"I know," Bart replied.

"But you didn't call back."

"I know."

"Seriously?" She studied his overgrown beard, the dark lines beneath his eyes, the swelling around his nose, each detail hinting at a story she would sign up to read any day. "Are you okay?"

"I'm good," he replied too fast. "Why are you even here? It's a school night."

Darah squared her shoulders, but Abe cut in. "D, why don't you stay with Geri and Joaquin while Bart and I get the car."

"We can go together," Geri said, stepping closer to Bart like gravity had pulled her to him.

Bart touched Geri's arm like she was glass, irreplaceable. "We'll be back soon," he said, glancing at Darah as if he wanted her to jump in.

"We can wait by the window," Darah said. "We parked pretty far away. It's been a mess since Harvey."

Geri scanned the terminal like someone might emerge from the crowd. "Okay."

When her brothers left, Darah led Geri to a bench by the windows. Geri adjusted Joaquin on her lap, her movements slow, like each motion brought pain.

"Isn't he heavy?" Darah asked. Geri as a mom still didn't feel real.

"You get used to it," Geri replied, her smile faint.

"Everyone's so excited to see you. Even Aunt Lina and Ms. Jen wanted to come."

"Ms. Jen?" Her lips twitched, a flicker of the old Geri peeking through. "It's been so long, hasn't it?"

"Way too long." Darah remembered those late-night calls when Geri had just moved to Nigeria, the excitement in her voice about the "motherland." Then like a candle wilting in the dark, Geri had met her dream man and the line had gone quiet, her world becoming too distant.

45

"You've grown so much," Geri said. "Taller than me now."

She'd passed Geri back in eighth grade. Her height was becoming a problem, draining the pool of potential boyfriends. "You should see Eli. He's talking more, growing like a weed."

Her smile lingered this time. "I can't wait to see him."

"I missed you."

"I missed you, too." Geri laughed, its old warmth giving Darah hope that the weird tension would pass with time.

The little boy in Geri's arms stirred, big brown eyes peeking out from under the hood of his puffer jacket. As Geri adjusted him again, Darah noticed the scar on Geri's arm, a jagged truth too loud to ignore.

"Joaquin's gonna love the playground we built at Bart's," Darah said to brighten the mood. "Swings, slides, the whole works."

"That's so nice. You guys are always looking out for me. Thank you."

"We're family."

"Family?" Geri repeated, quiet. She stood, shifting Joaquin onto her hip. "Bart's here."

Bart strode in, all smile and brightness. "He's awake."

Joaquin reached for him and Geri handed him over without hesitation. A seamless transition. They looked like a family.

Bart caught Darah staring and his smile wobbled. "Abe's out front," he said.

They made their way to the car. Darah took the back third-row seat while Bart helped buckle Joaquin in the booster seat, double-checking the straps like a doting dad.

The drive back stretched longer than usual along the cracked highway and collapsed fences, reminders of everything Hurricane Harvey had stolen when it hit Houston just three weeks ago. Those days had been full of uncertainty as the flood waters rose and forced them to evacuate to Bart's house in the next neighborhood.

As they sped past the turn to their house, Darah traced her finger on the cool windowpane. The blue tarp clung to the roof like a ghost refusing to leave. She missed the old house, the way things used to be, the sense of everything and everyone belonging in the right place. Now, it was just silence where her parents' voices once echoed.

"It really hit y'all area bad," Geri murmured.

"Need to replace the roof," Abe said. "We're staying at Bart's for now."

"You live nearby?" Geri asked.

"Two streets over," Bart replied.

"Wow, that close." Geri sounded surprised. "Your house didn't flood at all?"

"No, the whole neighborhood is on higher ground," he explained.

"He did a lot of research before he bought it," Darah jumped in, earning a grin from Bart.

When they pulled into Bart's driveway, Bart scooped the sleeping toddler out of the booster, and Joaquin burrowed against Bart's chest.

Darah trailed behind them. The front door flew open, and Phoebe pulled Geri inside with a warm hug. Bart followed, leaving Darah alone with Abe grabbing bags from the trunk.

"Wasn't that weird?" Darah asked, slinging a duffel bag over her shoulder.

"You mean Bart and Geri?" Abe said, his tone too casual to be innocent.

"They seem super close."

"I thought that's what you wanted."

Darah blinked. "Wait. Is that what you want?"

Abe rolled the suitcase across the driveway. "I told you—"

"Complicated," she finished, mimicking his exasperated tone just as Bart stepped out.

"What's complicated?" Bart asked, popping a candy into his mouth.

"You and…watermelon candy," she deflected, changing course under Abe's warning stare.

Bart laughed. 'You never stop, do you?"

"No, it's weird." She couldn't understand his obsession with watermelon candy, the only flavor of candy he ate.

"Girl, go to sleep. You gotta be at school in a few hours."

Her stomach sank. She'd forgotten. Tomorrow meant classes, rushed notes between bells, and the unspoken pressure to belong, to pretend she cared. High school was becoming an experience she could have lived without, a place she drifted through but never belonged. She'd hoped for at least one day to breathe before being swallowed up again.

She trudged inside, passing by the guest room they'd prepped for Geri and Joaquin. Light spilled from beneath the closed door, Phoebe's laughter mingling with Joaquin's giggles.

Their home felt different now. Warmer. Alive.

"Darah," Abe called from the living room.

"I'm going, sheesh." She slipped into the room she shared with Eli, his soft snores subdued by the hum of the white noise machine she'd insisted on getting last week.

As she slid under the covers, Joaquin's laughter lingered, light as breath. Geri wasn't the same woman who'd left for Nigeria. And Bart? He wasn't the same either. None of them were. Yet somehow, it felt like their makeshift family had stitched itself whole again.

Maybe this was how true healing began. Not with butterflies or neatly-tied up endings. Just quiet and steady. One returned voice at a time.

10

"Glory," Phoebe huffed, chasing Joaquin around the furniture.

"I think you should sit down," Geri said. But she couldn't stop laughing because her son's unrestrained giggles filled the room, a sound so rare it almost brought tears to her eyes. They had been back in Houston barely two days, and already Joaquin was a different child. Yes, he'd been getting stronger since their first week in Ghana, but now he clutched at the world with boundless energy, feeding off Phoebe's infectious energy.

Phoebe, the perfect picture of a mother-to-be, glowed with that irresistible warmth God had bestowed on pregnant women alone.

Geri couldn't remember glowing when she was pregnant. Those early months in Abuja, she'd been a shadow of herself, tormented by nausea and her in-laws, fleeing to Port Harcourt before anyone could discover her pregnancy.

"We should start heading out," Bart said as he stepped into the living room.

Geri caught Joaquin in her arms before he could run to Bart. Last night, it had dawned on her that she needed to start creating some space between her son and Bart. How would Joaquin cope without Bart once they moved in with her mom?

Phoebe laughed. "He really likes you, Bart."

Like was an understatement. Joaquin clung to Bart as if he'd always been in their lives. Bart didn't seem to mind. He welcomed the boy's affection like it was the most natural thing in the world. It was troubling how easily Joaquin—they—had come to rely on him. They'd spent every day together for the past month. Through the tough nights and long days at the hospital, he was always there. He'd seen her at her most vulnerable. Like that one week in Ghana when her period had hit harder than usual, he'd quietly gone out and returned with pads, painkillers, and chocolate. She'd joked that some woman had trained him well, but he hadn't laughed, just looked at her like he wanted to hold her. And that was the hardest part. Not knowing whether to run or let herself fall into him.

"We should pray before you leave," Phoebe said.

So they did. Then Bart drove them to the pediatric clinic Phoebe had raved about. He was quiet during the ride. Geri found herself glancing at him more than once.

"Are you going to get your nose checked?" Geri asked. He always acted like it didn't bother him, but she'd caught him wincing now and then.

"I'll get around to it," Bart said. "Are you sure you didn't want Phoebe to come?"

Geri nodded. She'd told Phoebe she wanted to handle this

first visit alone. She couldn't depend on the Tekas forever.

"Can I go in alone with Joaquin?" Geri asked when they got to the clinic.

"Sure," Bart said. He handed Joaquin his yellow toy car from Amsterdam. Joaquin clutched the car like it was Bart himself.

Once inside, the wait was short. Geri had barely gathered her nerves before a nurse called on them. The questions came fast and clinical as the nurse took Joaquin's weight and height. By the time they reached the exam room, Geri felt sure the visit would end badly.

"Do you have any concerns?" the nurse asked before leaving.

It took Geri a long moment before she shook her head. Where could she even begin? Today might just be the start of another long cycle of tests, sleepless nights checking out medical websites, fearing every possible outcome.

A rap at the door startled her. A fresh-faced man in navy scrubs entered.

"Hello," he said, as if talking to the ceiling. He scanned the room until his eyes landed on Joaquin. "I'm Dr. Song."

Phineas Song. Phoebe had raved about this young pediatrician who had helped Eli thrive after Mama Ester had switched Eli from another doctor.

"Nice to meet you, Joaquin," he said, voice warm but brisk.

Joaquin clung to her. "Sorry, he's—" Geri said.

"It's okay," Dr. Song said. "Takes time to get used to me." He sat on a stool by the door and stared at Joaquin with a depth that made Geri's heart race. "Joaquin is thirty-three inches. Is his father tall?"

Hakeem's face flickered in her mind. "Yes. He was."

Dr. Song adjusted the stethoscope in his pocket. This was the part where doctors sighed and told Geri what else was wrong with her son.

"You mentioned he sleeps more than usual, yet still seems tired? Was he a good sleeper early on?"

"I'm not sure. He was in the NICU, but around six months, he mostly slept through the night until he turned one." The timeline blurred in her memory.

"Children might sleep more during growth spurts." His voice was calm, conversational. "Joaquin, can you show me with your hand how old you are?"

Geri began to answer, but Joaquin raised two fingers.

"He's eighteen months," she said, stunned.

Dr. Song grinned. "That's a big age. Can you open your eyes really big for me, like this?" He made a silly face, and Joaquin mimicked him, giggling.

The doctor sat back, his eyes distant again as if his brain was conducting a rapid-fire drill of diagnoses. She held her breath, waiting for the dreaded verdict.

"You're expecting me to diagnose your son with something," he said finally.

Geri straightened on her chair. "Aren't you? You need to run more tests?"

He shook his head. "From what I've seen, we should take it slowly for now. I think Joaquin needs more time to settle into his body. If something's actually wrong, we'll figure it out together."

Air rushed out of her lungs. She bent forward, overwhelmed.

"Please, breathe," he said softly. "I keep telling the nurses we need a sign that says that."

Geri laughed, tears pooling.

"Sorry, I'm told I'm bad at this part of my job," he said, suddenly more awkward. "When I was young, my parents thought something was wrong with me. I didn't talk until I was three, diagnosed with a developmental delay. They homeschooled me, afraid I'd never make it in the real world." He smiled like a little kid, and Joaquin laughed.

Joaquin reached up to pat Geri's face. She held him tight, her thoughts spiraling back to those traumatic nights during her pregnancy, that nightmarish day she'd tumbled down the stairs, living with the constant regret that she'd failed her son before he'd even entered the world.

"Joaquin has a wonderful life ahead of him," Dr. Song said. "Let's give it time. Don't let anyone's biases limit his potential by comparing him to a standard. Help him break barriers. I'm here to help in whatever way I can."

"Thank you," Geri said. "You have no idea how much hope you've given me. And I don't agree that you're not good at your job. You're perfect, Dr. Song."

Later that night, Geri couldn't stop raving about him to Phoebe. When Phoebe finally stood to leave the room, Geri hugged her, her belly making the embrace awkward.

"Thank you," Geri whispered. "For everything. For letting us stay here."

"It's Bart's place," Phoebe teased. "And at some point, we need to talk about Ghana."

A knock spared Geri from replying. Bart opened the door, glanced at Joaquin asleep on the bed, and gestured at Phoebe.

"Your husband's looking for you," he said.

Phoebe left the room, her voice trailing with Bart's as they walked down the hall.

Geri climbed into bed, wondering if Bart would come back. She'd grown used to his voice reaching across the dark—from the couch by the hospital window—until she drifted off to sleep. Last night, sleep had been hard to come by.

She curled around her son, who still smelled of lavender from his bubble bath. The soft hum of the AC outside her window filled the silence. No car horns. No whirring overhead fan. Just quiet. A quiet she hadn't known in years.

Geri inhaled slowly, then let it go. This was the place she'd ached for all along. Maybe now that they were far away from the ghosts of her father's house, Joaquin could finally know what it felt like to have his own place in the world. A place he could call home.

11

Darah clenched her teeth until her braces groaned in protest. Someone had yanked her hair from behind, and she didn't need to look back to know who. Two junior varsity clowns with football dreams were sitting behind her.

She turned with slow fury to face them. Riding the school bus was like being in the eye of a senseless storm you could never forecast.

"Nice hairstyle, Puff-Puff," said the boy with the oversized Afro, hair-puller written all over his face.

"Thanks, Big Head," Darah shot back. "I can do your hair just like mine if you want."

Laughter scattered down the bus aisle. Thankfully, she wasn't the punchline.

Big Head stood up, looming over her. "Watch your back, Metal-mouth."

Darah rose to meet him, almost matching his height. If she didn't take a stand now, it would just keep going on. Their audience hollered louder, the chaos feeding itself.

"Sit down!" the bus driver's voice boomed through the noise.

Big Head's eyes flicked over her shoulder, and whatever he saw made him slouch back into his seat, grumbling under his breath.

The brakes screeched. Her stop.

Darah grabbed her bag and headed up the aisle, heart still thumping from the rush. Her foot caught on something— probably another cheap trick—and she lurched forward. A hand steadied her before she could faceplant into the dashboard.

Laughter exploded behind her like fireworks.

She turned and froze. Jeremy Walker.

"Easy," he said.

Darah brushed off his hand with surgical precision, careful not to make eye contact, because if she did, she might not look away. And that would be dangerous.

Jeremy's fan club—the sour-faced posse of girls who loved to orbit him—were already glaring daggers from their seats. Great. Just what she needed.

"You good?" His voice was maddeningly calm. Like a line from one of those songs you hated to love because it got stuck in your head for weeks.

"I'm fine," she mumbled, running down the steps like the bus was on fire. She'd barely hit the pavement when she realized he was following her.

"Why are you getting off here?" She almost tripped on the sidewalk.

"Why can't I?" he asked, with that same effortless shrug he used when dropping threes from half-court. "My truck's in the shop. When it's fixed, I'll give you a ride."

"No thanks." Riding with Jeremy Walker was signing a declaration of war. His horde of admirers would eat her alive.

She flopped onto the big boulder near the signpost—her unofficial waiting spot—where the neighborhood mom was already standing with her oversized tote and polite disinterest. She waved. The woman waved back.

"She seems nice," Jeremy noted.

Darah squinted up at him. "I thought you didn't do the bus."

He shifted, just enough to block the sun from her eyes. Of course he did. He was so perfect sometimes she wanted to roll her eyes.

He grinned at her like a toothpaste ad. Like he knew he was too charming for his own good. "How about we—"

"No."

"You didn't even let me—"

"I don't need to," she said. Her heart fluttered behind her ribcage like a moth caught in a jar.

Jeremy Walker wasn't just tall, smooth, and full of himself—he was dangerous. Caramel skin, a roster-listed 6'1", and that smile? Total YA author bait. The kind of guy who only existed on the covers of books she swore she read for the prose. The dream every literary heroine ended up kissing under the stars—and then regretted it, because wolves always bite.

This was real life. Boys like Jeremy didn't look twice at girls like her. Not unless it was a prank cruelly hidden behind a sweet smile.

She'd never guessed he knew who she was until SAT Prep, when he'd asked for her number out of nowhere, right before a crowd of girls descended like bees on a dropped popsicle.

"Your little brother's bus is next, right?"

Her spine straightened. "How do you know that?"

"I'm stalking you," he said.

She hated that she smiled. She turned toward the street so she wouldn't have to see his pretty face.

"Was there something you wanted?" She tried to be cool about it, but her voice betrayed her curiosity.

Jeremy tucked his hands into his pockets. "I'm looking at it right now."

Her cheeks warmed under his gaze. "Well, I'd rather not be looked at right now."

"Why?"

"I look a mess."

He tilted his head. "Well, thank God it's a free country. I like to look at beautiful things that make me happy." He kept staring. "Darah," he said softly, like he was testing how her name tasted. "Let's hang out. Just us."

"What, like a date?"

"Yeah. Give me your number." He was too much—too confident, too everything. "You want me to leave, right?"

Darah widened her eyes. Was he blackmailing her? "I can't believe you." She shoved her phone into his hand. "Put your number in and go."

He did, unbothered. His phone buzzed a second later, and he held it up in triumph. "Don't ghost me, Teks."

She snatched her phone back as Eli's bus rounded the corner. Jeremy winked before strolling off in the other direction like the whole exchange had been a casual win.

She couldn't help watching him go, her heart busting at the seams. Maybe she was overthinking this. Jeremy was only playing a game.

But maybe—just maybe—he actually liked her. And that

possibility felt dangerous, like the beginning of a chapter she wasn't sure she was capable of writing.

Eli's bus hissed to a stop. Elementary schoolers spilled out like leaves scattered on the wind. Neighborhood mom waved again, shepherding her crew away.

As the last kid skipped down the steps, the bus driver hooked a thumb over her shoulder. "Time to go, Eli."

He stood from the front seat, head still bowed, laser-focused on a worn puzzle cube.

"See you later, Mrs. H," he called, without looking up.

Darah matched his steps as they started toward home. "Dude, put that away before you trip and crack your skull." She nudged him toward the sidewalk's inner edge, placing herself closer to the street. "You should help me convince Abe to let me drive to school, then we both wouldn't have to ride the bus."

"I don't mind the bus," Eli said.

"But you don't have any friends." She cringed. "Sorry. That was mean."

"I have friends," Eli said, still unbothered.

She would have crumbled if someone had pointed out her social inadequacies. "Hannah doesn't count," she teased.

"I wasn't talking about Hannah. My friends ride another bus." He finally looked up. "You don't have any friends on your bus?"

Time to change the subject. "Did you fight with Hannah?" she asked, grabbing the low-hanging fruit. "Is your playdate cancelled?" She was scheduled to babysit Eli and Hannah this Saturday while Abe and Phoebe went out with Hannah's parents.

Eli scrunched his eyes. "Girls are complicated."

Darah slung an arm over his shoulder. "Don't beef with your girlfriend, E. Just apologize so we can have a peaceful weekend. I've already got plans for the money Phoebe promised me."

"She's not my girlfriend." He shrugged her arm off.

"Sure." She smirked. "So how was school? Besides fighting with your not-girlfriend?"

He let out a dramatic sigh, then his face lit up. "Guess what we watched in science class?"

There were exactly three things that got Eli Teka excited. Mario Kart marathons with Junior. Phoebe's lemon crunch cake. And "Penguins?"

"Rockhopper penguins," he beamed. "Do you know what they're known for?"

"Hopping rocks?" she deadpanned. He gave her the most exaggerated eye-roll. "C'mon then, Zoologist Eleazer Teka, educate me. What's so special about rockstar penguins?"

He launched into it, hands gesturing as he detailed their spiky eyebrows, oddly romantic mating rituals. She half-listened, content to just watch him light up. It never got old. Eli loved everything about penguins.

As they turned onto their street, her smile slipped. Construction crews crowded a nearby yard. Debris lined the sidewalks like scars—discarded furniture, ruined memories, pieces of people's lives waiting to be hauled away.

Their old house stood like a ghost, empty and hollow. Abe had asked them not to go inside, but they still walked by every school day, just to see if anything had changed.

Eli stopped, his gaze on the roof. The night the storm broke it open, he'd gone eerily quiet, just like in the months after their parents' death. Rainstorms always unsettled him, as if it made him remember things he wanted to forget.

Darah tugged his arm. They crossed the street into Bart's neighborhood. She'd once teased Bart for buying a house so close to theirs, like he couldn't escape them even if he tried. But that night, when they'd driven through rising waters to find his street untouched, her tears had been pure relief.

"Geri looks different," Eli said suddenly, stepping around a branch on the sidewalk. "What happened to her?"

Darah didn't answer right away. Even Eli—in his penguin-loving, cube-twisting bubble—had noticed. Geri was quieter now, as if the person they knew had been chipped away while she was gone.

"I don't know," Darah said.

Eli nodded like that was enough. "Can't believe she has a kid. You think he likes penguins?"

"You should show him your collection."

Eli grinned wide. "Cool. Race you?"

"No," she warned, but he was already sprinting. She ran after him, laughing, because in these moments, it felt like everything could be ordinary again.

Then she saw the red BMW parked by the curb. A woman stepped out in a hot pink dress, with sunglasses large enough to hide her lies.

"Knew it," Darah muttered, skidding to a halt.

Ms. Trouble in heels walked around Bart's truck. As much as Darah hated to admit it, the woman's style was always on point. A tad too flashy, but still, Kasey Hernandez was as cool as it got. And she was back.

Kasey—Bart's on-and-off girlfriend—strutted toward them in clicking stilettos, clutching a takeout bag from Canes like it was a trophy for showing up unannounced. Her voice wrapped in that sugary mean girl tone Darah knew too well.

"Hi guys," Kasey said. "You just got back?"

"Yeah," Eli said, with a big smile.

Darah didn't bother responding. Kasey always knew when to

resurface, right when Darah had started to forget her.

Darah unlocked the door with a little more force than necessary. Laughter spilled out as she stepped inside. In the living room, Bart and Joaquin were jumping from cushion to cushion. Phoebe and Geri were on the couch, laughing hard.

"Is this The Floor is Lava?" Eli asked, excited.

Bart scooped Joaquin up mid-jump, his grin wide, until he noticed them.

Darah didn't need to look to turn. She could feel Kasey behind her, that overpowering perfume which smelled like everything and nothing all at once.

She stepped aside and gave Bart a clear view of the doorway and the woman he strangely couldn't seem to shake. Since Bart moved to Houston, he'd dated a number of women, who came and went, but Kasey always seemed to be in play. Last Darah heard, they'd broken up. Again.

"Hi, friends," Kasey greeted, strutting in like a fashion ad.

Bart put Joaquin down. The little boy ran to Geri, who wrapped her arms around him.

"Hi, Kasey," Phoebe said, warm as always. "Long time."

Darah fought back a laugh. Nobody called you out like Phoebe Teka, every word landing like a velvet slap.

But that was just how Phoebe rolled. She actually liked Kasey. Kasey had been there for her after the miscarriage, and Phoebe never forgot that.

"Hope I'm not intruding, girl," Kasey chirped.

"Not at all." Phoebe turned. "This is Geri and her son, Joaquin, family friends. Geri, this is Kasey, Bart's—"

"Girlfriend," Kasey said, eyes locking onto Geri like a challenge. "Nice to finally meet you."

Geri nodded. Not even a blink of surprise. "Likewise," she

said, without a single glance at Bart, who was super interested in fluffing sofa cushions.

Dead giveaway. He hadn't told Geri about Kasey.

"I brought chicken for y'all," Kasey announced, placing the bag on the coffee table like a peace offering.

Bart finally faced her. "Hi."

An awkward silence landed until Phoebe—the peacemaker— spoke up. "Thanks. Darah, you got your wish—fried chicken for dinner."

"Yay," Darah deadpanned. She'd asked for chicken days ago.

"Of course." Kasey's hand slid onto Bart's waist. "Would love to stay, but I'm gonna steal Bart for a bit, if you don't mind."

Bart glanced at Geri. "Sure. Let me grab my phone." As he walked away, Kasey laced their fingers and followed him upstairs.

Darah went to sit beside Geri, who remained quiet, unreadable. Joaquin wiggled out of her arms and trotted over to Eli, who offered a high five.

Phoebe opened the chicken box. "I'm starving. Anyone up for an early dinner?"

Eli and Joaquin rushed to Phoebe. "Can I give some to him?" Eli asked, holding up a drumstick.

Geri jerked forward. "No, he's alle—"

Too late. Joaquin grabbed the drumstick from Eli and took a giant bite. Phoebe and Geri exchanged a look of horror. Phoebe reached for Joaquin, but Geri raised a hand.

"It's okay," she said. "Dr. Song said not to limit him. Let's see what happens."

They waited, watched. Nothing happened. Joaquin kept chewing happily, unbothered, while Geri took deep breaths.

When Bart and Kasey came down the stairs, Bart rushed to Joaquin.

"We're good," Geri said with surprising poise. "Enjoy your night out."

"But—" Bart started.

"It's okay, Bart," Phoebe cut in. "We got this."

Clueless, Kasey smiled at Joaquin. "Glad someone else likes Canes." Her hand found Bart's again, but he moved his hand away from reach. "Well, goodnight, everyone," Kasey said, her smile plastic.

"Thanks for dinner," Phoebe said, reaching for a wing. "Y'all be safe."

"You too, girl," Kasey said as she tugged Bart toward the door.

He looked like a man being dragged to the gallows. Once Kasey stepped outside, he hesitated at the doorway, eyes on Joaquin.

"I'll be back soon," Bart said, closing the door behind him.

12

Outside, the cool evening air slapped his cheeks like a wake-up alarm. "Wait."

Kasey didn't slow down. Her heels clicked against the pavement, each step as sharp as her posture. She was furious.

"Can we just talk out here?" Bart asked.

Kasey flung open the car door. "No. I need a drink. You drive."

Her tone invited no argument. He should have seen this coming: Kasey showing up at his house. The moment she'd introduced herself in front of Geri, she might as well have punched him. Kasey never referred to herself as his girlfriend. Complicated—that was the term she preferred. But coming face-to-face with the Geri she'd heard about for years must have rattled her. Enough to forget her usual detachment.

Bart glanced back at the house. The look Geri had given him

had been icy. And now Kasey was slamming the passenger door like she wanted to rip it out.

He climbed into the driver's seat, but didn't start her engine.

"So, she's back," Kasey said, voice edged like broken glass. "And you didn't think to tell me."

"You're acting like I didn't call you," he murmured.

"I called you back."

He sighed, leaning his head against the seat. "Kasey, please. Don't start."

"Don't start?" She let out a sharp laugh. "You're seriously telling me not to talk about the fact that Geri—the woman you've been hung up since before we even met—just showed up, and you couldn't even look at me when I called myself your girlfriend?"

"You don't even like being called that."

"That's not the point, Bart." She jabbed a finger toward him. "You never gave us a real chance. Be honest. Have you ever imagined a future with me?"

He couldn't believe she was putting it on him. From the beginning, Kasey had made it clear she didn't want anything serious. But when he'd finally gotten tired of the games, she'd decided to change the rules and upgrade him from a special friend—to what he wasn't even sure.

"I've tried to be what you wanted," he said. "But you always seem to want something else."

Kasey scoffed. "What I want is someone who isn't still in love with another woman."

Bart couldn't meet her eyes. Not when she said it that way. Not when she was right.

"It's not like that," he offered, though the words felt hollow to him. "Geri's..."

"Geri's what, Bart? Don't lie to me. I saw the way you looked at her. Don't sit here and tell me there's nothing between y'all."

He couldn't say that. At least not on his side. Geri probably didn't feel the same. After a month together, she was still holding him at arm's length.

Kasey turned her face to the window. "I need a drink. Drive. You know where."

Bart started the car. They drove in silence, the hum of Houston traffic the only sound between them. They ended up at their usual spot, a downtown lounge with mellow music and strong drinks. Kasey made her way to the bar and started tossing back shots, laying her words on him with every sip of her cocktail.

He didn't drink. Not tonight with his mind scattered, heart torn. He barely said a word, just sat there. She had every right to be angry, but he'd always kept it real with her. The way she was drinking, he knew he'd be driving her home. Then calling an Uber.

"Are you a sucker for punishment?" Kasey asked, twirling the stem of her glass. "Maybe I've been too nice to you."

Bart cracked a smile. "That's your definition of nice? Dumping me and picking me back up again when it suits you?"

Kasey gave him a guilty look. "It's not like that," she said, using his own words against him. "I was just taking my time. Trying to figure us out."

Bart leaned forward, elbows on the bar, waiting for her to finish. She stared into her drink, her face shifting, anger melting into a look like regret.

"Why don't you ever look at me that way?" she asked softly.

He reached into his pocket but didn't pull out a gummy. "What way?"

"The way you looked at her."

He didn't answer. Didn't need to. He snatched the untouched

glass in front of him and downed it, ruining the dry streak he'd kept for months.

The alcohol did nothing to loosen the knot in his chest. Seeing Geri again had wrecked him. He'd tried to bury her memory for years, under easy distractions, and Kasey. But it had always been Geri. Every failed relationship, every woman he walked away from, every time he pretended not to care, it all pointed back to her.

Kasey must have known that, from the beginning, right here in this lounge, the first night they met. She'd been newly single, venting about her ex-fiancé. He'd just been dumped by another woman who'd accused him of being distant.

But Kasey was different. They'd talked until the lounge closed, laughed, drank, danced. It wasn't love. It was just safe, easy.

"You always said you didn't want anything serious," Bart said.

"I changed," she said, her voice almost bitter. "You changed me. I've had time to think, since we broke up."

She looked at the shot glass like it held an answer. "Take me home, Bart." Then with a dry smile: "One more for the road." She tossed it back and stood.

Bart drove her home, the silence unbearable. He'd never thought Kasey could be so quiet, especially after drinking.

"I'm sorry," Bart said, the words slipping out before he could still them. He'd known Kasey was fighting her feelings for him, which was why she'd always treated their relationship like a fast-food romance.

"Me too," was all she said.

At her house, Kasey leaned into him for a hug. She'd called an Uber to come get him, but the Uber was late.

"I'm not giving up on us, Bart. When she flies away again, I'll be here. I'll be the one who puts you back together."

69

His stomach twisted, but he said nothing. His Uber pulled up as she closed the door behind her.

On the drive back, Bart kept his eyes shut most of the way, the ache in his chest spreading with every mile. Kasey was right. Geri would probably leave again, to a place he couldn't reach her. She had every reason not to stay.

Still, he loved her. Because love was the only answer for this all-consuming feeling that had stayed with him all these years.

Maybe that made him a fool. But he couldn't stop. Not anymore.

When he got to his house, he didn't go inside right away. He stood in the yard and looked up at the stars, brilliant, impossibly far.

Geri was back. And so were the feelings he'd spent years pretending didn't exist.

He drew in a deep breath, the words on his lips. But he didn't say them. Not yet.

It was time to face the truth. Whatever it cost.

13

Bart had a girlfriend. In the two weeks they'd spent together in Ghana—through long hospital nights and whispered prayers—he hadn't once mentioned a girlfriend, let alone that woman. That glamorous, caramel-skinned vision who clung to him like he belonged to her.

All night, Geri tried to banish the image of Bart and Kasey walking hand-in-hand, her stilettos clicking like exclamation marks on the hardwood floor.

After seeing that, she couldn't stay in his house anymore. She needed to leave. After everything Bart had done for her and Joaquin, the least she could do was give him back his life back, his home, his freedom, and the woman who seemed to fit him perfectly.

First thing in the morning, Geri called her mother. They hadn't spoken since Ghana—when her mom had told her the

Rockport house had flooded during Harvey, so Geri had been forced to rework her plans to stay with her mom. But in the week since Geri had returned to Houston, her mother hadn't called, not a single check-in to see if her daughter and grandson were alive.

"How did it go with the doctor?" her mom asked, casual as ever.

Geri looked at Joaquin snoring beside her on the bed. "It went great. He says Joaquin is going to be fine."

Her mom let out a scream of praise. "Look at God! What a miracle. My people, come and hear—"

A chorus of voices exploded in the background, a wave of shouting and tongues and hallelujahs. When her mom came back on, she sounded breathless.

"When are you coming to see your grandson?" Geri asked. Silence. Then the background noise surged again. "Mom?"

"Mija, can I call you back?"

Geri gripped the phone tighter. "You always do this."

"Do what?"

The clipped tone, that deflective pitch, Geri knew it too well. It always left her feeling like a child again.

"You know it's not that I don't want to come," her mom continued. "There's just a lot going on right now. You can't expect me to drop everything and come running."

"No one's asking you to drop everything. We need to talk about fixing the house. Shouldn't that be your priority?"

"I'm staying with my friend from fellowship," she said, far too cheery. "It's been such a blessing. So encouraging."

Of course. Her mother was tucked away in her bubble of church events and spiritual highs. Still conveniently unavailable when Geri needed her most.

"I thought maybe you'd want to see your grandson," Geri

said. Her mom had probably never once thought of coming to Nigeria when her own daughter was going through hell. "We're all praying for you," she would always say, those few times Geri had managed to get her on the phone.

"Sorry I can't right now," her mom said. "Our apostle from Rio is here this week. It's a big conference."

Another revival. Another excuse. Same old mother. Between the long shifts at work to keep them from being homeless and the long shifts at church to keep them from hell, her mother had been mostly absent. Geri had spent her teenage years waiting for her mom to come get her from the Teka's house. And now, even with her own child in tow, she was still waiting. Still hoping to be chosen first.

"Whatever, Mom."

"Don't be like that, mija. I'll call tomorrow. The sessions end late tonight. Please kiss my baby and tell him Abuela loves him."

When the line went dead, Geri tossed the phone on the bed, trying not to let the tears fall. Her mother had always been better at offering excuses than any real comfort, but it was the silence beneath the words that hurt the most.

A soft knock pulled her back to the present. She wiped her face quickly and opened the door to find Ms. Jen waiting in the hallway.

"Oh, my Geri," the older woman said, pulling her into a hug. "It's so glorious to see you again." Ms. Jen stepped back with those searching eyes. "Is everything okay?"

The warmth in her voice brought more tears to Geri's eyes. Before she could answer, Darah popped around the corner.

"Is Joaquin still sleep?" Darah asked, bright-eyed. "We're having a little party to celebrate you guys coming home."

Geri felt her smile falter, just before she caught herself. "That sounds like a blast," she said, staring at this tall girl-woman who used to play with dolls and dream of going to space. Just how much had she missed?

"You okay?" Darah asked, sounding careful now.

Of course they could tell. Her face was probably still blotchy from the phone call. Thankfully, Phoebe's voice rang from the living room, calling Darah and Ms. Jen away.

Geri slipped back into the room. Joaquin was awake. She scooped him into her arms just as Phoebe appeared at the door with Ms. Jen.

"Abe's going by the house," Phoebe said. "He wanted to know if you'd like to come, so he could pick your brain."

Geri hesitated. "I—no, it's okay, I'll see it another time."

"I think it'll be good for you," Phoebe said. "Ms. Jen and I can watch Joaquin."

"Yes, you should go," Ms. Jen added. "Abe needs your help."

That was how they framed it—like she'd be helping them. This was her chance to do something useful in return for all the love they'd poured out.

"I need practice," Phoebe said, patting her belly. "If I can't handle Joaquin with Ms. Jen, then I'm definitely in trouble." As she was speaking, Joaquin reached for Phoebe and wrapped his arms around her belly like it was familiar territory.

That settled it. Geri kissed her son's cheek and gave them a grateful smile. "Okay. I'll go."

Within minutes, Geri was in the passenger seat beside Abe, riding through the neighborhood toward the old house. A large dumpster blocked part of the driveway. The steady thrum of hammers and nail guns echoed from the rooftop above.

When she got out of the car, she stared at the house. She couldn't believe she was seeing it again. The porch had been repaired. The old heavy oak door was gone, replaced by a sleek fire-red fiberglass, one of the things Geri had suggested in her "renovation arguments" with Bart.

"We decided to replace the whole roof instead of patching it," Abe said.

Geri followed him up to the front steps. She paused at the threshold. The front room looked like a page torn from a home design magazine. The bulky leather sofas were gone, replaced by velvet chairs facing a white-painted brick fireplace, the framed photographs on the wall curated like a gallery. No more clutter.

Abe breezed past the den, now a home office with floor-to-ceiling bookshelves, lined with knick-knacks and more family pictures.

"I know, it's changed a lot," he said, heading to the kitchen.

The familiar yellow wood cabinets had been swapped for soft gray. A French-door refrigerator stood where the old one once hummed. Geri trailed her fingers along the smooth counters, almost disoriented by how little remained of what used to be.

"It's beautiful." Years ago, Bart had shot down many of these ideas. "Was there a lot of damage upstairs?"

"We had to rip out the carpet in Mom and Dad's room—our room now. Junior's old room is the nursery."

They started up the stairs, no longer squeaky, no longer faded, the railing polished and new. The old banister she'd helped Papa Yonas fix was gone. So many traces of her life here had been stripped away. The scent of fresh paint and lemon filled the air, but the soul of the house lingered, like a warm memory waiting for her to speak its name.

At Junior's room, the door stood open. Windows bare, drywall unfinished.

"Baby's room, right?"

Abe sighed. "It's taking longer than planned. That's why I told Phoebe not to come. She cried last time."

Geri walked to the center of the room that once reeked of teen boy sweat and dirty laundry. The room where they'd found Junior's gun. That same day they'd found out about Marcus, who was now Phoebe's adopted brother. Everything had changed since she last stood in this room.

"Yo," Bart's voice called from downstairs.

Geri turned toward the window to avoid him. She hadn't seen him since last night. Had he even come home? His footsteps pounded up the stairs. She wasn't ready to see whatever expression was waiting in his eyes.

"Bart, I thought they'd be further along in here," Abe said.

"Calm down," Bart said. "It'll get done."

Geri stole a glance over her shoulder. Bart was looking at her, his mouth working. He always seemed to be chewing something or walking around with a lollipop in his mouth. Yesterday, Darah had casually joked about Bart's obsession with watermelon, and Geri couldn't help connecting his fixation to her own past fondness for watermelon gummies. Up until she'd left for Nigeria, she'd always carried candy, not lollipops though. Still, it was a stretch to think Bart's sudden fondness for candy had anything to do with her.

"We don't want Phoebe crying again," Bart said, moving past Geri to look out the window.

"She's gonna ask me about the nursery," Abe grumbled. "Please, I need this finished before we can tell her anything."

Geri peered into the closet. Abe had changed. Marriage had softened him. Watching the two of them stand there arguing like old times, she couldn't help feeling like an intruder.

"They haven't even installed the shelves yet," Abe said,

pointing at the closet. "Nothing's ready."

"I can help," Geri blurted out, not even sure where the words came from.

Abe frowned. "No. You're supposed to be—"

"I need to do something," she said, firmer now. "It's been weird being back, so let me help. I can get this room ready in time. You know I'm good at this."

Abe looked past her, clearly asking Bart for his opinion.

"Please, Abe. I need this. I need to be part of something again."

Abe didn't look convinced. "It's a lot of work, Geri."

"I can do it," she said, meaning it more than she'd meant anything in a long time. Maybe this was exactly what she needed to feel a little more like herself. "I'll do anything."

"Anything?" Bart's voice cut through the moment.

Something about the way he said the word made Geri smile. Or maybe it was the thrill of making this space come alive with Phoebe's colorful vision. A baby's room, something she'd never been able to give Joaquin.

Bart extended his hand. "You're hired. Your first assignment: bring this room to life."

Geri stared at his hand for a beat before reaching out. His hand was warm, familiar. She glanced at Abe, who clapped a hand on Bart's shoulder.

"He's the boss," Abe said.

Bart's eyes were locked on hers. "You'll do anything I tell you?"

He held on to her hand and she didn't pull away. "Whatever you need, jefe."

And she meant it. After everything he'd done for her, whatever Bart Teka wanted from her, she was willing to give.

14

After Bart left the nursery, he stopped by the master bedroom. He'd thought he was in control until that familiar spark in Geri's eyes had unraveled him. Working together might be good for Geri, but it was terrible for him.

He caught himself smiling in the body-length mirror on the wall. This room used to be his parents' bedroom and had taken the worst of the storm. His crew had gutted it down to the studs to make space for Phoebe's vision.

Abe followed him in. "What was that about?" he whispered.

Bart shrugged. "Baby girl's due in two months. We need all the help we can get. And Geri needs a distraction."

Abe gave him a look. "You still haven't told me what happened in Ghana."

"What could've happened?"

"That's a weird answer."

"To a weird question. You know full well nothing happened."

Abe raised a brow. "And Kasey?"

Bart ran his hand along the smooth drywall. "She broke up with me."

"When hasn't she? I heard she came by with Canes."

Bart sighed. "You never liked Kasey."

"I never said that."

"You didn't have to. Just be honest."

"I am. I think Kasey's cool. Phoebe loves her." Abe pointed a finger at Bart. "The problem is you. The question you should be asking is: why don't you like her?"

"What are you talking about?" Bart scoffed, but he knew. Darah had asked him once why he kept dating women he didn't seem to like.

"It's not that I don't like her," Bart said. "I just never made space for her. Not the right way." He'd always kept Kasey at a distance, and his family had sensed that.

"You know she RSVP'd to the shower," Abe said.

Bart winced. He'd forgotten Kasey would be there. She was never one to miss a performance. "I'll text her not to come," Bart said, already dreading her response.

"No, Phoebe wouldn't like that."

"Then what am I supposed to do?" His relationship with Kasey was never supposed to become complicated, yet like all of his other relationships with women, it somehow had.

From the start, it was impossible not to compare Kasey to Phoebe. The family had embraced Phoebe immediately—even before she'd started dating Abe. Phoebe had just belonged. Until Kasey, none of the women he'd dated had behaved like they wanted to be part of the Tekas. They wanted him, but apart from his unusual family.

"You kept the tub?" Geri's voice sounded behind them.

She stood in the doorway, a different Geri from the one who'd once stood in this same bathroom, fighting to preserve Mom and Dad's old tub, and every other thing Bart had wanted to replace.

By now, she should have noticed. Half the updates in this house—the colors, fixtures, and floorboards—had her fingerprints on them. He'd once resisted her design ideas, but somehow, over time, her once silly ideas had started making sense to him.

"Someone said taking it out would be like ripping the walls off," Bart said.

Geri raised a brow. "I said that?"

She had said much more in her old spitfire way of talking, mixing English and Spanish insults while fiercely defending what she loved.

"Phoebe loves the tub," Abe said.

Bart had forgotten Abe was even still there, and Abe's smirk said he knew it too.

"Papa searched high and low for this tub," Geri said, running a hand over its edge. "Because your mom saw it in a magazine and loved it."

Abe nodded: "Geri, you ready to head out? I need to stop by the store."

"I'll take her back," Bart said, too fast.

"No, it's okay—" Geri started.

"I need to show you something," he insisted.

"I guess it's settled then," Abe said, giving Bart one of those don't screw this up looks before disappearing down the stairs.

"Thanks," Bart said. He'd missed their quiet rhythm in Ghana, the way she used to fall asleep talking to him. Now, he lay awake most nights, wondering if she did too.

"What did you want to show me?" she asked.

Bart leaned against the frame. "Joaquin had no reaction to the chicken yesterday?"

Her eyes lit up. "Nothing. I watched him all night, but he slept fine."

"Just like Finn said—Dr. Song."

Geri nodded. "I'm really trying to believe it. That Joaquin can finally have a normal life."

"Just give it time. He's in a better environment now. We trust God and see what happens."

Geri squinted at him. "It's always weird hearing you talk about God."

"You act as if I'm this bad person."

"How could you be?"

She stared at him with a smile so soft he couldn't help looking away.

"I've been praying a lot more since I got here," she went on.

He didn't speak, just let the moment stretch.

"I'm trying," she said, eyes flicking toward the window. "That's all I can do."

"You're doing great." Yes, he missed the old Geri, but this new vulnerable woman was too adorable. He waited for her to continue, but she didn't. "What about your mom?"

Geri rolled her eyes. "She's living it up at church conferences and prayer meetings."

"Good for her."

"I can't stay in your house forever, Bart."

His smile faded. "I know. But don't feel like you have to leave."

Her eyes narrowed. "How do I even begin to repay you?"

He nudged her shoulder to lighten the moment. "You're scaring me with all this niceness."

She laughed, but the warmth passed too quickly. "We should head back. Joaquin will wonder where I am."

They walked down the stairs. Bart's hand twitched at his side, aching to reach for hers.

He knew better. She wasn't ready to receive what he had to give.

But he was ready to wait. For as long as it took.

15

"What happened to your old tool belt?" Bart asked.

Geri walked ahead of him, her hips swinging just enough to keep him staring. He even missed that dusty old belt and her clunky work boots.

Geri paused at the edge of the driveway. "Mom probably sold it when she moved to Rockport."

He opened the truck door for her. She gave him a suspicious look but climbed in anyway. He drove across the highway to the same hardware store they'd gone to four years ago. When he pulled into the lot, Geri smiled, as if remembering how he once dropped his keys out there.

"What are we doing?" Geri asked.

"Getting you some tools."

That earned him another smile as they walked inside. "I don't need much. I'll have to find out what colors Phoebe wants for the room."

Once they reached the power tools section, her eyes lit up like she'd stepped into Tiffany's. "This is genius," she said, holding up a sleek rechargeable battery. "What a beautiful color."

Bart dropped the boxed set into the cart.

"I don't need all that," she said.

"You will."

"Yeah, but I—"

"Whoa, is that Bart?"

He turned and instantly regretted it. "Liz." His ex from high school. Of all the people, in all the places. He glanced at Geri, her mouth slightly open.

"I haven't seen you in forever!" Liz gushed, in that fake Valley-girl accent which used to annoy him. "Wow."

Bart plastered on a smile and—on impulse—reached for Geri's hand, expecting her to pull away. She didn't. "Yeah, it's been a while," he said.

Liz blinked at Geri. "Pena? Wow. You look—different. Whatever you're doing is really working for you. Go you."

Geri's grip tightened around Bart's hand, sending a current up his arm and down his spine. But her face stayed light, her smile believable.

"You look great, Liz," she said.

"Thanks." Liz tilted her head. "Wait, you two actually got together? That's so cute. What a small world."

"The smallest," Bart said, tugging Geri closer. "Hope you're well."

"We are. Me and hubby just opened our vet practice. He's already seeing clients, so I'm grabbing supplies." Liz's eyes dropped to their cart. "Still doing DIY projects? That's cute."

"Yeah, she is," Bart said before Geri could respond. "We've

got somewhere to be. Take care, Liz."

With a flick of her hair and a too-bright smile, Liz pushed her cart down the aisle. Geri watched her go, her jaw tight until Liz was out of sight.

He remembered what she'd once told him years ago—how girls like Liz had made high school miserable. Back then, he hadn't fully understood. But now it made sense. And he'd dated Liz, which meant he'd been part of the problem.

"It's funny how people change but still stay the same," Geri murmured.

Girls like Liz never really changed. They just refined their methods of making others feel small. But Geri, she had grown. She'd been knocked down and still found a way to keep standing, taller than ever before.

"You always did have bad taste in women," she said, shooting him a look.

Bart couldn't even smile. "Not anymore."

She looked away. "Why did you make her think we're together? Does your woman know you're roleplaying as my man?"

His heart skipped. "I don't have a woman."

Before he could say more, she walked off toward the flooring aisle. "Have they picked carpet yet?" she called over her shoulder. "I'm thinking we convince them to go softer. Maybe chenille."

"Let's grab a few swatches and show them later," he agreed.

After that, Geri went quiet. As they drove back, a thousand words tangled on his tongue, but Geri stared out the window like she was somewhere else.

He took the scenic route home. The neighborhood had changed since she left. As they turned a corner, the park came into view with its new swings and slides.

"Wow," Geri whispered. "The busted park is no longer busted."

"They replaced everything," Bart said. He'd contributed some manpower to the effort. "We should bring Joaquin. It's a five-minute walk from the house."

Geri leaned forward. "Why did you move here? You used to hate this neighborhood."

He shrugged. "It grew on me. My family's here. Why move someplace else?" He gestured toward a nearby strip of shops. "There's even a cool bookstore now—"

"You're acting strange."

"How?"

"You held my hand." She bit her lip. "I thought you'd change once we got back. But you're still being... really nice."

"I'm always nice."

Her brows went up.

"Come on now," he said. "After all that time together, you want us to go back to fighting?"

"Not fighting. Just..."

"Just what? You miss me calling you Geraldine? I can start again if it helps."

"Sure, if you're okay with me calling you Bartimeus."

He pulled into the driveway. "Bartimeus is a sexy name."

Geri laughed. "Sexy? Now I know you're tripping."

She climbed out of the truck, walking toward the house with that unintentional sway in her hips that got him every time. He unlocked the front door from his phone before she reached it. Once Geri stepped inside, she stopped short.

Darah was on the couch with a thick book in her lap. Joaquin was curled up between her and Eli, their grins mirroring whatever was on TV. It had to be penguins, of course.

Bart gently nudged a misty-eyed Geri inside, and closed the door behind them.

16

Darah watched Aunt Lina take a careful sip of the punch, her eyes lighting up.

"What do you think?" Darah asked, trying not to smile.

"Try it first." Aunt Lina handed her the cup like a secret.

Darah took a sip. Pineapple, raspberry, the zing of ginger beer, lime, just enough cinnamon to scratch her throat. Memory wrapped itself around her tongue.

"Wow," she breathed. "You nailed it, Ms. Jen."

Ms. Jen's brows lifted. "You sure?"

"Let me try," Phoebe said, reaching for a cup. One sip and her face broke into a grin. "That's the best punch I've ever tasted. Abe, Bart, come try this."

Cups were passed around like communion. Phoebe's mom—Mrs. Marsha—and her Aunt Bel grabbed extras for their husbands grilling in the backyard.

Abe looked at Ms. Jen. "Thank you. It's perfect."

Bart stared into his cup as though waiting for someone to appear in its depths. "Yeah, it is."

"Thank you, Bart," Ms. Jen said, a blush rising in her cheeks.

"It's almost like Mom's," Darah said, finishing her cup. It was nothing short of a miracle how Ms. Jen managed to hit all the notes of the punch Mom had served at every gathering. Almost like Mom had whispered the recipe to Ms. Jen in a dream as a blessing for her first grandchild's shower.

Aunt Lina swiped at her cheeks. "Ester would've made gallons for today's party. She'd be so proud."

Ms. Jen capped the jug. "It was my pleasure."

"All that's missing is that ridiculous punch fountain Dad used to pull out," Darah said. One Christmas, their dad had brought home an over-the-top drink fountain from an auction. Mom had scolded him for wasting money on it, but from then on, she requested it for every party. The last time they'd used it was the July 4th cookout, just before everything changed.

"I have no idea where that thing is," Abe said. "Do y'all know?"

Bart shook his head. "Maybe Junior?"

"It's in the attic," Geri said from the living room.

Geri was sitting with Joaquin and Thandi in a sea of pink and white balloons. Judah and Tari were tying decorations beside them while their baby girl, Nona, tried to eat a ribbon.

Geri handed a balloon to Nona before standing. "I can go look before the party starts."

"You don't have to," Phoebe and Abe said in unison.

"I'll take you," Bart offered.

"I'll come too," Darah added. "Need to grab something anyway."

Geri glanced at Joaquin happily squealing beside Nona. "Let's make it quick," she said.

They stepped outside into the warm Houston air. A car pulled up on the side of the road. Kasey hopped out from the back like she was ready for a photo shoot, and the car drove off.

"You came," Bart muttered, clearly not expecting her. "Did something happen to your car?"

"No," Kasey replied. "Just figured you could give me a ride back. Where are y'all going?"

"A quick run to our house," Darah said. "Phoebe's inside. We'll be back soon."

Kasey didn't take the hint. "I'll come too," she said, heading for Bart's truck. "Sounds like fun."

Darah opened the back door and slid in beside Geri. Bart fumbled with his keys while Kasey settled into the passenger seat like she'd been invited. On the drive over, Geri explained the story of the fountain.

"How do you even remember where something was stashed four years ago?" Kasey asked from the front.

"I helped Papa put it there," Geri replied. "The attic dust made him cough bad."

"Thought you were gonna say his knees," Bart said, chuckling. "Always sending folks up and down those stairs."

"He didn't like climbing that ladder unless he had to," Geri said, her voice warm.

"That Mr. Teka," Darah murmured, smiling at Geri. She'd missed this—them reminiscing together. For years, Geri's absence had left a void deeper than anyone had ever admitted out loud.

At the house, Bart parked beside the dumpster. Once they climbed out, Darah met Geri on the other side of the truck. Geri just stood still, her eyes locked on something across the street.

Darah followed her gaze, but there was nothing out of place on the quiet street.

"What's wrong?" Bart asked, placing a hand on Geri's shoulder.

Geri shook her head. "Thought I saw someone. Sorry."

"What's going on?" Kasey's voice called from the door.

Both Bart and Geri jerked like they'd been caught kissing. "Nothing," Bart replied, unlocking the door.

Once inside, Geri made a beeline for the stairs. Kasey wandered toward the kitchen. Darah waited until Bart closed the door, then shot him a look.

"You wanna tell me what we're really looking for?" Darah asked.

"Drink fountain," he said.

"Not that. Why was Geri spooked?"

A thump sounded from upstairs. Geri was already at the attic door.

"Go help her," Darah said. "You know the attic gives me the creeps."

Bart disappeared upstairs and Darah stepped into the study. After all these years, the room still smelled like Dad—aged leather, polished walnut. Her favorite place, a time capsule of their moments together.

She sank into the worn leather chair and it squeaked in protest, just like it used to when she'd climb into his lap. Those nights she'd wake from nightmares and tiptoe downstairs, only to find Dad already waiting in this room where the lights were usually on. Almost like he'd sensed her fear before it reached her. He would hold her, whisper prayers or funny stories until she stopped trembling. Then he'd carry her back upstairs on his back, no matter how much his knees hurt.

"I miss you, Daddy," she whispered, staring at the ceiling until her eyes stung.

"There you are," Kasey's voice sounded from the doorway.

Darah straightened, wiping at her cheeks.

Kasey eyed the floor-to-ceiling bookshelves cramped with hundreds of books. "Bookworm's paradise," she said, in an un-Kasey-like tone.

"You need something?"

Kasey smiled. "I don't see any romance novels. Your mom wasn't into reading?"

What a weird assumption. "She liked mysteries," Darah said, already standing. She walked past Kasey.

"You don't have to run off like that. What—I'm not allowed in here?"

"Did I say that?"

Kasey crossed her arms. "It's written all over your face."

Darah rolled her eyes. "Stay if you want to. No one's stopping you." She stepped into the hall, silently willing Kasey to follow.

She did. They ended up in the kitchen, where the tension finally snapped.

"What's your problem with me?" Kasey asked, in a low voice edged with heat.

Darah almost laughed. Finally, Kasey was taking the direct approach. "I don't have a problem. Maybe you do." Kasey clearly tagged along just to watch Bart. Was she threatened by Geri?

Kasey threw up her hands. "I actually like you. That's what makes this weird. When I first met y'all, I expected everyone but you to give me a hard time."

Darah scoffed. "If I were really giving you a hard time, you wouldn't be standing in my parents' house right now."

Kasey blinked, clearly caught off guard.

Darah took a breath, "I just don't think you and Bart are good for each other."

"And let me guess, you think Geri is?"

"We found it," Bart shouted from the foyer. "Let's get going."

Kasey instantly brightened, her mask snapping back into place. "To be continued, Darah Teka," she said with a tight smile. "Just so you know, I'm not giving him up."

Darah watched her leave, and waited for a bit, leaning against the kitchen counter. Her hands were trembling, just a little. After all this time, she'd finally seen the real Kasey. And it was Geri who had cracked the mask.

"I really hope you know what you're doing, bro."

"Darah!" Bart called again.

"I'm coming."

17

Darah met them at the door. Bart carried a box with Dad's old drink fountain. Kasey stood beside him with a fake smile.

Darah wasn't about to ride home with her. "I haven't found what I'm looking for," she said. "Y'all go ahead."

"I'll stay with her," Geri cut in. "You two head back first."

"I can't leave y'all here," Bart said. "Tell us what you're looking for and we'll help."

Kasey tugged on his arm. "You need to get the punch fountain back, and I need to help with the games."

"She's right," Geri said. "The party's starting soon. I'll help Darah here and we'll walk back."

After a pause, Bart handed Darah the house keys. "Don't take too long or I'm coming back." He walked out of the house with Kasey.

"You wanna talk about it?" Geri asked, once the door clicked shut behind them. Outside, Bart's truck rumbled to life, tires crunching the gravel as he pulled away.

"Nope." Darah went back to the study. Climbing a stool, she reached for the topmost shelf.

Geri ran a hand across the shelves, looking around the study with something deeper than Kasey's earlier detached curiosity.

From one of the shelves, Geri picked up an old cellphone. "I can't believe this is here."

"Yeah, we knew it was yours so Bart put it there," Darah said, searching for her book. She found it as Geri pulled a green book from a nearby shelf.

"A Dummy's Guide to Carpentry?" Darah smirked as Geri flipped through the pages like she'd reunited with an old friend. "I thought you already knew everything about carpentry."

"You can never know everything about anything." Geri lifted the book to her nose and inhaled. "Crazy how it still smells like him."

Darah swallowed. "I was just thinking the same thing."

Geri's eyes misted. "I miss him. He was the father I never had."

Darah squeezed the book in her hands. Mom had introduced her to the world of fiction, but Dad had stirred her love for writing. Your Little Author's Handbook—his gift for her eleventh birthday—had been tucked away since the chaotic move to Bart's place during the hurricane.

"We can go now," Darah said, before the moment stretched too long and turned into a cryfest.

Geri slipped her book back on the shelf and followed Darah out.

"Why didn't you take it?" Darah asked.

"I'll look at it on Monday. I'm working on the baby's room.

Don't tell Phoebe."

Darah chuckled. "She probably already knows. Bart is the worst at keeping secrets, except..."

Geri arched a brow. "Except what?"

"Let's go before Abe bites my head off," Darah said. No way Geri didn't already know how Bart felt. But if she did, why was she still acting like this?

As they walked back to Bart's house, Geri slid an arm around Darah's waist. "I owe you an apology," Geri said. "For ghosting you. I was too caught up in my life."

Darah returned the side-hug. "It's okay. You're here now."

From what she'd pieced together through Abe and Phoebe's carefully filtered responses, Geri's marriage hadn't been the fairy tale Darah had imagined. Maybe Geri had settled for a man who didn't love her. Maybe that was why she'd gone quiet, because she didn't want them to see where she'd ended up.

"I'm sorry I didn't return your texts," Geri continued. "I just didn't know how to answer your questions."

Was she ready now? Ready to talk about how it felt to leave behind the only life you'd known and become someone else? Belong somewhere else?

For four years, Darah had let herself dream. If Geri could be accepted in another part of the world, maybe she had a shot too. But that was the hardest pill to swallow. Geri hadn't been accepted there either. She'd left full of confidence and returned an anxious mother who flinched at every car that sped past. Even after two weeks being back in Houston, Geri still looked like she was just passing through and could disappear anytime.

"It couldn't have been easy for you," Geri said. "With Phoebe and Abe going through everything while you were just trying to grow up. And helping raise Eli."

"Bart stepped up when you left. Eli and I stayed at his place, so Phoebe's mom and Aunt Bel could be with Abe and Phoebe after they lost the first baby. We bonded a lot."

"That's good," Geri said, surprise clear in her voice.

As they neared Bart's subdivision, Geri's steps quickened.

"He's surprising you, isn't he?" Darah asked.

Geri smiled. "You're surprising me too. I can't believe you're going to be a senior next year. SAT Prep already? Soon you'll be telling us about your boyfriend."

"Yeah, right. Like that's gonna happen anytime soon." Left to her brothers, she wouldn't have her first boyfriend until grad school.

"Dating in high school is kinda weird, right?" Geri mused.

"Only people who didn't date in high school say that."

"Wow." Geri nudged her arm. "You're getting cheekier by the day."

Darah stuck out her tongue. Geri mirrored her, and Darah laughed. This was what she'd missed most—Geri being goofy, the easy banter, their inside jokes. The days of giggling over random silly stuff or roasting Bart. Geri had always felt like a big sister, which made her absence ache all the more. Back then, the fifteen-year age gap hadn't mattered. But once Geri moved away, it had stretched like the ocean that separated them.

"Did you have a crush in high school?" Darah asked.

"Who didn't?" Geri teased. "Do you?"

"I asked first."

Geri wrinkled her nose. "It's a secret."

"Then so is mine." Darah picked up her pace, grinning when Geri called after her.

"Geez, your legs are as long as Junior's now." Geri caught up, breathless. "I need to get in shape."

"Come for a run with me, Abe and Bart. Now that he's back, we go every morning at five."

"I'll pass." Geri smirked. "So...you like someone?"

Two faces popped into Darah's mind, uninvited. "I'll tell you mine if you tell me yours."

Geri groaned. "It was so long ago."

"Was it Abe?"

"What—? No way."

Of course not. Geri and Abe were like siblings. "Then it's Bart?"

Geri stopped walking, eyes wide.

Darah stumbled to a stop. "Wait. Seriously? Since high school?"

Before Geri could answer, a truck screeched to a sudden stop nearby. Geri jumped, pulling Darah back from the curb.

The truck reversed. Window rolled down.

Jeremy.

Her stomach flipped. Great. Now she was tripping, too.

"What's up, Teks?" His smile was blinding, like he'd just stepped out of a dream she was definitely not writing down.

It made her smile—no, she wasn't supposed to be smiling. Not now.

"You know him?" Geri asked, her grip tightening around Darah's arm.

"Just some guy from school," Darah muttered. As if her phone didn't have his contact saved under "J McTrouble."

Jeremy parked across the street and crossed over, easy and confident as usual.

Geri didn't let go. "That's not just some guy," she murmured. "That's the guy from school."

Darah sighed, heat rising in her face. Even Geri couldn't

ignore how good-looking Jeremy was. "What are you doing here, Walker?"

"Not sure how I feel about you still calling me that." He hooked a thumb over his shoulder. "My folks live a few streets over. Hi, Neighbor. Hi, Geri."

Darah's eyes widened. "You know each other?"

Jeremy nodded while Geri shook her head, then paused. "Wait, Jeremy as in Mrs. Walker's kid?" Geri crooned.

He nodded again. "It's been a while. Ma was just talking about you the other day. Said she hadn't heard from you since you went to Africa."

"Boy, you've grown like crazy," Geri said.

Darah looked from one to the other. This wasn't cool. She needed to break up this reunion fast.

"Your truck's back," she said, eyeing his black pickup. "No more bus rides. Good for you."

Jeremy grinned. "Yeah, which means I can drop you off after school now."

"Nope. I'm good." Her voice came out too quick. She could feel Geri's eyes boring into her like a heat lamp.

"I should probably let you two—" Geri began.

"Nope, we gotta go." Darah latched onto Geri like a lifeline. "Bye, Walker." She wasn't about to stand there and let Jeremy charm the sense out of Geri, who clearly approved of him. Mom would've liked him too. Phoebe? Maybe. Abe and Dad? They'd probably hate his guts on principle. But the worst part was none of that mattered. What mattered was how Jeremy was still looking at her. Like she mattered.

"I'll call you later, D," he said.

Her heart stuttered. D. Only her brothers called her that. Dangerous. She frowned at him, half-wishing he'd stuck to calling her Teks. That name felt safer.

"I'll tell my ma I saw you," Jeremy added.

"I'll check in on her soon," Geri said.

As he drove off, Geri raised a knowing brow. "D? He's pretty friendly for someone you're being so cold to. Why are you acting weird?"

"Weird how? There's a party we need to get to, remember? How do you know the Walkers?"

Geri kept walking. "I used to help his folks out with some home improvements."

They crossed the last few houses in silence, Bart's coming into view like a safehouse, though her heartbeat hadn't slowed one bit. She didn't have time for boys. Especially not ones like Jeremy Walker. But her pulse hadn't gotten the memo.

Geri didn't give up on the subject. "He seems your type. Tall, light-skinned, what was that one guy from that show you liked? Pretty eyes, curly hair?"

Darah laughed. "I know you're not talking. You and Bart made us all miserable with that ridiculous sexual tension."

"What the–?" Geri sputtered. "Hey, mija, that was ages ago. Don't start writing some fake love story."

"Fine. Let's just let it play out on its own."

"There's nothing to play out," Geri countered. "He has a girlfriend."

"Hardly."

Bart's front door opened. He stood in the doorway, his gaze on Geri. "I was about to come get you," Bart said. "You okay?"

"We're good," Geri mumbled, looking everywhere but at him.

"My lips are sealed," Darah said, grinning as she slipped past them both.

Today was gonna be fun. She could feel it.

18

The backyard buzzed with laughter, the golden glow of evening settling over the guests at the co-ed shower. Pink and white streamers fluttered in the breeze, wrapped around tables dressed with tiny white teddy bears, a theme Bart had—for some reason—insisted on. The scent of barbecue hung thick in the humid air. Children squealed with joy as water balloons burst against the grass.

Joaquin ran to Geri, hands dripping wet. "Mommy!" He dashed off again, squealing alongside Eli and Hannah, his laughter untouched by the shadows of his short, hard life.

Nearby, Darah, Thandi, and Adelaide—Uncle Harry's adopted daughter, whom Geri had met just today—were busy filling more balloons. Watching them, a pang of longing pressed behind Geri's ribs. All the moments she'd missed. All the time she could never get back. This was the kind of day she used to imagine on quiet nights: simple, peaceful, surrounded by people who loved her. A glimpse of the life she might have had.

After blowing bubbles with the kids, Geri wandered over to the grill, where Bart was with Abe, Judah and Daniel manning the meat like it was game day.

"Why's the guest of honor on grill duty?" Geri asked.

"'Cos he's tripping," Bart said, reaching for the tongs, but Abe held them away from him.

"Where's Pops Randall and Uncle Harry?" she asked, scanning the yard. "I thought they were on grill duty."

"They went to get more charcoal," Daniel said, sipping from a bottle of malt.

Geri stared at the unopened bags stacked in the corner. "But there's—"

"They said Bart bought the wrong kind," Abe muttered, nudging him aside.

"Phoebe's dad says we'll burn the expensive meat," Judah said.

Bart snatched the tongs from Abe and shoved him away from the grill. "You gotta learn to let go, man."

"He'll learn quick," Judah said. "Parenting humbles you. Right, D?"

Daniel groaned. "I feel like jam spread over dry toast."

"Geri, that's writer code for 'I'm exhausted,'" Judah said.

Daniel groaned again, and even Geri laughed this time. Daniel and Eden had twins nine months after their wedding, and three months in, fatherhood had him looking like he'd been wrung dry.

Judah slung an arm over Daniel's shoulder. "A man's needs come last when he becomes a husband and a father. At least that's how it's supposed to be."

"Happy wife, happy life, right?" Bart echoed, smiling at Geri.

She tried not to look at him. "But doesn't that breed resentment in the man?"

"Only if he doesn't understand why he has to sacrifice," Abe said. "It's not as simple as folks make it out to be, but you'll reap what you sow. If you sow the right seeds, you'll reap a good harvest."

"My man," Judah praised, pulling Abe away to the center of the yard. Once there, Judah blew a whistle, calling everyone to attention just as Uncle Harry and Pops Randall returned carrying charcoal and more groceries.

"Don't look now," Uncle Harry said. "They're glaring."

"It's you takin' forever to find the meat," Pops Randall grumbled, unloading sirloin like sacred offerings.

"Let's get this party started," Judah said. "Can we have the woman of the hour out front?"

Radiant in a soft blue gown, Phoebe joined Abe, their hands clasping under the swell of her belly. Kids shrieked around them, balloons bouncing off their ankles, adding their own chaotic charm to the moment.

"Move over, son," Pops Randall said, nudging Bart away from the grill.

"Why y'all gonna say I brought the wrong charcoal?' Bart asked.

"You did," both Uncle Harry and Pops Randall said at the same time.

Geri burst out laughing, and when she looked at Bart, he was laughing too.

"What's the joke? I want to laugh too," Kasey said, walking up to them. Kasey, the effortlessly beautiful, perfectly put-together woman who never had to wonder whether she belonged. She looped her hand around Bart like he was hers by right.

That was Geri's cue to leave. The games had started. In the center of the yard, Tari blindfolded Abe while Darah slipped earplugs into Phoebe's ears for the first game. The crowd roared with laughter, kids darting around like light beams.

Geri joined the other women near the back porch. She didn't look Bart's way again until the first game was over. And when she did, he was looking right at her. She blew up her eyes at him, trying to appear unbothered by it all. But he didn't smile. He just looked away when someone called for him, and he went inside the house.

As the games progressed, Geri didn't see him outside, so she took out her phone and started recording the games because she knew Bart had wanted to be there for them. After a while, she spotted Bart by the back gate talking to Kasey. At first, they looked like they were arguing, then Kasey hugged Bart, and when her hand slid over his chest, something twisted inside of Geri.

Geri stopped recording and put her phone in her pocket. Her knuckles ached from how hard she'd gripped her phone. Seeing them together shouldn't matter. She had no claim on Bart Teka. No right to feel whatever this was. He had saved her life. Joaquin's life. He hadn't abandoned her when she was trapped in Ghana and had no one else. She owed him everything. So why did it feel like the ground was shifting beneath her feet?

She swallowed the tightness in her throat. It was foolish, the very idea of her and Bart.

"Are you okay?" a voice asked. It was Adelaide, watching with quiet curiosity.

"Yes," Geri said, rising to her feet.

Adelaide gave a knowing smile, as if she saw through the lie but chose to let her be. She moved on, and Eden appeared, balancing a paper plate stacked with cake.

"Are you okay?" Eden asked.

Geri forced a smile. No twins in sight. If there ever was a moment to talk, this was it. Maybe if she could get Eden on her side, no one would question her decision to leave Houston.

"I need to talk to you," Geri said.

Eden put down the plate and gestured for Geri to follow. They slipped through the side gate, leaving behind the music and laughter.

On the front lawn, Eden stopped and turned to face her. "Is this about Asabe?"

Just hearing the name hit harder than expected. "I don't think staying here is smart. Doesn't that just make it easier for her to find me?" She'd left Port Harcourt over a month ago, but it still felt as if Asabe wasn't far away.

Eden held her gaze. "Wherever you go, Geri, she'll find you eventually."

Her body went rigid. "Not if I leave. If I lay low, if I—"

"Go hide out with your mom in Rockport?" Eden's voice was gentle, but the edge was unmistakable. "You don't really believe that's safer. This is Asabe Musa we're talking about."

Geri winced. Of course, Eden had already put the pieces together.

"To get to you," Eden said, "she'd have to get through all of us. Through me. And I might not look like much, but I'm harder to take down than I look."

Geri let out a shaky laugh, and Eden smiled. But then her tone sobered.

"That said, if Asabe does find you, we're going to be ready. She doesn't have strong legal ground here, but that doesn't mean she won't stir up trouble."

A chill spread through Geri's fingers. "What kind of trouble?"

"If she files for custody, she could claim you're unstable. That you have no permanent home, no steady income, a history of trauma. That you fled the country because you have a problem establishing roots. She'll twist everything. Say you're unfit."

"But I'm not—" The words broke on her tongue. "I'm not unstable."

Eden took her hands. "No, you're not. That's why you stay here, surrounded. The more people standing with you, the harder it'll be for anyone to tear you down."

Geri nodded, but her pulse was thundering in her ears.

"Just take it one day at a time," Eden added. "But if you get anything, a phone call, an email, a letter you don't recognize, you call me. I'm your attorney for as long as you need me."

Geri wiped the tears from her eyes. "Thank you." She knew Eden was right, but staying here felt like asking for trouble.

Mumbling something about checking on Joaquin, she hurried back to the yard with Eden trailing behind. Her son was still playing, laughing while Darah and Thandi launched another round of water balloons.

Everything looked normal. And it hurt, ached in a way she couldn't explain. She needed space. Quiet. To think.

She stepped inside the house, but the air felt thick, too clean, reminding her of antiseptic, those long nights in the hospital. Her room felt small, suffocating.

She left the room, slipped outside to the front porch, and slumped down on the steps. The street stretched in front of her, still and quiet. Long shadows spilled across the pavement, the hush of twilight sharpening their edges, like enemies waiting to pounce.

She took a slow breath, trying to settle the storm inside her.

Then she saw it. A black car idling near the curb. Tinted windows. Engine humming low.

Cold terror sawed up her spine, rooting her in place. The thought crashed through her with terrifying certainty.

Asabe had found her.

The car sat still, dark and silent. Was someone inside right now? Watching her? Joaquin.

The instinct hit her so hard she jumped from the porch, jolted out of her daze. Her breath came out ragged, panic thudding in her ears.

Run. The command exploded through her. She bolted into the house, rushing to the backyard, nearly tripping as she stumbled onto the lawn. The laughter, balloons, music—it all felt wrong. Distant. A world she didn't belong to.

She barely registered the startled glances as she rushed to the only thing that mattered. Joaquin was still there, still giggling, splashing water at Eli.

She dropped to her knees and gathered him in her arms, clinging so tightly he squeaked. Her hands shook as she buried her face in her son's curls, the scent of lavender anchoring her for just a moment.

"Geri?" It was Bart's voice, sharp with concern. "What's wrong?"

Anger flared in her chest. Why was he always there when she needed him? "Nothing," she said, handing Joaquin to him before she rushed into the house. She went into her room and closed the door and collapsed in tears.

She had to leave. This house. These people. This life—it wasn't hers to keep.

They would find them. They would take him.

The Tekas, Bart's warmth, this fragile new rhythm she'd

dared to settle into, it was all a mirage. A lie she wanted to believe. If she stayed, she would drag them all into her nightmare.

She had to run. Before it all shattered again. Before she lost everything.

19

Between everyone needing help with one thing or the other, Bart didn't get a chance to talk to Geri. Minutes after she ran into the house, she reappeared in the backyard, smiling as if nothing had happened and proceeded to avoid him for the rest of the party. Not that he had time. He wasn't even there for the games. Just when he thought he could settle down to watch Phoebe open the gifts, one of the kids had clogged the toilet with a roll of tissue.

By 9 pm, people started to leave. The shower was over, and Bart couldn't help his rising frustration, especially at Kasey, who wouldn't stop complaining about her stomach.

"It must be something I ate," Kasey said, hanging on to his arm as Bart walked her to the driveway.

He scanned the messy backyard. Cleaning would have to wait until tomorrow. "Just go home and rest," he said. "I already called you an Uber."

"No. I want you to take me."

She did look pale, but the playfulness in her tone made him pause. Why had she left her car at home to begin with? "I can't right now," he said.

Kasey clutched her stomach as Pops Randall and Uncle Harry were walking toward the house from their parked cars.

"What's wrong, Miss?" Phoebe's dad asked.

"Not feeling well," Kasey said, resting her cheek against Bart's shoulder.

"Then take her home, son," he said to Bart.

Bart opened his mouth, but the two older men gave him such stern looks that made him nod.

"Thank you," Kasey said, pulling Bart toward his truck.

He followed, each step heavier than the last. "Kasey, you have some real bad timing."

He drove her home in silence, except for the occasional groan from Kasey. When they got to her house, she walked through her door, kicked off her heels and disappeared into her bedroom without a word.

Bart lingered in the kitchen. Maybe she really was sick. Maybe he'd misjudged her, again.

He grabbed a bottle of water from the fridge. The glowing numbers on the microwave marked the time like a taunt. Where had the day gone? He'd missed most of the party. His first baby shower. His first niece. They'd prayed hard for her. He'd never prayed more for anything in his life. After everything Phoebe and Abe had been through, this baby felt like a promise kept. He'd dreamed about this day, stayed up texting ideas with Darah and the others. He'd created the perfect gift basket with onesies, swaddle sets, and tiny dresses he'd picked out himself. He hadn't known he'd care this much. Was that why it stung so bad to be here instead of winding down the day with his family? With Geri?

"You coming?" Kasey's voice called from her bedroom.

Bart exhaled and headed in. She was perched on the edge of the bed, her dress pooled on the floor. Sitting cross-legged, bare shoulders framed in her long, tousled hair. A perfect invitation.

He passed her the water bottle. "Do you have a fever?"

Kasey drank slowly, then held the bottle out to him with a soft smile. He placed it on the nightstand.

"Better?"

She licked her lips and fell back onto the bed, arms sprawled wide. "Can you stay?"

"No." He picked up her dress and sat on the edge of the bed. Was that why she'd left her car at home? To get him here? "Just try to rest. It's been a long day."

"I'm really happy for your family," Kasey said. "I can't wait to meet your niece. She's going to be spoiled rotten."

"Probably." That little girl would be their joy, a miracle, the living proof that prayers didn't always go unanswered. That God was listening, just like his parents always believed.

Kasey's fingers trailed up his back, breaking his thoughts. She was leaning on one elbow now, eyes full of something that didn't match her earlier smile.

"How are you feeling now?" he asked.

She shifted closer, her breath warm against his neck. "Can't you stay with me? I need you."

Bart stiffened. He knew this game; couldn't believe he'd fallen for it. Kasey wasn't sick. She'd never been sick.

She climbed into his lap, straddling him. "I can't even remember the last time you kissed me."

He didn't want to remember. "Kasey—"

She kissed him before he could finish, insistent, arms

winding around his neck. For a second, he forgot himself. She was the last woman he'd been with. It had been months. A man had needs.

"Kasey, please," he said, forcing himself to pull away. Her smile was seductive, calculated, eyes sparkling with the promise of a good time. "You need to rest."

"I'm not sick anymore." She tossed her hair and gave him a playful look. "You're my medicine. You always have been. I can feel how much you want me, Bart."

He peeled her arms off his neck. "Kasey, I need to go."

Her expression twisted. "I throw myself at you, and you sigh? What's going on with you?"

He stopped to look at her. He couldn't explain it even to himself. But he just couldn't do this.

Her voice came softer. "I miss you. We haven't been intimate in ages."

He couldn't listen to this. "I have to go." Her sultry voice was clouding his common sense.

Her thighs eased around him, her eyes flashing. "Seriously? You've never turned me down before."

He lifted her off his lap and placed her on the mattress. "I just have to go."

"Then go," she snapped.

He walked out of the bedroom, out of her house, got into his truck and took the fastest route back home. By the time he pulled into his driveway, most of the cars had vanished. Judah and Tari were just driving off as he parked in the garage.

Inside, the house had shifted into that post-party quiet. Aunt Lina, Ms. Jen and Phoebe's mom were boxing leftovers. The living room was a mess—deflating balloons, gifts bags piled like a small mountain. Pops Randall was snoring in the corner. Uncle Harry sat beside him, watching the muted football game with half-lidded eyes. Across the room, Abe and Phoebe sat curled together on the couch, his hand rubbing her belly.

"Is Kasey okay?" Phoebe asked. "She really tried for us today."

The words stabbed at him, but there was someone else on his mind. "She's fine. Geri went to sleep?"

Phoebe nodded. "She thinks Joaquin might've eaten something bad. He's sleeping now. Hopefully not food poisoning."

She didn't say it, but Bart knew she was thinking what he was thinking—an allergic reaction. Joaquin had been snacking all afternoon on tamales and cookies, way too much for a stomach that small.

Bart headed down the hallway toward Geri's room. The door was closed, so he went out to the backyard and started cleaning up.

Darah and Eli joined him, no questions asked. Darah told him that Marcus had sent a recording of him and Junior singing a lullaby to the baby. They sounded awful, but it made Phoebe happy since the two of them couldn't fly down from Pittsburgh because of Marcus' football game.

By the time they'd finished folding chairs, tossing water balloon scraps and stacking trays, Phoebe's family had left. Only Ms. Jen was still outside as Bart took out the trash.

"Is everything alright, Bart?" Ms. Jen asked, standing by the car.

In the past, he'd never paid much attention to Ms. Jen at their family events, but since she became Phoebe's doula, she was around more often. Phoebe trusted her. She was the kind of person who made you feel steadier just by being in her presence.

"I'm good," he said. "Thanks for coming."

But he wasn't good. Late into the night, he couldn't sleep. It took him several hours of lying awake in bed to figure out he was angry at himself. He had let his complicated relationship with Kasey go on for too long, simply because he wasn't man enough to let her go.

Kasey had always been dramatic, but tonight felt just too manipulative. Watching Kasey today reminded him of Liz, and that made him sick.

Thirsty, Bart made his way through the quiet house to the kitchen. He poured himself a glass of water, downed it in one go. The microwave clock blinked 2:06 a.m. His phone buzzed. A text from Kasey. He didn't open it. Instead, he scrolled to the most recent message from Tonye:

Looking more and more like an inside job. Still no obvious link to MIL. Keep you posted.

Bart stared at the screen, the water in his gut turning to ice. Geri was still in danger. They had to find out who sent that hitman.

He slid his phone into his pocket and noticed the punch fountain propped by the sink. Dad's ridiculous, beloved drink fountain. Geri had crawled into their dusty attic to find that thing.

She'd been skittish when they got to the house, maybe thought she saw one of Asabe's men. But she'd gone anyway, and walked back with Darah alone, hiding whatever fear she carried just to help bring the party to life. That was Geri. She always pushed through. Even when it hurt. But it had come back to bite her. The way she'd panicked at the party was probably because of what she thought she'd seen earlier at the old house.

Bart turned to go back upstairs. A door clicked open and a sliver of light spilled across the floor near the laundry room. He moved toward it, pausing when he spotted Geri tiptoeing toward

115

the bathroom, her back to him.

She was barefoot, dressed in a tank top and sleep shorts, her hair mussed from sleep, skin glowing faintly in the soft light. Kasey had worn even less earlier tonight, and all he'd felt was irritation.

Bart smiled despite himself. He had forgotten what it felt like—to have his heart kicking at him like he had no choice in the matter.

Geri turned, eyes widening when she saw him. She pressed a finger to her lips. The front of her shirt was stained dark with something. She hurried toward the bedroom, and he followed.

As soon as the door shut behind them, the smell hit him— sharp, sour. Joaquin stood near the bed in a fresh diaper, his big eyes wet with tears, silent.

Bart blinked at the mattress propped awkwardly against the wall. Had she lifted it by herself?

"The mattress protector needs to be washed." She balled up the soiled sheets and clothes and dropped them beside her open suitcase.

"Mommy," Joaquin whimpered.

Geri knelt and kissed his cheek. "It's okay. Don't cry."

"Why didn't you call me?" His voice came out sharper than he wanted. "I was right upstairs. You could have at least texted me."

Geri pulled a clean sleep shirt over Joaquin's head and tugged pajama pants up his legs. "I'm sorry," she mumbled. "I'll clean it."

"Jesus, Geraldine—" Why did she always act like she had to fix everything alone?

She finally met his gaze, eyes rimmed with exhaustion. "I said I'm sorry."

"Stop apologizing." He reached for the dirty sheets, but she

116

placed her hand over his. Someone knocked.

The door creaked open. Abe peered inside, only to wrinkle his nose. "What happened?"

"Go to sleep," Bart said. "We've got it."

Phoebe appeared behind Abe. "Is Joaquin okay?" she asked, slipping into the room.

"He's okay," Geri said with a wobbly smile. "Just needed to let it out."

Phoebe gently stroked Joaquin's curls. "Poor baby. I wonder what it was. Kasey also got sick."

Geri's eyes flicked to Bart and quickly dropped. "Sorry for waking everyone."

Bart grabbed the dirty sheets. She probably knew he'd left with Kasey. That was why she was acting like he was a stranger. He stormed out before the pressure in his chest made him say something he'd regret.

In the hallway, Darah stood squinting through bleary eyes. "What's going on?"

"Go back to sleep," Bart muttered, brushing past her. He dumped the sheets in and started the washer. He snatched a clean shirt from the laundry rack.

When he returned, Abe was moving the mattress from the wall. Phoebe sat on the carpet, humming softly to Joaquin, who wasn't crying anymore. Geri stood in the corner, looking lost, her arms wrapped around herself.

Bart held out the clean shirt to her. She blinked like she didn't recognize him, and the look in her eyes bruised something in him, more than he could ever have imagined.

Without a word, he draped the shirt over her shoulders and walked out of the room.

20

Like her mom always said: "God moves in mysterious ways." Somehow, Joaquin's blowout in Bart's guest bedroom had shattered whatever tension lingered between her and the Tekas. Since then, the house felt almost like it used to—laughter and easy banter filling the rooms.

With everyone but Bart.

On Sunday morning, Joaquin was back to his normal self, so they went to church with the Tekas. Joaquin loved it—his first time in a real service. He cried when it was time to leave.

Bart didn't go with them. He barely spoke to her the entire day. She still hadn't told anyone about the black car she'd seen during the baby shower, letting them believe her sudden panic had been stress. Maybe it had been nothing, just a neighbor waiting for someone. But fear didn't need proof. It lived beneath her skin now, a quiet, breathing thing.

Houston felt like a trap door—on the verge of springing open. Bart had been there in Port Harcourt. It was only a matter of time before Asabe connected the dots.

Geri knew she'd have to leave Houston, find a small, quiet town where Asabe would never think to look. But to do that, she needed money. She needed to work. She had to finally get her contractor's license and stop relying on other people to keep her afloat. Running away would have to wait until she could afford her own place. Her mother had always been a lifeboat with holes.

That same Sunday night, she cracked open the exam study guide she'd bought. She made good on her promise to Jeremy and called his mom. Mrs. Walker was so thrilled to hear her voice that she insisted Geri come over the next morning.

With the old cellphone she'd left at the Teka house years ago, Geri managed to reconnect with a few former clients and lined up a couple of small fix-it jobs—enough to feel like her life was moving forward again. Both Ms. Jen and Phoebe offered to watch Joaquin during the day so she could focus on her work.

The visit to the Walkers felt like a divine appointment. Mrs. Walker greeted her with tears and laughter, insisting she eat a full breakfast before leaving. Mr. Walker joined them halfway through the meal, and before Geri left, he pressed an envelope into her hand.

"Think of it as back pay," he said. "You undercharged me for all the work you did back then."

It was a check for one thousand dollars. Geri burst into tears right there in their living room. She was still crying when she told Phoebe about it later, and Phoebe cried too.

By Tuesday morning, hope felt new again. As she got ready to leave, her mother called. Joaquin was in the living room with Phoebe, cheeks full of pancake, while Geri stood in her borrowed room talking to her mom.

"We praise God for Joaquin," her mother said, near tears. She launched into a Spanish hymn Geri hadn't heard in years. "Being with the Tekas is good for him."

"No, Mom. We can't keep staying here." Geri's eyes fell on the folded shirt on her bed—Bart's shirt he'd given her three nights ago. "I need to leave Houston." The words came sharper than she meant, fear creeping into her voice.

A long pause. "What's really going on, Geri?"

"I have to go." She hung up before her resolve could crack. Asabe aside, staying with the Tekas couldn't be permanent. She needed to stand on her own.

Her gaze drifted back to the contractor's exam guide on her desk. Joaquin deserved more than survival. He deserved stability, a home, a future. She didn't know how she'd get there, but she had to start somewhere.

She reached for Bart's shirt again. The soft cotton still carried his woodsy scent. She pressed it to her chest, then shook herself out of it. Bart had a gorgeous girlfriend who knew what she wanted. Time to return his shirt before she started imagining things again.

In the living room, Joaquin's cheeks were round with food. "Mommy, I done!"

Geri smiled, heart melting at how healthy he looked now.

"He ate great," Phoebe said, smiling.

Maybe Mom had been right—about the Tekas, at least. Maybe this house really was healing him.

Geri bent to kiss the top of his head. Ms. Jen couldn't make it today, so Geri turned to Phoebe, ready to insist on taking Joaquin with her to the old house. But Abe walked in, sleeves rolled, laptop under his arm.

"I thought you left with Bart," he said.

Phoebe smirked. "She was just about to give me a speech."

"I just..." Geri started, caught off guard.

"Don't worry," Phoebe cut in. "Joaquin and I have a full schedule—reading, painting, my mom's coming over. You go do your secret home project." She nudged Joaquin's cheek until he squealed. Geri opened her mouth to object again, but Phoebe's face was determined.

"This isn't about Saturday, is it?" Phoebe asked.

"No, I just don't want to wear you out."

"I need the exercise," Phoebe said. "Pilates ain't got nothing on chasing toddlers."

"You're still allowed to do Pilates?"

"If I'm careful, sure." Her eyes twinkled.

Geri glanced at Abe, who looked like he'd personally drive his wife to Pilates if she asked. "Lucky woman," Geri said. Phoebe chuckled.

"Thank you," Geri said, deciding not to argue. Joaquin looked happy. Abe was home. She could move fast and be back before naptime.

Abe walked her to the porch. "Don't overdo it."

"I won't," she promised. "This is nothing. I once flipped a whole duplex by myself."

Back then, her projects had been about passion, building her skills. Now, it was about rebuilding from the inside out. She needed this—the sawdust, the sweat, the sense of progress.

"Thanks for watching Joaquin," she said. "And for everything."

Abe smiled. "Call if you need anything."

Geri started down the street, surprised by how easily the old route came back. What surprised her more was Bart's decision to live so close to the house he'd once wanted to escape. He'd changed. Less self-centered. Quieter. More... everything. The kind of man who picked up dirty sheets without flinching, who folded hers and Joaquin's clothes and left them stacked neatly by the dryer.

The house came into view, a heartbeat of memory waiting. Construction was in full swing. She stepped around the dumpster toward the fire-red front door.

Time to get to work.

The scent of fresh varnish hung in the air as she climbed the stairs. From the master bedroom next door came the sharp rhythmic bursts of nail guns. She pushed open the door to the baby's room. Near the window, a set of cordless power tools and more sat like a gift: gloves, a tape measure, pencils—everything she needed, down to the exact planks placed beside the closet. The only thing missing was a miter saw.

Geri ran her thumb along the slick handle of the nail gun. Brand new, just like the gloves. Footsteps sounded from the hallway. A middle-aged man in a dusty plaid shirt and jeans passed by the open door.

"Perdón, señor," she called, stepping out of the room.

He paused, his bushy brows lifting. "Hello," he replied in English. "You must be Geri."

"I am. Nice to meet you, se—"

"Call me Emilio." His voice had the easy rhythm of someone fluent in both languages. "How's everything coming?"

She held up the nail gun. "Perfect, thank you." Was he the general contractor?

"The boss said you'd need it. Seems like you've used one of these before?"

"Just pneumatic. This isn't too different. Any chance you've got a miter saw handy?"

His brows rose again. "Looks like you really know what you're doing. I'll grab one."

She nodded her thanks. It had been a long time since someone in her field took her seriously without hesitation. And it felt good.

Back in the room, she picked up the tape measure. She could frame the windows and closet door before lunch if she moved fast.

Emilio returned just as she finished the first measurements. He plugged in the saw near the corner. "Where'd you learn this stuff?"

"Papa Teka," she said, smiling. "The original owner. He had me working on projects around the house. I thought I was the luckiest girl alive."

She positioned the first plank and pressed down the blade. The saw whirred to life, slicing cleanly through the wood. The sound filled her chest like a breath.

Emilio crouched beside her. "Clean cut. You ever thought about joining a crew?"

Heat crept into her face. "I don't have my license yet."

"For what?"

"My general contractor license."

He waved a hand. "That's easy. And I'm not just talking. We don't just invite anybody onto our projects. What you did downstairs? You've got the eye."

She blinked. "You mean the study?" Who told him she'd put them up?

"Hard to miss." Emilio grinned.

"You hiring?" She laughed, but the idea planted something deep inside her. Could it really be that simple? A temp gig with a steady paycheck before moving.

"I'll ask the boss," he said. "You keep working."

She watched him leave and let out a long breath. Maybe this was it, the doorway back to herself. Not the woman who had merely endured, but the one who created.

Two hours in, she needed a rest. Sweat dripped down her temples. Her shirt clung to her back, and her arms ached from cutting and measuring. But the closet frame stood proud, solid, clean. She propped her hands on her hips, breathing hard.

By the door, a bottle of water and a granola bar waited on the floor. Her brows drew together. Emilio? No, she hadn't heard him return.

She unscrewed the cap, took a long sip, and nearly choked when Bart appeared in the doorway.

"Taking a break?" he asked, leaning against the frame.

She figured she probably looked a sweaty mess. "When did you get here?"

"Few minutes ago. You didn't hear me?"

Meaning he'd left the snacks by the door. "I was listening to something," she said, taking out her earbuds.

He studied the closet frame. "You've still got it."

She tried to sound casual. "You doubted me?" she asked, trying to sound casual.

"Never that, Geraldine Pena."

His voice was warm with a hint of pride. The way he called her name was as if he'd been waiting for her to get back to this, building things.

"What were you listening to?" Bart asked.

"Audiobook."

He smiled, waiting for more. Somehow, it had felt easier telling Emilio, a stranger.

"I'm studying for a licensing exam," she said. "I want to be a general contractor."

21

She came alive, like he hadn't seen since meeting her again. Those bright amber eyes stopped him cold, took away his breath, his words.

"Don't get too excited," she said. "I haven't registered yet. Not trying to jinx myself."

Bart could only smile. It would be weird if he said it right now, how proud he was. This was the Geri he remembered. She wasn't waiting around for life to hand her a break. She was reaching for healing, even with fear nipping at her heels.

"Sorry about Saturday night," Geri said, unwrapping the granola bar he'd left by the door. "It's just been a while since I had so many people looking out for me."

"I'm sorry too," Bart said. "I shouldn't have snapped."

"You didn't snap. You're just terrible at whispering."

Her half-smile made him laugh. "You're not mad?"

"How can I be mad at the guy who hand-washed poop out of my kid's pajamas?"

"His wasn't as bad as yours."

Her lips pressed together. "Sorry."

He studied her—the freckles on her nose, the familiar quirk of her mouth when she was teasing. "Why do you apologize so much now?"

"Do I?" Her smile faded. "I guess it's a habit."

"You never used to apologize. Even when you should've." That sass, that fire, he missed it more than he'd realized.

"I used to apologize. Just not to you." She turned before he could catch her smile and walked to the closet. "Which was childish. Now I'm all grown up." As she ran her hand along the trim she'd cut earlier, the corner of her t-shirt lifted, revealing the bare skin of her waist.

"Yes, you are," Bart said. She must have heard the longing in his voice because she turned to him. He didn't look away. He wanted her, and he wanted her to know, how every outfit she wore lately seemed to mess with his head.

Geri turned away first. "Anyway, I figured you were just grumpy about missing the games at the shower. Is your girlfriend feeling better?"

Just like that, the spell broke. "Ex-girlfriend," he corrected her.

Her eyes went wide and she looked down at the miter saw. "Well, it was a lot of fun."

Bart took a step toward her. He wasn't about to let her gloss over his relationship with Kasey. She needed to understand that Kasey was in his past.

"I actually recorded it."

He paused behind her. "Recorded what?"

"The games." Geri pulled her phone from her pocket. "I don't have the fancy iPhone or anything, but most of it's all here. Figured Phoebe might want to watch it later."

He reached for the phone, but instead of taking it, he grabbed her hand and pulled her to him, expecting her to push back. She didn't.

He closed his arms around her, and held her to his chest. "Thank you," he said. Holding her felt... so good.

She made a sound and he stepped back. "Sorry."

"Look who's apologizing now," she said, passing him her phone.

The video was already on. Why hadn't he thought of getting someone to record the whole thing? "You have no idea how much this means to me." Even he hadn't known until now. They were supposed to have a baby shower the first time. Instead, Abe had called him from the ER.

"I still can't believe that happened," Geri said.

"Me too." It was an impossible thing to believe, how a good God could let that happen to a good person like Phoebe.

Bart sighed. He hated talking about it. "There are better days ahead for all of us," he said. "You too, Geri."

She smirked. "Thanks, Hallmark. Go watch your videos and let me work."

Bart laughed as she nudged him out the door. He sat on the floor outside the room and hit play. The angle wasn't perfect, but he could see everything: Phoebe destroying Abe in the diaper game, Darah cracking up at Abe's cluelessness, kids running wild, the unfiltered joy of it all.

Then there was Geri. The sound of her voice on the video—her soft, sincere, entirely unguarded commentary. She laughed at the silly games, whispered sweet comments about Phoebe's glow to Ms. Jen, spoke to Joaquin in that stern, loving Spanish that always warmed his chest. During the prayer at the end, he caught a few quiet sniffles, her soft "amens" echoing under the chorus of voices. It filled his heart more than anything had in a long time.

By the time the video ended, he wanted most to take her into his arms again. He got up from the floor and peeked into the room. Geri was mumbling to herself as she reviewed her measurements, her brow furrowed in focus. She was in her element, loose strands of hair falling over her face. He'd seen a few of her sketches lying on the desk at the house—clean lines, clear images. He hadn't known she could draw, too. Was there anything she couldn't do?

She bent to grab another water bottle. Tossing her head back, she took a long gulp. A few drops slipped past her lips, trailing down her neck. His eyes followed the line of those drops, imagining what it might feel like to kiss them away, one by one, before they disappeared beneath the collar of her shirt. When she swiped her thumb across her lips, he nearly groaned aloud.

"There you are," Emilio called in the hallway. "I was looking for you," he said, eyes sparkling with mischief like he'd seen everything. "Need to talk to you about a new team member, Boss man."

"Hold up," Geri's voice broke in. "Bart's your boss? I thought you were a real estate agent."

Bart turned. "I was. Now I'm a real estate developer. I didn't have a chance to tell you."

She gave him a look. "There were plenty of chances, Bart. And you've been sitting here for like thirty minutes."

Was it that long? Had she seen him watching her?

She flashed a breathtaking smile that caught him off guard. "That's amazing, Bart."

All he could do was nod. He hadn't realized how much he wanted her to say those exact words.

"What made you change?" she asked.

He shrugged. He couldn't say "you did." She had sparked the whole thing, her passion for fixing things, her insistence on color palettes and crown molding. He couldn't tell her that he'd bought and flipped a house down the street with her in mind.

"Too many real estate agents in Houston," he replied. "Logical switch."

"Makes sense." Her gaze lingered a beat longer, like she knew there was more.

Emilio clapped a hand on Bart's shoulder. "His house was our first big project. After that, he asked me to be on his team. Rest is history."

"Well," Geri said, smiling. "Maybe I'll pick up a few tricks from you while I'm still here."

"Anything for our new recruit," Emilio said, with a wide grin.

"Still?" Bart muttered. She quickly turned away to the closet. Had she already made plans to leave?

Emilio squeezed Bart's shoulder again. "Need to talk for a minute."

Bart followed Emilio down the hall. They stopped near Darah's room, where a man stood on scaffolding beneath a small hole in the roof.

"This roof needs to be done before Abe comes by again," Bart said.

"Tomorrow afternoon," Emilio said. "Skylight slowed us down."

Darah had asked nicely for a skylight in her room. Phoebe thought it was romantic, and that had sealed the deal. "Let's at least finish the floors by the end of the day."

"Sure thing, Boss." Emilio turned with a smirk. "Your Geri's a carpenter? Match made in heaven if I ever seen one."

Bart squinted at him. It strangely felt good to hear the words 'Your Geri.'

"I like her," Emilio went on. "She's got something."

"You just met her," Bart murmured.

"Doesn't take long to know a good woman when you see one." Emilio gave him a firm pat on the shoulder before walking away.

Bart stared up at the hole in the ceiling, open like the possibility of him and Geri ever taking that next step. The warm light filtered through. He needed to stop imagining her lips under his.

He returned to the baby's room and found Geri standing with her back to him, arms planted on her hips, surveying her work. Framed by the windowlight, she looked like a snapshot from a life he hadn't dared dream of.

He wanted a picture of her right now. He pulled out his phone, wondering when exactly his heart had started following her around like a puppy. She turned around suddenly, and he hid the phone in his hand behind his back.

"It's crooked," she muttered.

Bart followed her gaze to the newly installed frame. "Looks fine to me."

She bent to pick up the nail gun. "So you bought all this?"

"We needed a new set anyway. The crew prefers pneumatic, but cordless is more convenient."

"It's gonna take some getting used to, hearing you talk like that."

Bart folded his arms. "Talk like what?"

"Like someone who knows what he's doing." Her eyes

sparkled.

"I do know what I'm doing. You trying to work, or you just here to roast me?"

Her smile faded. "Bart, I can't keep loafing off you. Plus, I'm a little jealous right now. I always dreamt of having my own business. Thought I could do something back in Nigeria, but it didn't happen."

He didn't have to ask why. Asabe had clipped her wings before she could even try to fly. He heard laughter and realized the audio from the baby shower was playing from her phone still in his other hand. He must have mistakenly turned it back on while trying to hide his phone from her. Light and free, Geri's laughter carried through the phone speaker.

"I forgot I was even recording," she said. "I was laughing so much that day."

He handed the phone back to her. "It was perfect. Thanks, Geri." Their fingers brushed in the exchange, sending a jolt up his arm. He dropped his hand fast, swallowing the rush.

"I might need to ride to the store again. For some more paint. Sorry."

"We might already have what you need."

She raised a brow. "You got Chantilly Lace and Raleigh Peach?"

Bart reached for his keys. "We can go in ten. Want to see them install Darah's skylight first?"

"Darah's getting a skylight?" Geri laughed, falling in step with him down the hall.

"She asked. Princess Darah gets what she wants."

"Good for her. I love skylights."

Of course she did. His own master bathroom had two, letting the light flood in. At the time, it seemed like a random choice.

Now, he couldn't help thinking it was fate.

They stepped into Darah's room as Emilio shouted instructions up to the crew on the roof. Geri stood beside Bart, eyes wide like a kid seeing fireworks for the first time. Bart didn't watch the skylight go in. He watched her.

Once the crew started sealing the edges, Emilio wandered over to them, wiping his hands on a rag. "Did you give her the job?" Emilio asked.

Bart smirked. "We're about to stop by the store. Want anything while we're out?"

"Nah, Boss man," Emilio said, twinkle in his eye. "Take your time."

Bart shook his head and turned to Geri. "Ready?"

She waved at Emilio and led the way to the stairs. At the bottom, she rushed to open the front door with a mock glare. "Don't even think about it. I can open my own door."

He darted past her toward his truck. "And I can open mine."

"You're so childish," she called, giggling as she followed.

Bart opened her door with a theatrical bow. "After you, Milady."

Geri rolled her eyes and climbed into the truck with surprising ease. Kasey always complained that the cab was too high off the ground.

"Thank you," she said once he got in. "You're full of surprises, aren't you?"

"Because I changed jobs? You don't like it?"

Geri didn't look away. "I didn't say that."

"Good."

He pulled out of the driveway and turned onto the road—the same one they'd driven down years ago, before everything fell apart.

But this time, it felt like the future he'd imagined was finally coming together.

22

Darah settled down on the plush carpet in Thandi's living room. "You think we'll finish my hair before your mom gets back?"

"Depends on the style," Thandi said, grabbing her hair kit from the counter. "If you're about to ask for waist-long braids again, then it's a hard no."

"No to finishing on time, or no altogether?" Darah grinned at Thandi's death stare. "Relax. Just mini twists this time."

"Very funny. I'm about to start charging your behind."

"Why would you charge your best friend in the whole wide world? That's criminal."

"What's criminal is you not lifting a finger to help. And every time I try to teach you, you zone out."

"Why do I need to learn a skill you enjoy doing? Isn't this bonding time? I pay you back in snacks and affection."

"You're such a brat." Thandi sat on the couch behind Darah. "Did you even wash your hair?"

"This morning. I did a quick detangle too." Darah opened her laptop and winced. "Go easy. I'm tenderheaded."

"Tenderheaded, my foot. And define 'quick' because I'm not seeing it."

"Give me a break, my hair's not like yours."

Thandi's curls were soft and springy, cooperative. Darah's hair was thick, 4C, always trying to prove a point. Other than Thandi, the only people Darah trusted to touch her hair were Thandi's mom—Aunty Mani and Phoebe. The one-time Phoebe took Darah to a salon, the stylist tried to upcharge her like she had a lion's mane. Phoebe walked her back out and spent the whole afternoon researching natural hair routines.

"Maybe I should get locks like your mom's," Darah said.

Thandi applied cream to Darah's temples. "Mom and I can install them for you. Maintenance isn't hard either. I help Daniel with his."

Daniel's thick locks were usually tied in a man bun with shaved sides. He still managed to look like a cool dad, even with spit-up stains on his hoodie.

"Okay, Ms. Saleswoman." Darah opened the game on her laptop. "If they'll look like your mom's sisterlocks, I'll consider it."

"If you can't take care of your hair, you're not getting to that level."

"Touche." Darah laughed. "Wow, you're feisty today."

"You asked for mini twists at noon. You know this takes hours. Why didn't you come earlier?"

"Got caught up with my Sims." Darah raised her laptop to show a young digital woman with locs. "What do you think? Cute?"

Thandi's hands stilled. "She looks like you, with locs. Is this a new legacy or a story?"

They'd been obsessed with The Sims since Efe and Chanel introduced it to them years back. Darah had entire neighborhoods filled with alternate-universe Tekas and every kind of fictional family imaginable.

"Haven't decided. She's gonna be my college version. Should I keep the locs?"

"She'll probably take care of them better than you do."

Darah nudged Thandi's leg. "Should I make a college Thandi too? We can be roommates. I'll give you a cute boyfriend."

"Give her a big Afro like yours." Thandi tugged on a clunk of Darah's hair. "So, how's the romance going at your place? Did Bart finally confess his love yet?"

Darah snorted. "Nope, and now Kasey's been coming around more."

"She gotta throw that Hail Mary."

Darah clicked on a sim. "Since when do you talk football? You even know what it means?"

"Hail Mary means she's desperate because she saw him drooling over Geri. It's already game over."

"It's been over. That relationship was broken before it started. All they've done is slap band aids on a sinking ship."

"You're so cold, D."

"But I'm right. Okay, I'm done with your sim. Now let's build her boyfriend. Want him super fit, skinny, or like Cornrows Cal."

"Girl, if you bring up that guy one more time, I'm giving you a weird hairstyle."

Darah cackled. "Football fit then. Make him like a running back?"

"Yes, dark-skinned, and give him a single gold earring."

"Very specific."

"Sit still," Thandi said, nudging her head down. "Honestly, I don't blame Kasey. If I were her, I'd be pissed too."

"It doesn't matter. If Bart marries Kasey, he'll be miserable. He deserves more than that."

"And that's Geri?"

"She's perfect for him. Always has been." Bart never argued with Kasey the way he'd argued with Geri. "You should've seen them back then. There was this tension, like they could just rip off each other's—"

"Darah!"

"Throats. I was gonna say throats."

Thandi gathered some finished twists into a loose bun. "You're so bad."

Darah shrugged. Now that she knew Geri had harbored feelings for Bart before, it all made sense. "Bart was a zombie when Geri got married. And every girl he dated after that sort of looked like her."

"His tastes definitely changed."

"But they could never beat the original. If he doesn't make his move on her now, that's on him." Darah eyed the screen. The sim boyfriend she was creating for Thandi looked familiar. "This doesn't look anything like Cornrows Cal."

"Mention him again and you're walking out of here with your head not done."

Darah closed her eyes as the mint spray hit her scalp with a zing.

"Did you finish your own sim's boyfriend?" Thandi asked.

Darah opened one eye. She'd finished two versions, but Thandi would roast her for that. "I still can't decide between Scholastic or Suave."

"Why can't he be both?"

Darah sighed. "Do you think it's actually possible to end up with your high school crush?"

"End up like... date them?"

"No, I mean end game. Marriage. Babies. HEA."

Thandi's fingers paused in Darah's hair. "That would be incredible."

"Like Geri and Bart. What if they ended up like their sim versions—"

"If they saw what you did in Sims, they'd flip," Thandi said, laughing. "You gave them six kids and they're not even together yet. You're insane."

After Phoebe's first miscarriage, Darah had coped by building dream families in the Sims for all her siblings. Abe and Phoebe had five kids in the game, including the two they'd lost in real life. Darah had even started simulating their grandchildren. What if she put in as much effort into real life as she did her game saves? What if she nudged Bart and Geri a little?

"What are you thinking about?" Thandi asked.

"My end game. Your end game." Darah turned her head to look up at Thandi. "Can you imagine what your guy might look like?" She caught the wistful smile before Thandi could tuck it away. "Wait—there's someone?"

Thandi shook her head, but that shy smile betrayed her.

Darah spun around and blew hair from her face. "You better spill or I'm telling your mom."

"And I'll leave your head looking like Chewbacca if you do."

"That's cold." They worked in silence for a while as Darah perfected Sim Thandi's boyfriend from head to toe.

"So... is Junior's brother still moving down with Aunt Phoebe's parents?"

"Marcus?" Darah said. "I think he's considering it. U of H football might tip the scales."

"What about Junior?"

"Who knows?"

Three years ago, Marcus had been adopted by Phoebe's parents. Junior chose a college in Pittsburgh to stay close to Marcus. Now Phoebe's parents were selling their house and moving to Houston in time for Baby Teka's arrival.

"It would be cool having everybody in the same city again," Thandi said.

Darah stared at the screen. Football. Running Back. Hail Mary. Marcus. "Wait a hot minute."

Thandi tugged her roots. "Stop moving or we'll never get done."

Darah jerked around. "That's why your sim looks familiar. Is this supposed to be Marcus?" Thandi was always asking about Marcus and Junior.

Thandi couldn't even make eye contact.

"Seriously? Marcus?"

Thandi waved one hand. "We just text and call once in a while."

"You're calling him?" Darah clamped her mouth shut. To think her righteous best friend would actually get a boyfriend before her. "It's that serious?"

"C'mon, we're just talking. He's probably doesn't even like me like that."

"But you made him your sim boyfriend. That's definitely serious. And I can't even believe you just said that." Of course, Marcus would like Thandi—she was gorgeous. Just last week, some agent at the mall had asked if she'd ever considered modeling. At fifteen. Thandi didn't even try and still turned heads.

"It's not that serious. Just delete him," Thandi said quietly.

"I'm not deleting Sim Marcus. He's already in the world and I have plans for him and Sim Thandi. How long has this been going on?"

Thandi didn't answer.

"How long, Thandi?" She sounded more intense than she meant to. But Thandi never talked about boys. Not seriously. Darah had always been the one gushing, while Thandi simply listened.

"Since Abe's wedding," Thandi said with a small shrug. "When Marcus came back the next summer, he gave me his number, so I texted him after I got my first phone."

Darah turned forward so Thandi wouldn't see her face. The summer after Abe's wedding meant they'd been talking for two whole years.

"Wow, that's quite the surprise."

"Don't be like that," Thandi said quickly. "I don't want it to be weird."

"It's not," Darah said, forcing herself to smile. "Just a surprise that you didn't tell me." She saved Sim Marcus and closed the game. She didn't feel like playing anymore. "Has he asked you out?"

Thandi's laugh was nervous, childlike. "Yeah, right. That dude's living his best life in college. I'm probably the last person on his mind."

"Right," Darah mumbled. She'd seen too many guys ogle Thandi to believe that.

"Besides," Thandi added. "Mom would flip if she knew I liked him."

"Why? Marcus is a good guy. He's Phoebe's brother."

"It's not him. It's dating in general. She thinks dating in high school is pointless," Thandi said with a sigh. "I just like talking to him. He's sweet."

"Marcus, sweet?" Darah chuckled.

Like Junior, Marcus was rough around the edges. As a freshman running back already over six feet, he had an undeniable gravity about him that pulled people in. And Thandi? She looked like she belonged in a high-fashion spread, the kind you tore out of magazines to post on your wall. Darah often felt like a lanky giraffe next to her, even though they were only a couple of inches apart. Somehow, Thandi made everything look effortless. Guys were intimidated by Darah, but not by Thandi. They tripped over themselves for her. Smiled wider. Except maybe Jeremy.

Again, he'd slipped in like a splinter beneath her thoughts.

He'd texted her again this morning, offering her a ride home. The text was short, casual, but she'd reread it at least five times before pretending it didn't exist.

She hadn't responded. Not after how she'd acted on Saturday. She'd been cold to him. She always was. And yet, he was still trying. Why?

She didn't know what to do with that kind of attention, kindness. Not showy like she would have written it in one of her stories. No moonlit declarations. Just steady pursuit. Like she was some sort of prize and he'd take all the time in the world winning her heart.

Darah pulled her knees in. Maybe Jeremy didn't see her the way she saw herself. And somehow, that terrified her even more than the idea of being overlooked. Because what if he really meant it? What if someone like him really was choosing her?

"Are you upset?" Thandi asked. "He and I are just friends.

Don't be mad at me, D. Please?"

Darah stared at Thandi's sweet, sad face. "How could I be mad at you about that?" It was the right thing to do. Be happy for her best friend. "I'm not upset. Let's check when Pittsburgh plays this weekend."

Darah pulled up the guide on the TV. "Let me guess, he's the one who explained 'Hail Mary' to you?"

"Oh my gosh," Thandi groaned. "Please stop."

They burst out laughing.

It was impossible to stay annoyed at Thandi. Thandi couldn't help being so... Thandi.

Darah's phone vibrated on her thigh. She glanced at it and her heart stuttered—again. This guy. His timing was ridiculous. He had a radar for showing up when her defenses were low.

She waited until Thandi left for the restroom before checking her phone.

Another message from Jeremy.

Friday? Just us. My treat. Don't ghost me.

Her thumb hovered over the screen, her lips parting before she quickly erased the smile from her face.

What was he doing? No—what was she doing? She shook her head, setting the phone face down. Just how long until he figured it out? That she wasn't like the girls he usually talked to. She wouldn't flirt back or fling her underwear at him. That behind the sarcasm and dodged texts, she was mostly trying not to care too much. Because caring would make it real. And if it became real, it could fall apart.

The sensible part of her—the Christian girl who had been raised to do what's right—understood the dangers Jeremy posed. But when every message felt like a soft knock on the door she didn't know how to open, what was she supposed to do? Especially when the other side of her—the fluttery, ridiculous girl who wanted to be like everyone else—was starting to hope he wouldn't stop knocking.

"Who keeps texting you?" Thandi asked, skipping back into the room.

Darah slipped her phone under her leg. "A secret."

"Who, RJ?"

Rohan Joel Obed, the young immigration lawyer and chronic volunteer at House of Hope. He was one of the characters in the novel she was currently writing in her dreams, the Indian heartthrob with the prettiest soft hazel eyes and exquisite shirt cuffs.

"In what universe would Rohan have my number, much less text me?"

Thandi worked the last section of hair. "Good point. Then who is it?"

"No one important, Nosy." Darah pinched Thandi's thigh. "This is about you. When did you start hiding things from your mom? First, Marcus. I bet you haven't even told her about that modeling agent guy. That's the second time, right?"

Thandi frowned. "How am I supposed to tell her that when I already know what she'll say? No, thanks, I don't need that smoke in my life."

"But if she didn't have an opinion, would you do it?"

"Modeling?" Thandi shrugged. "I don't know. Seems like a lot of work."

"My little fashionista, you've already done half of it just waking up," Darah teased. "You're gorgeous."

"So are you," Thandi said, matter-of-fact. "Your height, your face, that attitude. You'd kill it."

Darah snorted. The agent hadn't even looked her way, but

she knew why. Her skin was too dark, hair too thick and frizzy. With her golden skin and camera-ready curls, Thandi was the one they wanted.

"They're drawn to you," Darah went on. "Just like Marcus. Honestly, I can't believe I missed it. That dude lights up whenever you talk."

"Stop it! Putting stuff in my head." Thandi laughed, throwing a twist at her.

When Aunty Mani returned hours later, Thandi was gathering the final mini twists into a ponytail.

"Well done," Aunty Mani said. "You've gotten really good."

"Thanks Mom," Thandi said, beaming.

As the mother and daughter embraced, Darah felt that familiar pang. She missed those fierce, soul-deep hugs from her own mom, their inside jokes, how Mom would fuss over her hair, pulling it into tight, clean braids while listening to African Christian music. When Mom died, the beauty of her touch left with her. No one could touch her hair the same way again.

Minutes later, Bart picked up Darah from Thandi's house. The sun had already dipped behind the row of townhomes in the distance.

"Did you guys play basketball?" Darah asked once they drove off.

After dropping her off at Thandi's, Bart went to volunteer at House of Hope. Their whole family volunteered at the children's home. Since their parents had found Darah, Clement and Eli through House of Hope, it only made sense that they served now, honoring them by giving back.

"Yeah, Tevin destroyed all of us," Bart replied.

"That dude is special," Darah agreed. "He just might make it to the NBA."

Bart nodded. He lowered the music, tapping the hard beat against the steering wheel, waiting for the light to turn green.

"You're in a good mood," Darah said, side-eyeing him. "Is this the perfect time to ask you if you'll let me drive the car in the garage?"

"No."

"Not a good time, or no, period? I mean, it's just sitting there. And Junior said I could have it."

"It's not his car to give. The original owner's back. So, no."

"Geri doesn't even know you have her car. You know I can't keep bumming rides forever." She turned to face him. "When are you going to tell her?"

"When I'm ready. And you can take the bus. That's what living in the city's for."

"Be serious. I'm not riding the bus downtown every Saturday."

Bart glanced over. "Whose idea was it to let a sixteen-year-old take college courses, huh? What's the rush to grow up, Squirt?"

Darah faced the window. "It just feels like everyone's leaving me behind," she whispered, the words escaping before she could stuff them back into her silence.

Bart was quiet for a beat. "I got you, D. Just a bit more patience."

Darah shook her head. How could he understand? Bart had always been the coolest sibling. But then, he had changed since he got back from Nigeria?

"You didn't tell me about your dad," she said. "Was it the reunion you dreamed of?"

Bart snorted. "There's nothing to talk about. He'll be gone soon."

His tone was so cold it unnerved her. "How does it feel then, to find a parent only to lose them again?"

He didn't answer, so she glanced at him. His hard face betrayed nothing.

"It's wild to think Dad knew about your father this whole time," she said. "I wonder what else he and Mom knew."

Dad had found Marcus, and now Marcus and Junior were really cool. What if Abe's parents were still alive? Or Eli's? Her birth parents were long gone, but what if there was someone out there for her too? Someone who knew her parents. What if she had a sibling she didn't even know to look for?

"I'm not sure I want to find out," Bart muttered as he turned onto their street.

Darah studied him, the way his shoulders hunched, the weariness in his eyes. He looked older than he did a few months ago. But maybe it had less to do with his father and more to do with Geri.

"Why are you looking at me like that?" Bart asked. "I'm not changing my mind about the car, D."

She smirked. "Just when I think about saying something nice, you ruin it."

He chuckled. "Brat."

Her smile lingered. "Be honest. If they knew about your birth mom, you're really saying you wouldn't want to know?"

"Nope," Bart said, firm as ever.

As they pulled up to the house, the garage door lifted, revealing Abe's SUV and the hooded car beside it.

"So back to the car—" Darah began.

"Don't want to hear it," Bart cut in as he opened the car door. "The car's off the table."

"Then what about its owner? Is she off the table too?"

Bart stopped in his seat. "What?"

"Can we finally talk about your feelings for her?" She tried to keep her voice light. "Because honestly, you're wasting time, and I'm not sure why."

Bart opened his mouth, then closed it. "It's complicated."

"Sure," Darah said, pushing open the car door. "Just don't take too long, bruh. Good women like Geri don't wait around forever."

She hopped out, leaving him sitting there in his car, looking like she'd just handed him a truth he wasn't ready to face.

23

Geri reached for Joaquin sliding down the blue slide, his laughter bubbling up as she caught him. The morning sun bore down hard, and the new plastic slide was too hot to keep playing on.

"Time to go inside," she said.

Joaquin wriggled out of her grasp and darted around the backyard. Geri waited until he circled back close. She scooped him up, blowing kisses on his cheek. No matter the tantrum or meltdown, it was better than watching him stuck on a hospital bed. Holding him close, she walked them both back into the house.

It was quiet today. Phoebe was out with Aunt Bel and Uncle Harry. The kids were at school, Abe was at work, and Bart was across town at one of his properties. Geri didn't mind the silence. It gave her space to think without answering a dozen questions.

She had barely stepped inside and locked the back door behind them when the beeping of the electronic lock sounded again. It was the front door. She glanced down at her soft, faded T-shirt dress. It was too late to scramble to her room.

The front door opened. Instead of Bart, Kasey stepped in. Alone.

Kasey's polished smile instantly faltered when she saw Geri. "Oh, hi there."

"Good morning," Geri said, willing herself to stay calm as Joaquin slipped behind her legs.

Kasey breezed in with a large gift bag swinging from one hand, designer purse in the other. She wore sky-high heels, a red halter dress that hugged a tiny waist and showcased her hourglass figure most women would pay a fortune for. She was nothing like Bart's ex—CJ, the slender, top model chick, or Liz who didn't have any curves to speak about. Bart's tastes had definitely changed.

Geri tugged at the hem of her dress. Compared to Kasey, she felt like a frumpy housekeeper.

"I thought Phoebe would be home," Kasey murmured.

"She's out with family."

"This is for her," Kasey said, placing the gift bag on the couch. "Forgot it for the shower."

"I'll let her know you brought it by."

Kasey smiled at Joaquin. "It's okay. I'll text her." She glided up the stairs without waiting for a response.

Geri sat down, watching Joaquin push his yellow toy car across the floor. She'd only gone upstairs a handful of times, but Kasey had the run of the place. She knew Bart's door codes, his rooms. She belonged here.

"I hungry, Mommy," Joaquin said, little hands tugging at her shirt. "Bobfish, please, Mommy."

She smoothed his curls. "How about apple and peanut butter? It's almost nap time. You can have goldfish after."

"How do you moms do that, understand what they're saying?" Kasey's voice floated down from the top of the stairs.

Joaquin darted behind her again. Geri glanced down to reassure him, and heard a yelp. The sharp skid of heels on wood. She looked up just in time to see Kasey tumble forward, arms flailing, body twisting, her ankle snapping sideways.

Geri jumped forward, and the world tilted, rewinding the scene to her old nightmare she thought she'd outrun. The day someone had pushed her.

It had happened in the weeks after Hakeem's funeral. While Geri waited for Asabe to release her passport, Asabe had banished her to one of Hakeem's houses, where she lived alone with a maid. She'd thought the maid had left to get supplies, but as she came down the stairs to get some food, she felt hands at her back, and the floor vanished beneath her feet.

She could still feel it. The blur of motion, her hands grasping at empty air, her body pitching forward in a helpless freefall, the rush of gravity yanking her down, the sharp crack of bone and wood colliding.

After that incident, she was in the hospital for weeks. That was when she found out she was pregnant, and made the decision to run away from Abuja.

Now, as she watched Kasey fighting to stay upright, the cry tumbled out of Geri's throat.

"Jesus."

That was all she could muster. But somehow, that was all it took. At the last possible second, Kasey's hand latched onto the railing and her descent jolted to an abrupt stop.

"Kasey," Geri cried, rushing to the bottom of the stairs.

"I'm okay," Kasey gasped, still clutching the railing, her face pale.

Geri started to climb, but Joaquin clung to her legs. She stood there trembling as Kasey hobbled down the last few steps. The echoes of that old fall kept tolling, like a doorbell she couldn't stop answering.

Kasey frowned at the tear in her dress. "Great. This was for my meeting later today."

"It doesn't look too bad." Geri stretched out her hand. "Take it off. I'll fix it you."

Kasey stared like Geri had offered to patch up her wedding gown.

"You don't want me to?" Geri asked.

Kasey nodded. She still looked dazed from the fall.

"I'll grab my sewing kit," Geri said, adjusting Joaquin on her hip.

By the time she returned with her kit in hand, Kasey was gone. Her purse was on the couch, her towering heels discarded at the foot of the stairs.

Geri got a bag of goldfish and a juice box from the kitchen and settled Joaquin on the couch.

A minute later, Kasey reappeared wearing one of Bart's baseball jerseys. She handed Geri the torn dress. "You sure you know what you're doing?"

Geri took the delicate fabric in her calloused hands. "Don't worry. At least you won't have to leave here half-naked."

Joaquin giggled, crunching goldfish crackers while Geri threaded her needle, fingers moving with practiced ease.

Kasey sat on the recliner, buried in her phone, long legs tucked beneath Bart's oversized jersey.

The dress was an easy fix, mending the rip along the delicate seam. One stitch at a time. Just like everything else in her life these days.

"You're not who I expected," Kasey said suddenly. "I don't know what I expected, but it wasn't you."

Geri's hands faltered. Had Bart painted her as some horrible person? "Sorry to disappoint."

Kasey shifted on the recliner. "I was determined not to like you. But here you are, being nice to me, sewing my dress."

Geri's needle paused midair. Kasey's expression was strangely open, not at all like when she'd first met her.

Geri turned back to the luxurious fabric. "Why would you not like me?"

"Because," Kasey said, folding her arms, "my boyfriend's been tripping over you for years."

The needle pricked Geri's thumb and she hissed, sticking her thumb in her mouth.

"Mommy?" Joaquin toddled over to touch her knee.

"I'm fine, baby." She kissed his forehead before her gaze snapped back to Kasey. "What did you just say?"

"You heard me." Kasey tilted her head. "Do you know where I first met Bart? At a bar downtown, three years ago. He looked like he'd lost his best friend. Or maybe the woman he loved."

A startled laugh escaped Geri. Both Joaquin and Kasey stared at her. "You're talking about CJ, his girlfriend from four years ago."

Kasey's eyes sharpened. "You really have no clue, do you? Bart broke up with her before he moved back to Houston." She tugged Bart's jersey lower over her bare legs. "Why am I even doing this? Are you almost done with the dress?"

Geri lifted the garment, showing the half-finished seam. "You've got it all wrong. Bart hated my guts before I left. We're just... barely friends now."

Even as she said it, the words tasted strange. Was that all they had been, that whole month in Ghana? All those late conversations, those moments she'd wondered about him in the dark, convincing herself that his actions meant nothing more than charity.

"Where's your kid's father?" Kasey asked.

Geri stiffened. "He died before Joaquin was born."

"Sorry. Touchy subject, huh?"

"It was a long time ago," Geri said, keeping her voice calm.

Kasey didn't drop it. "Must've been hard, raising him alone. Do you miss your husband?"

Geri took her time, pretending to be distracted by the fabric. It was impossible to explain how she missed the idea of having a partner, even when the reality had been nothing like she'd imagined.

"It's complicated," she admitted, watching Joaquin twirl a spool of colored thread between his fingers. How would he feel once he was old enough to understand what had happened between her and his father? Would he resent her for leaving behind his heritage and birth country?

"Why?" Kasey's voice was low now. "Because of Bart?"

Geri caught her own gasp, her face flushing hot.

"This is crazy, right?" Kasey leaned forward, a glint in her eyes. "Do you get what I'm saying?"

Geri shook her head, pulse thudding wild. "I think you're imagining things. Maybe you should rest upstairs until I finish the dress."

Kasey grinned. "I should just go, shouldn't I? Pretend I didn't notice. But here I am, trying to convince you that my boyfriend's been in love with you this whole time."

Geri sat frozen, her face burning, mouth dry.

Kasey gave a little laugh. "I'm a sucker for those stories, you know, the enemies-to-lovers romance. Thought Darah and I might bond over that, but that girl? She hates my guts."

"Darah can be difficult sometimes," Geri managed to get out.

"Not with you." Kasey's voice rose. "She loves you. Every time she wanted to jab at me, she'd bring you up. And Bart would just go all quiet, like he couldn't hear a word anyone was saying. Like he was thinking about you."

Geri stared at Kasey, struggling for words. "I... I don't know what to say."

"Don't say anything." Kasey reached out. "Just give me the dress. I'll wear it as is."

Numbly, Geri handed it over, her hands trembling in her lap. She was pretty much done. She watched Kasey rise, smooth the repaired fabric down her sides, and walk confidently up the stairs. Back to Bart's room. To Bart's bed.

The realization made Geri's stomach twist. Bart's girlfriend somehow thought Bart was in love with her.

Moments later, Kasey descended again, her heels stabbing the floor. She paused near the door, one hand brushing her hip. "Not bad," she said. "Thanks. You didn't have to do this for me. You're making it really hard to dislike you."

Geri couldn't even muster a smile, her throat thick with questions she didn't dare ask.

"And maybe I never stood a chance against you," Kasey said. "The minute he met you in Nigeria, it was probably already over for me."

Geri shook her head, unable to form a single defense.

Kasey smiled. "It's alright. If you don't care about him, let's just forget I said anything." Her eyes flashed, like a challenge. "But for now, Bart is my man. And I'm his woman. And I need you to start respecting that."

With a sharp turn, Kasey walked out of the house, leaving Geri alone with Joaquin in the living room.

Geri fell back against the couch, taking deep breaths, feeling like a storm had torn through her chest.

24

Bart saw it coming. Kasey wanted to talk, and he was ready. She picked her favorite breakfast café. As usual, it was half-packed when he got there. He chose a corner booth at the back. When Kasey arrived, she didn't even smile before seating across from him.

"Hand me the menu," she said, flipping her long hair over her shoulder. She always looked at the menu, even though she always ordered the same thing: bottomless mimosas, a sizzling crab omelet, and brioche bread.

Kasey scanned the menu for all of five seconds, then peeked up at him through thick lashes. "I'm surprised your phone still works. You were mad when you left my house."

Bart lifted his coffee cup. Mad didn't cover it. He'd stormed out, tangled in emotions he hadn't understood. He wasn't angry at her anymore. He was angry at himself for waiting so long to have this conversation.

A strange look crossed her face, like she'd seen an insect at the bottom of her water glass.

"Are you okay?' he asked.

Kasey smiled. "Still processing."

"Processing what?" He sipped his coffee. It was bitter today. Too bitter.

She pinned him with a glare. "Why you haven't slept with me in months."

Bart choked on his coffee. He wiped his mouth with the napkin. "Why are we talking about this here?"

"You act like I'm gonna jump you anytime we're at my place." Her voice turned sharp, accusing. "Like we're doing something wrong. Even when I kiss you, it's like you're looking over your shoulder."

She wasn't wrong. He'd changed, and he wasn't sure why. Maybe it was a mixture of things. The last time they were together was after he'd found out about his father. He'd been unraveling, and she'd been there. Since then, it felt like they were stuck in neutral. They hung out, but neither one really showed up.

"Ever since you came back from Nigeria, it's like pulling teeth to get you alone," Kasey went on. "And even that last night you stayed over? All you wanted to do was talk about your father, having to go to Nigeria, about understanding God's plan."

A flush crept up his neck. "God's plan? Me?"

"That's not what I want to talk about." She leveled a pointed look at him. "Geri... you're still in love with her?"

Bart stared at her, the tension creeping from his temples to his forehead. He almost sighed out loud when the waiter approached their table.

Kasey handed the menus over. "I'll have the crab omelet,

sunset mimosa, with brioche."

The waiter turned to Bart. "Chicken and waffles," he said.

Kasey raised a brow. "No tres leches pancakes? Watermelon juice?" She smirked, as if it was a harmless joke, but it always felt like a jab, like she thought those choices didn't fit him.

"Trying something different." Bart sat back. Joaquin loved fried chicken. And waffles. Geri had liked waffles too. He opened his mouth to ask for an order to go—then caught himself.

Kasey frowned. "You just thought about her, didn't you?"

"Kase–"

She held up a hand. "It's fine, I get it. You spent a lot of time together. It was intense. Close quarters. It's normal. I read about it. It's called a savior complex."

"That's not it, Kase."

"Then what is it? You didn't correct me when I said you're still in love with her. What, you never stopped? You've kept her in your heart all this time, and now that she's a widow, you finally have your shot?"

He couldn't answer. How could he when he himself was still figuring it out? He'd let go of Geri once he heard about her wedding. He'd met Kasey that same night, drinking, trying to bury his complex feelings because it never made sense how he could be in love with a woman he barely knew or had anything to do with. Before Geri left, they'd never even hung out or gone out on a date, much less had sex. Was that really how love worked?

He'd had a front row seat to Abe and Phoebe's relationship. They had somehow fallen in love without doing most of the stuff—like going on dates and sleeping together—that other couples did to fall in love. No, Abe and Phoebe were different. No one fell in love like that, the way those two had, without any bells or whistles. He'd watched enough dramas and romcoms to know that love was supposed to hit you like a storm—no, like the sun breaking through dark clouds. Love was a moment, when everything finally came together and you just knew. And this thing—obsession with Geri felt like love, but it hadn't happened in any of the ways those movies had said love was supposed to happen. It had just happened.

"Did something happen between you two?" Kasey asked.

The long hospital nights with whispered prayers. The way she'd trusted him with her grief, her hopes, her fears. It meant everything to him. But had it meant anything to her?

"Be honest with yourself, Bart."

He shook his head. This rift with Kasey had started long ago, maybe from the beginning. Going to Nigeria, meeting his birth father—seeing the fleeting fragility of life and how a man who once had everything now had nothing—had opened his eyes to the truth.

"I want more," Bart said. "A family. Like Abe and Phoebe. I want that forever kind of love."

Her lips parted, but she said nothing.

"Even if it's not Geri," Bart said, more to himself than to her. "I want that. But I'm not sure how to get there."

Kasey sat back, arms folded. "So, it's not just me?" Her smile was bittersweet. "You're saying I'm not the problem—you are."

Bart's throat worked. "Yes."

"Bull," she spat. A tear slipped out, then another. "We both know it's me. If I were that kind of woman, then we could have that kind of love."

Bart forced himself not to look away from her pain. He didn't fully understand what she meant, but Kasey had always struggled with rejection.

She had poured out her fears to him the night they first met, the night Phoebe had told him about Geri's engagement. He'd found himself at the lounge. Kasey had walked up to him with a drink and a bright smile. She told him he was cute, asked for his number. They'd spent an entire weekend together, and somehow stayed friends while dating other people. The ghosts of what-ifs kept both of them from giving it a real chance. She'd just gotten out of a two-year engagement and wanted fun.

"You sound just like him," Kasey whispered. "I'm the kind of woman you have fun with not marry, right?"

He made sure to meet her eyes. "I never said that."

"You don't have to," she said, letting out a breathy laugh. "You're right, I could've tried harder, but I feel like I never really had a chance no matter what I did. Not with you always thinking she was the one who got away."

"Kase—"

"I fell down the stairs at your place yesterday."

He leaned forward, scanning her arms, her face. No bruises he could see. "Are you okay? That's why I always tell you to take off your heels before you go upstairs."

Kasey smiled, as if glad he was concerned for her. "I'm fine. Geri was more shaken up than I was."

His voice dropped. "She saw you fall?"

The waiter returned with another mimosa. Kasey picked up her glass.

"If it had been Darah, she probably would've laughed in my face. I'd have laughed too, if it wasn't me. But Geri, she looked terrified. Like it was her who fell."

He could picture it—the horror in Geri's amber eyes. "She fell once. When she was pregnant with Joaquin. Down the stairs."

"That explains it," Kasey murmured. "Yesterday was so weird. Sitting there, watching the woman my boyfriend's been pining for sew my dress and be nice to me."

"She sewed your dress?" His mind spun, trying to picture what had happened.

"I told her," Kasey said, with a bitter laugh. "That you had feelings for her."

The bottom dropped out of Bart's stomach. Last night, she'd gone to bed early. He'd thought she was tired, but she was clearly avoiding him.

"It's your fault," Kasey went on, sipping her drink. "Sure, I waited too long with all that breaking up and coming back together. But you should have..."

Her tears slipped out, and she looked at him like she was waiting for him to speak.

"I'm sorry," he said. She was right. He hadn't fought hard enough for her, for them. For anything but his career.

"For the record," Kasey said, "she looks nothing like me. Your sister's a brat."

Bart almost laughed. "Yeah, she is."

Kasey leaned back, her expression softening. "So, what are you gonna do now? Confess your feelings and sweep her off her feet?" Her eyes glistened with unshed tears. "If she breaks your heart—and she probably will—don't expect me to take you back."

He nodded. His chest hurt, full of words he couldn't seem to say. "You're a good person, Kasey. You deserve a good man."

She stared at him. "You're a good man, Bart."

He swallowed hard. How could she say that when he hadn't been able to protect her heart? She'd come to him broken from her first love, and what they'd shared had only been a bandage over wounds neither of them wanted to name. And now, he was sending her away, broken again.

"I'm sorry," Bart said again, overwhelmed by the heaviness

in his eyes.

"I'm sorry too." She reached across the table and squeezed his hand. "You tried. And I'm grateful. It was just bad timing." She let go and stood, grabbed her purse. "I'll head out first."

He watched her walk away. No hug. No goodbye.

A minute later, their confused waiter arrived balancing a tray with her crab omelet, his chicken and waffles. Kasey's favorite meal sat untouched, steam curling upward like a ghost quietly slipping away.

Bart handed the waiter his card. "I'll pay now. Please can you pack the chicken and waffles to go? Just leave the omelet here."

As the waiter left to pack up his food, Bart remained seated, staring at the empty chair across from him. He let out a slow breath, the weight of silence pressing into his chest.

Kasey was gone. And it was his fault, thinking he could give her more than he ever had to give.

"Oh God," he whispered. "Help her find a good man. Someone who'll love her the way she deserves. Better than I ever could."

And as the last curl of steam rose from her untouched plate, Bart finally understood. That 'good man' had never been him. All along, he'd been holding a place he was never meant to fill.

"Amen."

25

Darah slumped in her chair in the youth center. Not another awkward sermon about sex.

The guest speaker—imported from another church because none of the resident pastors had the guts—stood stiffly at the pulpit. A scrawny white man with reddish-brown hair and bright blue eyes, looking every bit like someone who married his college sweetheart and hadn't uttered the word "sex" since their wedding vows.

Abe would have sounded just as nervous, prattling on about purity and waiting for marriage. Several boys in the chapel burst out laughing. It was now officially embarrassing.

"They don't want to talk about it till they're forced to," Darah whispered to Thandi beside her. "And when they do, it's this weird charade."

A sharp shhh cut through the pews. Thandi nudged her arm

but kept her eyes glued to the speaker. They'd grabbed seats by the back door, where the crowd of teens packed in for the midweek service. The preacher fumbled through metaphors about preserving the body as a temple, looking like he wished the earth would swallow him whole.

The whole thing was weird. Didn't Christians have sex? Judging by the number of babies in church, you'd think they would have figured out how to talk about it by now. He probably had five kids and still couldn't say it with his chest. Even the young married couples she knew weren't upfront, though they clearly couldn't keep their hands off each other. Eden was the worst culprit, always touching her husband—stroking his locs and kissing him. Once, she'd caught Abe and Phoebe making out, and Abe would often stop mid-sentence if Phoebe so much as looked at him funny. But whenever Darah wanted to talk about dating, everyone clammed up like she'd asked about bank fraud.

The service mercifully ended in a rush, the sanctuary emptying faster than a school bell dismissal. Darah and Thandi took their time down the stairs to avoid the stampede.

"It wasn't that bad," Thandi said, as they strolled down the main hallway.

"Nobody wants to hear about sex from their youth pastor," Darah said. "They act like it's the devil's invention. Just saying the word makes adults squeamish."

"Well, the devil did corrupt it."

"Human nature corrupted it. Same way a toddler lies without being taught. You gotta show us younger people how not to mess up something good, not just telling us 'Sex is bad.'"

An older man walking past gave them a disapproving glare as he exited the church doors.

"See?" Darah smirked. "Everyone's allergic to the word, but

it's everywhere—books, TV, movies, comics. Shoot, you can read a steamy at the library without showing ID, not to mention going online." Darah chuckled. "Judging by my brothers, I'm pretty sure all of them lost their virginity in high school. Bart, maybe in middle school. What a joke!"

Thandi side-eyed her. "Well, my mom's still a virgin."

Darah stopped mid-stride. "Still blows my mind every time you say it. Your mom's a saint."

"She's amazing." Thandi's grin was pure pride.

"Phoebe too. But the second she got that preacher stamp of approval, you know she couldn't wait." Darah laughed again as they reached the busy lobby. "True Love Waits only works until a fine man's asking for more than a dance."

Thandi snorted. "That better be from a novel you're reading. You're not getting any action, right?" She whispered the last words.

Jeremy's smile flashed in Darah's mind. "Nope. I barely have time to hit the library."

"You're so bad," Thandi nudged her arm.

"Hey, Thandi."

They both turned. A guy leaned against the wall by the stairs, waving. Cornrows Cal, looking fresh as usual with spotless Jordans.

"Oh, God," Thandi groaned under her breath. With her fair skin and waist-length curls, half the youth group had a crush on Thandi. Since Calvin was probably the cutest guy, he always stepped to Thandi like she owed him her attention.

"Time for me to bounce." Darah made to slip away.

Thandi's grip locked on her arm. "Don't you dare leave me with him."

Calvin approached, smiling wide at Thandi. "Hey, gorgeous."

"Hey," Thandi mumbled, monotone.

"How's your week been?"

"It's fine."

Darah bit back a laugh, thinking she should invite Marcus to youth group next time he was in town. If Calvin saw Thandi with Marcus, Calvin would finally back off. She'd pay money to see that showdown.

"I didn't see you in the chapel," Calvin went on.

"I was there," Thandi said, like she'd rather be anywhere else. It was wild how the usually friendly and reserved Thandi got borderline rude when she was dealing with guys who thought they were all that.

Darah scanned the hallway. A cluster of college students and singles trickled out of another chapel nearby, their laughter echoing under the high ceilings. Among them, she spotted RJ. He wore a blue button-down tucked into dark slacks, looking more suited for a courtroom than a midweek church service. Everyone else wore hoodies and sneakers, but RJ walked alone, his steps purposeful, as if he had a million-dollar case waiting for him.

"I'll call you later," she said, tugging Thandi's sleeve. "Night, Calvin."

Thandi's eyes blew up, pleading, but Darah hurried away, weaving through the crowd until she caught up with RJ. She tapped his shoulder, and those hazel eyes turned, soft and guarded all at once, like she'd interrupted a serious thought.

"Hey, pretty eyes," she said.

Right on cue, his face broke, a mixture of confusion and panic. He quickly looked around, as if wondering if anyone else heard her.

Darah laughed. It was so easy to mess with him. Still, the old RJ would have taken a cautious step back, avoided her stare.

Tonight, he held his ground.

"You look really nice, Rohan," she said, flipping a beaded twist over her shoulder.

His eyes lit up. "You changed your hair."

Of course, he noticed. "You like?"

"It suits you."

A simple response, but it warmed her down to her toes. She absently toyed with the beads on a twist, then realized he was watching her play with her hair, transfixed, like she'd cast a spell. He snapped out of it with a smile, his gaze sharpening again.

She dropped her hand. It was time for her weekly food for thought. Whenever she ran into him, she liked to drop some random knowledge just to mess with his head.

"Life is short, Rohan," she said, teasing softly. "You should spend more of your time doing the things you really want to do."

He simply stared, wide-eyed and quiet, like she'd handed him a puzzle he wasn't sure he wanted to solve. He was so adorable. Every time she saw him, she wondered if she'd ever stop teasing him. Probably never.

"RJ?" Abe's voice floated over. He approached them, hand extended.

RJ's professional expression slipped easily into place. They shook hands and said goodbye. Darah walked with Abe outside to the parking lot.

"I almost want to see him in a courtroom," Darah mused aloud. "He's too young to be a lawyer. Didn't he go to college at fifteen?"

"That'll be you soon, Miss I wanna graduate early." Abe never shied away from expressing his displeasure at her trying to graduate early.

A car horn beeped behind them, and Auntie Mani pulled up.

"Glad we caught you," she said, getting out of her car. "Need to give you something for Phoebe."

Abe followed her to the trunk, and Thandi materialized beside Darah, glaring.

"You abandoned me to flirt with RJ."

Darah put a finger on her lips. "Are you trying to get me in trouble?"

"Then don't pretend you weren't flirting."

"I wasn't. He's so innocent, I just like to mess with him."

"You don't think I saw your googly eyes? You showed off the hair I did. Flirting. Traitor."

"Will you hush?" Darah glanced at Abe and Kimani unloading bags.

"Now you're shy?" Thandi lowered her voice. "What happens when he actually bites and you can't handle it?"

"Bites what—"

Abe reappeared carrying half a dozen gift bags. Darah rushed forward to help.

"Our women's Bible study group sent gifts for Phoebe," Thandi's mom called from the driver's seat. "Some couldn't make it to the shower."

Abe and Darah exchanged knowing glances. After returning the gifts from the last baby shower—because Phoebe couldn't bear to keep them—they hadn't invited many people this time.

Thandi stuck out her tongue at Darah as her mom drove off.

"That was very nice of them," Darah said, trailing Abe to the SUV.

Abe unlocked the doors and ducked inside. "You've got a thing for RJ?"

Darah nearly dropped the bags. Thandi was so dead. Play it cool. "A thing?" She chuckled. "Am I allowed to have those?"

"You can like whoever you want. Just no dating allowed." Abe took the bags from her and arranged them in the backseat.

Darah rolled her eyes and climbed into the car. "I'm not entertaining that silly rule. Besides, crushes are a waste of time. He's simply a peer of mine."

Abe snorted. "What does that even mean?"

"We rub shoulders as cohorts, share similar interests, and enjoy occasional discourse."

Abe chuckled as he started the car. "RJ's your peer?"

She clicked her seatbelt. "Maybe when I start going to the singles class next year, we can revisit that silly rule and squash it once and for all."

"Yeah, right. Who's letting a seventeen-year-old into the singles class?" Abe pulled onto the main road.

"I'm graduating next year whether you like it or not, Abe. What other class would I go to?"

"You could stay with your agemates."

"Forget it. I'd rather stay in the sanctuary with the grown-ups."

"Why are you in such a rush to grow up, D?"

Darah rested her cheek against the window. He wouldn't understand. He never did, no matter how many times she tried. "Then at least let me go to Homecoming this year."

At a red light, Abe sighed like a man carrying too much on his shoulders. "Homecoming's a waste of time."

"You don't get to say that. Y'all got to go, so why can't I? It's the only one I'll get before graduation."

"Junior didn't go to his. And it wasn't fun when I went."

"That's you. I bet Bart had a great time."

Green light. Abe drove on, ignoring the jab. There wasn't any point arguing. Forget homecoming, forget dating. If Abe had his

170

way, he'd lock her in the house till she turned thirty.

"I just don't get the rush," Abe said, his voice quieter now. "Why skip a grade when you could just have a normal high school experience?"

"Well, I'm not normal."

"That's not what I meant—"

"Homecoming, prom, they're normal high school experiences. Dating's normal. But I can't even like a guy without y'all flipping out." She folded her arms, looking straight at him. "All my friends are dating, but no one's allowed to like me back."

"No one said you couldn't like someone," Abe countered. "But RJ's too old for you. Pick someone your own age."

Darah groaned. "Then why talk about wanting me to have a normal high school experience if y'all won't let me have one?"

Silence stretched between them. She could feel his gaze flick toward her at the next light, but he didn't speak.

"You're the one who thinks crushes are a waste of time," Abe finally muttered.

"If I can't do anything about a crush, what's the point?" The words slipped out sharp. A quiet ache hollowed her chest. She'd never even gone on a single date. "It's suffocating."

"What is?"

She pressed her temple against the glass. "Forget it." There was no point explaining this part either. She couldn't wait to be in college, around people who might finally take her seriously. People who wouldn't treat her like a precocious child trying too hard to grow up. This was the only way she knew how to be. High school felt like a waiting room she couldn't escape. Waiting for the rest of her life to begin. Her classmates obsessed over dances, parties, and trivial heartbreaks she couldn't relate to. After Harvey hit, some had whined about missing tournaments while families around them had lost everything. They didn't get it. None of them really saw her, so how could they ever understand what she'd been through?

She rubbed her eyes. "Can we stop for fried chicken? I'm starving."

"Phoebe said just come home. Geri's cooking."

Darah gaped at him as the streetlight illuminated his hesitant grin. "Do I need to remind you about the last time Geri cooked?"

"Let's have hope." Abe chuckled. "She can't have gotten worse."

"I'll just eat cereal," Darah deadpanned.

He laughed as they turned into the garage. Bart's side of the driveway was empty. He wasn't home yet.

Darah eyed the car under the hood. "When's he gonna tell Geri this is still here?"

"Why? 'Cos you want to drive it?" Abe smirked at her. "Be patient, Darah."

"You're not the one riding the bus and dealing with crap every day."

"Someone picking on you?" His face flashed that same protective look from back in seventh grade when those girls had mocked her at the zoo trip. By the end of that week, two of them had cried their apologies; the other two mysteriously reassigned to another homeroom. She never did learn what exactly Abraham Teka had said to the principal, but it had been enough.

"Nothing I can't handle," Darah said. She was too old now for rescue missions. One last glance at the car—its sleek silhouette like a sleeping promise—and she went into the house.

A warm, fragrant wave of spices enveloped her. Inside the living room, Eli sat reading aloud from a marine wildlife book, Joaquin nestled against him. Around Bart's sprawling coffee table sat a mountain of tiny clothes. Geri, Phoebe, Aunt Lina, and Ms. Jen were folding the clothes, each piece handled with quiet reverence. Their smiles lifted toward her and Abe as they walked in.

"Ready to eat?" Geri asked.

"If what I'm smelling is what we're eating? Heck yes." Darah picked up a tiny pink onesie, folding it carefully.

"Language," Abe warned, lifting a matching onesie.

"Soon you'll be dressing your little girl in that," Ms. Jen said.

"Can't wait," Abe said, his voice wrapped in quiet wonder.

With one hand on her belly, Phoebe's lips curled in a misty smile. Their love had been tempered through loss, two storms survived, and now this fragile hope rising from the ashes.

For a moment, Darah watched them, the way Abe's steady hand covered Phoebe's. She wondered what it might feel like to have that. Someone steady. Someone sure.

"I'll set the table," Geri said.

"I'll help," Ms. Jen offered, patting Darah's shoulder as she passed. "How was midweek service? Anything worth sharing?"

"Nothing to write home about," Darah replied.

Geri pulled a roasting pan from the oven—golden-brown chicken glistening under a lacquer of honey and herbs. Joaquin scrambled from Eli's lap to join Darah in the kitchen.

"You made this?" Darah asked in wonder. "From scratch?"

Geri set the pot down, steam curling from the lid. "There's rice too."

"Jellof rice," Eli announced, climbing onto his chair.

"Jollof rice," Darah corrected, strapping Joaquin into his booster. Tari's rice was the standard, smoky and layered with flavor, but Geri's version looked pretty convincing.

As the table filled—laughter weaving between plates passed

hand to hand, voices overlapping like threads—Darah stopped by the sink and let the joy settle around her, fragile and fleeting. She caught her reflection on the microwave: beaded twists framing her face, eyes shining a little too brightly beneath the kitchen lights.

"Looking good, Darah," she whispered to herself. Maybe RJ had noticed more than just her hair. Maybe it wasn't so silly to wonder why Jeremy was interested in her after all.

She slid into her seat, surrounded by family, their warmth, by love woven through loss. Tomorrow, it was back to the complicated web of life. Waiting to grow up was the hardest part of growing up. But tonight, at least, she could live in this moment.

Tonight, she belonged.

26

Bart pulled into the driveway, eyeing the familiar line of cars parked along the curb. Aunt Lina's dusty pink sedan stood out like a faded rose under the streetlights.

"And there's no way to trace it back to her mother-in-law?" Bart asked, his phone connected to the car's speaker.

"No trace," Tonye replied over the line. "I don't see how she did it. The woman in the room, Fatima, was badly injured. It makes no sense for Asabe to go after her grandson like that."

Tonye wasn't saying anything Bart hadn't thought about. "But there's no way she's innocent," Bart grumbled. "She's connected somehow. We just haven't found it yet."

"Maybe indirectly. But right now, she's asking around, the same questions we're asking."

Bart didn't press him for details. Tonye's political ties ran deep. "Either way, that woman is dangerous, and if she catches wind that Geri and Joaquin are here, she's gonna try something."

"I'll let you know the minute I hear anything," Tonye assured him.

"How's Geri and my godson?" IB's voice chimed in from the background.

Bart's shoulders eased. "Happy. Healthy. Joaquin's a whole different kid." He checked the clock. "Isn't it crazy early for you guys?"

"We had a prayer meeting," IB replied, yawning. "Thanks for taking care of my girl."

"My pleasure," Bart said.

"I'm sure it is," Tonye teased. "We know she's in the best hands."

Bart laughed. "Yeah, she's in God's Hands."

"Right," Tonye drawled. "We'll catch up later, bro."

"Wait." Two days ago, Tonye had updated him on Peter's condition, and even though he knew Tonye would tell him if anything changed, it felt wrong not to ask about the man.

"He's still unresponsive," Tonye said, as if reading his mind. "I'll keep you posted. You know how we do."

"Thanks for everything, man."

He waited until their goodbyes faded before disconnecting the call. His gaze lingered on the glowing windows of his house. There was a time he'd come home to an empty loft in LA. To think his own house could be this full. A heartbeat within its walls.

But as warmth settled in his chest, it quickly tangled with doubt. Was his house this full because of him, or were all these people here for Abe and Phoebe? Was he capable of building the kind of love Abe had with Phoebe? Or Tonye with IB?

He stepped inside to the scent of roasted chicken and spices that curled around him like a welcome hug. "Smells amazing."

In the living room, the women sat folding baby clothes. Joaquin and Eli zoomed toy cars across the rug. At the dining table, Abe fiddled with a baby monitor while Geri sketched in her notebook.

"That time already?" Bart called, his pulse giving a familiar, restless thrum. Geri didn't look up.

"Might as well get it installed," Abe whispered, and turned to Geri. "We're still good for tomorrow, or you need more time?"

"Maybe one more day," Geri answered, her soft smile aimed at Abe, not Bart.

"Whatever you're scheming, let Bart eat first," Phoebe teased from the couch. "Bart, your plate's in the microwave."

Geri shook her head at Abe's grin. "She knows what we're up to."

"Pretty sure," Bart murmured, walking toward the microwave.

He retrieved his plate—mound of rice, roasted chicken glistening with glaze, and a colorful spread of vegetables. His stomach gave a happy lurch as he carried it back to the table and sat opposite Geri.

"Thanks for the food," he said, letting his gaze linger.

Without looking up, Geri got up and went to the sink, rolling up her sleeves to wash the dishes.

Bart's throat worked around a swallow. After what Kasey had told her, she still wasn't ready to face him. He scooped a bite of rice into his mouth and almost groaned aloud. The smoky, spicy richness melted over his tongue. He tore into the roasted chicken, tender and juicy beneath the crisp skin.

"Tari gave you her recipe, Phoebe?"

"That's all Geri," Abe said, with a nod.

Bart froze mid-chew. "Geri made this?" His voice pitched

high.

"She did," Phoebe and Darah chimed together, giggling.

Abe's phone vibrated on the table. He checked the screen and left the kitchen, answering the call on his way out.

Geri stood by the sink, sleeves pushed to her elbows, the kitchen lights framing her in warm gold. Bart didn't know how long he stared at her, fork idle over his plate. The next bite he took tasted like home, and every glance her way felt like standing outside a door he wasn't sure he deserved to knock on.

The food was that good. The rice tasted like it belonged at a Nigerian party. He pushed his fork through the grains. This was from Geri? The woman who once couldn't boil water without setting off the smoke alarm? Each layer she revealed made him more curious, more undone. If he kept peeling back her mystery, if he kept following these quiet breadcrumbs she left scattered around his house, his heart would collapse at her feet.

A loud crash snapped him out of his reverie. He twisted toward the sound—glass shattering near the sink. His fork clattered onto his plate as he shoved back his chair and rushed over.

Joaquin was already toddling toward Geri, reaching for the broken pieces scattered at her feet.

Bart swooped him up before his small fingers could touch the shards. "No, buddy." He carried the squirming boy to the living room and dumped him into Darah's waiting arms. Joaquin whined, craning his neck to peek back at his mother. Phoebe blocked his view.

Geri stood frozen by the sink, one hand lifted in the air, a smear of red gleaming across her palm. She hissed, cradling her hand.

Bart crossed the floor in two strides. "Let me see."

Geri took a step back, but Bart caught her wrist. He turned on the faucet, guiding her hand under the stream of cool water. The blood swirled away in thin crimson rivulets.

He checked her fingers. "Any pieces stuck?"

She shook her head, lips pressed tight.

"Good." He cradled her fingers in his palm, pulled a napkin from the counter and pressed it against the cut. His thumb brushed over the long, pale burn scar curling up her forearm. Just how many scars did she carry? How many stories she'd never told?

"I'm sorry."

"Stop apologizing."

Her wide eyes met his, so close he could see flecks of amber swimming in their depths. Her lips parted slightly as if she had something else to say. He wondered—just for a heartbeat—what it would feel like to destroy this space between them once and for all. Her soft and spicy scent wrapped around him as his hand lingered at her wrist. His body leaned forward—unconsciously, foolishly—drawn to her like a magnet he'd been resisting for years.

"You okay, Geri?" Darah's voice floated from behind.

Geri snatched her hand back so quickly she almost knocked over the dish rack. "Sorry," she squeaked, her face flushed as she hurried out of the kitchen.

Bart cursed under his breath. Darah's playful smile flickered across the doorway. Even Joaquin stared at him with an accusing pout, as if he too knew Bart had crossed a line.

Movement stirred by his leg. Bart looked down to find Ms. Jen crouched by the sink, quietly cleaning the mix of water and broken glass.

He bent down to help, but she lifted the rag out of his reach. "It's okay," she said. "I'm almost done."

There she was again, always ready to help. How long had she been standing there? How much had she seen?

Abe returned, glancing between Bart and the kitchen. "What did I miss?"

"Everything," Darah said, laughing as she walked away.

Bart watched the hallway where Geri had vanished, a quiet ache spreading beneath his ribs like the continuation of the pain he couldn't shut off. How could he have nearly kissed her? Here, in the middle of his kitchen, with her blood on his hands and her life still so fragile?

He braced both palms against the counter, his breaths unsteady. He needed to get a hold of himself. He was Bart Teka, not clueless Abe who never knew how to get what he wanted from a woman. He wanted Geri, so why was this so hard?

Bart pushed away from the counter and caught Abe staring at him. "What?" Bart asked.

"You doing too much, bro," Abe replied.

Bart scoffed, but then it hit him. What if Abe was right? What if doing things his way would never work with Geri?

He nodded. "Yeah."

He needed to chill before she built another wall between them. Before she found another reason to run away and disappear again, this time for good.

27

Geri closed her bedroom door behind her, trying to quiet her wild heartbeat. Her knees gave way and she sank onto the bed. She sucked on her palm to make sure the bleeding had stopped.

"What was that?" she muttered. Had he tried to kiss her in the kitchen?

His eyes had locked with hers like they held an answer she didn't have the courage to ask for. His hand had closed around her wrist like he belonged there. Like she wasn't someone broken, but someone he wanted.

She dragged her palms over her face, trying to chase off the heat rising to her skin. Kasey's voice echoed in her ears again, that quiet, infuriating certainty: "My boyfriend's been tripping over you for years."

It didn't make sense. She wasn't Bart's type. His exes were exotic, glamorous, long-limbed beauties, women who knew how to command a room.

She didn't command anything. She was only trying to survive.

But there was that unmistakable look in his eyes. The way his voice caught when he asked if she had cooked dinner. She'd imagined it before—what it would be like to feed him, to sit across from him and watch him eat something she made with her own hands. One time, when Hakeem had left the table without touching her food, she had pictured Bart smiling at the first bite, marveling in her newfound ability.

That fantasy had been her escape. And tonight, watching him eat her food and groan with pleasure felt like watching a dream step out of the shadows and ask her if it could stay a while. That last groan of his had made her hands fumble and drop the porcelain plate.

Geri fell back on the bed. The last mouth that touched hers had been cruel and punishing. Her last kiss had tasted like shame and regret. She'd convinced herself she'd never want to be touched by a man ever again. Never trust herself to want anything. She had her son. She needed nothing else.

Then why had she leaned in? Why had her body betrayed her, aching toward Bart like it remembered something sweeter than fear?

A knock at the door jerked her up. "Come in."

A smiling Darah peeked inside. "Ready for Joaquin? He's sleepy. Is your hand okay?"

"I'm good," Geri said, glad it was Darah. She couldn't face anyone else right now. Who else had seen him try to kiss her?

Darah brought Joaquin inside. "We're practicing walking to bed on our own. I already brushed Big Boy's teeth."

"Thank you." Joaquin rubbed at his eyes and crawled up onto

the mattress. "We need to change your clothes, baby."

Instead of moving, Joaquin slid off the bed and barreled into her legs. She lifted him into her arms. He wrapped his arms around her neck and rested his cheek in the crook of her shoulder. Darah stood there watching them with one of those girl-woman stares Geri had come to recognize. The kind that saw more than it said.

"Can I show you something?" Darah asked, cocking her head toward the door.

She wasn't leaving this room if Bart was still out there. "What is it?"

"It'll be quick. Bart already went upstairs."

Her heart gave a treacherous flutter. "Okay, if it's quick. Joaquin needs to sleep."

Geri followed Darah out of the room. Thankfully, no Bart. As they passed the kitchen, Ms. Jen looked up from cleaning the sink.

"Wait," Geri said, reminded that she hadn't finished cleaning up.

"It's okay. Go," Ms. Jen muttered, waving her on.

Geri nodded her thanks. Darah opened the door to the garage and flicked on the light, spilling brightness across the concrete. She circled Abe's SUV and stopped beside a covered car, tugging at the faded cloth until it slipped free to reveal a freshly painted, gleaming red Chevy. Her old car.

Joaquin squirmed in her arms. "Red car," he squealed.

Was this really her car? The dents she remembered were gone. The hood gleamed like glass.

"I don't understand."

"Remember when you told Abe to give Junior the car or sell it?" Darah's smile grew. "He didn't. Because Bart wouldn't let him."

"I don't..." But she did.

"He saved it for you," Darah said. "Said it was yours. Always would be."

Geri shook her head. After four years, why was her car in Bart's garage?

"He wouldn't even let me use it for driving practice."

Geri stared at Darah, this girl who spoke like she'd been cracked open by life and knew everything there was to know about pain.

"This is crazy," Geri muttered. She didn't dare ask the question that had been stirring ever since Kasey walked out of the house yesterday.

"I think you know what I'm trying to say, Geri." Darah folded her arms. "When everyone else moved on, when even I thought you'd left us behind, Bart kept hoping. After Junior left for college, he fixed everything on your car. Just in case you came back. It's been sitting in this garage since he got this house. He just never stopped believing you would come back."

Geri brushed her free hand along the car's smooth hood. It looked nothing like the dusty version she'd left behind. Her first big purchase. Her first taste of freedom. She'd cried the day she handed over the keys to Abe, thinking she might never see it again.

"I was mad salty when he wouldn't let me touch it," Darah added with a soft laugh. "But now I get it. And I think you do too."

Geri couldn't speak, her heart stuck in her throat.

Darah gave a wink. "Let's get back before they start wondering."

Back in the guest room, Geri tucked Joaquin under the covers. He fell asleep quickly, his little hand curled near her ribs.

She lay wide awake, staring at the ceiling, her mind spinning.

Wasn't this the same Bart who couldn't bear to stay in the same room with her? The one who always knew how to make her feel like she didn't belong? Yet it was his voice that calmed her at the hospital. His laugh made something ache and uncurl inside her. She could still feel his hand wrapped around hers under the faucet—warm and gentle. That wasn't the Bart she remembered. He was someone else. Someone who stayed.

Was that why he hadn't left them behind in Accra? Why he bunked in that tiny hospital room for two weeks, sleeping in a chair just so Joaquin could have someone to cuddle through the night? He never once complained. Not when the pain of his dislocated nose showed in the shadows beneath his eyes. Not when his comfort was gone, his life disrupted. He had stayed. When no one else could.

Geri wiped her eyes as more tears slipped out. Was she allowed to long for something again? Allowed to believe that someone like Bart could see every scar she carried and choose her anyway? How could she trust a man who had changed girlfriends like he did his cars?

But like a soft answer in the dark, the image of her own car returned, gleaming and quiet in the garage. Waiting. For her. Just like Bart.

Geri turned into her pillow, her heart aching with hope she wasn't ready to speak aloud.

For Bart Teka, she could. She really could.

28

Bart trudged up the steps like weights were strapped to his legs. The crew at his parents' house was light today. Emilio had pulled most of the workers to a site across town. Aside from the landscapers touching up the backyard, it was just him and Geri inside. The silence had never felt so loud.

He paused at the top of the stairs. The scent of primer and open windows drifted down the hallway. After last night, the almost-kiss and the way she'd bolted, he wasn't sure if showing up today was brave or just plain stupid.

The old Bart wouldn't show up. Old Bart would have been angry. So he had to come. Because Abe would have come. Abe always showed up no matter how he was feeling.

He stepped forward just as she emerged from the nursery, her breath catching like she'd run up the stairs.

"Hi."

"Hi."

She lifted a bottle in her hand. "I'm just getting some more water."

He reached for it without thinking. "I'll get it."

Their fingers brushed. She dumped the bottle in his hand and ducked back into the room. He stared at the door for a second too long before heading down to the kitchen. He filled her bottle and grabbed a glass for himself. The water was ice-cold, but it didn't put out the fire in his chest.

When he returned, she was crouched in front of the paint buckets, studying them like they held the future. "I'm trying to decide. Peach or lace white?"

He handed her the water, trying not to watch her lips close around the bottle. "Peach trim. White for the walls."

"Good idea." She put the bottle down, already pulling out brushes, rollers, and trays. "I'm thinking we might only need one layer of primer."

"I'll help."

She met his eyes for a second. "I saw something yesterday."

Was she talking about the kiss? "What did you see?"

She handed him a tray. "The car."

His grip nearly slipped, tipping the can. He looked up and caught the amusement in her eyes. He wiped off paint from the side of the bucket.

"You saw it," he echoed.

"I did." She was smiling. Actually smiling.

He shrugged, heart hammering in his throat. "I couldn't sell it."

"Why?"

Because I was in love with you, he wanted to say. Because you mattered more than I could admit.

Instead, he reached for the roller. "Because I was sorry. For everything. I treated you badly. And I never got the chance to say it."

"I wasn't exactly nice either."

"I deserved worse." He dipped the roller in the paint. "After you left, I looked up old yearbooks."

With Abe's help, he'd pieced the truth together, how their mom had met Geri in middle school while she was serving in PTA. Mom had seen Geri crying and invited Geri and her mother to their house for Thanksgiving. Geri had been bullied for being overweight, so Mom and Dad had helped her through some tough times.

Geri tilted her head. "If you're talking about Liz, it's not your fault she made school miserable. You didn't even remember me. You had no idea who I was."

"That's what makes it worse." He'd said nothing to stop the bullying. He only broke up with Liz because she was annoying and he wanted to date someone else, not because she was mean. He'd ignored the rumors, and now he expected Geri to simply forgive him after all the cruel comments he'd made in the past, or how he couldn't remember her from before four years ago?

"You're a good guy, Bart."

The words stunned him. More than any apology or affirmation ever had.

She rolled her eyes. "A slightly annoying, arrogant, know-it-all good man." Her freckles glowed in the sunlight. She was beautiful, and she was looking at him like he was still worthy.

"You care about your family," she said. "You moved back home. You fixed up my car."

"Because you were supposed to come back." He'd planned it out. Give her the car, say the words, finally tell her what he'd never known in that short time they'd spent together.

Instead, he'd watched her life unfold from the outside like a stranger, never knowing, never wanting to know. And now, here she was. In his house. In his heart.

"I hoped you'd come back." He drew out a slow breath. "I missed you."

It sounded too small, too neat for the chaos inside him. "I missed you so much, Geri, I couldn't get through a day without thinking of you."

Her eyes widened, like she didn't quite believe it, or didn't want to.

"When I found out you got married, I really wanted to be happy for you." He couldn't tell her how it had gutted him, imagining her with another man.

She looked away. "You were the only one who never reached out."

"Don't know any man who'd enjoy watching the woman he wants build a life with someone else."

She nodded and covered her mouth. He reached for her hand, half-expecting her to pull away. She didn't. He lifted their joined hands and kissed her knuckles.

"I really like you, Geri. A lot."

Her fingers tightened around his. Take it slow, he told himself, but inched a little closer anyway, mesmerized by the freckles scattered across her cheeks like a map he couldn't wait to study. She was so close now he could feel the flick of her lashes, the tremble in her breath. But then she gently pulled away and stepped behind the paint cans like they were a barricade.

"Let's get the walls painted first," she said, sounding breathless. "No slacking."

He bit back a smile. She didn't say no. "Yes ma'am," he said, grabbing the roller and falling into step beside her.

An hour later, after priming all the walls, Bart stepped back to scan their progress. If they finished early, maybe he could convince her to take a break, go get lunch. A light jab of a paint-tipped finger smudged his cheek.

"Sorry," Geri said, grinning. "You looked too serious."

He caught her hand. "Why do you apologize so much?"

"Why do you mind so much?"

He tugged on her hand until she faced him, and stole the breath from his lungs. There was nothing left to think about. He leaned in, kissed her cheek, the bridge of her nose, and settled on her lips, her hand sliding to the back of his head. Her sigh deepened the moment and quieted all his doubts. He wrapped his arms around her, grounding himself in the feel of her, the scent of lavender and something distinctly Geri. She belonged here. In his arms.

"I love the way you feel," he whispered against her mouth.

"Bart," she breathed.

He pulled back at the tremble in her voice. Tears shimmered in her eyes, spilling down her cheeks. He reached to wipe them away, but she raised a hand between them like a shield.

"I—I need water," she stuttered. Before he could speak, she fled the room.

He didn't follow her. He couldn't. Not with her fear still hanging between them like smoke in the empty doorway, his chest hollow, like he'd reached for a fragile flower and it had blown away in the wind. He'd thought the hardest part was telling her how he felt. But maybe the real question was if she could ever let herself be loved again.

His phone buzzed on the floor, pulling him from the silence. Tonye's name glowed on the screen.

"Bart," Tonye's voice was lower than usual. "I've been trying to reach you."

"What's wrong?"

"It's Uncle Peter." A long pause. "He passed away this morning."

Bart sank onto the windowsill, a slow ache sawing up his spine.

"The family wants to bury him on Wednesday. But you don't have to come."

Bart let the words settle as the hollowness from before spread across his chest. It wasn't grief exactly. Just a heavy finality. An entire book folding closed.

"I'll be there," Bart said. "I have to see it through to the end."

"You sure?"

"Yeah. I need to. Thanks, Tonye."

When he ended the call, he stared out the window, soft light spilling gold over the bare nursery walls. A breeze rustled the trees outside, and the rage inside of him finally quieted.

His father's life had ended. Complicated, unfinished, weighted with too many shadows. And yet, in this house, in this room, a new life would soon begin.

Bart pressed a hand to the cool glass. In the end, that was life. Some doors had to close for good, so others could open, leaving behind the shadows of the past to walk into a new hope.

29

The funeral was in Bonny Island. He arrived on Tuesday. Since none of the relatives knew Peter had a son, both Tonye and Uncle Paul had advised Bart to stay away from the burial rites, to avoid any complications.

On Wednesday morning, Bart drove alone, trailing Tonye and IB to the gravesite. When he reached the cemetery, he couldn't bring himself to join the mourners. He stayed in the shade of a nearby mango tree, shirt clinging to his back in the Bonny sun.

A faint breeze stirred the air, lifting the scent of freshly turned earth, perfume, palm wine, and sweat. Dust clung to his shoes. His jaw ached like his face might snap in two. He couldn't believe he'd come back, but he knew it was the right thing to do.

IB and Tonye paid their respects to the dead. Over a hundred others crowded the burial ground. Some stood in clusters beneath parasols. Others fanned themselves under striped canopies. Uncle Paul wept. Camera phones lifted as if in worship. Prayers rose like vapor amid the rustle of wax-hollandais. The women wore matching deep-purple lace, the men's black *dons* starched stiff, lumbering through the heat, murmuring condolences Bart doubted were sincere.

None of these people had come to the hospital. Maybe they were cousins. Old friends. Coworkers. Maybe they came for the spectacle. Or the food. The man they were burying barely knew his own son. Peter Banigo. A man who shattered lives and rebuilt none. Who whispered apologies too late. Who never held his child. Never carried even a fragment of his son's pain.

And yet, here he was, saying goodbye, wishing he'd said the words when they still mattered.

The officiant snapped a small Bible closed and stepped away from the grave. A dust cloud hovered over the fresh mound. Someone had put a circle of flowers at the base of a framed photo—Peter, beaming in a blue *woko*, as though he'd been halfway decent.

Bart didn't buy it. Still, something gripped his chest and didn't let go. He waited. This wasn't his stage. Let the others say their piece. Some dropped hibiscus petals. Some poured libations. A few lingered to talk. Most wandered off. Tonye and IB looked his way, but they didn't approach him before leaving.

When only stragglers remained, Bart stepped forward. The grave looked too shallow, the earth too soft, like Peter might claw his way out and ask for another chance.

He waited until it was only him. No one needed to hear what he had to say.

"I should've said it," he murmured, voice low, eyes trained on the soil. "I should've told you I forgave you when you—"

A car pulled up behind him. He didn't turn, didn't care until footsteps crunched the grass.

"Bartimeus Teka?" A woman stood a few feet away, tall, composed, skin a warm coppered mahogany, her braids swept into a low bun. No makeup, no jewelry, and yet no hint of grief. She looked like she'd come to settle a contract.

"My name is Hope," she said, cool and casual, but her eyes were sharp.

Hope Banigo. His half-sister. He recognized her from a picture Tonye had showed him.

She offered a dry smile. "I would've come sooner, but I didn't want to make a scene. I figured I'd let the mourners mourn."

Bart glanced at the grave. "But you knew him better than most of the people here."

Hope gave a humorless chuckle. "You mean the ones who came for the rice and drinks, or the relatives sniffing around for inheritance?"

"I'm not here for any of that."

"That makes two of us." Hope folded her arms. "I stayed away for years. My father…" She shrugged. "Well, he's dead now. Let bygones be bygones." She smiled. "But you—you're alive. And I didn't even know you existed until last month."

"That makes two of us," he echoed, this time with a real smile.

Hope shook her head as if still in disbelief. "You look like him."

"Is that so?"

"You're my brother. And I believe in family. So I came. To help you."

Before he could ask what that meant, Hope glanced behind her at the car. The door opened and a second woman stepped out. Her steps were careful. Her face was familiar. Too familiar.

"No," Bart muttered, backing away. "What is this?"

Fatima. The woman from the hospital. One of Asabe's people. The last time he saw her she was bloodied and barely alive.

"Please," Fatima said softly. "Just give me a minute. That's all I ask."

Bart glanced at Hope, who calmly met his gaze. "She's a close friend. Whatever trouble passed between you, I can assure you she means no harm, brother."

That word—brother—landed with strange weight. There was something familiar in her steadiness wrapped in ease. It was like looking at a grown-up Darah.

"You saved my life," Fatima said. "You helped Joaquin get out. I owe you. So please, just listen to what I have to say."

Bart let the silence stretch. It wouldn't kill him to listen.

Fatima stopped short of arm's length. She looked thinner, worn out. "It wasn't Mother who sent that man. She would never put Joaquin in danger. And if she wanted to harm Geraldine, she could've done it long ago. She knows where you live in Houston, down to your zip code, even the oak tree in your front yard."

His stomach cracked like ice. "You're lying."

Fatima shook her head and recited his address. Every digit, including the nearest street.

They knew. They had always known. Where Geri was. Where Joaquin played.

"I don't know what you've heard," Fatima continued, "but she would never harm the mother of her grandson. Someone else is after Joaquin. We believe it's one of Geraldine's people. Her father's family has enemies, and some relatives have reasons to make sure Joaquin doesn't live to grow up."

"Why are you telling me this?" Bart asked.

"Because you can protect them," Fatima replied. "If something happens, you'll never forgive yourself. And she said she trusts you with them."

The words came sharp—unwelcome, and yet they warmed him. A grudging, broken gratitude. Asabe trusted him? After everything, she expected him to believe her?

Hope stepped forward. "I can help. I've got contacts. If you don't want to deal with her directly, I'll be your bridge. You don't have to carry this alone."

Bart said nothing at first. The wind moved through the cemetery like a whisper of betrayal. He didn't have a choice. He could talk to Tonye about it later, but he couldn't afford to sit still anymore. If Asabe wanted to work with him, fine. He'd use her and keep his eyes open.

"Alright," he said to Hope. "It's only because it's you asking. If you're the one I'm dealing with, I'll go along." He turned to Fatima. "But if anyone shows up at my house uninvited, the deal's off. I won't ask questions. I'll shoot them, for Geri, for Joaquin."

A strange smile tugged at Fatima's mouth. "Mother will be glad to hear that."

Hope pulled out her phone. "Let's exchange numbers."

She called his number. He saved hers.

"I'll be in touch," Hope said with a grin. "And don't ghost me, bro. I'm serious. We've got some catching up to do."

He almost smiled. She really was like Darah.

Hope looked at the grave for a long moment before the two women turned and walked back to the car. The car rolled away in a quiet swirl of dust.

Bart stood alone again. The soil had already begun to settle around the grave.

"I forgive you," he said, the words sinking into the pit in his stomach. "But if you get another shot at life, try to do better. Be a better man."

Around him, leaves rustled like a final breath released. The name on the stone, Peter Banigo, the man whose blood ran through him. The man who'd failed at everything that mattered.

"The craziest part is I was heading down the same road," he whispered. "But then my real father died, and everything changed." He blinked fast, opening his eyes wide to force back the swell. Not here, at this man's grave. These tears weren't for him.

"Now that I look back, I realize you were always there. In me. In my anger. In the way I shut people out. In how I protect myself more than I love."

He swallowed hard. "But I'm done with that. I'm going to fight not to become you. Not for me, for them. For the people who count. I'll be the kind of man you couldn't be."

He wiped a hand down his face. "Goodbye... my father."

He walked away without looking back. The dust didn't bother him anymore. Only the urgency. He needed to get back to Houston. To the boy. To the woman who made him want to try. He'd promised she would be safe. And this time, he wouldn't be late.

30

She missed him. He'd been gone three days for his father's funeral. But his confession played on loop in her thoughts. Her skin still hummed with the imprint of his mouth. The press, the heat, the slow, aching fire of a kiss that waltzed into a tango she didn't want to end. His touch had seared through her like flame, like the scar on her arm. She'd burned herself frying plantains, and for days it hurt like the devil, then itched like fury.

That was how it felt thinking about him. An itch she couldn't help scratching. His kiss had undone her. Made her feel something dangerous. Longing. She'd even dreamed of him last night.

"Mommy," Joaquin called, jumping across the squares in the hospital lobby, his imaginary version of hopscotch.

"Be careful," she warned. Her thoughts fell right back to that moment, her arms clinging to Bart's strong shoulders, her lips chasing his like she didn't know how to stop. The shame came after the panic, the look of pity on his face as he pulled back, as if he'd glimpsed her pain, the darkness Hakeem had left behind.

She had run away before he could say what he was thinking. The drive home had been silent. He hadn't touched her again, had barely looked at her. He'd stayed out of her way, and that cut deeper than words.

He had awoken something in her, and these last three days, his kiss haunted her like a melody she couldn't stop humming. But so did the past, the final memory of Hakeem's hands on her. The past and present tangled and taunted each other, memory and desire warring inside her like flame and smoke.

She hadn't slept much, crippled by thoughts of what she'd given up by choosing Hakeem. If Bart had been waiting for her the whole time, she should have come straight home and spared herself all the suffering.

But as she watched Joaquin, she knew it was senseless to think that way. If she'd never married Hakeem, she would never now have the greatest joy of her life, Joaquin.

Still, regret chewed on her thoughts, and longing. She missed Bart. She'd missed him all that time in Nigeria. And she was missing him now. His steadiness. The quiet way he saw her, even when she wasn't sure she wanted to be seen.

"Geri," Eden called, pushing a sleek twin stroller into the waiting room. Dressed in soft white as usual, her platinum hair shimmered under the light, making her look almost celestial.

Joaquin ran to the stroller and peeked under the hood.

"You have an appointment?" Geri asked, looking at the twins sleeping in the stroller.

"Yeah." Eden's violet eyes flicked between Geri and Joaquin. "You heading in for your visit?"

"We just finished. Waiting for Phoebe and Abe."

"How was it?"

Geri exhaled. "Really good." How often did a doctor's visit feel like balm on a bruise you stopped hoping would fade? Dr. Song's quiet kindness had become a touchstone—proof that healing wasn't always dramatic. Sometimes it just whispered, Breathe. Relax. It's gonna be okay.

Joaquin stayed near the stroller, watching the babies under the hood, but thankfully keeping his curious fingers to himself.

"You know I was sickly as a baby?" Eden said. "Probably obvious."

Geri had never known anyone with albinism, but Eden carried herself like someone who had already survived the hard questions. She was probably bullied too.

"I used to hate how different I looked," Eden went on. "But Mema, she helped me find myself."

"Your mom?"

"My second mom," Eden said. "Raised me from when I was two."

Geri's eyes drifted to Joaquin waving at the twins. She still couldn't believe how okay he looked. Not fragile. Not sick. He looked like a boy with a future.

"Healing," Eden said, "can be slow. Sometimes we fast and pray and plead and scream, and all we get is silence."

Geri nodded. So many nights she'd stared at the ceiling, silently screaming, watching Joaquin cry with no strength to comfort him. Blaming herself for staying too long in Abuja, for leaving too late.

Joaquin giggled. The babies were awake.

Eden smiled. "But healing comes in ways you never expect."

The glass doors opened. A woman in her late fifties rushed

in, eyes scanning the waiting room until they landed on Eden and Geri.

"Sorry I'm late. Are we late?"

"Nope, we're good." Eden gestured toward the stroller. "Mema, this is my friend Geri."

Mema's eyes brightened like she'd been waiting for this moment. "Nice to finally meet you, Geri. You've been in our prayers for a long time."

Heat flushed Geri's face. Phoebe's people always made her feel like family. Like someone expected, and wanted.

"Nice to meet you too, Mema."

Mema and Eden exchanged a look. Mema reached out and gently touched Geri's hand.

"I don't want to make you uncomfortable," she said, "but I feel God wants me to tell you this. You are safe here. No one is going to hurt you or your son anymore."

Geri stilled. The words landed like a blessing. Or a promise she didn't know she'd needed. God told this woman to speak to her? God was thinking about her.

Her eyes welled up, and Mema hugged her.

"Oh, precious child," Mema whispered. "Your Father loves you more than you'll ever know."

Tears came faster. Geri didn't even try to stop them. She buried her face in Mema's shoulder, this woman who had unraveled her with the exact words to a prayer she'd prayed a few nights ago. She'd asked God to remind her of his love.

Phoebe had a women's group. Eden, IB, Tari, and a few others gathered to pray, talk about marriage, and support one another. But they didn't just pray. They acted. IB and Eden had moved mountains to help her and Joaquin get out of Nigeria. These weren't just church women. They were warriors.

The door swung open and a nurse peeked out. "Audrey and Zachary Keshi?"

"That's us," Eden said.

Mema reached for the stroller, chuckling as Joaquin pushed it toward the nurse. She held out her hand, and he slapped it with unfiltered joy.

Eden rested a hand on Geri's shoulder. "Before I forget, you should come to Family Night at our fellowship. It'd be good for you and Joaquin."

Phoebe had already extended the invitation. Everyone here seemed kind, but fellowship sounded like the sort of place where people prayed in tongues, laid hands on you, and acted holy while staying silent and detached when it mattered most.

"I'm not sure," Geri said.

"It's not a church," Eden explained. "Just a bunch of people doing life together. No pressure. It's tonight. Phoebe and her crew usually come."

What about Bart? Geri nodded slowly. "I'll think about it."

Eden and Mema disappeared into the back offices with the twins. Geri took Joaquin down the hall toward the elevators. The doors opened with a chime. Inside were Phoebe, Abe, and Ms. Jen.

"Great timing," Phoebe said. "How'd it go?"

Joaquin leapt inside and Abe caught him mid-air. "I'm guessing that's a good sign," he said, tickling Joaquin until the boy giggled.

Geri stepped in beside Ms. Jen, who greeted her with a warm hug. Did Ms. Jen come to all her clients' appointments? Or was this just for Phoebe?

"Dr. Song is incredible," Geri said.

Phoebe touched her belly. "I can't wait for our little girl to have him as her doctor too."

"How was your appointment?" Geri asked.

"Fantastic," Phoebe beamed. "Baby Girl's measuring on track. Date's still first week of November."

"Or any day now," Ms. Jen said. "Countdown's officially begun, so it's time to slow down."

The elevator chimed again, doors opening to the ground floor. They all stepped out.

Abe passed Joaquin back to Geri while Phoebe slipped her hand into his. "We need to stop by my aunt's house," Phoebe said.

"I'll take Geri home," Ms. Jen said, holding up her keys. "I've got a toddler seat in the back. Don't ask."

Geri grinned. "I didn't."

"We'll get the groceries and meet you at home," Ms. Jen added. "Wanna go shopping, little man?"

"Yes!" Joaquin ran after Ms. Jen, his curls flying as they headed out of the building.

Phoebe did her familiar jog-shuffle to catch up with Joaquin, and when Geri turned back, Abe was watching her.

"What?"

"Are you okay? You and Bart were acting strange before he left."

"Nothing happened," she said, too quickly.

Abe raised a brow. "Something's always happening with you two." They crossed the street together. "You know I don't talk just to talk," he added.

"I know."

"Bart cares about you. Probably more than he knows how to deal with. But he means well. So if he's bothering you, just say so. He'll hear it now. He's in a better place to listen."

"He's not bothering me," she said, with conviction.

"Good," Abe said. "Then take it easy." He smiled at her, like a father checking on his daughter.

Geri was still smiling when Ms. Jen pulled out of the parking lot.

"Was that about Bart?" Ms. Jen asked once they merged onto the highway. "Y'all looked serious."

"Abe's always serious," Geri said with a soft laugh. She glanced back at Joaquin, content playing with a bin of toys in the backseat.

When she was in high school, Ms. Jen would sometimes pick her up after school. Her backseat always had snacks, drinks, and random little knick-knacks, as if her car was just another room in her house. Not much had changed since then.

"Abe just wanted to know about Bart," Geri admitted.

Ms. Jen let out a knowing laugh. Bart was her favorite topic. After every Teka holiday gathering, Geri had vented about him during those long drives home. Ms. Jen never corrected her or told her she was being dramatic, just listened with that glint in her eye and a soft chuckle that said she knew more than she let on.

"Did something happen?" Ms. Jen asked.

Joaquin babbled on behind them. "We kissed," Geri said, in the most casual tone she could muster.

Ms. Jen gasped. "Geri!"

"I know," she muttered, turning the AC vents toward her face. Just saying his name made her pulse jump. What was wrong with her? Did every widowed woman fall apart over one kiss?

"What do you know, dear?" Ms. Jen's voice took on that familiar maternal tilt. "You didn't like it?"

"That's not the issue. Am I allowed to like it? Isn't it wrong for me to want that?"

Ms. Jen frowned. "Wrong, why? Because of Joaquin's father?"

That almost made her laugh. Hakeem had forfeited every

right to her affection long before he died. "No. Because I'm a widowed, single mom with no degree, no job, and a whole lot of baggage. And Bart, he could have anyone."

Ms. Jen sighed. "If this is about Kasey, you should know, that thing was over before it even began. He wouldn't have kissed you otherwise. They broke up more times than I can count. Toxic from day one," Ms. Jen said with uncharacteristic bite. "She played games with that boy."

Ms. Jen never spoke ill of people. For her to sound this sharp meant she knew something.

"Trust me, Geri. That man adores you."

Adores? Her throat went dry. It wasn't supposed to make sense, but it did. The tender way he always looked at her, talked to her.

"I don't know what to do," Geri admitted. "Especially now that he's being weird."

"Weird how?"

"Right after we kissed, something shifted. Like he regretted it."

"Baby girl, what you saw wasn't regret. Maybe something you didn't recognize." Ms. Jen was quiet for a beat, her hands steady on the wheel. "What's really going on, Geri? Talk to me."

Geri's hands trembled in her lap. "It's just the worst time possible to be thinking about this. I need to get my life together."

"Why can't you do both? You've always had a thing for him, since—" She stopped when Geri shot her a look. "I'm just saying," Ms. Jen continued. "Is it so bad that he finally feels the same way? We all saw how wrecked he was when he heard you were getting married. And when he came back to Houston with you and Joaquin, he wasn't the same man."

Geri looked down at her hands. "All of this sounds like an

impossible dream."

Ms. Jen pulled into the grocery store lot. "You're the best woman for him."

"Of course you'd say that. You've always liked the idea of us together." Ms. Jen had always been partial to Bart. "But what if it's not meant to happen?"

"What is for you is for you," Ms. Jen said, shutting off the engine. She got out of the car and took Joaquin out of the seat as Geri stepped out. "For now," she said, meeting Geri's eyes, "don't make any rash decisions. Just wait. Go along and see what happens."

Geri walked beside her toward the store, Ms. Jen blowing air kisses at Joaquin. It was easy for Ms. Jen to tell her to wait, but she was running out of time. Every day here was another day Asabe could find her. She couldn't stay here much longer, but she had to wait until the baby was born. Then she would leave for good.

"I'll try," Geri said. But that was what scared her most. Because if she went along, she wouldn't want to ever leave. Right now, for the first time in years, she was happy staying exactly where she was.

31

She'd expected Jeremy to pull something, but not like this. Not on an early-release day. Everything always felt upside down on early-release days, like the universe had forgotten its script and was winging it. Coach Myers had canceled after-school softball hitting drills, so for once Darah had a free afternoon before Eli's bus.

Avery, her teammate and part-time drama queen, invited Darah over to binge-watch some new Taiwanese romance about polar opposites. Avery promised popcorn, commentary, and mockery of all the angsty stares. But as they walked toward the buses, Darah saw him. Jeremy Walker.

He walked like the pavement belonged to him, like he knew he didn't have to try and still somehow did. Her pulse tripped over itself. She was a second from turning her head and pretending not to see him when Avery waved.

"Hey, D." He walked up to them as if he didn't notice the air around them had changed and everyone was watching him—them—right now.

"I have a question," Avery declared, chin tilted.

"Shoot," he said.

"Why do birds always appear every time you pull up?" Avery asked.

Jeremy raised an eyebrow. "What?"

Darah stared at Avery in horror. Birds? Why would she say that when a group of Jeremy's fans were watching them right now?

"Right." Jeremy laughed like he understood. "You got plans right now?" he asked Darah.

"She's not doing anything," Avery replied. "Feel free."

"We were going to your house?" Darah reminded her.

"Were we?" Avery batted her lashes.

Jeremy's grin deepened. "Thanks, Avery."

Before Darah knew it, he'd grabbed her hand. Her hand. In front of everyone. Like it was nothing. Like he'd already decided they were something and the rest of the world—including her—was just catching up.

The noise around them silenced as Jeremy led her across the courtyard toward the student lot. Heads turned. Conversations dipped. His fans—especially the sour-faced girls from bus duty—stared hard. He didn't say a word. Just walked like they'd rehearsed this.

At his truck, he finally let go to open the passenger door like some old-school rom-com hero. The kind who ruined a girl's ability to settle for less, who made you believe he saw you when no one else did.

"Jeremy, I don't—"

"Hey, Jeremy," a voice sang from behind.

Two cheerleaders—glossy-haired irregulars in Darah's world—strolled up to their car, ponytails and polish sparkling in the sun.

"Are you coming to get ice cream?" one asked, as if Darah wasn't standing right there.

Jeremy glanced at Darah as if he was waiting.

Then—shockingly—the other girl turned to her. "You should come too, Darah."

Darah nodded before she could stop herself. How did she even know her name? It was like stepping into someone else's life. She knew better than to believe in moments like this, but still, it felt good. To be seen. Chosen. Noticed.

She slid into the passenger seat, even with every emotional fire drill she'd ever rehearsed going off. Jeremy Walker was showing her off to everyone—and her heart, the traitor, fluttered like a page in the wind. Because part of her wanted to know how this story went.

She peeked at him as he started the car. The cheeky smile on his face said everything. Then he blew past the turn to the ice cream place and veered toward the highway.

"I'm guessing no ice cream?" she said.

"Let's go to that tea spot near SAT prep," he said. "You'll be more comfortable there, right?"

All she could do was nod. He clearly knew her better than she thought he did.

"It's our first date," he said, with that unruly grin. "I don't want to share you with anyone."

She turned to face the window, her heart pounding in a wild rhythm.

When they pulled into the familiar plaza, she smiled despite herself. She was actually going on a date. Apart from studying, softball was her only real constant, and even that was off-season till February. She was used to structured chaos: practices, pitching drills, batting cages, adrenaline and dirt. She wasn't used to... this.

She was unbuckling her seatbelt when a guy in a red hoodie and red Timberlands approached.

Jeremy quickly stepped out and shut her door behind him. "Wait in here."

She watched Jeremy and the stranger through the windshield, the guy gesturing with urgency while Jeremy stayed calm, nodding. Then came the long handshake, the kind that carried weight, as they locked eyes and the guy held on to Jeremy's arm and kept on talking. By the time Jeremy returned to the car, his mask of charm had slid back into place.

"I have to be on time to get Eli from the bus stop," she reminded him.

"Of course. I'll drop you off there," he said, like he understood exactly why she had to be there for Eli.

As they headed toward the tea shop, she asked: "Who was that guy?"

Jeremy paused at the glass door. "That's just GT. My brother's homie."

"You have siblings?"

"Why do you look so shocked?"

"I just didn't think you did." Another thing that didn't match what she thought she knew. Things she hadn't written into the character she'd created in her head. He wasn't just the guy with perfect cheekbones and a cult following. He noticed things—her tea order, her comfort zones, the fondness in her voice when she talked about her brother. The more she looked, the more she realized she didn't know him at all.

And yet, here she was. On a date. Her first date. With him, Jeremy Walker, the most popular guy in school, the one her classmates obsessed over. And for whatever reason, it didn't feel like a cosmic prank. Not yet.

"I've got two older brothers," he said.

"Wow. So you're the baby?"

"Pretty much." He opened the door for her, a small, polite gesture that made her heart do a slow roll in her chest, just like how the characters in books described it, a way she'd never thought she'd feel.

"The one right before me works at NASA," he added. "Robotics division."

"Geez." She stepped inside behind him, the door jingling as it shut. The teahouse was syrupy and warm—sugar, spice, a whisper of nostalgic sweetness. She'd never once felt safe in a place like this, but today was different, and she didn't need to ask why.

A line stretched past the counter. Some students she recognized from SAT prep, others were upperclassmen who normally wouldn't look her way. But today, everyone looked, and said Hi. With his arm around her shoulder, Jeremy introduced her to anyone with a question in their eyes.

She stood a little taller before realizing she was a head above half the guys in the store, the tallest girl around. She bent her head again.

"You don't have to do that," Jeremy whispered. "I love when you keep your head up."

Tears sprung to her eyes, so she looked away, at the clock. Two whole hours before she had to meet Eli.

"We can bounce if you want."

"It's okay," she said quickly. "What schools did you apply to?"

They needed a neutral subject to talk about.

"Rice. Stanford. A&M. Clark. Syracuse."

"Clark and Syracuse?" She laughed under her breath. "You're trying to touch every time zone?"

"Gotta keep my options open."

Rice? His brother worked at Nasa? He wasn't at all the boy she'd built in her head. He joked a lot but also opened doors while finding the time and grades to apply to both Ivy-League schools and HBCUs. He was the boy moms prayed their daughters would date. The boy who charmed all the aunties at church camp.

"It would be a shame to leave Texas now though," he said.

"Why?" The way he stressed his words made her pause.

"Anywhere I don't get to see that pretty face is too far for me."

And just like that, she forgot how to breathe. He nudged her forward, and she moved, letting the line carry her like a tide. Her heart pounding against her ribs like it was begging for permission to hope. What was she doing here? Letting him in. Playing with fire. But maybe fire could be beautiful too.

More people kept walking up, guys dapping him, girls waving and smiling at her. It was disorienting, not being invisible. Not just the tall pitcher on the softball team, or the tall girl on the bench with a book and earbuds. They even knew her name. And maybe that wasn't only because of Jeremy. Maybe she'd gotten them wrong all along.

"You going to Homecoming?" Jeremy asked.

"Don't think so," she replied. "Feels weird thinking about it after the city was just flooded a few weeks ago."

"That's why we should go. We only get a few high school dances. Might as well make the memories while we can. Besides, it's my last one before college."

"Right, Syracuse? That far? You sure you're not cold-blooded?"

"Only when I need to be."

She didn't realize how much she was smiling until they reached the counter. Jeremy ordered before she could speak. A taro tea with boba for her and a mango smoothie for himself.

"How did you know I like taro?" she asked.

Another one of his wicked grins. "You forget where we met?"

He flashed another one of his heart-stealing grins. Calling him fine was an understatement. His smooth voice drawled like it was tuned to a private station only she could hear. It did something to her insides she didn't have the vocabulary for—not yet, not fully. He was unraveling her slowly. And she was letting him.

"I remember," she managed.

It had been during a break at SAT prep. She'd escaped to the campus café with her favorite drink and a novel she'd already read before. He'd sat down across from her like it was the most natural thing in the world. Technically, it wasn't the first time they'd met. But it was the first time he seemed to notice her. He'd joked about her boba tea order and made her laugh.

"Had me at smooth chocolate skin and braids," he said, as they now waited for their order.

"Don't joke around."

"I'm not." He leaned in. "I mean, look at you. After all that test prep, you were still reading."

"I love to read. A lot."

"I know."

Their number was called. Jeremy grabbed the drinks and walked to the back, a small table tucked in the corner away from the crowd.

Darah glanced at the clock again, trying to ground herself. It didn't help.

"We've got time," he said.

His smile always did something strange to her, like a door creaked open where she hadn't realized one existed.

"Why are you being so nice to me?"

Jeremy hummed a tune she didn't recognize. "Because you're being nice to me."

"How?"

"You're giving me your time," he replied.

What could she possibly say to that? She sipped her taro tea, the sweet creaminess sliding down her throat.

"You got a boyfriend, Darah?"

She almost choked on a boba pearl. "You've seen me hanging out with any guy?"

"Had to ask." He took a sip of his smoothie and held it toward her. "Try some."

She stared. "You want me to drink from your straw?"

"I ain't got nothing, girl."

"I'm allergic to mango," she lied.

"Since when?"

"Stop flirting with me," she said, her voice softer than she intended. "It's distracting."

He laughed and she turned toward the window. Light danced along the parked cars outside. She couldn't believe she'd said that out loud. She needed to change the subject to him, anything to shift the current pulling her in.

"What about your other brother?" she asked. "You didn't say."

He went still. "He's gone."

Darah's heart clenched. "I'm sorry."

"It's a'ight," he whispered, gaze drifting to the parking lot.

His jaw was tight, then softened, his pain rippling across his face. His loss had shaped him, too. Maybe not as visibly as her pain, but it was there, shadowing the way he carried silence in pockets of grief. Whenever people found out about her parents, they either asked questions or mumbled clumsy apologies like they'd stumbled into a tragic slice-of-life genre they hadn't meant to read. The worst were the ones who tried to patch the silence with hollow hope, like a fresh coat of paint could fix a crumbling wall.

She didn't ask him anything. Didn't try to fix it. And Jeremy sat there, letting the silence be what it was. No awkwardness. Just two people who had learned how to keep their pain quiet.

Suddenly, she didn't feel so alone. And she hated how much that meant to her. Because even with all the stories and longing, this was more than she'd let herself want. And part of her was terrified she was starting to want it anyway.

"It's hard," she said at last. "Losing someone you love."

Their half-forgotten drinks sat between them. The buzz of the café blurred behind the weight of what neither of them needed to say aloud. But for once, Darah didn't want to run, didn't want to shrink or deflect or build another wall. Not with him. She wanted him to keep talking, about the things he'd lost, how he managed to walk through the world without looking broken.

He told her about his childhood, his family, the weird way life changes when someone you love leaves and never comes back. He never said the word died, but it clung to the edges of his stories like smoke.

She listened, and laughed too. He had a way of weaving pain with wit, warmth with sorrow, a voice that was beautiful not just for how it sounded but for what it carried. A voice life had torn and stitched back together.

"I heard your parents passed away some years back," he said

after he'd talked for a while. "That must be hard."

Must be. Not must have been. He understood what others couldn't: how grief didn't end, it stretched, lived in your routines, hid in your laughter, buried you at unexpected times. You learned to walk with it, even when the world expected you to sprint. Struggling to remember while trying to forget. Having to pretend you were fine. Because after a while, everyone expected you to be fine.

"Yes," she whispered, and took a long sip of her tea. The sweetness coated her tongue like armor against the burning ache in her throat.

"My mom died when I was born," Jeremy said.

She turned to him with wide eyes. "So, the one you've been talking about—"

"My stepmom. She's cool people. But yeah. My real mom? She never even got to hold me."

His voice didn't crack. But her face did. So much loss. Quiet, unspoken, and somehow still alive. Maybe that was what drew her, the sadness in his eyes no matter how big he smiled. It was grief in disguise. And she knew its language.

She glanced down at his arms—smooth, corded with muscle—and hated herself a little for how easy it was to get distracted by how beautiful he was, instead of holding space for the sacred quiet between them. But it was all too much. Too raw. Like a thread ready to snap, there really was only one place she and Jeremy could end up, and still.

The bell above the door jingled. A crowd of kids tumbled into the café, all laughter and backpacks, led by two older women.

Her stomach flipped. Elementary schoolers. Her phone. 3:12 p.m. Eli.

She lurched to her feet, her cup falling sideways and rattling on the floor.

"Sorry," Jeremy said, moving with her.

"I can't believe myself." The sharpness of her own voice startled her. Why was she yelling at him?

"It's my fault," he said gently. He opened the car door for her again, no trace of defensiveness.

She climbed in, knowing she'd ruined it, whatever this was. Jeremy would probably stop trying now. And maybe that was for the best, right?

That's what Bart always warned her about. Her tone, her walls, her constant bracing would drive people away.

Jeremy didn't say much on the ride. His hands gripped the wheel, but his silence didn't ooze with tension.

He pulled up to the curb several houses away from Eli's bus stop. "Need help finding your bro?"

"No, it's fine." She scanned the sidewalks. Kids everywhere, no Eli.

"I'm gonna FaceTime you tonight," Jeremy said.

"I have an Android."

"There's an app for that."

She squinted at him. "Are you a masochist or something?"

That grin again, full of mischief. "I know what that means, you know."

"Of course you do." Most boys at school wouldn't.

"Thanks for hanging with me, Darah."

He said her name like it was a lyric in a song he was writing. A song called Something Worth Waiting For. Then he drove off like he hadn't just rearranged the insides of her heart.

His taillights disappeared around the corner. The sound of children's voices surrounded her again. 3:37 PM. Eli could already be home.

She sprinted back home, the whole time thinking about Jeremy, and the strange, impossible feeling blooming in her chest.

By the time she reached Bart's house, her heart was pounding harder than her feet. A black Mercedes sat in the driveway, meaning Hannah and her mom were here.

Inside, Phoebe and Rue were on the couch, laughing over a picture on Rue's phone. At the dining table, Joaquin, Eli and Hannah munched on Oreos and almond milk.

"Rue picked up the kids, but she said she didn't see you at the stop," Phoebe said. "Eli said you had something at school. Wasn't today a half day?"

Eli's face was as blank as stone.

"Yeah, I'm gonna go change," Darah said, darting off to her room, shame clinging to her like sweat. Eli had covered for her. Because of her, he'd lied.

She closed her room door behind her, halfway through pulling off her socks when someone knocked.

"Come in," she called. Phoebe peeked in, belly first. She had that look—part mom radar, part prophet. "What's up?"

Phoebe perched carefully on the bed. "I'm just amazed by how quickly you're becoming a beautiful young woman."

Darah tossed her socks into the dirty bin. "Okay. What's bringing this on?"

"It's true." Phoebe's smile didn't waver. "Sometimes I get caught up in everything going on and forget how fast you and Eli are growing. And I'm sorry for that."

Darah's tears came fast. "It's…" She didn't expect this right now. After losing two babies, Phoebe had seemed so wrapped in a silence so thick it bruised the air. It was devastating how pain could make someone disappear while they were still there with you. Why was Phoebe apologizing when she was the one who had gone through hell?

"It's okay, Phoebe," she whispered. But inside, something cracked just a little more. Because it wasn't just Jeremy she wasn't opening up to. It was Phoebe. Her family. This whole strange, beautiful life she hadn't asked for.

Phoebe gently tucked Darah's twists behind her shoulder. "I miss hanging out with you. Miss doing your hair. It's gotten so long. I can't keep up anymore." Her eyes watered. "We're good, right? You know no matter what, I'm here for you. We can still have our Teka girl nights. Get our nails done. Or a massage. Well, you can get one. I'll live through you."

Darah snorted. "What do I look like getting a massage when you're the one who needs it?"

"We both need it." Phoebe grinned. "I know it's not easy sharing a bed with Eli kicking you half the night. And I've seen you trying to find new corners of the house to do schoolwork."

"It's fine." Only it wasn't, not really. Some days, she felt invisible, like she had faded into the background noise of everyone else's survival. The grown-ups were tired, the house was full, and she didn't want to take up more space than she deserved.

Phoebe reached for her hand. "You'll always be my girl, D. My one and only little sister I love more than you know. Don't ever think you can't come to me. If you ever need a break from your knuckleheaded brothers," she leaned in with a wink, "we'll take one together. My treat. Always."

Darah smirked. "You're married to one of those knuckleheads, remember?"

"Exactly. I might need a break too."

"Even after Baby Girl's here?"

Phoebe smiled as if she'd been waiting for the question. "It's gonna be tough. But my mom's coming, and my aunt. Abe can hold her down while we sneak away."

A familiar squeal echoed down the hall—Joaquin.

"I should go." Phoebe stood with a groan.

"Maybe we can invite Geri too. Someone needs to talk to her."

Her eyebrows lifted. "You think?"

"He's been in love with her for years," Darah said, like it was common knowledge. "But it's up to Geri now."

Phoebe's smile deepened. "It always is, isn't it?" She paused at the door. "You're still coming to Family Night tonight?"

So much for a FaceTime with Jeremy. "Yeah."

Barely a minute after Phoebe left, Eli walked in. He went straight to the built-in shelves by the window and grabbed a couple books.

"Eli," she started, but the apology caught on the back of her tongue.

He turned, face still blank. "Don't wait for my bus anymore."

Darah reached for his hand but he shrugged her off. "C'mon, it was one time—"

"I'm not a kid. It's okay."

He walked out before she could explain. That was Eli. He didn't need many words to make a point—his silence did the work for him. He carried hurt like a soldier, quiet and unspoken, and it broke her heart every time.

She sat there, staring at the empty doorway, feeling the mess of her world settle back onto her shoulders.

Her phone buzzed. A text. Jeremy.

Found your bro yet?

She didn't even know she was smiling until she felt the ache in her cheek as she typed back a reply.

Yes.

Simple. Safe. Enough.

But the word lingered on the screen like it meant more than it said.

Yes. To everything.

She fell back against the bed, phone still in hand, fingers brushing her chest where her heart refused to calm down.

Somehow, she felt lighter. As if something buried had shifted. Something inside her long-hidden—coiled tight by fear—had finally dared to stretch and breathe. The room seemed to spin in a carousel of thoughts she wasn't ready to name. It held her like a soft breath. And for once, she let it unravel her bit by bit, like water dripping from a leaky faucet.

She thought about his voice, the curve of his smile, the way he listened without needing to fix her. The way he remembered things she hadn't realized she'd shared. She was terrified of what it could mean, but part of her couldn't wait to find out, to learn that not all stories needed to start with a bang. Some simply began on a quiet Wednesday—no, it was actually Friday—in a café, where an invisible girl starts to wonder if someone's been seeing her all along.

And God help her. She didn't mind being seen by Jeremy Walker. Not one bit.

3 2

Bart's first day back in Houston was packed. In the morning, he met with one of the founders of a small nonprofit rebuilding homes after the hurricane. They'd set up in an old church, where stacks of donated drywall and tarps filled the rooms. A huge, white board listed addresses, families praying for someone to show up for them. When Bart had promised to help with manpower and materials, he hadn't realized how many promises that would mean.

By noon, Bart and Emilio were walking the neighborhood, meeting dozens of people. A single mom who'd been sleeping in the church with her two kids. A grandmother whose porch had buckled, her kitchen in shreds. A father of four burst out crying and hugged Bart. They thanked him like he was a savior, and it broke him each time. He kept thinking about his parents, how they would have probably turned the church into a feeding station. Emilio and the crew had been helping since last week, but Bart felt as if he needed to do more.

By the time he left, he'd given his word to repair at least six homes before winter. It was going to cost him—time, money, more than he probably had—but walking away wasn't an option.

His exhaustion dragged at him, but his mind wouldn't rest. Doing good hadn't quieted the noise inside of him. He needed clarity, someone who could talk him away from the restlessness that had followed him home. So he drove to see Daniel.

"I kissed her," Bart said, the first thing out of his mouth once he sat down in Daniel's office. "And now she's tripping," he went on in a whisper. He'd expected only Daniel to still be at work, but tonight was family night at fellowship, so Judah and Tari were in the front office.

"Just to be clear, who exactly did you kiss?" Daniel asked, then laughed. "Wow, I'm happy for you, bro."

"Don't be," Bart said. "When I kissed her, she started crying. Pretty sure I triggered something. Maybe a memory of her ex-husband."

Even now, he could still feel her. The heat of her skin. The urgency of her mouth. Touching Geri had been like pouring gas on a long-smoldering flame. But then she'd cried, tears running down her cheeks like water dousing fire.

"You know what she's been through," Daniel said. "Abuse doesn't disappear just because someone new walks in. Even if she wants to move on, she can't until she's ready."

"You have to be patient with her," Daniel continued. "Love isn't just words, it's showing up, over and over again. That's how God does it for us. So why should we love any less?"

Bart stood, pacing the floor in slow circles. Back in Ghana, Geri had screamed in her sleep. The way she'd called her husband's name, not like she missed him, but like she was trapped, still reliving a nightmare. He had held her that night like his arms could block the demons of the past. But what if loving her just made it worse?

Daniel chuckled. "Just yesterday, Eden asked me if I still found her attractive. I couldn't believe it. Bro, I'm over here losing my mind over this woman, just praying she'll feel like having sex with me, and she's worried about stretch marks and her hair falling out. I tell her every day she's beautiful, that she's my number one, but she just can't hear it right now. Sometimes it's like that, and you just have to be patient."

Bart dropped back into the chair. He'd never seen Daniel look so defeated.

"Love is sacrifice," Daniel continued. "Both people have to sacrifice. We men love to talk about sacrifice, but we don't really understand it. I mean, if someone pointed a gun at Eden, I would jump right in front of her. But when she hits me with a sharp word or doesn't respond the way I want, I start tripping. And that's what we all do, man. We say we'd die for them, but we can't even die to our pride. Doesn't make sense, right?"

Bart let out a half-laugh, half-sigh. He'd leaped into Geri's hospital room ready to die, so what was he now tripping about? "You and Judah should start a marriage counseling firm. Call it The Dying Men."

Daniel shook his head. "I have enough dying of my own to manage."

"So what do I do now?" Bart asked.

Daniel didn't hesitate. "Find out her ring size."

Bart blinked. "You're serious?"

"Why not? You want to marry her, right? Then just get the ring and wait. Give her time and find ways to show her you're not going anywhere." Daniel's phone buzzed on the desk. He picked it up. "Eden says you should stay for family night, Geri's going to be here."

Bart stood to leave. "I'm just gonna head out." He needed to think about how to tell Geri about Asabe. He'd spoken to Tonye about meeting Fatima at the funeral, which had only made things murkier. If Fatima was right, it wasn't Asabe they should fear. It was Geri's family, fighting over legacy and bloodlines, threatened by a grandson in the way of their inheritance.

Once Bart and Daniel stepped out of the building, Bart held open the door for Judah carrying in a box of groceries.

"Can y'all help out?" Judah asked. The van behind him was full of boxes with groceries that the fellowship was donating to some immigrant families coming by tonight.

By the time they were done offloading the groceries, half of the fellowship had already arrived. Geri came with the rest of the family. Joaquin ran to Bart when he saw him, and Bart picked him up. While Abe and Phoebe went inside with Darah and Eli, Geri stopped at the van beside Bart.

She threw her arms around him. "I missed you."

Bart froze with her and Joaquin in his arms, the words he'd never expected to hear stirring his blood. "I missed you too," he said.

With a smile, Geri pulled away and took Joaquin from Bart. "We'll see you inside," she said before disappearing into the hall.

Four days since he last saw her, and with one simple hug, she'd reminded him all over again why he couldn't let go of her.

As he stood outside gathering his thoughts, Ms. Jen was walking toward the building.

"Are you ready to go in?" she asked, with that disarming smile.

Bart nodded and followed her inside the lobby. It would be less awkward than going in alone.

"I always feel a little strange coming here on such nights," Ms. Jen whispered. "After all, it's called Family Night for a reason."

At first, he didn't understand the sadness in her voice, but then he'd never heard anyone mention her having a husband or children.

"I think a lot of people here see you as family," Bart said.

Her expression turned sheepish. "Do you think of me as family?"

He stopped walking at the entrance, but she went on through the doors into the main hall. From inside, a cheer broke out.

Bart followed Ms. Jen into the packed hall. A spotlight beamed on the small stage, where an elderly man, a teen girl, and a little boy were reaching into a barrel, pulling out apples with letters written on them, trying to spell words. The crowd was cheering and offering clues with laughter. Everyone was distracted by the game.

Ms. Jen made her way to the back row, and Bart took the seat beside her without thinking. His eyes locked onto Geri standing in the front row.

A wave of cheers erupted as Judah hoisted the smallest kid into the air like a champion.

"He's one of the first babies I helped deliver," Ms. Jen said, like a proud grandmother.

Bart joined the applause for the kid. Even though Ms. Jen was older now, the beauty of her youth still shone through. Did she really have no husband? No kids? Maybe she was a widow. If he had known her circumstances, he would have been nicer to her.

"How could I not think of you as family?" Bart muttered over the noise. "You've been so good to my family. And Geri thinks you're the best. How long have you known her?" he asked, suddenly curious.

"Since she was in high school," Ms. Jen replied. "We met at one of your parents' holiday parties."

"Really?" He'd been too self-absorbed to notice anyone who didn't orbit his world.

"She's one of the sweetest people I've ever met. Responsible, kind, warm, like you wouldn't expect, given what she's been through."

Bart nodded along. "You don't have to convince me."

Ms. Jen smiled as if she knew exactly what he meant. "I'm glad you know."

When the games ended, Judah stepped on stage and spoke about the importance of forgiveness and unconditional love in building a family. It wasn't a sermon, more of a casual conversation between friends. He was interrupted several times by questions, or people who had something to add to his thoughts on family.

After the discussion ended and Judah prayed, he told everyone to wait before leaving. "Our Family Night has grown," he said. "Our families are growing. And that's because of the women who keep showing up for us."

A wave of applause rose from the crowd.

"Mother's Day was long ago," Judah continued, "but we don't need a calendar to show love. We want to celebrate our mothers. The new moms. The seasoned moms. The soon-to-be moms carrying life right now. And the potential moms, which should pretty much cover every woman and girl here."

Daniel and Abe stepped onto the stage with baskets of flowers.

"A wise man once told me," Judah said, "that we should give

people their flowers while they're still here. So tonight, the men of this fellowship want to tell you—our ladies that we see you. We see your sacrifice. Everything you do that no one applauds. Every day you show us love. You carry us. Forgive us. Thank you for not giving up on us. You are a gift. You are a treasure."

Daniel and Abe moved down the aisles with the baskets of roses, passing one each to the mothers first, then to the younger women and girls.

Abe handed Phoebe a rose, then Geri. The applause soared into a standing ovation with whistles and cheers.

Bart felt a shift beside him. Ms. Jen's head was bowed. Was she praying, or crying? She suddenly shot to her feet and rushed out of the room, but he'd already seen the tears. The double doors slammed shut behind her.

A few people turned. Geri looked straight at Bart. She'd noticed.

He got up and went after Ms. Jen, turning the corner past the bathroom. In the dim hallway, she was crouched beside the wall, her soft cries barely muffled by the music and laughter still echoing from the hall.

"Are you okay?"

Her eyes were red. "I—I'm fine," she whispered, turning her face away.

"You don't look fine," he said, with as much gentleness he could muster. "What happened in there?"

She sniffled. "It's nothing. Please, just go back in. I'm fine."

Bart crouched beside her. "Well, I'm not okay either. That whole thing just reminded me of my own mom, and how..." He let the sentence fall apart. Regret pulled tight across his chest.

Ms. Jen made a sound between a gasp and a sob, her shoulders trembling.

"Sorry," he said. "I didn't mean to make you upset. You and my mom were close, right?"

She nodded without looking at him.

Bart sighed. Maybe this was too much for her. She hadn't needed to be here tonight. These things never factored in women who'd never had the chance to be moms. Or maybe she'd been a mother, and lost more than he could see. Was she crying because she had lost a child?

Hearing footsteps, he turned as Geri appeared in the hallway with Joaquin perched on her hip.

She touched Ms. Jen's back. "Do you need to go home?"

Joaquin reached for Bart and he took the boy from Geri's arms. Joaquin snuggled into his shoulder, little fingers clutching his shirt like he hadn't seen him in weeks.

"I'm fine," Ms. Jen murmured. "I just needed a moment. That's all."

"Bart?" Phoebe's voice reached him from behind.

The doors to the fellowship hall were wide open, and families were spilling into the corridor with laughter and farewells.

Phoebe stopped beside Ms. Jen. "What happened?"

"She just needed a moment," Bart replied. "What's up?"

"One of the families needs a ride back," Phoebe said, as Tari walked toward them.

"Bart, please can you drop some people off in Montrose?" Tari asked. "The van's already full."

Bart glanced at Geri, but her face gave nothing away. He was exhausted from his long day plus the jetlag.

"Yeah," he said, and the way Geri smiled at him made it all worth it. "I'll pull up out front."

"Thank you so much," Tari said, walking down the hallway with Phoebe.

229

"I'll hang out with Ms. Jen for a bit and she'll drop me off," Geri said. "Okay?"

The way she looked at him—like she was really asking for his permission—left any protest trapped behind his teeth.

"Cool." He left her there with Ms. Jen and walked to his car. He pulled up to the front and waited for the family while thinking about Geri.

Something must have changed while he was away. She wasn't as guarded anymore. He needed to talk to her about Fatima, but not yet.

Bart popped open the glove compartment in his car. His gun lay tucked inside its black holster, cold and daring.

"Forget taking bullets for love," he said, with a smile. If anyone came for Geri or Joaquin, he would be the one firing the shots.

3 3

The drive back home seemed to fly by, mostly because Geri was waiting for Ms. Jen to talk, but Ms. Jen stayed tight-lipped, staring into the night as they drove down the highway.

"Sorry for keeping you out so late," Ms. Jen said, breaking the stretch of silence.

Geri flicked her eyes toward Ms. Jen in the passenger seat. "I'm just glad you're feeling better." She had insisted on driving at least to Bart's house.

She peeked at the rearview mirror. Joaquin was fast asleep in his booster seat. Getting him changed and into bed without waking him would be an Olympic feat.

"Nights like this always remind me of what I gave up," Ms. Jen said. "I'm sorry for the drama I caused."

"Don't say that. We were all just worried. Even Bart."

Her lips twitched as she said his name. He'd looked so

helpless crouched beside Ms. Jen, like comforting a woman was a foreign language he never mastered.

Ms. Jen smiled and faced the window, the traces of her earlier breakdown still lining her eyes in the soft glow.

"We're about fifteen minutes out from home," Geri said. "I mean, Bart's house," she corrected. It was strange how in less than a month she'd already started calling it that.

Ms. Jen chuckled. "Sweet Geri, what are you really scared of?"

"Tonight's not about me. We're talking about you right now." Ms. Jen had always been a master deflector. Whenever Geri got too curious about her past, Ms. Jen always redirected the questions away from herself and back to Geri's messy life.

"You're worried that you might be wrong again," Ms. Jen said. "What if I lean into this and fall flat on my face, again?"

Geri glanced at Joaquin's sleeping face hidden in the shadows. "I hate that I regret marrying him. Because Joaquin is the best thing that's ever happened to me." She could feel the tears swelling in her eyes.

"I truly wish I could spare him all of it," Geri went on. "Before I left here, I thought I'd buried what I felt for Bart. And meeting Hakeem gave me a perfect excuse to move on from a silly crush. But I didn't. I started thinking about him again, and I felt horrible."

"That's not your fault," Ms. Jen said. "Your marriage wasn't what you hoped it would be."

Geri swallowed hard. That old ache crawled up her throat. "When I saw him in the pharmacy, I thought I was hallucinating. I wanted to touch him, just to make sure he was really there. And then in the courtyard, he was crying so hard, and I just wanted to hold him. I was happy that finally, he needed me."

She waited, but Ms. Jen said nothing.

"Those nights in Ghana, they were the scariest—and the safest—I'd ever felt. Joaquin slept better there than anywhere else. Because Bart was there. And every night I told myself, this is a dream. You'll wake up and it'll all be gone."

Her voice dropped to a whisper. "But it wasn't gone. He was there. He laughed with Joaquin and read Psalms to me like he actually believed what they said. And I hated how much I started believing him, expecting him, but still waiting for the dream to be over."

Ms. Jen let out a heavy breath. "You're not dreaming, Geri." The words were so soft they nearly got lost in the hum of the road. Her hand was shaking as she reached across the console and tapped Geri's arm.

"I'm so glad you're back home," Ms. Jen whispered. "I missed you. Terribly."

Tears flowed now. "I'm glad to be back too."

They drove without words for a while, a silence that bottled time and was hard to break.

"That first day I saw you at Bart's house," Ms. Jen said, "I went home and cried. I knew you'd come back changed, but I didn't know how much. And when I saw Bart again..."

Geri waited, but Ms. Jen took her time.

"He looked just like," she went on, voice small, like she was afraid to hear herself uttering the words. "Someone I used to know."

Geri didn't turn to look. Ms. Jen's voice had shifted, like it was personal, like she needed to say something but didn't know how to get it out.

When they got off the highway, Ms. Jen turned toward Geri. "Can I ask you something?"

"Of course," Geri replied.

"Did you get to meet Bart's father in Nigeria?"

Geri shook her head. "But I wish I did. Meeting him might have explained some parts of Bart. And I still wonder what kind of man he was. To abandon his child. But Bart still went all the way to Nigeria to bury him. He crossed an ocean for a man who never wanted to know him."

Ms. Jen drew a breath. Then softly, with a strange finality, she said: "He didn't know."

"He didn't know what?"

Ms. Jen's eyes filled again. "I mean, maybe he didn't know Bart existed."

Geri tried to keep her face straight. "Why would you think that?"

Ms. Jen looked away. "I just... I knew someone once. A long time ago. And I never told him."

Geri opened her mouth but closed it. She couldn't bring herself to ask what. But she couldn't let this go. Ms. Jen was finally hinting at answers to her past, and as crazy as it sounded, that past seemed to have something to do with Bart.

"Ms. Jen, did you know Bart's father?"

The question hung in the air for what seemed like eternity. Just the thought made Geri's skin prickle.

Ms. Jen pressed a hand to her mouth. "I'm sorry," she rasped, breaking into quiet sobs. "I shouldn't be talking about this. Not now. Not like this."

A red light caught them near the turn away from the feeder. Geri pulled into a quiet spot on the side of the road and shifted the car into park.

"You don't have to explain anything." She grabbed Ms. Jen's hand and held it. "But maybe talking about it will help."

"I'm sorry," Ms. Jen whispered. "I shouldn't have kept it from

234

him this long."

"Him?" Geri swallowed the lump rising in her throat, trying to stitch the pieces together, but the thread kept breaking. Ms. Jen had always loved the Tekas. She'd always shown up like family. But she wasn't. Not officially. But now, she was crying like someone mourning. For Bart's father?

The thought pulled her back to the image of Bart crouched beside Ms. Jen at the fellowship. The way she'd looked at him, how they'd sat in silence.

"Ms. Jen, please tell me the truth." In that moment, they'd looked just like... "Does Bart—"

"Mommy."

Geri turned around. She had forgotten he was there. "It's okay, baby. We're almost home."

She shifted the car into drive. What was she thinking parking here? This area wasn't exactly safe at night. Their talk would have to wait. Once they got home, she would unravel this mystery once and for all.

34

After dropping off the family from fellowship, Bart went back home. The porch light was on, but Geri's window was dark. When he entered the house, he found Abe sitting in the living room.

"Is Geri here?" Bart asked.

"No. She stayed with Ms. Jen."

The thought of her out there at night made him walk back to the door. "It's nearly eleven."

"They're fine," Abe said.

"How do you know that?" Bart snapped. Didn't anyone understand Geri was in danger? "You forget what's going on? Or do you just not care?"

Abe gave him a long look. "You need to calm down, bro."

"And you need to do better." He looked out the window. Only his truck sat in the driveway.

"Okay, I'm just going to charge that to whatever's going on with you," Abe said, in that condescending tone that pissed off even Phoebe.

"You're the one tripping. I'm peachy."

Abe stood from the couch. "Can you just chill? How did it go with your father's funeral?"

That cracked him wide open and he stormed back into the living room. "So now you wanna talk, huh? You didn't want to talk about nothing before."

"What in the world are you talking about now?"

"You always keeping secrets." He didn't mean to yell, but didn't care anymore. "You could've just told me. You knew where she was, you knew she was in trouble and needed help, but you said nothing. Just watched me walk around like a fool while she was out there suffering."

Abe's eyes flashed. "You told me not to bring her up again. After the wedding—"

"That's bull. That never ever stops you from telling me stuff I need to know. I'm sick of you deciding when you're gonna meddle and when you sit back like some jerk. You only do what suits you and keep quiet when it doesn't, then act like you're doing me a favor."

"You need to calm the—"

Bart shoved him and Abe returned the shove.

"You'd better chill out before I—"

"Hey!" Phoebe's voice whipped across the room. "Are you two insane?"

Bart dropped his fists and stepped back, chest heaving. "I'm sorry," he ground out, "but your husband's a jerk. A controlling, calculating jerk."

Phoebe looked between them like she couldn't believe her

eyes. "What is this? What's going on right now?"

Bart turned to her, his voice raw. "You know what, Phoebe, you too. I expected it from Abe, but not you. You both knew what was happening to her, and you kept it from me. You knew I would've dropped everything to bring her home."

Phoebe's face collapsed with guilt, which instantly destroyed Bart.

"I'm sorry, okay?" he whispered. "Don't you need to sit down or something?"

"No, I'm sorry too," she said.

"You see, this is exactly why we couldn't tell you," Abe muttered.

"Abe, please stop," Phoebe said, and faced Bart again. "She didn't want you to know, Bart. You were the last person she wanted to find out."

The words hit like a punch to the chest. He staggered back half a step.

"Imagine if you'd shown up," Abe said, quieter now. "You know how you do. You shoot first before you even get to asking questions. You think that wouldn't have made everything worse?"

"Geri was in a bad place," Phoebe said. "She didn't trust anyone. IB and Tonye barely got her to trust them. We couldn't risk losing her again."

Bart moved toward the front door. It didn't matter anymore. Now he had a chance to be there for her. He pulled out his phone to call her.

"It's cool. I understand."

"You understand what?" Abe asked.

Bart glared. "I heard you."

"And where are you going right now?"

"To find her."

"You need to chill," Abe said. "You're doing too much. We all know you love Geri, alright. But you need to slow down and let her figure out what she wants."

Bart turned to face him. "Don't you get it? Until we know who's after Geri, she's in danger."

"Wait, Geri's in danger?" Darah cried.

"Bart loves Geri?" Eli mumbled, standing near the stairs like he'd stumbled into a soap opera.

"Of course he loves Geri. How could even you not see that?" Darah said before turning on Bart. "And you need to stop. I threw you an alley-oop and you're tripping over your shoelaces. Geri didn't even want me to know. And I'm practically her little sister."

Bart scoffed. "That's not the same. What could you have done?"

"Nothing," Darah said, unfazed. "But neither could you. Only God could have fixed it. Only God could have brought her back to us, so what you need to do is not mess it up."

Phoebe was nodding. "Just slow it down, and let her come to you."

"What? I think he needs to pick up the speed not go slower," Darah said. "But back to the most important thing. What do you mean 'Geri's in danger?'"

"It's nothing," Abe replied, and turned to Bart. "I'm sorry. For not telling you about Geri. We just had a lot going on."

The heat behind Bart's ribs cooled enough to let guilt slip in. He shouldn't have exploded at them, not with everything Abe and Phoebe had been carrying. The miscarriages, waiting in silence, the pressure of holding broken things together while the rest of the world looked on.

Bart slid his phone into his pocket. "I need some air."

"Where are you going?" Phoebe and Darah asked in unison.

"Just to the car. I'm not even going to call her, don't worry."
He pulled the door open.

"He's so whipped," Darah whispered as it clicked shut behind
him.

Bart didn't argue. He walked down the paved path and
stopped at the edge of the driveway, the chill of the night hitting
his face like a reprimand. The street was still, quiet, no headlights.
No laughter. Only silence, and the endless list of things he
couldn't fix.

He climbed into his truck and rolled down the window
halfway to let in the breeze. He wanted to call her, but Darah was
right. He needed to trust in God more. Because it was God who
had taken care of Geri all this time.

Geraldine Teka wasn't a broken thing waiting for him to fix
her. She was the woman he loved, maybe since the moment he
first saw her storm through their front door four years ago.

Bart sat up, wondering if a drive would help clear his head.
He reached for the ignition. Headlights swept across the street. A
car turned into the driveway beside his.

On instinct, he lowered himself in his seat. From the driver's
side, Geri stepped out, and opened the back door to get Joaquin,
cradling him against her shoulder. Ms. Jen came around the car
rubbing her arms like she couldn't get warm.

"Call me as soon as you get back," Geri said. "You promised
we'd talk."

Bart couldn't see their faces well in the dark, so he leaned
forward.

"Okay," Ms. Jen whispered, glancing toward the house. "But
please don't let Bart know I asked about his father."

His breath stopped.

"I won't," Geri said. "But you have to tell me everything. You knew him, didn't you?"

Bart's hand slid to the door handle. A hundred thoughts collided in his chest. Who exactly was this woman? She'd been part of their lives for years, always there, but somehow, even Abe didn't know much about her. Why would she ask about his father?

Ms. Jen's voice broke the night. "Yes," she said. "He wasn't a bad man."

Bart didn't know when he opened the door. In the next breath, he was standing in the driveway with the two women caught in the act of rewriting his entire life. They froze under the porch light, wide-eyed, in startled silence.

Standing there in front of them, heart pounding in his ears, Bart knew it in his bones. This was the moment he finally broke. And there was nothing he could do about it.

"Why did you say that?" he asked. "How would you know if he was bad or not?" His eyes never touched Geri. "You knew Peter Banigo? Do you know me, too?" He felt the fury rising, too fast, too hot. He sounded unhinged. He didn't care.

"Bart—" Geri's hand clutched his arm.

He jerked away. "Geri, take Joaquin inside. I need to talk to this woman. Alone." He took a step toward Ms. Jen, her hand over her chest like she couldn't breathe.

"What's your deal? Why are you asking about Peter Banigo?"

"Bart, stop!" Geri pulled him back again. "What's wrong with you? You're scaring her."

He couldn't look at Geri right now. "Tell me the truth. Is 'Ms. Jen' even your real name?"

The woman—this woman who had lingered around his life like furniture that had always been there—put her hand to her mouth. Tears poured silently down her face.

Geri yanked him again. "That's enough. You're being hostile

for no reason."

"She just said she knew him!" Bart shouted, facing her for the first time. "Can you really say I'm tripping?"

That stopped Geri cold. She looked between the two of them like she saw something she wasn't ready to understand.

"Please," Geri said softly. "Can we talk about this tomorrow? She was just worried about you."

"No," Ms. Jen cut in. "I won't make him wait any longer." Her fake smile collapsed into a trembling line. "Just take Joaquin inside."

Geri shook her head and grabbed Bart's sleeve, her eyes pleading: *Please don't do this right now. Not like this.*

For a moment, Bart felt his anger soften, but he yanked his hand away from hers. "Just give me some time with her."

Geri said nothing more and carried Joaquin into the house. Once the front door closed behind her, the driveway fell into a silence that made it hard to breathe.

Bart didn't speak. He didn't have to. She was already breaking.

"I'm sorry." Her voice shattered like glass. "I'm so, so sorry."

He stood there watching her cry, the truth slowly cracking him open, memories clicking and locking into place.

It wasn't just the way she cried at the fellowship. Not just the years she'd been around their family, never fully explaining why. It was everything. The time Mom and Dad had asked if he wanted to know about his birth parents, and how Ms. Jen had kept looking at him a few days later at that family party, like she'd swallowed a secret that might never come back up. How hadn't he noticed until now?

"No." He threw the word at her, his heart thrashing in his chest. The thought wouldn't stop rising like a tide within him.

Peter had called the underage girl "J."

Jen.

Jen.

His back hit the side of his truck as he stumbled away from her like she was a cursed spirit climbing out of a grave.

"You're J," he whispered.

She gasped, and then trembled. Sobbing.

"Are you..." His voice fell apart before he could finish.

Her eyes told him, but she still mouthed "Yes."

"No," he said again, and turned from her. She called his name once, maybe twice.

He sprinted across the driveway, past the house, away from the light, into the darkness. His feet crushed the pavement. Fast. Too fast. He had to get away from her. Because it wasn't true. She couldn't be his mother. No woman would do that to her son. How could she have been by his side for so long and said nothing?

She hadn't lost him. She'd abandoned him. Watched him grow up and never once said, That's my son.

She let other people raise him. Let him grow up not knowing. Let him ache through life for a woman who never came back. Until now.

Too late. She was far too late.

Her rejection clung to him like wet concrete settling into his bones. But he didn't stop running. Not even when her voice cracked through the night behind him.

"Bart, please!"

Her voice. Other voices screamed out to him.

No way. Not today.

She'd run away from him once.

And now, it was his turn.

3 5

After Geri put Joaquin to bed, she sat beside him watching him sleep. Then she heard a shout—more like a roar from outside the house. She looked out of her bedroom window and saw Bart running down the street. Ms. Jen shouted his name and started after him before collapsing onto the driveway with her hands on her head, sobbing.

Geri dashed to the front door. Abe was already there. She followed him out into the night. Ms. Jen's cries got louder as though her soul was unraveling.

Geri grabbed her arms to keep her upright. "What happened?" she asked, eyes scanning the empty street. "Where's Bart going?"

"Oh God, help me," Ms. Jen kept saying.

"What's going on, Ms. Jen? Talk to us." Abe pressed his phone to his ear. "Voicemail."

The front door opened behind them. "What's going on, babe?" Phoebe asked, stepping out.

"Where's Bart?" Darah followed close behind. "I thought I heard him yelling."

"Let's get her inside first," Abe said.

They helped Ms. Jen back inside and sat her on the couch. Geri dashed to her room to check on Joaquin, still sleeping.

"Ms. Jen, you've got to talk to us," she said, once she returned.

Ms. Jen looked up, eyes swollen and glassy. "I thought I had time. Time to say it in a better way. But there's no good time for something like this."

Geri grabbed her chest. A sinking sense of inevitability coiled in her chest. But it was too far-fetched to even think it. Not Ms. Jen. This kind, wonderful woman would never have kept such a mind-blowing secret for all these years.

"I was only sixteen," Ms. Jen whispered. "And, Peter, he didn't know. I didn't tell him. He left before I had the courage."

"Hold up," Abe began. "Peter as in Banigo?"

"I didn't mean for it to come out like this," she replied.

"This is crazy," Darah blurted. "Are you saying you're like, Bart's mom?"

Ms. Jen bowed her head in a trembling nod.

Geri covered her mouth, feeling like she might throw up. The silence was complete and decisive. No one said anything for almost a minute. They just stared at Ms. Jen, the woman they thought they knew but clearly didn't.

"I have to go find him," Geri said. "Darah, please watch Joaquin for me."

Abe moved to block the door. "No way. If Bart finds out I let you leave alone right now, he'll be so pissed. It's not safe, Geri."

"I'm not going far. Just down the street," she said, her voice barely holding steady. "Please, Abe. Let me go. I need to be the one."

He stared at her, and something in her eyes must have told him there was no stopping her.

Abe sighed and stepped back. "At least take a car."

"I'll be fine."

She rushed outside before he could stop her, ran along the quiet sidewalk, the wind cold on her face. The farther she ran, the harder her chest ached. Too many questions. All the clues she'd missed all this time. It explained why Mama and Papa Teka had kept Ms. Jen close all these years, inviting her to every gathering, every milestone. They had kept Bart's truth hidden from him, just as her own mother had kept her father's family hidden from her.

Geri slowed as she neared the Teka house. The porch light glowed like a beacon. She turned the front door knob, praying. It opened. She burst through the door, breathless.

"Bart?" Silence. The house was too still. A light glowed under the door to the study.

Her hand hesitated on the knob. There was nothing she could say to him right now. She just had to be there for him.

She pushed the door open. Bart sat on the edge of the desk, facing the wall. His broad shoulders hunched forward like the weight of the world had collapsed onto his spine.

"Bart?"

He didn't turn. The air in the room was thick and hot with his pain.

She moved closer and stopped short of taking him into her arms. Tears rolled down his face, falling onto an open photo album in his hands. The pages—faces—blurred beneath his grief.

She didn't have to look to know what he was seeing. His parents. His childhood. Second-guessing every moment. Every memory now marked by a quiet shadow.

Geri placed a hand on his back, burning hot, trembling.

"Why are you here?" His voice was low, raw. "How could Abe—"

"Shh," she whispered, squeezing his shoulder. "I told him I had to come."

"I'm not going back." He exhaled, the sound hollow. "I can't leave right now."

"I'm not asking you to. I'm staying with you, until you're ready." His shoulders shook harder, and she leaned his head against her.

He let out a groan, deep and broken. "You shouldn't."

She didn't let go, his grief rooting her to him. He pressed his face into the curve of her neck and inhaled like he was trying to breathe through the collapse of a lifetime.

She wrapped her arms around him, the edge of the photo album digging into her side as she pulled him closer. His cries came out raw, unrestrained, and she wept with him. For the boy who had never wanted to know his mother. For the man who had found her, only to lose the ground beneath his feet.

It made sense now. All those times Ms. Jen defended Bart. Her pride whenever he was mentioned. Geri had thought it was fondness, but now she understood what she'd been seeing all along. Motherhood, bruised and buried, waiting for the right moment to speak.

Had Ms. Jen approached the Tekas knowing Bart was her son? Or had fate woven her back into his life like some twisted miracle?

She rubbed his back in slow, steady circles, waiting for him to speak as his sobs finally quieted.

He clutched the album like it was the only thing anchoring

him to his life. "Did that woman tell you she was my mother?" The word mother came out like it hurt his tongue. "It's a lie. She's no one. I don't have a mother. I don't have anyone."

The words gutted her. Bart had always been the loud one. The flirt. The magnetic center of every room. But beneath all of it—the banter and bravado—he was alone. He'd been alone for a long time.

Geri leaned back, searching his handsome face, tight with shame, rage, grief. She reached for his chin, gently tilting his face toward her.

"You have me, Bart." The words came from a place so deep in her soul it shocked her. "You'll always have me."

He turned his face away. "You're just saying that to make me feel better."

He didn't believe her—of course he didn't. She'd been pushing him away all this time.

"No, I'm not," Geri whispered, pulling his chin back so he'd look her in the eye. "I've always had a thing for you, Bartimeus." She swallowed hard. "Being with you feels like coming home."

His gaze searched hers like he was afraid to believe. "I know you're trying to comfort me—"

She silenced his words with her mouth. Softly. Slowly. A kiss full of trembling certainty.

She pulled back and forced herself to meet his eyes. "Then what does that mean?"

Bart dropped the album on the desk, never breaking her gaze. His hands slid to her hips, guiding her to stand between his legs, his eyes dropping to her mouth.

"Tell me to stop," he whispered, "and I will."

"I won't," she said, placing her hands on his shoulders. She'd resisted this feeling long enough.

Their lips met again, deeper this time, like taking a first breath after almost drowning. She melted into him as he pulled her flush against him. His tender, spiraling dance sent shivers across her skin. She gasped, and he smiled against her lips, chasing her breath with one more kiss, and another. By the time they pulled apart, she was breathless, shaking.

Minutes later, they went outside and sat on the porch steps. The air was cool with fall, crickets chirping, their music steady and unseen.

Geri leaned into Bart's solid frame, resting her chin on his shoulder. The city sky was hazy—only a few stars tonight—but somehow, it didn't matter. Her lips still buzzed from the kiss that felt like a lifetime overdue. It was nothing like the first time she'd kissed him. Middle school Bart fumbling around in a dark closet had nothing on grown-up Bart.

Four years ago, they'd stood on this same porch arguing, hurting each other with careless words and unspoken wounds. But pain had softened them. Loss had grown them. And love— real love—might be waiting beneath it all.

Bart took a deep breath, and she wrapped her arms around him. He caught her hand and held it to his chest. She closed her eyes. No matter how much she'd lied to herself, or tried to hate him over the years, she'd always been hopelessly in love with him. Her love for him wasn't something she could ever take back.

"Did you walk here?" he asked.

"I ran." She sighed. "Regretting it now. Should've taken Darah up on that exercise offer. My thighs are on fire."

He chuckled, his hand moving over her leg as if to ease the sting. "I don't want to go home," he murmured after a moment. "I can't even tell her not to come back. Phoebe needs her."

Geri pressed her cheek to his shoulder. "Sorry. But

everyone's waiting for you."

He didn't say anything for a while. Then he got up without warning and reached for her hand. "Come on. Let's get this over with. I'll piggyback you home."

"Boy, please." She laughed, swatting at him.

He stepped in front of her and knelt. "I'm serious. You ran all the way here for me. Least I can do is carry you back."

Geri stared at his broad back, inviting her to lean on him. Like something out of those over-the-top dramas Phoebe and Darah were always watching, where the guy did something outrageously romantic right when the girl was falling apart.

She'd always rolled her eyes at those scenes. But now, it made sense why those women seemed to melt into nothingness in an onslaught of joy. Because she too felt it now. Because it was Bart Teka kneeling in the moonlight.

"I'm heavy," she warned.

He smiled like he understood more than what she'd said. "Me too, Geri."

She almost laughed. Stepping forward, she glanced at the shadowed house behind them. The house that raised the Teka siblings, that held their grief and secrets like sacred ground. The place where Mama and Papa Teka had quietly made room for redemption, while sheltering their children from truths too heavy to bear. What else had those walls seen? What more had been kept at bay, for the sake of love, for the sake of peace?

Geri leaned into him, resting her chest against his back. It was time to hope again.

His hands slid over her thighs to steady her and curved around her hips before adjusting her higher. When his fingers brushed lower, she squeaked.

"I see why you volunteered," she teased, breath warm against his ear.

"I don't know what you're talking about."

He jerked forward into a sprint, and a startled laugh escaped her, rising like music into the night. Then he stopped running and walked slowly, his boots crunching over fallen acorns on the sidewalk.

"Let's go somewhere tomorrow with Joaquin," Bart said. "Is there anywhere you want to go?"

She didn't need to think about it. "Corpus Christi. To see my mom. She still hasn't met Joaquin."

His steps slowed. "We're just visiting, right?"

Geri tugged gently on his ear. The thought of running to Corpus and choosing anything but him now felt like closing a door God had cracked open.

"Yeah. I'm coming back with you," she said, and felt him relax under her.

"Cool. We can leave early tomorrow and come back Sunday."

"Thank you." She tapped his shoulder. "Now put me down so I don't mess up your back."

He didn't move at first, so she squeezed her thighs around him in playful warning. A low laugh rumbled from his chest as he finally set her down with care.

"You wrong for that," he said.

"I don't know what you're talking about."

She slipped her hand into his, and they walked the rest of the way home mostly in silence. The road stretched before them like a path carved through thorns and vines creeping over the worn-down fences.

She wasn't going to run anymore. Not from him. Not from this longing for something higher than survival. Tonight, he had touched her heart, not with his bravado, but with the trembling hands of a man who'd been transformed through pain. A man who hadn't yet realized he needed to stop fighting the storm, and let the stream of grace carry him to wherever God willed.

God had brought her here, and she couldn't run away when he needed her. She had to be here for him, and help him get through this pain. Not on the run, but as a woman daring to hope. Because grace had found them tonight. And hopefully, that same grace would carry them home.

36

"This is beyond crazy," Darah said, staring at the woman still crying on Bart's couch. The same woman who'd come by every chance she got—Phoebe's doula, their stand-in auntie who knew how to braid Phoebe's hair just right when she was too tired to care, who always brought that weird ginger tea everyone drank under protest but finished anyway. Ms. Jen had been woven into the fabric of their lives for years. She belonged. And now, she was the reason Bart had run off into the night. His mother, the woman who gave birth to him.

"How can she be Bart's bio mom?" Her gaze bounced between Phoebe and Abe. "Did Mom know about this? All those Christmases and Thanksgivings?"

Abe stood by the window, his attention fixed on Phoebe trying to console Ms. Jen. Her cries cracked through the quiet room like thunder, and all Darah could think was: How long? How long had she sat with them, laughed with them, prayed with them, knowing what none of them did?

"I was scared," Ms. Jen finally managed. "I didn't know how to take care of a baby. But I couldn't get rid of him, even when my parents insisted—" She groaned, curling into herself.

A chill slid down Darah's back like an unwanted hand. She glanced at Phoebe, whose face had gone dark with horror.

They wanted her to abort Bart. The idea of a world without him—no brash loudness, no relentless teasing, no fierce loyalty—punched Darah square in the chest.

Tears pricked her eyes. "Why stay close to him all this time and not tell him? Did Mom and Dad make you stay quiet?"

"D," Abe said, using the same tired voice he did when he wanted her to calm down but knew she wouldn't. "This isn't the time—"

"Then when? If she was gonna keep this secret forever, then she shouldn't have gotten caught."

"Easy, Darah," he said. "Ms. Jen, I think Bart should hear this explanation from you first. And right now, I don't think he wants to see you."

Darah folded her arms tight like that could keep the ache from spilling over. She didn't blame Bart for running. She didn't want to look at the woman either.

Eli was at the window, peering into the dark like he could will Bart home.

"Nothing's going to be solved tonight," Phoebe said. "I think you should go home, Ms. Jen. Bart needs space."

Phoebe needed Ms. Jen, especially this close to her due date. But even Phoebe—sweet, soft-spoken Phoebe—sounded resolute. Right now, Bart's well-being came first.

Ms. Jen sniffled. "Can you at least call him? Just to make sure he's okay?"

"How can he be okay when—?"

"Stop," Abe snapped at Darah, then gentled his voice. "Geri probably found him, or she'd have called. Go home, Ms. Jen. We'll keep you posted."

The silence that followed Ms. Jen's departure was so complete that Darah could hear her own pulse in her ears. When Abe shut the door behind the woman, the siblings let out a collective sigh, but Phoebe was covering her face. All the heat left Darah's body and she hurried to Phoebe's side.

"I'm fine," Phoebe gasped, holding up a shaky hand.

"No, you're not—" Darah started, until Abe shot her another look.

Phoebe breathed slowly, a practiced rhythm. "I just can't believe..."

Darah slid onto the couch beside her and laid a hand on hers. "Abe's right. Please breathe, Pheebs. We all need to calm down."

Tears traced Phoebe's cheeks. "What was she thinking? Coming to this house over and over, knowing it was her son's—" She choked on the last word.

Abe rubbed her back. "It's gonna be okay," he said, in that gentle voice reserved only for Phoebe, even though his eyes were brimming with worry.

"Maybe Mom told her to stay quiet," Darah said. "Maybe she wanted to tell him but didn't know how. I mean, imagine if knucklehead Bart from years ago had found out before now, that would've been way worse."

They sat in silence, the weight of secrets past and present pressing down on them. Bart didn't handle betrayal well. Months ago, after Junior had revealed the truth about Bart's birth father and how Dad had contacted the Banigos, the house had felt like the Cold War. Abe, defender of honor and reputation, clashed with Bart for weeks. And then—just like that—Bart decided to go to Nigeria to meet the man.

But if Junior had only mentioned Bart's father, not his mother, maybe even Mom and Dad hadn't known the whole truth.

"He's here," Eli said, moving away from the window.

The front door opened. Bart walked in, holding hands with Geri. He looked like he'd run through a storm and come out drenched. But he was smiling.

"Sorry, Bart," Phoebe said, still on the couch, Abe's arms around her.

"I'm good," Bart said, clearly trying to keep it light. "When did she leave?"

"A while ago," Eli answered.

Bart ruffled Eli's hair. "Y'all need to sleep. It's late."

Darah caught Geri's gaze for a second, but Geri looked back at Bart. She wasn't fooled either.

"I'm fine," Bart said again, like if he said it enough times, it might become true. "By the way, Geri, Quinn, and I are going to Corpus tomorrow."

Darah smiled. "Quinn?"

Phoebe stood. "To visit your mom, Geri?"

"Yeah. It's time she met Joaquin. Bart wants to come."

Darah held her tongue. Ms. Yelena could have come down herself. But that wasn't the point. Not tonight. This whole scene felt off. Bart was smiling too much. Through the years, Darah had seen every version of Bart. She'd seen him shattered, furious, numb, but this wasn't any of those. This was worse. This was him pretending. Something had broken in Bart tonight, and Geri was probably the only person who could help him put it back together.

Bart said goodnight and walked Geri down the hall, murmuring that he was okay. He walked past the living room again and headed up the stairs.

When they heard his door close, the house seemed to let out a collective breath like it too had been struggling to breathe.

"Bart's right," Phoebe said. "Eli, please go to bed."

Eli nodded and shuffled off. Darah turned to follow him.

"You wait, Darah." Abe's voice had that familiar edge, the one that usually led to a lecture.

Darah turned with the best innocent expression she could summon. "Is something wrong?"

"Nothing's wrong," Phoebe said quickly, her smile too gentle.

Abe's scowl said otherwise. "We have something to tell you."

Phoebe blinked. "We do?"

"We might as well tell her now," Abe said.

Darah braced herself. Was this about how she spoke to Ms. Jen? Or worse, for coming home without Eli again?

"I don't think this is the right time," Phoebe murmured. "Especially after—"

"That's exactly why it's the right time," Abe countered. "I feel like I'm keeping a secret."

Phoebe nodded. "Okay, go ahead, babe," she encouraged, patting his arm.

Abe's eyes did a full lap of the room before landing back on Darah. "You're getting your car this year. For your birthday."

Darah's mouth fell open. "Are you serious?"

Abe frowned, like her reaction was too much. "You were always gonna get one. You just needed to be pa—" Phoebe elbowed him.

"Yes, we're serious," she finished for him, smiling.

Darah's joy broke free like a bubbling spring. "Thank you."

"Thank Bart tomorrow," Abe said, almost begrudgingly. "He said it had to be a new car."

Darah laughed. Her brothers were softies. "I will. I love you guys so much." She threw her arms around Phoebe, who hugged her back as much as her belly would allow.

"There's more," Phoebe said.

Abe groaned. "Phoebe—"

"You can go to homecoming this year. If you want."

Darah blinked. "What? For real?"

Phoebe tucked a loose twist behind Darah's ear. "You're becoming an incredible young woman. We trust you to keep making us proud."

Abe rubbed the back of his head. "Phoebe said we need to let you enjoy high school a little more."

Phoebe chuckled. "We haven't even mentioned prom yet, and you're already tripping hard."

Darah gasped. "I can go to prom too?!"

"Of course you can," Phoebe said. "You only get one senior year. You deserve to enjoy it. We'll find your dress, get your hair done, the works, and your date—"

"What date?" Abe grumbled. "We didn't talk—"

"Or you can go with friends," Phoebe added.

"Yep. Friends," Darah said, pasting on a smile as her heart skipped to Jeremy. "Thanks, Abe."

Abe wore his usual mask of reluctant affection. "We're proud of you. For being a good sister. For being steady. For honoring Mom and Dad even when things got hard. They'd be proud too."

Hearing him cracked her open. She rushed into his arms, wrapped herself in the familiarity of his warmth and strength, the way she'd done when nightmares used to chase her awake.

He held her tight, just long enough. "Get some sleep."

Darah thanked them again and went to her room. Eli was sprawled across the bed, blanket halfway on, snoring softly.

She didn't even mind anymore. She slid in beside him, lips curled in a smile. She was actually getting a car. A dance. Prom. It felt like she'd been handed the keys to a future she hadn't dared ask for.

When her eyes fluttered shut, her phone vibrated on the nightstand. Another buzz, and another. She rolled over. Two missed calls. Five texts. Jeremy.

Her heart raced as she opened the first: Just checking if you're good. Text when you get this.

The second: Have to leave town for a week. Won't make it to prep class tomorrow. See you when I get back?

Where was he going? Why now? Not that he owed her an explanation. They weren't anything. Not really.

She turned the phone face down and stared at the ceiling, letting the silence stretch over her like a blanket. Now that she could go to Homecoming, if Jeremy asked, it wouldn't be awkward. He seemed genuinely interested, though she couldn't fathom why. But if he was trying this hard, maybe she could try too. Wasn't that what they were all doing? Trying.

Bart had been cracked wide open, but he hadn't shut himself off. Geri had come back carrying a mountain of sorrow but still choosing to build something new. Phoebe and Abe were trying, loving through the ache of what they'd lost and the uncertainty of what might still come. Eli had started to laugh again.

Like some slow miracle, they were all learning to breathe again, each finding their way toward wholeness, being pieced back together stitch by stitch in a fragile mosaic of faith and grief and family, held together by something stronger than any of them. Someone.

"Sorry, God," she whispered into the dark. "I haven't been talking to you recently. I'll try to do better."

She closed her eyes and let herself dream of the future, about hope. The kind that slips in through the cracks like a small voice in the whirlwind of life. The kind that doesn't need testimonies or big miracles. Sometimes it simply looked like a kitchen full of siblings who could still laugh in the aftermath of a storm.

She remembered Harvey, that first night after everything fell apart. She'd come to Bart's house soaked and scared, but she'd slept like a child for the first time in weeks. Because she was with her brothers. And in spite of all they'd lost, they'd gained one another.

Maybe that was what healing really was. Not the absence of pain. It was the presence of love to open the doors even in the storm. And right now, maybe that was all she really needed. To open her heart and let love in, no matter the cost.

3 7

Ms. Yelena Pena laughed as Joaquin belted out his ABCs in Spanish, clapping her hands with delight. Her eyes sparkled as she swooped him into a big embrace.

"He's so smart," she beamed at Geri, kissing Joaquin's curly head with pride.

"He can count to ten in Spanish too," Bart said.

"Un genio!" She bounced Joaquin on her knee. "Mi chiquito brillante."

Geri watched them quietly, like someone seeing a memory unfold in real time. When they had first arrived at Corpus, her mother's welcome had been stiff and guarded, eyes darting between them like they were strangers selling religion door to door. But Joaquin's brightness had unlocked her heart. She'd gone from startled houseguest to doting abuela in a matter of minutes.

Now she accepted Joaquin's empty fruit pouch like a gift. "He has a good appetite, mija. What were you worried about?"

"He wasn't eating much before we came home.," Geri replied.

"Home," Ms. Yelena repeated, her gaze pinging between the two of them.

Bart's eyes wandered around the stuffy room again—the worn couch, the TV blinking in the quiet background, the large-print Bible laid open beside a half-drunk mug, the faint scent of roasted corn and cinnamon.

Joaquin nestled against Ms. Yelena. "He likes me," she crooned.

"Why wouldn't he like you?" Geri said. "You're his abuela." That smile—the one Bart had missed for years—curved her lips.

Ms. Yelena's expression softened too. "Thank you for coming. It's really good to see you two." She nuzzled Joaquin's cheek and looked over at Bart. "And you too, Bart."

Bart tried his best to keep smiling. He couldn't shake the feeling of being watched. Had Geri told her everything? How cruel he'd once been? Maybe that was why Ms. Yelena looked at him like she was still deciding.

"What are your plans for today?" she asked Geri, her tone breezy.

"No concrete plans. We're here till tomorrow."

"Tomorrow? Where are you staying?"

"We got rooms at a hotel. Since there's no space here." Geri handed her mom a wet wipe for Joaquin's sticky cheeks.

Ms. Yelena only nodded. "Will you go to church with me tomorrow?"

Geri looked at Bart. He shrugged, noncommittal. "We'll see," she replied.

Ms. Yelena smiled like it was already settled. "I want you to meet my family. They've been a great help to me. I can't wait for them to see how beautiful my grandson is." She smothered Joaquin's face in kisses until he squealed with laughter.

Bart couldn't help smiling. Joaquin deserved this—a doting grandmother. She wasn't perfect, but at least she was trying.

When he looked back at Geri, she was staring blankly at her mother and son, like she didn't know how to enter the moment. Bart fought the urge to reach for her hand.

"Are y'all going to the beach?" Ms. Yelena asked.

"Yes, ma'am," Bart said before Geri could shut it down. "You should come with us."

Ms. Yelena laughed. "No, I stay with my chiquito. You two go enjoy."

"We want Joaquin to see the beach too," Geri said.

Bart covered her hand with his. "Maybe we let your mom watch him for just a little while?" The look Geri shot him could have melted asphalt.

"That would be nice," Ms. Yelena offered. "He can nap on my bed. It's low to the floor. He'll be safe. Mija, let me babysit my grandson."

Bart turned to her with a grin. "He's a great sleeper."

"Just like his abuela," she beamed, stroking Joaquin's curls. "Go now. Come back soon."

Geri hesitated, but Bart gently urged her up. "Mommy will be back soon," she said. Joaquin touched her cheek with sticky fingers. She kissed him, then her mother. "Thank you, Mama."

As soon as they shut the door behind them, Geri spun toward Bart. "What was that?"

He pulled her toward the car. "Your mom wants time with Joaquin. Isn't that good?"

"She wants to babysit him. I didn't ask for that."

He opened her door. "Just let them be. Let's go chill for a bit."

Geri paused for a moment, then got into the truck. "Just because you asked nicely," she said, with a small smile.

Bart got in and drove off. They didn't talk about her mom again, but Bart couldn't stop thinking about Ms. Yelena, how hard her life must have been raising Geri alone. She too had been abandoned by Geri's father, but she hadn't given up Geri to the system. She had fought for her child, unlike the woman who'd stayed close all this time but never claimed him.

How was he ever supposed to forgive her for that?

Last night, in his restless rage, he'd stayed awake until almost dawn, thinking about the insanity of his life, about Geri and how she finally seemed ready to move forward with him. Geri loved Ms. Jen, and Phoebe loved Ms. Jen. He couldn't make himself the reason why the woman walked away from his family. He had to make peace with her, somehow.

"Are you okay?" Geri asked.

"Yeah. Just happy for Joaquin. He gets to be spoiled today. Isn't that what you wanted for him? A grandmother who makes a big deal out of everything he does?"

"Of course I want that." Her voice was tight. "But you know. I mean, I don't know. She needs to…" Geri drew a breath. "Either way, he already gets spoiled plenty with Ms. Lina and Ms. Jen—" Her eyes widened at him. "I'm so sorry."

Bart forced a smile. He knew Geri wanted to talk about it, but he didn't want her name in the air right now. Not here.

"You saw your mom's face," he went on as if she'd said nothing. "It was like Christmas morning when he climbed into her lap. She's probably trying to make up for lost time."

Geri stared at him for a moment before looking away. "If she cared so much, why didn't she come see us in Houston?"

He had no answer. Parents could be selfish. Absent. Unapologetically late. Like Ms. Jen.

He tried to banish the image of her tear-streaked face, but it slipped in again like mist under a door. No matter how hard he shut it, she found her way in. She didn't even look like he'd imagined his mother would. And maybe that was the hardest part, how someone so soft-spoken and kind could have lived her life hiding from him.

A long breath escaped Geri's lips. "I'm sorry. I'm over here complaining about my mom, and you're still trying to wrap your head around... sorry again."

Bart gave her a sidelong glance. "At least you know."

Geri wrinkled her nose at him. "Brat."

"No scowling on our date."

"We're on a date?"

"What else would you call it? I've been thinking about this for a while. Get ready."

"Okay, now that look in your eyes has me nervous."

"Don't fear, my heart. I've got you."

Her eyes widened at the words. She smiled and patted his arm, but said nothing more.

The neighborhood passed in quiet rhythm. Narrow streets, old homes in faded hues, kids' bikes parked on front lawns, elderly folks sitting on porch swings. It felt like stepping into the past. The kind of place where stories floated in the wind, the sea breeze tangling through Geri's curls. She looked like she belonged here, basking in the pure light of endless possibilities.

He parked across from McGee's Beach and hurried to open her door. "My heart," he said with a mock bow, hand outstretched. Her fingers slid into his. "After this, we can get some corn dogs and rocky-road ice cream."

Her mouth parted. "How did you know that's my favorite junk food?"

"You're the only one I ever saw eat those weird crusted corn dogs. And you and Darah were the only rocky-road fans in the house. Darah stopped buying it after you left for Nigeria."

He led her down the beach to the water. It was early, so they were able to find a spot where it was only them for a good distance. The sea stretched wide before them, sky reflecting in endless blues. Seagulls swooped overhead, cawing like they too had something to celebrate. It was cliché. It was perfect.

"Just curious. What's your love language?" Geri asked.

"Touch," he said without hesitation, and she laughed. "Isn't that obvious? I'm always trying to touch you, you know."

"Yeah, I've noticed."

"And?"

"And what?"

"Do you like being touched by me?"

She looked away, but a smile tugged at her lips. "I forget how slick you can be," she said, then tugged her hand free and darted toward the water.

"You're not going to answer," he called, jogging to catch up.

"It's just weird," she shouted back. "Us being like this. I can't get used to—"

He caught her mid-sentence with a kiss. She yelped and shoved him, laughing as she ran away. Her laughter filled the air like wind chimes. He chased her through the sand and seashells, until she tripped and tumbled into the dunes.

"You okay?" he asked, kneeling.

"I'm fine." She pulled him down beside her.

Together they sat as the waves lapped at their feet. "Thanks for coming here with me," he said.

Her fingers found his again, and he felt the tension loosen in his heart, like an old rusted steel door giving way. Here, by the sea, next to the woman he never deserved, he let himself feel it without thinking about what the future held. And for a moment, he heard a quiet voice, as if the sea had spoken to him. But he knew it wasn't the sea. Because he'd heard the voice before. It was the same voice that had calmed him last night. A whisper that maybe broken things could still be rebuilt.

As more people arrived, a group of kids dashed in and out of the shallows, playing chase across the shore. The sun shimmered on the waves like it too was laughing. Geri tucked a few curls behind her ear, squinting into the wind.

"Why'd you cut your hair?" Bart asked, gently catching a stray curl between his fingers.

"I didn't. It just fell out." Her dry laugh didn't reach her eyes. "Pregnancy was hard. Postpartum was worse. My hair started falling out in chunks. Postpartum alopecia is a thing. It's brutal."

He looked at the full crown of curls that somehow still framed her like a halo, even after so much loss. How much had she endured alone, bleeding joy by the day?

"I'm sorry," he murmured.

"Not your fault," she said, folding her arms around her knees. A seagull shrieked overhead. The waves responded in rhythm, their roar a steady pulse. "I haven't been happy in a long time. Maybe my wedding day, for a moment. But by the next week, I felt like I couldn't breathe. Like my life had been traded for something cold and unfamiliar." She was staring at the water, but he could tell she wasn't really seeing it.

"When I gave birth to Joaquin, I cried. Because I felt so sorry for him. Sorry that he was born into a family that cared more about appearances than people. And I was angry with my mom.

She left me to figure it out all alone. Didn't even visit. Not once."

She grabbed a handful of sand and let it fall back to the ground. "She said Hakeem and I were unequally yoked, and if she supported the marriage, she'd be failing God. And after that, when I told her I was unhappy, nothing she said helped. And everything she didn't say made me feel worthless. My goodness, am I complaining again?"

"No, you're just telling your truth," Bart said, scooting closer. "Please, keep talking."

Her hands trembled as she drew lines in the sand with one finger. "I felt like I was sinking. Like I got so far off course, I didn't know how to come home. People tried to help—IB, Tonye, Abe and Phoebe—but I was scared. What if I brought Joaquin home just to fail him again?"

Her fingers found his. "You have no idea what I thought when I saw you that day. Sitting alone in the courtyard."

It was the kind of moment he would never forget, the echoing silence, and then her.

"Like a mirage," Geri said. "I kept blinking to see if you were real. And I thought to myself, is this a sign?"

He squeezed her hand. "I wasn't going to let you walk through that alone."

"It still feels like a dream sometimes. Like I'll wake up and be back in Abuja. Alone."

"You're not alone, Geri." He lifted her hand and pressed it to his chest, right where his heart beat steady and true. "This thing between us—it's real."

She finally looked at him, eyes searching his like she was trying to find the bottom of what he felt.

He wanted her to find it. Smiles were cheap and she needed more than words. She needed time, proof, before she could understand how those years of pent-up feelings had scarred him for life. There was no other woman in this world for him.

She drew back a little, a teasing look in her eyes. "I get it."

"You saying that means you don't. But it's okay." Theirs was a long road. He couldn't run his way into her heart. He had to walk, step by step until she gave herself completely to him.

A mother and daughter passed by, chasing their golden retriever down the beach. Geri's smile turned soft, wistful.

"You should tell your mom how you feel," Bart said.

Geri sat up straight. "That's a horrible idea."

"Maybe. But I don't think you can heal if you don't. You know, I still regret never asking my mom why she named me Bartimeus. Of all the B names in the Bible, she picked the blind guy."

Geri laughed. "You're so random."

"Just saying. The things we hold inside fester, no matter how small they seem."

"Are you talking about Ms. Jen?"

He stared past her at the shoreline. A dad was helping his daughter launch a bright green kite. It danced like a sermon in the sky.

"I don't even know where to start with that," he admitted.

"Maybe just start with talking to her first."

"I just found out yesterday, Geri. She's the last person I want to talk to."

She shrugged. "I get it. You don't want to talk to her."

"Your mom and Ms. Jen aren't the same. You actually know your mom."

"Right. But some days, I feel like I don't know her at all."

He brushed his hand through her curls. "But you want to. And you deserve to tell her how you feel." Her healing could only truly begin on the other side of a heart-to-heart talk with her mother. "There's a reason you came here. And now she's not at church, you should talk to her."

Geri rolled her eyes. "She practically lives there."

"Maybe it's her way of hiding," Bart said. He'd seen it in Ms. Yelena's eyes, the way she watched her daughter and grandson as if she was hurting in silence. "Your mom looks like she's holding back a lot. And maybe what she's holding is the closure you need."

Geri looked at him like she'd rather dive headfirst into the ocean than sit down with her mother. "I hate when you're right. But yeah, I think God wants me to have a real talk with her." Her expression suddenly shifted from sadness to serious, focused. "But I think He wants something from you too," she said, tugging on his arm. "So, let's make a deal."

"Uh-oh."

"I'll talk to my mom," she said, leveling her gaze with his. "If you talk to yours."

His stomach flipped. "That's not fair."

"It is," she said softly. "You can't move forward without it. You said it yourself."

But he hadn't meant it for himself. "You're asking a lot."

"I know. But I'm not asking more than what you've already given me." Her voice softened. "You've carried me this far. Let me carry this with you."

He stared at her—this woman with fire in her spirit—and felt his resistance melting to her gentleness. Maybe this was what love was: not guarding the door but opening it, and giving someone else the power to influence your life.

She raised her pinky. "Deal?"

He looked at her finger, at the trust and challenge in her eyes. It was wild how he was ready to do anything to make her happy, even if it meant making himself sad just a bit longer.

"Deal," he said, linking his pinky with hers.

"Seal it," she teased, holding up her thumb.

"Not that way." He leaned in and kissed her. A soft, playful brush of lips.

Once he pulled back, a loud crack split the sky. A fat droplet smacked his forehead. The sky had gone from bright blue to dark gray in minutes. Yesterday, he'd checked the weather in Houston, not Corpus.

The downpour came fast and hard, sending people scurrying. Bart grabbed Geri's hand and they ran to the parking lot, soaked through and laughing. Bart unlocked the car and held the door open for her before diving in himself.

Rain drummed the roof. He reached under the backseat and tore off a few sheets of paper towel, handing them to Geri.

"I can't remember the last time I got caught in the rain," she said between laughs, dabbing her face and neck. Her curls clung to her skin, glossy and wild, cheeks flushed, freckles bright like flecks of copper dust.

He wanted to memorize her like this. Hold her still in time. Frame this version of her in his memory, the one who felt free and alive.

She paused mid-wipe. "Why are you smiling like that?"

He brushed a drop of water from her lashes. "I can't stop looking at you. You have no idea how irresistible you are."

He framed her face with his palms, and made as if he was going to kiss her again, but stopped. He couldn't have asked for a more perfect moment.

"I love you, Geraldine Pena."

His voice trembled like a prayer whispered after years of silent unbelief. He didn't say it to get something back. He said it because it had become truer than the sky thundering above them.

Outside, the rain raged, but inside, everything fell still. He wasn't sure what she'd say. He didn't need her to say it back. But he needed her to know. He wasn't going to run from his feelings. Not from her. Not from his past. And not from the God who had tossed this beautifully-flawed wonder of a woman into the whirlwind of his life.

"I love you," he said, again.

3 8

At first, she couldn't find her voice. His words set off tiny explosions inside her. He cupped the back of her neck, his fingers sifting through the damp strands of her hair.

It really was like a dream, being here with him, and she never thought he would have said it just like that.

"I love you too, Bartimeus Teka."

The words didn't sound foreign, didn't tremble on her tongue like a borrowed truth. They rose from deep within, like they'd been waiting to be spoken, words meant only for him.

His fingers grazed her cheeks, sending a thousand nerves humming to life beneath her skin. When was the last time a man touched her and she didn't flinch?

When he lowered his head, she met him halfway. Their mouths found each other like they'd always known how. She clung to him, chasing the heat of his kiss, tasting safety and risk all at once, knowing she could kiss him forever.

But he snatched her out of the trance. "I want to marry you, Geri."

A cold shiver rushed up her spine and she pushed him back. The warmth of his arms fell away.

"No," she said, sharper than she meant, but she couldn't help it.

His eyes searched hers like he was trying to catch up. "What?"

"I'm not—" Geri dragged in a breath. "I'm not getting married again."

Confusion cracked his features. "I thought we loved each other."

"Yes, I love you," she said, trying to steady her voice. "But marriage? I can't, Bart. I just can't."

He looked stunned. "I don't understand."

"We're starting something beautiful here," she tried to explain. "Why spoil it now by talking about marriage?" The rain had slowed, but her heart pounded like the thunder still rolling somewhere in the distance.

"That makes no sense, Geri. I don't want to just date you, I'm crazy about you, I want to build something real." His voice was softer now. "I've factored you into my future. You, Joaquin, even your GC license. You'd be the boss of the job site. I'd just show up and carry wood."

She wanted to cry. Why did he have to be so beautiful? So serious? So sincere? "I told you already," she said, trying to sound as gentle as possible. "I'm not good at marriage. I've done it once, and I failed. Miserably."

He said nothing. The only sound was the rain murmuring against the roof of the truck.

She took his hand in hers. "I want to be with you. I won't ever want anyone else. But I'm not made for vows and veils. I'm not that girl anymore. After Hakeem, I swore never again."

Pain flickered through his eyes. "Sorry for bringing it up. It's just hard to be near you and not want forever."

She didn't want him to pull away from her. "Do we really need a traditional marriage to be together? I love you. You love me. Isn't that enough?" The thought sounded even more ridiculous after the question had left her mouth.

"Geri," he said softly. "We can talk about this later." He peeled her arms from his shoulders and kissed her wrist. "Let's go back to your mom's."

"That's it?" she asked, stunned.

"Joaquin's probably awake and the rain has chilled out, so it's best we go now."

He was calm, too calm. He drove away from the beach like nothing had happened. But the look on his face, that quiet smile, the way he nodded to a beat she couldn't hear, it made her stomach twist, like she'd missed something.

She watched him the whole way back, trying to read him. What happened to their date? Their moment? The warmth of his hand still lingered on her wrist, but everything else felt off. She couldn't name it, and that made it worse.

When they got back to the house, he was all smiles again.

"Are you angry with me?" Geri asked.

She'd barely finished speaking when he swept her up into his arms like it was nothing. She screamed and covered her mouth as he spun her around.

Laughing, he set her down on the driveway. "Now we're even."

Her mom opened the door. "Joaquin's still asleep," she whispered, eyes flicking between them as they stepped into the house.

Geri stiffened at her mother's stare full of judgment. Just then, Bart's hand brushed over the back of her head, a gesture so instinctive, so tender, it pulled a breath from her.

"Let me check on him," Mom whispered loudly and padded into the hallway.

"She's not great at whispering either," Bart said with a grin.

Geri chuckled under her breath. Thankfully, Joaquin could sleep through thunderstorms and Port Harcourt traffic—he wasn't waking up over a whisper.

When her mom returned, she reached for the open Bible on the coffee table. "I read to Joaquin after lunch. He likes the stories. I should get you one of those picture Bibles from church."

Geri swallowed the lump in her throat. "That would be nice. Thanks, Mom."

Bart's hand tapped her knee. "Guess I better go make that call."

Geri turned, panic flashing in her chest. "What call?"

"I'll be right back." He held her gaze for a beat too long before walking out and closed the door behind him, his absence creating an ache she didn't expect.

Her mother's eyes lingered on the front door. "Is something going on between you two?"

The question was casual, but Geri heard the disappointment underneath.

"I'm not sure what you mean."

"Are you dating him? Is this a fling?"

Geri clenched her jaw. "No, it's not a fling."

"So, what is it?"

"We're still figuring it out."

She sighed. "You need to focus on Joaquin right now. On

getting your life back in order."

"Bart's the reason we're here right now."

"And I'm grateful he brought you home. I am. But the way he looks at you, it makes me uncomfortable."

Geri's cheeks burned. She'd seen that look, felt it in her bones, and for the first time in years, she was starting to let herself believe she deserved to be looked at like that. But all her mother could think about was the wrongness of it.

"I don't think now's the time to be dating," her mom continued, "when your son needs stability. He comes first."

That did it. Geri's pulse kicked into gear. She forgot how easily her mother could put her on the defensive. She needed to pivot or end up in another endless argument.

"Can we talk about Bart later? I need to talk to you about something else."

She closed the Bible. "What is it, Mija?"

Geri glanced down, her hands clenched in her lap. She needed to dive in without filtering her thoughts.

"After Hakeem died... why didn't you come?" Geri asked. "When Joaquin was born and we were in the hospital for months, why didn't you come?"

Her mother blinked, lips parting. She looked like she was searching for the right answer, or maybe a version that didn't feel like a betrayal.

"I couldn't come."

"Couldn't or wouldn't?" Geri's voice cracked. "Because I married someone you didn't approve of?"

"You said you loved him. I couldn't stop you. You're old enough to—"

"No," Geri snapped, tears rising. "You punished me. With your silence. With your absence."

"That's not true. I prayed for you. I texted you the prayers we lifted up to God every morning. You were always in my prayers."

Geri bit her lip, but the words exploded out anyway. "While you were lifting me to your God in heaven, I was already in hell."

Her mother flinched like the truth struck her face. "My God? Is He not your God too?"

Geri gasped, her own words strangling her. "Where was He when I was being abused and tormented in that house? Where was He when I was alone, bleeding in a hospital bed with no one to hold my hand? If He was my God, why didn't He make you come?"

Her mother's eyes brimmed, lips trembling. "Mija—"

"You said I should put Joaquin first. But you never put me first. Not when I was little. Not when I begged you to stay home from church for once. Not when I needed you most."

"You're not being fair. I did the best I could. Do you think it was easy raising you on my own? Do you know what I gave up to feed you, to keep you safe, to get you into good schools?"

Geri scoffed. This wasn't about what her mother gave up. It was about what she didn't give. Love that wasn't performance-based. Presence that didn't need a pulpit. A hug after school. A conversation that didn't start with scripture. A mother who chose her, not ministry. She would have eaten cereal and frozen taquitos for months if it meant her mother didn't work double shifts and vanish into church every weekend. While her classmates traded stories about boring weekends with their parents, she was stuck in the back of a chapel watching her mother and the faithful congregation whip themselves up into a frenzy, praying to God for breakthrough.

"We needed the church, Geraldine," she whispered. "If I didn't have them, I would've fallen apart. I was barely holding on as it was."

"At least you had them." Geri's voice broke. "I didn't even have you."

The silence between them collapsed like a roof giving way in a storm. Tears ran freely down her mother's cheeks, and she made no move to wipe them.

Geri just stared. A piece of her—some younger, angry version of herself—felt vindicated by the way her mother was breaking. But it didn't feel like victory. It felt like loss, a big old lump rising in her throat. All the old pain—those nights curled in fetal position with Joaquin crying beside her, her body bruised and soul gutted—rushed back like a flood. And always, always, that aching question: Why didn't Mom come?

Now she had her answer, and it didn't provide a single drop of satisfaction to quench her thirst, for what, revenge? What exactly did she want from her mother? In the end, her mom was a victim too. They were simply two hurting women, broken by men, staring at each other across years of silence, trying to discover a new language to share their grief.

She was tired of feeling this way, waiting for her own mom to reach out and love her in the way only a mother could love. Because no matter what excuses she made for this woman, through all of her suffering, in the deepest moments of her pain, Mom had always been far—thousands of miles—away. Praying.

Geri looked up, voice trembling with fury. "Prayers don't mean much without action. I needed you, and instead of supporting me, you and your God punished me for not living life your way. I know, Mom, I married the wrong person, but I refuse to believe that the God I'm starting to know and the one you always pray to can be the same. Because the God I've seen these past years in the people around me would never allow you to behave so badly with your own child."

Her mother sat frozen, eyes wide. Geri couldn't tell if it was the weight of her accusation or the sting of truth that stunned her.

"Do you know how I felt when I found out I was pregnant? I was ashamed, Mom. Ashamed that I would one day have to tell my son who his father was. Just like you were ashamed to tell me about mine." Her mother's eyes dropped and Geri stepped closer. "I fell in love with the wrong man. But so did you, so why am I the one still being punished for it?"

It landed like a backhanded slap. Her mother flinched and silent tears slid down her cheeks.

"Mommy?" Joaquin stood at the hallway door, rubbing his eyes.

Still in a daze of rage, Geri rushed to him, scooping him up like she could shield them both from the moment collapsing around them.

"We have to go," she rasped.

Her mother didn't move, didn't speak, didn't rise to say goodbye.

Geri's vision blurred as she grabbed Joaquin's bag and fled toward the door. Behind her, Joaquin reached back, crying for his grandmother. Her heart twisted as she stumbled down the porch steps.

Bart stood by the car, glancing up from his phone. His face changed when he saw her.

"Are you okay?" he said, striding toward her.

She pushed past him, barely able to breathe. "Let's go. Now, Bart." You were wrong, she wanted to yell. The sooner they left Corpus, the better. The more she talked about her mother's abandonment, the deeper and more painful the wound felt.

She fumbled Joaquin into his seat. Of course, the belt was

twisted. Joaquin whimpered, shifting around.

"I'll do it," Geri snapped, brushing Bart's hand away. She buckled Joaquin in, slammed the door and stalked to the front seat. "Let's go."

She didn't look at him, didn't want to see his expression. She hated how her voice kept coming out sharp, like a weapon she couldn't put down.

Bart started the car. "Maybe we can still stop for i—"

"I'm not hungry. Just drive." She cringed. Her tone was all wrong. But she couldn't fix it now. Not with her chest burning like this.

The drive was silent except for Joaquin's soft sniffles in the back seat. She couldn't bring herself to look at him. Had he heard what she said about his father? Was he crying because of her? Because she kept breaking things before they had a chance to heal?

She bit her lip to keep from crying. What had she done to her precious son?

Bart pulled into the hotel parking lot. The hotel overlooked the ocean—he'd chosen it just for that. A view, a memory, a gesture of love. But Geri only wanted to curl up with Joaquin and sleep off the knife in her soul.

Bart stepped around to help, but she pushed ahead.

"I've got him," she muttered.

"I know you do." His voice was maddeningly calm. "But let me help."

Joaquin reached for Bart, but Geri pulled him closer to her, instantly snapping at herself to stop making things worse. But she couldn't. Somehow the pain kept edging her on.

With a sigh, Bart walked toward the hotel lobby. She followed, clutching Joaquin tighter than she needed to.

Inside the lounge, he gestured to a couch. "Wait here. I'll get the room keys."

She collapsed onto the cushion and tucked her face into Joaquin's neck, breathing him in. He was still warm, still hers, still safe—for now. But the room felt off-balance. She stared at Bart's back as he stood at the counter. This was supposed to be a beautiful trip with her son and the man she loved, their first night in a space not haunted by grief or loss. Just the three of them trying to figure out how to move forward. Maybe they would have walked along the shore, let Joaquin play in the sand. She might have laughed. They might have kissed again. Instead, she'd let everything unravel, because she just had to open her mouth. Why had she thought a conversation with her mother would give her closure?

Bart returned with two card keys. That gentle look from earlier was gone, replaced by guarded courtesy.

It chilled her. Had she ruined more than the evening? He clearly regretted coming with her. What if—after everything—he'd finally decided she was too much?

"They had to give the last connecting room away," he said, eyes not quite meeting hers.

Once they got in the elevator, the silence stretched between her and Bart like an invisible thread she didn't know how to take hold of. He stood at a polite distance, as if proximity might snap whatever hope he was still trying to hold. When they reached the room, he set down the overnight bag beside one of the beds and handed her a key.

"I'm down the hall if you need me. Room 210."

If she needed him? The words hollowed her chest. "Thank you," she murmured.

He gave her a small smile—a poor imitation of the warmth

he usually showered on her—and left the room, taking the last fragments of her anger with him. The soft click as the door shut behind him felt like finality.

The room suddenly felt too quiet, too cold. She unpacked their stuff, but Joaquin refused everything she offered—snacks, a change of clothes, even comfort. He hid under the covers and curled his tiny arms around his chest like a fortress, his message clear. He didn't want her. He wanted Bart.

She sat on the bed, pleading with him. How had Bart become the one her own son clung to? And why in the world had she pushed him away?

Because she was afraid? That was silly.

Because part of her still believed love was a trick—that promised everything only to take everything and leave you out in the cold.

But Bart hadn't left her, had he?

Later that night, Joaquin woke up screaming, his diaper soaked. Geri changed him, hushing his cries with kisses to his cheeks.

She reached for her phone. No texts. Nothing. Where was Bart?

She hit call. It rang and rang until an automated voice took over. She nearly screamed. She tossed her phone onto the bed, threw on a hoodie, and scooped Joaquin into her arms. Once she cracked open the door, her foot knocked something on the floor.

A bag. Still warm. Corn dogs, two sandwiches, and bottles of water.

Her chest burned. When had he come by? Why hadn't he knocked? She left the bag inside the room and marched down the hall to Room 210. She knocked. No answer. Called again. No answer. A horrible panic rose in her throat. Had he really left?

Breathless, she took the elevator to the lobby and rushed out into the parking lot. The space where Bart's truck had been was empty. She walked the entire perimeter of the building to make sure she wasn't seeing things. Nothing. Just her and the night, and her son falling asleep in her arms.

Back in the room, she fed Joaquin corn dogs while her mind spiraled in every direction. "I just hope he's okay," she said, and Joaquin flashed her another judgmental stare. "I know, it's my fault, calm down."

Once Joaquin fell asleep, Geri sat down on the floor. She was alone. Again.

The tears came slowly, like a faucet turned loose by a hand that had long refused to turn the knob. The hand of pain, gut-wrenching and sharper than anything she'd ever felt. She was the problem. Not her mom, not Bart.

Bart had said he loved her and wanted to build a future with her and Joaquin, and she'd shut the door in his face, afraid that if she opened it, the winds of loss would sweep through again. But right now, sitting on this hotel floor, the thought of losing him felt worse than anything else.

She couldn't keep lashing out at him. She needed to stop sabotaging her future, and maybe love wasn't enough. She felt hollow, like she was holding a puzzle with missing pieces in the middle. She needed something to keep her from free-falling and slipping into old patterns. And the only thing that came to mind was... God.

"Are you still there?" she whispered, amazed at how easily she'd forgotten Him again.

Geri leaned her head back against the mattress and closed her eyes. She didn't know if Bart was done with her, didn't know if her mother would ever understand her, or if she could undo the damage done to her son's heart tonight.

But maybe she could start with this. A simple whisper.

"Please, help me."

The wind pressed against the windows like a gentle, sweet song echoing in her ears. The rain had stopped hours ago, but the sky still felt heavy,

Geri drew her knees to her chest, weeping. Waiting for her joy to return in the morning.

39

He needed a drink, so he went looking for a bar. He drove through the same neighborhoods, down streets that looked like old Houston suburbs before the storm, before he became the man who carried too many regrets.

The night wrapped around his truck like a raincoat, headlights slicing through the darkness. He didn't know where he was going, only that if he stopped moving, he'd have to feel it all, and feeling right now might drown him.

He kept driving, blinking against the burn in his eyes. His GPS led him down a dead end, and when he got back on the main road, he recognized a gas station. They had stopped there earlier on their way to Geri's mother.

Bart made the turn and his instincts took over, anger rising within him. His memory served him well as the familiar porch came into view with the front light on. Just hours ago, he had stood out here watching the porch while everything went wrong inside. He'd asked Geri to talk to her mom, and it had backfired against him. Now he had to fix it.

Before he could get out of his truck, the front door creaked open. Ms. Yelena stepped out, wrapped in a shawl like she'd been waiting for someone she knew would come.

Bart got out and met her at the porch. The breeze smelled of the Gulf—briny, damp, alive.

Ms. Yelena didn't smile. "I stayed up for you. Come in."

That quiet welcome stunned Bart more than anything, reminded him of his mom, how she'd sometimes known things before they happened.

Inside, the house breathed silence. A quiet where not enough had been said. Invisible words whispered through shadows. The hum of a wall clock filled the gaps between them. Tick, tick, daring him to speak. She clicked on a small lamp in the living room and gestured toward the couch.

Bart sat down, unsure if he was here to defend himself, confess, or beg. She sat across from him like some dignified saint of old, ready to die for her cause, Bible resting by her side, hands clasped over one knee as if she were holding something together.

He cleared his throat. "I came to let you know... your daughter loves you. She doesn't hate you. She just wants, just needs to hear you're sorry. For the silence. For the absence. For what you both lost in the past."

The words hung between them like fragile glass shattering the air.

Ms. Yelena studied him. "Why are you so concerned about her?"

Wasn't it obvious? "I didn't come here to talk about that."

Her eyes didn't waver. "Are you in love with my daughter?"

It struck him so clean he felt himself flinch. "Yes, ma'am."

"And I assume you want to marry her?"

"Yes. With all my heart."

She still didn't smile. "Geri's father loved me too, or at least that's what I wanted to believe. But love is not enough. You need something stronger when the fire dies down. Something that doesn't break under pressure. You know what that is?"

He shook his head slowly.

"What do you think held your parents together?" she asked. "They were good people. The kind you don't forget. I was grateful for how they cared for Geri. Back then, you were never at home all those times I came."

He looked at his hands, the guilt washing over him again. "I wasn't around much. Thought it was easier for them if I stayed away, made room for the others. My younger siblings, they needed more. I thought I was doing the right thing by disappearing." He still couldn't believe he'd once thought like that. "After they passed, I realized how wrong I was. And now, I see what they were trying to leave us. Not just memories. A legacy."

"So, do you feel like you've changed?"

"I'd like to think I have. I'm trying."

Ms. Yelena tilted her head, her voice gentler now but laced with truth. "People don't change on their own, Bart. Not really. When pain hits hard, when life presses, we go back to our roots. To the unhealed version of ourselves we buried but never surrendered."

He went still. Her words like a ragged truth wiping clean a fogged mirror.

"How do you expect me to trust you with Geri? After what her father did to her? After what her husband did? How do I know you won't become the same story in a different voice?"

Bart sat on the edge of the couch, his heart thudding like a drum in his chest. "My father walked out on me too. Once when I was born, and again, when I tried to forgive him." His words slurred like he was dragging them through gravel. "I just met my birth mother, and I don't even know what to do with that yet. It messed me up. But I know I have to forgive her too. Because I'm tired of being mad. Of letting that anger run my life. Of carrying everything and feeling like I'll never be enough."

He looked up and found Ms. Yelena watching him. Her eyes flowed with gentle sorrow, understanding.

"Maybe that's how Geri feels," he said. "She's mad at you for not being there, and wants to forgive you, but doesn't know how."

Ms. Yelena folded her hands in her lap like she was bracing herself for a wave. "And you think me saying sorry would help her forgive?"

Bart nodded. "You mean the world to her. And meeting you tonight, I think I finally get it. I didn't understand before, why she even wanted to come here, after everything. Why she still reached for you. But now I see it. You're a good person. You're just hurting, too. Maybe that's why you stayed away."

Ms. Yelena exhaled slowly. "I see why she cares for you. You're a good one. Yonas and Ester, only good fruit could grow from that tree." She paused, the grief in her voice curling around her words like fog. "But goodness doesn't keep people from breaking each other's hearts. Goodness can still walk away. It can still abandon what it should've stayed and fought for."

Her words pierced through the anger he'd been holding in since last night. He'd gone to Nigeria to bury a father who wasn't really a father, and now he'd met a woman who claimed to be his mother. How was he supposed to make any sense of this chain of events?

"You're right," Bart said, the truth behind her words piercing deep. If he could call Geri's mom a "good person," and offer her that kind of grace, why couldn't he do the same for Ms. Jen? Why couldn't Ms. Jen also be a good person who made a horrible choice? Didn't she deserve the same mercy?

He nearly laughed. When had he started thinking in words like grace? Abe. Daniel. Judah. Tonye. All of these men had somehow come through their broken pasts with quiet strength and unflinching hope. Their thoughts had bled into him, changed the way he thought without him even noticing. Now he felt the weight of his own hypocrisy press down on his shoulders. He'd offered everyone grace but withheld it from himself.

"Maybe I'm all wrong for her," Bart said. "Maybe I'm just like Peter Banigo, or Hakeem. Men who ran when it counted. Men who didn't know how to stay." His words hung there, trembling. "My parents threw me away like I didn't matter, so why do I think I'd be any different? Why would someone like me think I won't leave Joaquin too?"

It was a confession that felt like bleeding out. He'd named a fear he'd never said aloud.

"You won't if you surrender."

He looked up. "Surrender?"

Ms. Yelena leaned forward, her gaze maternal. "Do you know why your father—Pa Teka—stayed? Why he never gave up when the storm came for all of you? Children who aren't even related to him by blood."

Bart swallowed, heart in his throat. "Because he was strong. He was a far better man than me."

"No. He didn't do it in his own strength. He surrendered." She held his gaze. "He gave his whole life to God, and let God carry the weight."

As much as Bart wanted to scoff, he couldn't. His father had been too steady, too hopeful for anyone to think that was normal. The heavier the burden, the more he'd seemed to smile. Those quiet mornings he would sit with his Bible, praying out loud when he thought no one was listening. And then there was that light in his eyes that Bart had always loved, and envied.

"He stayed because he had Jesus," she said.

A simple word. No, a name. But it landed in the room like muffled thunder. A name he'd heard his whole life but never leaned into. Dad had always told them that through it all, no matter how hard it got, he was able to keep going because of his faith.

But as he looked up at Ms. Yelena, instead of her words offering him comfort, a tear slipped down his cheek. The woman who hadn't gone to her own daughter when she was suffering was talking to him about God.

"If you have Jesus," she continued, "you can do anything."

It made no sense that she could say that without shame. "But you had Jesus, and yet, you didn't do right by—" He froze before he finished his sentence, an accusation wielded like a knife. "I'm sorry—"

Her hand rose and quieted his apology. She turned away, her eyes already wet. And for a long while, there was only silence, festering between them like an old wound.

"I really tried to do better," she said at last, her voice so faint it escaped like a breath. "But you have no idea what it does to you. To try and do everything right, and still end up on the losing end. You make one mistake and love one wrong person and suddenly, it paints the rest of your life."

She looked at him, her grief plain. "I tried. But I was alone.

He left. After everything he promised, he left anyway, ran like a coward and left me to pick up the pieces. You don't know how hard it was. Raising her alone. Watching my dreams vanish, all these things I'd planned to do with my life. And still, I loved her with everything I had."

She choked back a sob, reaching for a box of napkins on the ledge. "Geri is the best thing God ever gave me." Her hands trembled as she dabbed her eyes. "But back then, I didn't see it. Every time I looked at her, I saw him. I saw what I had lost. And I struggled."

She sank back down onto the couch, seeming to crumble into her own memories. "I know I wasn't a good mother to her. And somehow, I just didn't know how to be better."

Her voice disappeared. Her broken sobs filled the space like rain on a roof, a cleansing stream that washed away his rage.

Sitting there watching her fall apart, he no longer saw her as Geri's mother or his judge. She was just a woman who had tried, who had bled for years in silence, living with the ghosts of her choices.

He couldn't help imagining Ms. Jen sitting across from him, wondering if she'd ever come undone like this. Would she have said the same? That she was scared after Peter left her? That she loved him but didn't know how to be the mother he'd needed?

The questions screamed at him like a bitter symphony of pain. Most people didn't start off wanting to hurt others. They just got lost somewhere along the way, and some never found their way back.

Ms. Yelena was probably like that. Right now, she looked so small and human, her tears unwinding the last thread of bitterness he'd carried for far too long. All these years, without realizing it, he'd wanted to punish his birth parents for leaving him behind.

And now that he'd met them—and they weren't monsters, just flawed people with too many wounds—he didn't know what to do with his pain.

He had been denied his vengeance. And somehow, that was harder than the hatred.

Maybe this was what Geri felt too, watching her mother and her son bond while she stood in the middle like a bridge born out of pain. Not the fruit. Not the root. Just the scar in between the disappointment that made it all possible.

"Geri loves you," Bart said, gentler now. "She always has. You tried, and even though it wasn't enough back then, it can be now. You can still show up. We both can. We can choose to do better. Not perfectly. But faithfully."

He smiled, his voice thick. "I'll try to do that. And you try too. For her. For Joaquin. Deal?"

Ms. Yelena's face melted, her frozen expression dissolving into awe. She nodded twice, and stood, surprising him when she pulled him into her arms.

"My Geri's lucky to have you," she whispered.

Bart stood there in her embrace, stunned to silence by the softness of it. And there, in the quiet circle of her arms, he let himself yield. He put his arms around her, and it washed through him. Something he'd never realized how much he needed until that moment.

Even after he left the house, the feeling stayed with him, like being wrapped in a warm blanket of rain.

As he drove back to the hotel, he couldn't stop thinking about what she'd said—about God, about surrender, about Yonas Teka's quiet strength and how God had carried him through the hardest days. The invisible threads of grace that somehow held people together, even after everything else had unraveled.

The rain had started drizzling again. The roads were ghostly, empty. The sky above was ink-black and heavy, like the night had paused to listen.

When he parked at the hotel, he didn't move. The silence didn't threaten him now. He wasn't afraid to hear his own thoughts. All the things he'd once thought could satisfy him, he could see now how empty they'd been.

He let his head fall against the steering wheel and drew a ragged breath. But it didn't fill him. Not deep enough. Something had shifted inside him. And it wasn't grief.

"Wow," he said, realizing it was surrender. The sudden collapse of every wall he'd ever built to keep the truth out. The silent fall of a thousand invisible weights that had kept him from feeling what he needed to feel. And it came not like a shout of thunder, but in a slow uncurling of the scared little boy who had once prayed that someday, someone would love him enough to take him home.

"I can't do this alone," he whispered. "And I'm really tired of pretending like I can."

Even before the words left his lips, he knew he was breaking. The little boy was finally getting his chance to speak. The boy who had carried the world on his back, taught to never ask for help, to act like the hurt didn't matter. A boy who had been passed over, let down, and learned to wear his detachment to life like armor. A boy who had lost everything and had finally found what he didn't know he was searching for.

Like the tearing of a veil ripping down the middle, his tears poured down, soaking his sleeves, his collar, baptizing his fear, drowning his pride.

He wept until the pressure gave way to something lighter. Freer. It felt like he was truly breathing for the first time. Like God

Himself had reached in and taken the weight from his chest.

When he finally stepped out of the car, his face was still damp. The rain washed over him as it fell, but the night no longer felt heavy. He laughed without knowing why.

He marched into the hotel like he was walking on air. Maybe this was what it felt like to be born again.

40

Darah blinked awake to the pale light of dawn filtering through her curtains. Then she heard it—a low laugh. Someone was sitting in the chair beside her dresser.

She shot upright. "Junior?"

"Morning, Squirt."

She launched across the bed into his arms, nearly toppling the chair. "You trying to give me a heart attack?" she muttered, muffled in his sweatshirt.

"How can you still sleep like a rock? I've been here ten minutes." He hugged her tight, then leaned back, mock disgust on his face. "You still drool, by the way."

"Shut up." She wiped her mouth anyway. "What are you doing here? It's Monday."

"Wanted to surprise you before school," he said, settling deeper into the chair like he'd never left. "You look taller."

"Liar."

He chuckled. "You didn't even reply to my last text."

"Because you didn't send one."

"Exactly." He raised an eyebrow. "Lucky for you, I'm still your favorite."

Darah snorted. "That's up for debate."

But the truth was: it wasn't. Junior had always been the brother who made space for her, who didn't talk at her but with her. When she ranted, he listened—start to finish. He was her safe place. The only person who ever made her feel younger without making her feel small.

"You good?" he asked, his voice softer.

The question felt bigger than it should have. "Trying to be," she admitted. "The world's moving along, so we keep moving too, right?"

But she had felt the shift. Ever since Friday—ever since him—her mind had been spinning. The melody of that old Carpenters' song had wrapped itself around her brain like ivy. She didn't know where it was all going, only that the axis of her world had tilted.

"Still a little poetic nerd, huh?" Junior teased.

"Says the philosophy major."

"Touché."

She stood and stretched. "Can I ask you something?"

He looked like he already knew where this was headed. "Sure."

"Since Dad went digging on all of us... did he ever find anything? About my family?" She hated how her voice thinned at the end.

"What brought that on?"

She sat on the bed. "I've just been thinking lately. About

where I came from. You have Marcus. Bart's got Tonye. Abe fought to keep us together. I just, I guess I want to know where I started."

Junior's fingers drummed lightly on the armrest. "Even if it was bad, you'd really want to know?"

Darah nodded. "Even the bad's still part of the truth, right?" If there was someone out there who knew about her past, she wanted to know.

He stared at her for a long moment, then shook his head. "I don't know anything. Not really."

Not really. It wasn't a lie, but it wasn't the truth either.

Before she could press him, her alarm blared. "This is officially the weirdest Monday ever."

Junior stood. "Hurry up. Geri whipped up some tight breakfast. Not just eggs."

Darah paused. "You saw Geri already?"

"Yeah. You were right. She's different."

Darah nudged him toward the door. "Go before I start crying. I need to get ready."

By the time she finished breakfast and headed out the door with her gear, her heart felt steadier than it had in days. Junior was home. She didn't know how long he'd stay, but they'd at least get to hang out and talk some more.

Still, as the day wore on, a restless wind curled through her thoughts. She couldn't focus in any of her classes. At lunch, Avery poked at her salad while humming the song again, the new version from the drama, a little more upbeat, spicy.

Darah begged Avery to stop. She still wasn't ready to face what it meant. But the music—like the feeling—was everywhere now, even when the song wasn't playing.

As she jogged onto the softball field after the final bell, she was wound tighter than a pitch in mid-spin. Coach Myers was already yelling before they started warmups, and when the whistle blew for a water break, Darah was sore, sticky, and exhausted.

"Bring it in, girls!" Coach's voice sliced across the field like the first commandment.

Darah jogged in from shortstop, rolling her throbbing shoulder. These fall workouts were technically optional, but Coach Myers treated them like sacred rites of passage. They'd just wrapped a live scrimmage with split squads—half the girls playing defense, half batting. Darah had rotated between short and pitching today, and it showed.

"You good, Teka?" Coach Myers asked.

"Yeah. Just a little stiff."

"We'll work on recovery throws," Coach said. "Solid command today. Real promise in that curve." She called a water break, and the girls scattered toward the coolers near the dugout.

Darah squirted water on her face and neck, letting the cool droplets ease her. Her muscles ached from the drills. She wasn't even supposed to be a pitcher, but Coach had made her a project since last spring, insisting she had the arm—and the fire—for the circle. From the start, the woman had seen something in her that Darah wasn't sure she saw in herself.

"Look at you, girl," Avery raved.

"What?" Darah asked, patting down her face with her towel.

"You pitched three strikeouts in four batters," Avery said, with a fake swoon. "I'm just basking in your goddess glow."

Darah rolled her eyes. "I gave up a hit."

"To Lea, who's built like an F-150." Avery tipped her head. "Anyway. When are we gonna talk about you-know-who? You never told me he was your soulmate."

Darah choked on her water. "He's not—"

"The way he was looking at you Friday?" Avery fanned herself. "It was giving childhood promise under the stars. Slow-dance-on-the-rooftop. I'm just saying."

"You've been watching too much of that drama," Darah muttered.

"And your life is now a drama," Avery teased. "You started watching it, right?"

Darah tugged the towel over her head. Against her better judgment, she'd started watching the drama on Saturday night. One episode had turned into two, then four, and the worst part was now she couldn't stop imagining kissing Jeremy.

Early this morning, he'd sent her a sweet text: Good morning, beautiful. Simple. Casual. But she hadn't responded. Not because she didn't want to. But because she did.

"Please tell me you're wearing something amazing to Homecoming," Avery said.

Darah shrugged. The sky was thick with moody clouds and the threat of rain. Ever since Harvey, storms felt personal. Louder. Sometimes she woke up with her heart pounding, unsure of where she was.

"Are you sure you don't need help with your dress?" Avery asked again.

"Geri and Phoebe are helping me this weekend," Darah replied.

Avery winked and started humming that same haunting tune. A group of their teammates sat in a row near the dugout, shoes off, sipping from their bottles and groaning about sore quads.

"I can't believe we have practice the day before Homecoming," someone grumbled. "You think we can get Coach to cancel?"

"As if," said Lea, their catcher. "Coach probably thinks Homecoming is a Shakespearean tragedy."

"Maybe it was for her," another girl joked.

They all looked up at Coach Myers pacing the outfield like a linebacker looking for the enemy on the field.

Darah muffled a giggle. Coach taught AP Lit and was infamous for weaving Macbeth and Hamlet into game strategies. Once she'd compared an unplanned bunt attempt to King Lear's descent into madness.

"You're her favorite, Teka," Lea said. "Go ask her to cancel. Maybe she just forgot."

"No, I'm not. She makes me pitch extra innings," Darah reminded them.

"Exactly." Avery nudged her. "She believes in you. Our star pitcher in the making."

When all the girls turned toward her with the same wide-eyed plea, Darah knew there was no getting out of it. She sighed dramatically, rolled her shoulders, and jogged away.

"Got a minute, Coach?"

"You're almost out of minutes, Teka," Coach said, not glancing up. "I see you all scheming like a coven of Lady Macbeths."

Darah laughed despite herself. "We were just wondering if— hypothetically—you might consider cancelling the practice right before Homecoming."

Coach Myers finally lifted her head, but she didn't look at Darah, her gaze fixed toward the bleachers. "What are y'all gawking at?"

Darah turned. The whispers were already rippling across the field. Her teammates had stopped pretending to stretch. One girl was half-standing on the bench. Avery had her phone out.

By the fence, five boys stood shoulder to shoulder, each holding a hand-painted sign.

The first read: Darah in bold purple script.

The second: **Please**

Then: **Pretty Please**

Then: **Come to Homecoming**

And the last walked it off with: **With Me?**

A crooked heart was doodled beneath the letters, like someone had added it last minute. The whole thing was all over the place, and yet, it was a bonafide homerun.

Shrieks and giggles exploded around her. Girls clutched each other's arms, squealed her name. "OMG, Darah."

From the far edge of the bleachers, Jeremy emerged like he'd been waiting for the exact beat in the song. His hoodie sleeves were pushed to his elbows, and the moment seemed to bend around him, as if the world knew who the main character in the story was.

When he smiled at her, her own world cracked wide open. Time slowed in step with that relaxed swagger, the opening bars of the melody threading through her bones. From the beginning, it had never been a fair fight.

"Darah," Coach said. "Is this a Teka-approved emergency or a literary allusion I haven't deciphered yet?"

"I..." Darah blinked at the field, the signs.

Coach gave her a rare smile. "I think you should take five."

Darah's legs moved before her brain gave permission. She crossed the field, heart pounding so loud it muffled the world.

Jeremy met her at the edge of the grass, smile cocky and unsure all at once, as if he thought she could actually say no. It was the cutest thing ever.

"Hey, beautiful," he said, like it was nothing. Like it was everything. "Was watching your practice. You're pretty good."

Darah tried to speak. Failed.

He rubbed the back of his neck. "Still weird seeing Coach Myers in cleats. I keep waiting for her to quote Othello."

Darah laughed, breathless, dazed. Behind her, her teammates had lost it—screaming across the field—but she didn't dare look back. If she did, the spell might break.

Jeremy gestured toward the boys still holding the signs behind them. A few of them were from JV basketball, probably willing to make a scene for the sake of a big ask.

"So, what time should I pick you up?"

Her throat dried up. "Are you serious?" she managed to get out.

"I am." He leaned in, voice low and meant only for her. "If you haven't noticed, I really like you a lot, Darah Teka."

Her heart thudded in her ears. Was she dreaming? Was this fine boy really confessing feelings for her?

"I..." It wasn't a joke. It wasn't a line. That same quiet intensity she'd seen in his eyes at the café was back, laid bare for everyone to see. "Are you asking me to Homecoming?"

"I'm asking for more than that," he said, eyes unwavering. "But we can start there."

The words hit like waves crashing against a little shell until it cracked open. This was the same boy who seemed so out of reach, his world too far away from hers. Now he sent texts that made her heart flutter and her brain scatter, even though she knew that liking someone like him couldn't possibly end in anything but heartache. And yet, here he was, proving her wrong. Proving she was worth it.

"You still don't believe me," Jeremy said, his smile half-laugh, half-challenge.

"I just can't believe you're actually serious," she admitted.

"I've never been more."

He reached for her hand and she didn't pull away. It was too late to run. The old voice—the one that told her to stay safe, stay small—was drowning beneath the waves. This was nice, the way the world tilted when he looked at her.

Above them, birds wheeled across the lavender sky streaked with the promise of rain. They flew with ease, like they'd never doubted they were made to fly. Maybe that could be her, if she only gave in and let life carry her wherever it willed.

"Okay," she whispered.

"Okay?"

She nodded, heart in her throat. "Pick me up at six."

That smile again—boyish, awestruck, like she'd just handed him a petal of the sun. And then, slowly, he leaned down.

Her entire face went up in flames. "What are you doing?"

"I think you know."

Before she could think her way out of it, before she could hide behind another clever line or sarcastic net, she stepped forward and kissed him first, softly, slowly, every doubt falling away, like a bird falling from the sky. A bird choosing the fall.

The field behind them erupted, teammates shrieking. But she didn't break the moment. All she could feel was his mouth on hers, the warmth of his hand, the dizzy thrill of being wanted. Not just noticed, but needed.

She clung to him as the kiss deepened. Not fast. Not frantic. Just... right. Like the last piece of her puzzle falling into place. A piece that was always meant to be there.

When they finally pulled apart, Jeremy was looking at her as if she was a riddle he didn't know how to solve. "So," he said, "you'll be my girlfriend?"

Darah tilted her head. "I don't remember you asking me."

He arched a brow. "Do I need a sign for that too?"

She laughed—really laughed—until her cheeks ached.

They walked off the field together, her hand in his.

No, she wasn't dreaming. But what if she was making a mistake? Maybe it would all fall apart. Maybe the next chapter would hurt more than she was ready for.

She didn't care. She was already in love with him. After a lifetime of writing stories about girls who didn't believe they could be chosen, maybe it was time she started writing something new.

A story about letting go, where the heroine didn't hide behind masks and metaphors. A story where the girl got the boy, the dance, and her kiss in the rain. Where the birds didn't disappear, and the stars didn't burn back to the sky.

A story about love.

A story about belonging.

41

When the waiter placed the towering stack of pancakes in front of Junior, Bart couldn't help laughing.

"You're really gonna eat all that?" Abe asked.

"Bet," Junior replied. "Bart's paying."

They'd snagged their dad's favorite table, early enough to beat the Tuesday Special crowd. Behind Abe's shoulder, the family inscription on the wall caught Bart's eye, a carved reminder of what they'd built together.

As they ate, they talked about the past, their parents. Bart reached into his jacket and placed the small red velvet box on the table.

Junior's mouth dropped open. "That what I think it is?"

"Was that why you went to see her mom?" Abe asked.

Bart nodded. Last week in Corpus, Ms. Yelena had given him her blessing before he left her house that night. She'd promised to visit them in Houston next week.

Bart flipped open the box. Rose-gold, a little stunning diamond. He'd designed it himself and picked it up this morning.

Junior whistled. 'That must have cost a pretty penny."

"She's worth more than that," Bart said.

Abe smirked. "Can't believe you lasted this long with her living in your house."

"I wasn't planning to go see her mom with her, but I'm glad I did. It made everything clearer. And harder."

When he'd gone back to the hotel after leaving Ms. Yelena's house, he'd knocked on Geri's room door and she'd opened at once. He could tell she'd been crying, but she'd simply thrown her arms around him and kissed him like she never wanted to let go of him again.

Since then, things had been going better between them. They had talked every night and she was letting him in more and more. He didn't think it was wise to wait too long and give life a chance to spoil what they had going on.

"I want to propose soon," Bart said.

Abe shook his head. "She's not ready, bro."

Junior closed the ring box. "Don't listen to him. He's still traumatized from his first proposal to Phoebe."

Bart chuckled. "I mean, she did say no in front of the whole fellowship."

Abe groaned. "I told y'all she hated big gestures."

"But she said yes later." Junior smiled. "Just do whatever you feel. Stick it out. If it's real—"

"It is."

"Dad would be so proud of you," Abe said.

That hit Bart harder than expected. He glanced around the café, the ghost of their father's laugh echoing in the quiet corners.

He could picture their parents right here, Mom cutting her pancakes, Dad telling stories with that dramatic African flair. Had he spent enough time with them? Had he said thank you enough?

"Mom and Dad always liked Geri," Abe added. "They knew."

"Everybody knew she liked you," Junior said, grinning. "You were just blind."

Bart shook his head, blinking moisture from his eyes. He pocketed the ring again, heavier than before, but somehow it steadied him and sealed what he knew he had to do.

Abe tapped the table. "First things first, how are you feeling about today?"

Junior stopped mid-chew. "Today?"

Bart sighed. "I'm meeting Ms. Jen after this." After talking with Geri again, he had finally called Ms. Jen. "She said she'd meet me wherever I had time, so I told her to come to the Cane Island site."

Junior frowned. "That's awkward. Abe, let me tag along with you."

"I need you there, bro," Bart said. "She'll understand if I said I had to dip."

"That's why you played me into coming with you?" Junior quipped.

"You'll hang with Emilio and the crew. We won't talk long." Bart sipped his coffee.

"I still think you should've picked somewhere private," Abe said.

"That would be more awkward. What would we even talk about? She had years to reach out. She didn't."

"Would you have listened back then?" Abe asked. "You were angry, and you had every right. But she's here now. That has to count for something."

Junior leaned back. "If I ever saw Big Eddie again, I'd have no words."

"You'd throw hands," Bart said.

"Exactly."

"It's not the same," Abe insisted. "Ms. Jen's not trying to defend what happened. She's just asking to be heard."

Bart clenched his jaw. "She's a stranger."

"She's the woman who carried you for nine months," Abe said softly. "You don't owe her your trust, but you do owe her something. And you owe yourself the truth. That's how you move on."

Bart almost rolled his eyes. "I already agreed to meet with her."

"Yeah, I'm just asking you to try," Abe said. "Don't be unkind to her."

Bart sat in silence. Wasn't he entitled to be unkind? But he knew what Abe was saying. Looking at his brothers, how could he not? Junior's mother was murdered by his own father. Abe never knew his mother. And yet, right now, against all the odds, Bart had someone—a completely normal and seemingly kind woman—who wanted to be in his life, no strings attached, and he was angry about it?

"You always tell people to face their past," Abe said. "Maybe it's your turn."

Bart stared at the table. "We'll see what happens."

Abe's phone buzzed. He checked it with the urgency of a man waiting on news.

"Phoebe?" Bart asked. The baby's due date was in less than two weeks.

"No. Work. I gotta go." Abe stood, slinging his lanyard around his neck.

They all got up to leave and Junior started laughing. "I can't believe this dude here is actually about to join you in the Happy Married Fools Club."

Abe shrugged. "Emphasis on 'happy.'"

"More like sorry."

Abe drank the last of his coffee. "Three things to say to your woman for a happy life: I'm sorry dear, you're right dear, and I love you dear."

Bart snorted. "Catchy. And tragic."

"Yeah, sounds like bondage," Junior said. "I'll pass on marriage."

"We'll see," Abe said. "I know a girl you'll—"

Junior didn't let him finish and rushed out of the restaurant. After saying goodbye to Abe, Bart and Junior drove to the job site in Cane Island. Junior wouldn't stop clowning Bart about finally falling for Geri, which made Bart laugh.

"I'm glad you're back," Bart said, as they got on the freeway. "You good, though? We weren't expecting you until after the baby was born."

Junior leaned back in the passenger seat. "Just wanted to see y'all. Sorry I missed the shower. And the anniversary."

The silence lingered. Four years since the accident. Four years of grief and rebuilding.

"But I came right on time," Junior said. "I mean you're about to propose. Smiling back there like Geri gave you winning lottery numbers."

Bart didn't bother hiding his grin. "She did, bro."

Junior's eyes narrowed. "You've changed, man. What happened to you while I was away? This can't just be a Geri thing. I mean, you're just... different."

In the silence, the sunlit road stretched ahead. Junior wasn't wrong. There was something deeper behind the ease in his chest. He'd felt it since Sunday morning in Corpus.

"I don't know how to say it without sounding corny," Bart admitted. "But... I prayed." How could he explain what had happened to him?

Junior stared at him with raised brows, waiting for more.

"I prayed. Like for real. The kind of prayer Mom and Dad always wanted us to pray."

Junior leaned back in the seat. He didn't speak, didn't tease.

"I asked God to help me figure everything out," Bart continued. "And then, I don't know. Something changed. I just started feeling different about many different things."

Junior nodded slowly like he understood the weight of it. "So, you... became a real Christian?"

Bart exhaled, the words uncomfortable in his mouth. "I guess I did, bro."

Junior's face was blank. "Wow, that's what's up, B."

Bart kept his eyes on the road, but Junior said nothing more.

After a long minute of silence, Bart spoke again. "Do you ever think of y'know..." Why was this coming out so wrong?

"Bruh," Junior said, giving him a low-lidded stare. "You need to get your weight up first. You just barely made it and you're trying to pull me in too?"

Bart barked a laugh as they pulled into the parking lot of the shopping center site. Emilio was waiting near the curb with his trademark grin.

"Jefe," Emilio called out, handing each of them a hard hat. "Welcome to your kingdom."

Junior saluted him. "I see the empire's growing."

"Yeah, this shopping complex should be done by year's end," Emilio said, as they walked toward some of the workers on a scaffold tower near the entrance.

Bart studied the rising beams and fresh brickwork. "It's coming together."

Emilio pointed at the parking lot. "You expecting someone, jefe?"

Bart turned, and his whole body went still. A white sedan was parked beside his truck. Ms. Jen stepped out, a beige shawl wrapped around her shoulders like a shield. She paused at the edge of the lot, eyes scanning the site as if unsure she belonged in this picture.

"Ayayay... la belleza," Emilio crooned. "Who's that?"

Bart shot Emilio a glare, and Emilio shrugged.

Junior slapped Bart's shoulder. "We'll leave you to it, B. Good luck."

Bart handed Emilio his hard hat and started toward her, each step slower than the last. He wasn't sure what he was feeling—nerves, guilt, confusion—but the bitterness wasn't there anymore. It was as if he'd left most of his pain behind in Corpus.

"Morning," Bart said, trying to sound as casual as possible.

"Good morning." Her voice came out shaky, and she cleared her throat.

"Hope the traffic wasn't rough," he said, feeling bad for making her drive all the way through Katy traffic to meet him.

"I would've driven anywhere," she said, without meeting his eyes. "I was so happy when you texted me."

He didn't know what to do with that, so he gestured toward the pavement. "Want to sit for a second?" he asked, hoping she would refuse.

She followed him, clutching her shawl. Once seated, she folded her hands in her lap like a schoolgirl bracing for detention.

She didn't look at him, so he looked at her. She looked the

same as she always had—calm, elegant, warm. It was strange how she hadn't changed, but he had. Maybe that was why the anger didn't come like it had that night. He didn't want to hold on to his rage anymore.

"How old are you?" he asked. If she'd been friends with Mom, she was probably in her late fifties, but she didn't look her age.

"Forty-eight. In March."

He did the math. "You were sixteen."

She nodded. "Peter didn't know. Not at first. I lied about my age. He found out, and he left. I never got a chance to tell him."

Bart didn't need to hear the rest to imagine the frightened teenager, abandoned by a man who should have known better. A girl too young to be a mother. Still, she had been his mother. She hadn't ended the pregnancy. She'd chosen to carry him.

"Why didn't you just—" He turned to find her eyes on him. How many times had she sat there gazing at him like this? All this time, she'd had access to him and he had no idea who she was.

"I couldn't," she said, as if reading his thoughts. "I was young, and my parents..." Her eyes teared up and she looked away. "I just couldn't. I didn't want to. My parents were well-respected, so I was sent away to live with my aunt. Here in Houston, I had you here. Then I signed the adoption papers, and went back home. Tried to forget."

Forget him. She'd probably returned to her normal life and finished high school and college. Did she ever remarry? Did she have other children? How did she know where he was?

She spoke again before he could bring himself to ask. "But I came back," she whispered. "Because I couldn't forget."

They sat in silence, the air between them heavy with all the years lost.

"I was very angry," Bart said at last. "But I asked God to help me. And somehow, He did."

Ms. Jen's lips parted as if to say something, but no words came.

"I'm not saying I'm okay with all this," he went on. "But I know I don't want to be bitter anymore."

Her eyes filled. "I know I can't take back the years." Her hand reached out, and hovered in the air like a question. "But if you ever find it in your heart to want to know me... I'm here."

He didn't answer right away. He didn't know where all of this would lead. But he wasn't the same man who'd run away from her that night, so he just had to take it step by step.

"One day at a time," he said, quoting a song his dad used to sing.

She wiped the corner of her eye. And like that, the ache in his chest felt a little less sharp.

He turned his gaze toward the road, suddenly reminded of a friend in college who'd resented his own mother for having him too young. Because she'd never been a mother at all, just a string of boyfriends and broken promises. But what could a sixteen-year-old really know about motherhood? Where would he be now if Ms. Jen hadn't chosen adoption?

"Did my mom and dad know?" Bart asked.

Her voice wobbled. "I tried to keep track of you over the years, so when Pa Teka came looking for your birth parents, I wasn't hard to find, especially since I was already living in Houston. He invited me to their Bible study, and I just kept going. Ester—your mother—was so warm, so kind. She reminded me of a Sunday school teacher I had when I was a girl."

Bart turned to find her eyes glassy, her mouth curved in a smile too full of memories to contain.

"They just welcomed me in, like I'd always belonged. You

were already in college by then. And when I saw your picture, I couldn't believe it."

There was no pity in her face, no pleading. Just a soft openness, like she was willing to take whatever he gave her, whether it was silence or fire.

"I know you probably have a hundred questions," she said. "And I'll answer all of them."

He swallowed the knot in his throat. He hadn't ever imagined his birth mother being this nice. Her gentleness and love spilled out of her.

His boots scraped lightly against the stone beneath the bench. He tried to smile at her and failed. But it didn't matter. The pressure to untangle everything had somehow eased. He didn't need all the answers before they could start moving forward.

She flashed the warmest smile. "If it's okay, I would just like to say..."

He met her eyes. "Just say whatever you want to say. It'll take some time for any of this to make sense, but you don't have to hold back around me."

She nodded, as if understanding the depth of his request. "I just wanted to say that I'm just so proud of you, Bart," she said softly, her gaze drifting past him toward the hum of construction. "It suits you, this life you've built. You're doing what you were made to do."

He raised a brow, surprised by how certain she sounded. But as strange as it was, she'd known him longer than he'd realized. His parents' hospitable nature—which he'd found frustrating at times—had made it possible for his birth mother to watch him grow up. She had been in his life for years, baking casseroles during hard weeks, praying quietly in corners of rooms, watching his story unfold from a distance.

Just like Geri.

"About Geri and Joaquin," he began.

"I love them," she said. "Geri's my girl."

"That makes two of us."

She fiddled with the sleeve of her shirt. "She's always been the one for you."

He didn't argue. He didn't need to. Her gaze lingered on him, soft and maternal, in a way that cut right through his defenses.

"Ms. Jen—" Suddenly, it seemed so wrong calling her that.

"It's okay. I don't expect you to call me anything else. I'm just here, whatever you need me to be. I'm just grateful for a second chance."

Bart stared at the sky. "I appreciate you saying that."

"But back to Geri, you should give her time."

"I plan to," he said, grateful for the shift in tone.

"She loves you. She's always loved you. Even when you didn't remember her or notice her. Even when she tried not to." Her voice turned wistful. "You were always it for her."

He finally looked at her, but before he could respond, a whistle echoed from the site behind him.

Ms. Jen stood, smoothing the shawl over her shoulders. "I'll let you get back to it."

Bart rose with her, but still couldn't find the words.

"Hopefully I'll see you soon," she said, voice soft, not demanding.

Phoebe's due date was near, but he knew she wasn't just talking about the baby.

He nodded. "We'll figure it out." And he meant it.

Smiling, she turned, slowly walking back toward her car. The sunlight caught her hair, and the breeze nearly blew off her shawl.

Bart stood on the pavement, rooted in place, watching the

woman who gave him life—the mother he'd never asked for or looked for—walk back into his life with grace, expecting nothing in return.

He hadn't gone searching for her, but somehow, she'd still found her way back. He couldn't begin to imagine what came next, but not knowing didn't feel like something to fear.

As Ms. Jen reached her car, his phone buzzed. A message from his half-sister, Hope: We need to talk.

He looked up as Ms. Jen turned and lifted her hand in a final wave.

Bart raised his in answer. "Goodbye, M—"

He smiled and waved back.

It would take time. But for now, this was enough.

42

"So you're in love with Bart, right?" Phoebe asked, bouncing on an exercise ball, her eyes sparkling with that same mischievous glint Joaquin had when he was about to cause trouble. "And don't act like you don't know that man is crazy about you."

Geri simply shook her head in amazement, watching her son circle Phoebe like it was a game. "As if love solves everything."

Phoebe laughed. "It can. First Corinthians, remember?"

"Please don't start with the scriptures."

"You love him, though, don't you?"

Joaquin tumbled across Phoebe's legs. Geri dropped the spoon into the bowl of oatmeal she'd already reheated twice. "Joaquin, please come and finish your breakfast."

With a mouthful of oatmeal and a cheeky grin, he climbed onto the couch and sidled closer to Phoebe.

"Don't you dare," Geri warned, glaring.

Phoebe scooted back with a laugh. "He's excited to meet his cousin. But J, you gotta wait. She's still getting ready to come out and play."

Geri arched a brow. "Y'all finally picked a name?"

"We did," Phoebe beamed, patting her belly. "You'll find out soon. I just hope she gets a little of his energy. Don't want her too fragile or dainty."

"There's nothing wrong with dainty. She's your little girl." Geri had always thought of Phoebe as delicate and soft-spoken, but there was a core of steel beneath. Maybe that's what Abe had seen.

"I want her to be like Darah," Phoebe mused. "Sturdy. Decisive. Not like me. My parents treated me like an egg." Her voice drifted. "Sometimes I wonder if that's why I couldn't—"

Geri stilled, watching her fall into a silence too heavy for words. Two miscarriages. Years of trying.

"When I lost them, I thought maybe I wasn't ready. That's why they didn't stay. But then I realized that all the pain prepared us for her. All the waiting, it shaped us."

Phoebe's hands curved protectively over her belly. In days, those hands would cradle a promise fulfilled.

"Nothing about our story is a mistake," Phoebe continued. "Our babies are in heaven. And one day I'll hold them. But this journey, it's made me stronger. Abe too. And now, I'm starting to understand what it means when God says He gives beauty for ashes. This—girl is our beauty."

The raw hope in Phoebe's voice pricked Geri's chest. She needed more of that truth in her life, to believe for herself what she'd seen in other people's lives: how the most beautiful flowers could bloom in the toughest places. That her pain could be remade into something good.

Phoebe touched her hand. "Even though I hate what you went through, Geri, I see you now. You're strong, resilient, and you're the perfect mom for this warrior of a boy."

Right on cue, Joaquin fell off the couch like an exclamation mark to her words. He popped up grinning. Both women burst into laughter.

"Don't make me cry," Geri said, swiping at her face.

"I'm already crying for both of us," Phoebe murmured. "Bart's different now, Geri. He's not the man you left four years ago."

Of course he wasn't. The Bart she once knew ran from responsibility like it burned. But the man who took her to Corpus was a man who stood in the fire and stayed.

"He's ready to be Geraldine Pena's man," Phoebe said. "I'd bet anything he's about to propose." Geri tried to keep her face straight, but Phoebe must have seen through her as she raised a brow. "Wait, did he? Y'all came back from Corpus looking really chummy."

Heat rushed her face. "Yeah, he kind of did. I said no."

Phoebe winced, then framed Geri with a patient smile. "It's not no forever, though. Just not yet?"

Her stomach clenched. "I don't know. I can't get married again. It was a horrible time." She hated the way the words tasted. Words that were once her shield. Now they felt more like a prison.

"I get that." Phoebe's voice softened. "When the guy I thought I'd marry betrayed me, I swore off love too. I almost let Abe go."

Geri smirked. "For like a day."

Phoebe giggled. "It felt longer. But I was scared. If someone I trusted that much could betray me, why wouldn't Abe?"

"He wouldn't."

"Exactly. Because you truly know him. And you know Bart

too. You know they're not blood brothers, but the legacy of Yonas and Ester Teka lives in both of them. They have their faults, but they're good men, honest, loyal, the kind who love hard. If you'd let him, Bart could be a very good man to you."

Geri stood abruptly, nearly dropping the cold oatmeal onto Bart's white carpet. "I need to warm this again." She hurried to the kitchen.

"Don't bother, Sis," Phoebe called after her with a laugh. "He's clearly over it."

Geri set the bowl in the sink. Outside the window, the pristine backyard blurred behind the glass. Bartimeus Teka was a walking contradiction, a man both rough and tender, a man who shouldn't know how to love but still loved in spite of it. He was supposed to talk to Ms. Jen today, and she couldn't help wondering how it went, but she'd decided to wait until he came back home.

She felt a small tug at her leg. Joaquin was looking up at her with that look—which usually meant he wanted Goldfish and fruit snacks.

"You ready to eat now?"

He shook his head and pointed behind him.

Geri turned toward the living room. "Phoebe?"

"Yeah?" Phoebe's voice sounded breathless. She stood hunched over the exercise ball. The once-pristine carpet was wet beneath her feet.

"I think," Phoebe gasped, clutching her belly. "She's coming."

Geri nearly tripped over Joaquin in her rush. "Sit down first. L-let me call—"

"Abe." Phoebe lowered herself to the couch. "Call Abe. Ms. Jen. And—" She winced, folding in on herself.

"Joaquin, sit here," Geri said, putting him on the sofa beside Phoebe. "Don't move, okay?"

He snuggled close to Phoebe. "We're fine," Phoebe said.

Her own phone was in the bedroom, so Geri yanked cushions aside until she found Phoebe's phone wedged between them. Her hands fumbled as she hit "1"—Abe's speed dial.

He picked up on the first ring. "Babe, you okay?"

"Phoebe's water broke," Geri said. "Where are you?"

A sharp clang in the background. "I'm on my way. Let me talk to her."

She tapped the speaker and held the phone out.

"Sweetheart, are you okay? I'm calling Ms. Jen now."

Phoebe groaned, her face twisting. "I don't think I can wait."

Joaquin whimpered and Geri pulled him into her arms. "Should we go now?"

"I'm leaving Fulshear," Abe said. "Might take thirty—"

"We don't have thirty." Geri steadied her breath. "I'll take her. Phoebe, should we go now?"

"Yes, please. I think this is the real thing."

"Abe, just meet us there. You're closer to the hospital than to us anyway. Hold up." The only car in the garage was her old Chevy that Bart had fixed. "I'll check the car. Joaquin, stay with Aunty. Abe, talk to her. Keep her calm."

She bolted to the garage. The car was unlocked. A booster seat was already strapped in the back. But no keys.

She ran back in. "Where are the keys?"

"Upstairs," Phoebe gasped. "Abe?"

"Bart's room. Check his side drawers," Abe said. "You sure about this, Geri?"

"We don't have a choice. Start heading over there."

Geri darted up the stairs two at a time. She froze as soon as she touched the doorknob. She'd never been in his room before. She shook her head. She didn't have time for this. She pushed open the door. Bart's room was surprisingly simple. The only major furniture was a king-sized bed flanked by two dressers. But then there was the skylight right above the bed.

Everything smelled like him—clean, woodsy, safe. She opened the top drawer, filled with random stuff, a pocket Bible that looked new. The next drawer held another surprise. A big bag of watermelon gummies and a second bag of lollipops.

For a second, she couldn't look away. Again, what was with the watermelon? It was silly to keep acting as if his choice of flavors had nothing to do with her.

"Did you find it?" Phoebe's muffled yell came from downstairs.

A key was in the next drawer, a single key on her same old keychain, alone by itself. Swiping her cheeks, Geri snatched the key and raced downstairs. She could process all this later.

It took only minutes to get Phoebe ready to leave. Abe was already on the highway by the time both Phoebe and Joaquin were strapped in. With Phoebe's hospital bag slung over one shoulder, Geri grabbed Joaquin's diaper bag, shut off the lights, and hurried into the garage.

She said a prayer under her breath and pressed the garage opener. Joaquin sat quietly in the backseat, his eyes wide at Phoebe as she gripped her belly and breathed through the pain.

"Aunty is gonna be okay," she whispered to him. As the door creaked upward, Geri started the engine. The Chevy roared to life like a different creature—fierce, rumbling, tuned to run. She almost cried at the sound.

"Geri," Abe's voice came through the speaker. Phoebe's phone chimed—low battery. He had stayed on the phone the whole time.

"Leaving now," she said, easing the car out of the garage.

She parked on the driveway, hopped out to manually close the garage, and came back outside through the front door. Once she locked the front door behind her, she heard the doors close. Three men, walking away from a black SUV across the street. Muscular, all dressed in black, dark sunglasses hiding their eyes. Strangers. They could have been anyone, but the way they moved toward the Teka house—cautious, like they expected her to run—made blood rise in her throat.

Geri bolted into the driver's seat and slammed the door. Her hand flew to the lock and clicked. She checked her rearview mirror. The men were running now.

"Oh God—" She threw the car into reverse, tires screeching, backing up over the sidewalk. The men scrambled out of her path.

"Sorry," she yelped as Phoebe and Joaquin lurched forward. She shifted to drive and floored it, wheels screaming as they peeled away. "Hang on!"

"Easy, Geri, you don't have to—" Phoebe's voice caught mid-sentence, probably swallowed by a contraction.

Geri's eyes bounced between the road and the mirror. The black SUV roared into the street behind them.

"Abe, are you still there?" she asked, her voice high with adrenaline.

"I'm here," Abe said. Phoebe's phone dinged again—low battery. "Ms. Jen's on her way. Drive safe."

She wanted to laugh. There was nothing safe about this. But she couldn't tell Abe. Her foot pressed harder on the gas. The other car surged after them. She couldn't let them catch up. Not with Joaquin in the backseat. Not with Phoebe in labor. If they caught up—if anything happened to her—at least the two of them had to make it. She would die before letting them take Joaquin and Phoebe.

"I'll call you back," she said, already shifting focus. "Phoebe, my phone's in Joaquin's bag. Can you grab it?"

"What's going on?" Abe's voice had sharpened.

"I..." Phoebe grunted, digging in the diaper bag. "Forgot to charge this one. Found hers."

Geri scanned the road, heart racing. She just had to get to the hospital. A shortcut came to mind. Maybe it would buy them time. Maybe it wouldn't. She didn't care. She'd try anything.

"Phoebe—" The call dropped.

Phoebe looked at the screen. "Battery died."

Geri blew out a breath. "Call Bart. He's number one in my contacts."

Phoebe chuckled. "Bart's your number one?"

"Not now, Phoebe."

"Calling," she said. Then, with a touch of disbelief: "He is number one."

The phone rang once on speaker.

"Hey," came Bart's voice.

Just hearing him made her want to break down in tears. "Bart—" She couldn't get the words out.

"We're having a baby!" Phoebe announced, winded but cheerful. "Heading to the hospital now."

"Whoa," he cried. "Is Joaquin with y'all?"

"Yep. Geri's driving like a speed demon."

"Geri, be careful," Bart said, suddenly sharp. She could hear the shift in him—protective, alert.

There was no more hiding. "She's here, Bart. They found me," she blurted out, voice shaking. "Three men just showed up at your house."

A hard curse. "I was already heading home. Where are you now?"

"Westpark and Beltway," she said, swerving lanes. "Trying to lose them."

Geri met Phoebe's eyes in the mirror. Her smile had vanished. She clutched her belly now with both hands.

"Does Abe know?" he asked.

"He's headed to the hospital."

Wind tore through the background of Bart's call. "We're on our way. Geri—"

"I love you too," she cut in. If it was the last time she heard his voice, she needed him to know. "I'm sorry for saying No when you tried to—"

"Geri, I won't let anything happen to both of you. Now focus. Drive like you want the police to notice you. Flash your lights if you see any. Blow past a red light if you have to."

She hadn't thought of getting help from the cops. But she couldn't slow down. "Copy that." She had to get Phoebe to the hospital.

Once Bart hung up, Phoebe held up the phone. "What do you mean Asabe's here?"

Her grip tightened on the wheel until her fingers hurt. She couldn't answer, not with the SUV shifting lanes behind them, matching every move she made like a shadow. She took the tollway ramp fast, catching the EZ Tag sensor overhead. The light blinked green. Bart truly had thought of everything, even registering her car under his account.

"We're taking a shortcut," she said. "Just hang tight."

"I'm calling 911," Phoebe said, turning her head to glance behind them. "It's Asabe, right? They're after us?" She didn't wait for a response. She tapped the screen with shaking fingers, muttering, "Come on, come on…"

"911, what's your emergency?"

Phoebe clutched her belly. "We're—" a wince stole her breath— "we're being followed by a suspicious car. My friend's driving. I'm in labor—please."

The dispatcher's voice crackled. "Ma'am, are you in a moving vehicle?"

"Yes. She's driving—we're in a red Chevy—there's a baby with us. They're following—please—" Phoebe buckled over.

"Are you okay?" Geri asked, trying to balance the wheel while reaching behind.

"Ma'am, what's your location?"

"Tollway—Beltway—" Phoebe's voice broke as another contraction hit.

"Units en route. Stay on the line—ma'am?"

The phone slipped to Phoebe's lap as her body clenched forward. Geri tried to balance the wheel while reaching for Phoebe. They had to get to the hospital faster.

Geri checked her rearview mirror again. The black SUV was still behind them. Three men dressed in black. They weren't here to ask questions. They were here to take Joaquin back.

"Breathe, Phoebe," she said, stepping on the gas, pushing well above the speed limit. "It's okay, baby," she added for Joaquin. He hadn't made a sound. His small face was frozen in silent terror, eyes wide, lips pressed tight, hands clinging to the edge of his car seat.

Her chest cracked open. No, not again. Not today. She'd built a new life for him, filled with laughter, bedtime prayers, pancakes for breakfast. A life with music and safety and healing. A life that didn't belong to Asabe anymore.

"They won't catch us," she said through her teeth. "Not today."

Geri swerved off the toll road onto the service lane. She made a tight U-turn under the bridge and shot back up the entrance ramp heading in the opposite direction.

She checked the rearview. The SUV was gone. She didn't slow down. The road blurred around her. No police sirens. No flashing lights. Just traffic, exits, and the thunder of her own fear.

Taking deep breaths, Phoebe clutched her side. Her other hand trembled as she reached for the fallen phone.

"Hang on, Phoebe."

"Right back at you," she said, with a small smile.

When they pulled up to the hospital's front pavilion, Abe sprinted toward them, wild-eyed, hair tousled, face tight in panic. He yanked open the car door and helped Phoebe out.

"I've got you," he said, breathless. "Thanks, Geri."

"Abe—" Phoebe panted. "Geri—"

"Just go," Geri said. The baby was more important right now. "Go have our baby. I'll park the car and find Bart."

Phoebe hesitated, clearly torn. A nurse rushed toward them with a wheelchair. Abe and Phoebe disappeared through the sliding doors.

Geri peeled away and sped to the parking garage. She left the car half-cocked in a spot, grabbed Joaquin and the hospital bag, and sprinted toward the lobby. The more people there, the better.

The wide glass doors of the hospital entrance gleamed in the Texas sun. Inside, the fluorescent lights were harsh. The lobby stretched too long. Her boots echoed on the tile, every step pounding like a warning. For a second, she dared to believe they'd lost the SUV on the highway.

Joaquin clung to her like he knew what was happening. He felt heavier than usual, or maybe she was out of breath. She rushed toward the front desk. Her phone rang. Bart. She lifted the phone with trembling fingers. The glass doors behind her slid open.

Two of the men she'd seen earlier stepped into the hospital. They passed casually behind an elderly couple. One of them turned his head, and recognition lit his face. He made a beeline toward her.

Geri jerked away from the counter, her eyes darting around. There had been three men in the SUV, so where was the third man?

The nurse behind the counter looked up. "Can I help you, ma'am?"

Geri tried to whisper the words. "Please—call the police."

"Excuse me?"

"Now," she hissed. "They're here—please—"

A security guard stood at the other end of the lobby. He was looking in her direction, but was too far away to help her, and he probably didn't know what he was seeing. Maybe she could scream to get everyone's attention. But Joaquin was with her. What if they had guns and started shooting? She couldn't take that chance.

Geri bolted from the desk, gripping Joaquin as he whimpered in confusion. She turned the corner and crashed into a woman in a wheelchair. Joaquin nearly slipped from her hip.

"S—sorry," she gasped, barely registering the woman's shout behind her. She kept going, boots pounding the tile, heart in her throat. "Please, God, help me," she breathed, tears breaking loose. "Please."

The first man was right behind her. She raced down the corridor, past nurses, past stunned visitors who didn't know what to do, their eyes wide, necks craning, nobody moving fast enough to help.

"Geri!" Her name echoed across the corridor like a

thunderclap.

She knew that voice anywhere, but when she looked around, she couldn't see him. She ran in the direction she heard his voice, but the moment she stepped outside into the courtyard, someone blocked her path. The second man in black.

She stumbled back. Too late. A hand gripped her arm from behind. It was the first man who had chased her.

"Give us the boy," he said. "If you give him up, you live."

Geri's pulse screamed in her ears, but she clutched Joaquin tighter.

"No," she shouted.

Over her dead body. She was never letting him go.

4 3

As Bart approached the pavilion, a tall man in black cut across the hallway at a clipped pace. Bart ran after him, following the figure from outside the hospital, tracking him through the tall windows until the man disappeared around a corner.

Bart veered off the walkway, checking the building for a side entrance. "Junior," he said, turning around. His brother was gone.

He scanned the area, the parking lot, but Junior was nowhere. He ran around the corner until he came to another stretch of windows, and he saw her inside, Geri, running down the corridor with Joaquin in her arms—frantic, looking over her shoulder.

"Geri!" he shouted.

She stopped mid-step, head whipping toward the sound, searching. But she didn't seem to see him from inside.

Bart bolted along the sidewalk, looking for another way in. Just ahead, there was a side door. He shoved through, bypassing the front desk. Nurses and visitors turned at the rush of movement, but he didn't stop. When he reached the hallway where he'd seen her, it was empty.

"Geri," he called again, louder now.

A muffled voice called his name. He pivoted and ran down the adjacent hallway, through the automatic doors and emerged outside in a small veranda between two hospital wings. Ahead, halfway across the courtyard, two men in black were hustling Geri and Joaquin toward the back parking lot.

Before Bart could close the distance between them, the man holding Geri turned, drew a gun and pressed it against her ribs.

"Don't move," the man barked. "Let us walk or she dies."

Bart skidded to a stop, hands raised halfway, heart thundering. He took in the angles, the grip, the space between them. Geri's eyes were wide with panic, but she wasn't crying. She was locked in on Joaquin, talking softly to him.

Bart's own weapon—tucked at his lower back—burned against his spine. He could reach for it. He might even get a shot off. But not before the man fired point-blank at Geri.

His fingers twitched. "Okay, we'll do it your way," he said to the man.

Geri finally met his eyes. "Please," she said, voice cracking. "Bart, just let us go."

She was trying to save them both. But he couldn't. Every instinct screamed at him not to reach for his gun. One wrong move could snatch her away from him, forever.

Footsteps. From the far side of the courtyard, a child's voice chirped, "Mommy!" A little girl, no older than five, came bounding out from the side building with a juice box in hand. Her mother stepped out a second later, eyes widening in horror.

"Bailey! Come back here—"

The second man lunged, grabbed the child and spun her to his chest, one thick arm around her throat. "Don't scream," he growled to the mother. "Unless you want to see her neck snap."

"No," the woman gasped, frozen in place, hands over her mouth.

Bart's stomach turned to fire. He shifted his weight, testing his angle, but there was no way to draw without someone getting shot. Geri, Joaquin, the little girl—they were all too exposed.

The man with the gun tightened his grip on Geri. "Don't be a hero."

Bart glanced at Geri, her eyes silently pleading with him— don't do it. Don't make this worse. He swallowed hard, and then he saw him.

Junior. Tucked around the corner of the building, crouched low, eyes locked on the man holding the child.

Bart gave the faintest shake of his head, but Junior was already moving. Too quick for even Bart to register. Junior exploded from the side in a full-body tackle, slamming into the second man with all his weight. With a scream, the girl tumbled free, rolling across the grass and into her mother's arms.

The first man flinched, his eyes flicking from Bart to Junior.

Now. Bart launched forward, closing the distance. The gun went up, but Bart barreled into him with a shoulder to the ribs, his eyes on the gun the entire time.

He grabbed the weapon and jerked it sideways, away from Geri, then slammed an elbow into the man's jaw. The gun flew out of the man's hand.

Geri twisted free and yanked Joaquin out of reach, shielding his head as she stumbled back.

The man swung at Bart, catching his jaw. But Bart was done hesitating. He drove him to the ground, fist connecting with bone and the man raised his hands to guard. Bart drew his pistol and slammed the gun into his head—again and again—until the man went limp beneath him.

Bart looked up. Geri was crouched behind a column, Joaquin tucked into her arms, shaking but safe. The little girl was crying into her mother's sweater. The woman hadn't moved an inch, probably still in shock.

Sirens wailed in the distance, getting closer. Bart staggered to his feet, chest heaving. The man beneath him was out cold, blood trickling from his temple where Bart had pistol-whipped him. Across the courtyard, Junior's knee was pressed into the back of the second man, who groaned beneath him.

"That's two," Junior spat. "But Geri said three showed up at the house."

Bart turned, searching. "Geri, where's the third man?"

Geri shook her head, eyes darting around. She held Joaquin tighter and slowly backed toward the outside wall, scanning the shadows. "I—I don't know. I didn't see him at all."

Bart's gaze swept the perimeter—pavement, windows, the parked vehicles in the lot near the fence line. There, a man half-concealed behind a van at the far end of the courtyard, away from the chaos, holding a gun, his eyes trained on Geri and Joaquin with the cold steadiness of someone sent to finish a job.

Bart jerked to his feet with his gun. He didn't have a clear shot. What if he missed? There was too much distance between them.

He didn't get the chance to pull the trigger. A single shot cracked the air.

The third man jerked backward, knees buckling. He dropped where he stood. Dead.

At the west edge of the courtyard—on the other side of the

dead man—stood two armed men, guns raised, sweeping the scene military style.

Behind them stood a tall woman. Asabe. Geri's mother-in-law. Her face was like carved stone: unreadable. She moved forward with unhurried purpose.

Bart scrambled to Geri, wrapping her in his arms. She sat there frozen, shielding Joaquin's face. It was amazing how the boy had stayed quiet through all of this.

"It's gonna be okay," Bart whispered.

Geri didn't respond. She simply stared at Asabe like she was in shock.

Bart turned his attention to the imposing figure. "What are you doing here?"

One of Asabe's guards stopped beside Junior, who was still subduing the second attacker. Once Junior released the man, the bodyguard stamped his boot into the man's head. Junior's eyes darted to Bart, as if he was trying to understand the situation.

Bart positioned himself between Asabe and Geri. He too was still trying to unravel what had just happened. Asabe had saved their lives, and that turned upside down everything he knew about the woman.

"There's no time," Asabe said, eyes flicking between the two of them. "We need to get our story straight. You can pin everything on me and my men. We'd already contacted the authorities. They were told to expect a security threat. I'll take all the responsibility."

Bart stared at her, stunned. "You knew?"

She shook her head. "Only too late."

Her attention turned to Geri, and her face broke like she'd been shot herself. 'Geraldine... you were right about... Hakeem's death. It wasn't your fault. It was mine."

Geri gasped as if struggling for air.

Asabe took a cautious step closer, stopping well out of reach. "Is Joaquin hurt?" she asked, scanning the boy still clinging to Geri's shoulder. "Are you?"

"Joaquin?" Geri muttered.

Asabe nodded. "That's his name, isn't it?"

Bart scoffed. Was this maternal concern or practiced diplomacy? He opened his mouth but closed it when Geri touched his arm, steadying herself and him.

Her voice was cold and clear. "Say what you need to say, but we're not going back."

Asabe's gentle expression didn't change. "I'm not asking you to come back. I know now that this is where he's safest. Where you're safest."

Geri didn't blink. "Why the change of heart?"

Asabe's voice trembled. "Because I forgot what it means to be a mother trying to protect her child. I have everything I ever wanted, and still... I lost my son." Her eyes lingered on Joaquin, just enough to betray the weight of what she'd once had. Then her gaze shifted, as if looking too long had cost her more than even she had thought.

"My Hakeem would be alive today if he'd had a mother like you." Her voice caught again on his name and she glanced at Bart. "And a father who would run in front of a gun like that." She rubbed her hands together as if she was cold. "I underestimated my enemies. I won't make that mistake again. They came after my precious grandson. I will return the favor."

She didn't need to say any more. There was a dead man on the ground, and the other two men were being held at gunpoint by Asabe's bodyguards. "Return the favor" meant blood.

Now freed up, Junior wandered over to Bart's side. "The cops

336

are gonna be here any minute."

"I'm surprised they took so long," Bart said, hearing the sirens scattered all around them. People were watching them from inside the buildings and the parking lot. He placed his gun on the grass away from him. Legal piece or not, he would get shot in a heartbeat if the cops saw him holding a gun.

Asabe spoke again, softer this time. "I won't ask for your forgiveness."

"I don't plan on giving it," Geri said.

Asabe's lips twitched, almost a smile. "Insolent as ever." Her tone shifted. "Until we meet again, Geraldine, I wish you well—"

"Police! Hands where we can see them!"

The courtyard exploded. Voices shouted from every direction. Uniformed officers poured in from the parking lot and from both wings of the hospital, guns drawn, barking commands. The clatter of boots on pavement, the strobe of red and blue lights electrified the air.

Asabe dropped to her knees. "I have diplomatic immunity. We're the ones who called you in."

One of her bodyguards placed his pistol on the ground and followed suit. "I shot the man," he called out. "I have diplomatic immunity."

The second guard knelt without a word.

It didn't matter. The cops weren't listening. Protocol took over.

Someone tackled Bart from behind, slamming him into the concrete and knocking the breath from his lungs. His face scraped the pavement as his arms were yanked behind his back. Cold metal bit into his wrists.

He grunted, trying to lift his head. Then he heard her.

"Please—he's my son! Let me hold him—please—"

Bart twisted his head in time to see an officer dragging Geri backward, prying her arms away from a screaming Joaquin. An officer carried him toward the hospital doors.

"No—" Bart thrashed against the cuffs. "Don't take her. She didn't do anything—"

Something hard struck the back of his neck, choking off his words. His skull rang. Pain splintered through him. The cold ground. The blinding lights. Boots rushing past. Radios barking orders. Geri's voice—ragged and broken—still calling for Joaquin.

He tried to rise again, but it felt like the world sat on his back. His cheek hit the ground, in his line of sight, the pistol he never fired. Blood warmed the inside of his mouth.

Everything blurred as Junior's face came into view. He was on his knees now, hands behind his head, an officer pinning him down. His eyes met Bart's, wide, breathless, but still calm. A flicker of relief in Junior's expression, almost a smile.

His wild little brother. Not so little anymore. Even now, the kid wasn't shaken. But Bart understood. Junior had always been cut from a different cloth than the rest of them.

He turned his head again, enough to glimpse the building past the chaos.

Geri was upright. A nurse was guiding her toward the entrance. Joaquin was cradled against her shoulder, still crying, but now in her arms.

They were together.

Even as the cuffs dug deeper and the noise swelled around him, Bart's chest loosened with that one image.

As the officers led him away, he craned his head to keep looking at her, hoping she'd look his way.

She didn't.

Still, he smiled. Even if he never saw her again, she was alive.

Joaquin was alive.

She was the most important person in the world to him, and he'd kept his promise to her.

And that was the best feeling in the world.

44

The next days passed in a blur of whispered prayers of gratitude and restless waiting. By all accounts, Phoebe's delivery went smoothly, an angelic little girl God sent into the world. But Bart and Junior remained in police custody. Everyone they knew tried to help get them released, but nothing moved until Eden's billionaire father got a senator involved.

After three days, Bart was finally coming home. Geri got the news while she was folding a pile of Joaquin's clothes—tiny socks, animal T-shirts, soft pajamas. Her hands moved on autopilot, but her mind spun in circles, wondering if Bart was okay, if he was already on his way home. What would she say when she saw him?

Yesterday, IB and Tonye had called, marveling at how Asabe had somehow turned from villain to savior. "This God of ours is beyond me," IB had burst into song.

Once the call ended, Geri lay down in bed and wept. These

past days, she'd mostly kept her thoughts to herself. Yes, God had finally answered the thousand breathless prayers she'd scattered into the dark. But Asabe showing up wasn't simply a miracle. It felt like something had been rewritten in the heavens. The same woman who'd made her feel powerless and small had shown up at the last minute to save her life.

"Diplomatic immunity," Asabe had told the officers, and it was no bluff. The woman had left the country without spending a single night in jail.

After Geri finished folding Joaquin's clothes, she left the bedroom for the kitchen, where Joaquin and Eli sat at the table coloring. Penguins, peacocks, pterodactyls, an explosion of wildlife in bright crayon chaos. Eli, ever precise, colored within the lines. Joaquin scribbled with the passion of a boy trying to outrun his feelings. Even when Geri gently ruffled his curls, he didn't look up.

In the living room, the TV was on. A local news anchor gestured beside grainy footage of the hospital courtyard. The bold headline read: Local Heroes Save Girl from Armed Attack.

The footage cycled through chaotic scenes of the aftermath—flashing lights, stretchers, a flurry of uniforms. Bart's face never appeared, but Geri remembered every one of his heroic movements like she was reliving the scene again. It was amazing how he'd jumped into all of that without a second thought. And he had paid the price. But thank God, now he was coming home. And she still had no idea what to say to him.

"Thank you" wouldn't come close. He had risked everything for her; shown her a kind of love she'd only read about and longed for but never expected to receive. She couldn't deny him any longer. She had to show him in turn that she was ready to move forward.

"I can't believe you guys were actually here," Darah said, curled up in the armchair with a bowl of popcorn. Her eyes stayed glued to the screen even though the footage had aired at least a dozen times. The Houston reporters were enamored with the story of two adopted brothers who took down a kidnapper in broad daylight.

Geri and Joaquin's names were never mentioned, but images of Bart and Junior in their teenage years flashed across the screen—grinning and full of mischief. The press spewed facts mixed with lies. One reporter even claimed that Junior was a member of the military.

Even Yonas Teka made an appearance, regal as ever in his old photos. More beloved in the greater Houston area than she'd realized.

It was a good story. A clean one. The press ate it up like a redemption arc from a Lifetime movie. Witnesses—including the mother of the rescued girl—had praised Bart and Junior as if they were the last real heroes in the world.

"My brothers are famous," Darah said, shaking her head like she still didn't believe it. "I'm telling you—these Tekas? Every time things quiet down, they strike again."

Geri laughed, her first real one in days. "And you're talking?"

"Please," Darah said, flipping her braids over her shoulder. "I'm the calm one in this house."

"No, I am," Eli called from the dining table.

"Yeah, right," Darah shot back. "Wait until—"

A car pulled into the driveway. Geri ran to the window.

It was Daniel's car. Bart stepped out of the passenger side, hands in his pockets, head slightly bowed, like he wasn't sure he deserved to be still standing on this earth.

Geri's body moved before her mind caught up. She rushed

to the front door and flung it open, her heart surging with a wordless dream. Of longing? Relief? A love she was ready to fully embrace now.

She stepped onto the porch as Daniel pulled away. Bart turned, mid-wave, caught sight of her and stopped cold. They stared at each other across the stretch of driveway, suddenly unsure of the script.

"Where's Junior?" Why that was the first thing out of her mouth, she had no idea.

"At the hospital," he replied. "Phoebe gets discharged in a couple of hours."

"What?" She'd completely lost track of time. "We need to start heading to the house to make sure—"

"We've got time," he said, looking her over like he was still making sure she was real. "Are you okay? A lot happened—"

"I'm okay," she said too fast. Right now, he was more important. He looked tired, bruised, stiff. But good. The kind of good that made her stomach jump.

She glanced back at the front door. No one was coming out. Darah was probably giving her space. Thank God for that. It had to be now, before things spiraled again.

"Come," she said, reaching for his hand.

He followed without hesitation, a quiet smile tugging at the corners of his mouth like he was amused—and moved—by this unexpected boldness. She led him through the gate to the backyard, her pulse thrumming as if it had a mind of its own.

Once they stepped into the quiet yard, he stopped. "Seriously, are you okay?"

She turned to him and her face cracked. The way he asked, so gently, like he knew she was unraveling, broke her wide open. Tears slipped out before she could stop them.

"What happened?" he asked again, urgent now.

"You happened," she said, her voice shaking. "I was trying everything not to get caught up in this, and you just kept being there. Being kind. Brave. And then I thought I was going to lose you."

He stepped closer and leaned his forehead against her temple. "Thank God we all made it out alive."

Her hands clutched his arm, knuckles tight. "Please don't ever do that again." The reckless way he threw himself in danger for them, why didn't he value his life like she valued his? "If I lost you, I don't know what I would have done." She hadn't slept a wink the first night he was in custody. Could barely eat. It felt like her soul had stayed suspended in fear.

He brushed away her tears, his callused palms warm against her skin. "I'm sorry you were scared. But if I had to, I'd do it all again. For you. For Joaquin."

Geri studied his face, fresh bruises and fading cuts. "You'd die for someone who refused to marry you."

His eyes softened. "I'll love you, no matter how long it takes."

Her eyes filled with tears. The ache had nowhere else to go. It was now or never.

"Then you should just marry me."

"Yeah, that's—" He blinked. "What?"

"I'm asking you to marry me," she said again, marveling at how normal it sounded in her own ears.

"Don't play me like this. You said you weren't—"

"Forget what I said. You asked me to marry you, and now I'm saying yes. A thousand times yes. I love you, Bart. And I want to spend the rest of my life loving you."

He stared at her for a moment, then a smile, slow and full, rose like the sunrise she'd waited for all night.

"I love you," he said, dropping to his knees. In a flash, a red velvet box appeared in his hand. "That's why you should marry me, Geraldine Peña." He opened the box. Inside sat the most delicate, beautiful—perfectly sized—ring she'd ever seen. "Will you?"

Her hands flew to her mouth. "Where did you get this?"

"Been carrying it for a while now."

He looked up at her, the shadows of the past eclipsed by the strange light in his eyes. This past week, a lot had changed about him. He was somehow more patient, more kind, slower to talk, more ready to listen.

"In Corpus, you said all that I needed to hear," he said.

She felt herself flinch. "Really? I said not nice things."

"You were hurting. I was willing to wait if you needed more time. If you still do, I'll wait."

Geri shook her head, her tears spilling freely now. "I don't need more time. I want you. Forever. Now, if you want, we can—"

He kissed her. A kiss that said I'm here. I'm yours. We survived.

"I'm not going anywhere, Geri. Let's take our time."

"But we can start now," she whispered back, flinging her arms around him. Her chest felt like it was on fire—in the best way. Every broken place was coming together again.

Bart pressed a kiss to her cheek. "Need my ring around your finger first."

"In a minute," she said, burying her face into his shoulder. After everything they'd been through, after three days of aching separation, she knew now—she never wanted to spend another day without him. If he hadn't proposed, she probably would have marched to some random store, bought two cheap rings, and asked him herself.

"What are you thinking about?" he murmured against her ear.

The thoughts came easily now, flowing like her tears. "All it took to get us to this point."

Bart pulled back to look her in the eye. "I had to lose two fathers to finally find you." He wrapped her tighter in his arms. "But without Mom and Dad, we would be strangers. And without my biological father, maybe we still would be."

If she hadn't been trapped in Port Harcourt, they wouldn't have reconnected the way they did. So many improbable things had to happen to bring them to this point.

"I know they'll be very happy," Bart said quietly. "Mom and Dad."

Geri rested her cheek on his shoulder. How had she only now realized that this was her favorite place in the world? In his arms. No guards up. No pretending to be fine.

"Short engagement," Bart murmured. "I look forward to finding all your freckles. I've been dreaming about you since Ghana, God forgive me."

Heat flooded her, catching her off guard. "Me too."

His eyes widened. "Girl, don't get me started."

"A short engagement it is." She leaned into him, laughing. Her eyes drifted over the backyard, the hedges and young trees stretching quietly toward the sun. This place was becoming home. Would they raise Joaquin here? Would Bart want more kids? Was she ready to face pregnancy again, relive all that trauma and risk?

"Don't overthink it," he said. "One day at a time."

She blinked up at him. How had he read her like that? She touched his cheek, the slope of his nose, the curve of his ear. She couldn't stop touching him. "I guess I better move out then."

He curved a hand around her hip. "What on earth for?"

She gave him a pointed look and gestured to where his hand had landed. "Do I really need to spell it out?"

Bart didn't move his hand. "Trust me, I'm not going to cross any lines. I know you're serious about your faith. And I am too."

"Am what?"

"I'm going to do right by you, Geri." There was no hesitation in his voice.

She believed him. Still, she gently palmed his fingers and moved his hand. "I could get a temporary lease."

"No way. Joaquin's with us. And Darah too, our resident human boundary enforcement. She said she'll stay here a while to give Phoebe's peeps more space in the other house. So, yeah, I get it, you're a walking temptation, but we'll be careful."

His tone was so firm she almost dropped the matter. "My skin still buzzes every time we kiss," she whispered.

His brows went up. "Okay, we're definitely doomed. Might as well just ask for forgiveness right now."

She shook her head but couldn't stop laughing. "I still can't believe you don't remember taking my first kiss."

"What first kiss?"

Geri rolled her eyes. "It's okay, I was probably your most forgettable kiss."

He looked genuinely confused. "Wait, exactly what are we talking about here?"

"Back in middle school," she started, both amused and horrified that after all this time, she'd chosen this wonderful moment to bring it up.

"Middle school?" he spat, eyes wide in shock.

Just then, the back door creaked open. Darah peeked out, a mischievous smile curling her mouth. "Someone's here for you," she said to Geri.

It was like being hit with a bucket of cold water. Geri's eyes flicked to Bart.

He met her gaze with calm reassurance. "Asabe's on a flight back to Nigeria. We're safe." He led her inside, following Darah to the living room.

"Hola."

Geri nearly tripped on the carpet. Her mom was sitting on the couch with Joaquin in her lap, rocking him with the same lullaby she used to hum to Geri.

"Mom." Geri's eyes dropped to the two large suitcases beside the sofa. "What's going on?"

Her mother's smile was big. "Bart invited me to stay with you for the holidays. Thank you, son, for everything you did."

Geri stared at the man beside her. "Son?" When had he found time to speak to her mom alone?

Bart gave Geri's hand a gentle squeeze. "Glad you made it. We're about to head to the other house. Abe and Phoebe are coming with the baby. You'll come?"

Her mother's eyes lit up like it was Christmas morning. "I'd love to."

Geri instantly teared up. That pure smile reminded her of those rare days when Mom had put everything aside to watch old movies with her. "Thanks, mom," was all she could muster.

From that point, everyone was scrambling to get ready. Joaquin got colored markers all over him, so Geri had to give him another bath. When they finally made it to the old Teka house around evening, Geri went upstairs to make sure the baby's room was perfect.

Sunlight spilled through the window, casting soft shadows across the nursery walls as she hung the last newborn onesie in the dresser and slid it shut. The room hushed like a lullaby, quiet lighting, a fluffy white rug waiting for tiny hands and feet—was finally ready.

She turned at the sound of Bart's footsteps. He scanned the room before wrapping her in his arms.

"It looks great. I knew you could do it. You can do anything."

She cradled his face in her hands. "I'll make you a happy man, Bart. You won't regret being with me."

"That's my line." Taking her left hand, he slipped the ring on her finger. "Not waiting another second."

She glanced down, heart fluttering. Delicate and stunning, light on her hand but heavy with meaning. "It's beautiful."

"You're beautiful," Bart said, guiding her gently toward the wall.

The same wall where he'd first confessed his feelings, where they kissed for the first time. As his head dipped against her cheek, she gripped his shirt and inhaled his scent. Yes, she was ready.

He nuzzled her ear. "A walking temptation, I tell you." He pressed light kisses along her jaw, and her skin came alive beneath his lips.

Geri glanced at the open door. Everyone else was downstairs. Her mom and Darah were baking rolls. Joaquin was hanging with Eli and Junior, who had arrived some time ago.

"I can't wait to—" Bart whispered against her neck, his words cut off by the roar of the garage door opening under them.

Bart pinched Geri's cheek and they hurried downstairs. Darah and Junior had already gone to the garage to help, so Geri waited in the living room.

Moments later, Abe walked in carrying the car seat with the baby girl inside, followed by Phoebe, looking tired but all smiles.

Phoebe settled down on the couch, and Abe handed her their sleeping bundle of joy while he hovered protectively, his gaze soft with awe. Their baby girl was absolutely perfect—round cheeks, chocolate skin, a face like an angel painted in velvet tones. After all they'd endured, here she was. A miracle.

"She's unreal," Darah gushed, tears in her eyes.

From her mother's lap, Joaquin frowned at the baby like he didn't know what to make of her.

"Are you finally going to tell us her name?" Bart asked, standing beside Geri.

Abe and Phoebe exchanged one of their signature glances, full of quiet love.

"Selam," Abe said, with reverence, like just the name told a story. "It means..."

"Peace," Phoebe finished with him.

What a name. What a gift. "Selam Teka," Geri whispered, "I love it."

Phoebe looked at her, misty-eyed. "I owe you, Geri. You're my girl for life." She smiled softly, glancing down at her daughter. "I'm so glad you're here with us. We want you to be Selam's godmother."

Geri's hand flew to her mouth, stifling the sob that broke free. If anyone owed anything, it was her. Abe and Phoebe had fought for her when she didn't have the strength to fight for herself.

Bart rubbed Geri's back. "She's gonna be Selam's aunt too."

Phoebe blinked, her eyes darting to Geri's hand. "Girl, is that a ring on your finger?"

Darah gasped, bouncing where she stood. "Oh my gosh!"

Geri lifted the sparkling diamond on her hand, and her mother's eyes shimmered with tears.

Junior clapped Bart's hand into a hug. Darah and Eli exchanged a gleeful high-five like they'd been waiting for this moment. Joaquin looked around at everyone with wide, curious eyes, as if trying to piece together what all the joy meant.

Geri pressed her fingers to her lips, the laughter bubbling up inside her, impossible to hold back.

"When did this happen?" Phoebe asked.

"Earlier today," Bart said, throwing Geri a smug grin that made her cheeks burn.

Abe clasped Bart's hand in a proud shake. "Good for you."

"When's the wedding?" Darah leaned forward, eyes alight with mischief.

"Soon," Bart and Geri answered in unison. "Very soon," Bart added, his gaze locked on her like she was the only person in the room.

Phoebe laughed as Baby Selam stirred in her arms. Abe made a gentle shushing sound, but even the baby seemed to sense the joy humming through the room.

"I can't wait to go dress shopping," Darah whispered to Geri. "I already know what'll look amazing on you. You can get married in—"

"The backyard," Geri said. "I want to get married right here where it all started."

"OMG," Darah cried. "That would be awesome."

Phoebe's thumb went up. "We can absolutely make that work."

Bart smiled at Geri, and his gaze made her warm all over. How had she gone so long without noticing the way he looked at her?

"Looks like fixing up the back garden was a smart move after all," Abe said.

Phoebe laughed. "You two argued over that garden so much. Abe said it was fine, but Bart kept insisting it had to be perfect. It's like he knew."

Geri turned toward Bart, their eyes locking in that silent language they'd grown fluent in. She didn't need to speak the gratitude threading through her heart.

"Y'all gotta give me a date, though," Junior said from the corner. "I need to plan ahead."

"Just don't book anything for the next two months," Bart said. "I need you here."

Junior's voice was firmer this time. "I might get stationed out."

Everyone seemed to freeze. Bart was first to ask: "Stationed out where?"

Junior looked at all of them with the quiet confidence of someone who had chosen his path in life. "I just finished ITB. Came to visit before I move on to my assignment."

A beat. They all looked at one another.

"What in the world are you talking about?" Darah asked.

"Might be a while before I get another set of free days," Junior went on, as if she hadn't said anything.

Geri's heart dropped. "ITB?"

Bart's hand fell away. "That's the Marines, right?"

Junior nodded, and the whole room groaned.

"Why would you do that?" Darah shrieked, loud enough to jostle the baby, but no one shushed her.

Junior didn't flinch. Even the way he sat now—shoulders squared, back straight—spoke of discipline, resolve. In his own way, Junior had always been chasing something. Not just survival, but a legacy to live up to. He'd been shaped in the shadow of Yonas Teka, so it made sense he'd want to give back. Junior had found his own way to be a Teka.

Every piece clicked into place. That reporter from the news had been on point after all. That was why Junior had managed to stay calm through it all, even after the police showed up at the hospital. Handcuffed and lying near Bart on the ground, Junior had looked like none of it was a big deal.

The room fell quiet. Even Joaquin fixed his big eyes on his uncle like he'd grown antlers.

"I can't believe you did this without telling us," Abe finally said. "But why the Marines, Junior?"

Junior shrugged. "Why not?"

The silence that followed could have been sliced clean through. No one moved. No one spoke. Slowly, their attention drifted back to Phoebe—cradling Selam as if peace itself had come to live in her arms.

"You really suck, dude," Darah said suddenly.

That did it. Geri burst out laughing. She couldn't help it. The sheer absurdity and beauty of the moment cracked her wide open.

Bart looked over, that crooked grin she loved tugging at his mouth. He reached for her hand.

Abe shook his head with a smile. Darah punched Junior's arm and muttered something about "drama queen." Eli gave him a solemn, proud pat. Geri's mom looked like she couldn't decide whether to cry or start praying.

Just like that, the tension unraveled. Because of course it was Junior. He'd always danced to his own drum.

And these were the Tekas—wild, loyal, brave, and broken all at once. No matter what happened next, they would figure it out. Together.

Geri looked around the room, at her son curled up beside her mom, her fiancé sitting quiet beside her, her new niece tucked into Phoebe's chest. Laughter bounced off the walls like music. It was messy. It was hard-won. But like a quilt stitched from scars and second chances, she finally felt whole.

If she hadn't gone searching for her father, she would never have ended up in Africa.

Never would have met Hakeem.

Joaquin.

If she hadn't been forced to leave Nigeria, Bart would be married to someone else, and she'd be across the ocean trying to build a life for Joaquin while quietly letting go of her own happy ending.

But that wasn't the story God had written. In His hands, the shattered pieces had become beautiful. Against all the odds, through grief and chaos, and divine intervention, they had found each other again.

And this time, she wasn't letting go. Not ever again.

THE END.

Dee Osah is a husband-wife team with a godly passion for weaving their personal experiences into stories anyone can enjoy. They live in Houston with two young daughters who already love to whip up compelling tales. When not writing, they enjoy watching Anime and K-dramas, and learning to grow food for their ever-growing family.

Teka Homecoming is the second novel in the *Teka Family Series*. If you enjoyed this book and would like to read more of Dee Osah's stories for free, please scan the QR code below to visit our library or join our community.

Thank you for reading *Teka Homecoming,* and stay tuned for more.

If you would like to read more about Geri's first kiss that Bart didn't remember, visit our library and check out "**Seven Heaven**".

OTHER BOOKS BY DEE OSAH

Teka Legacy
My Sugar in Sugar Land
Queen of Trades